"In her debut novel, Frances Peck m⋯⋯ of complex characters, each broken in⋯⋯ n-pelling story set against the backc⋯⋯ e. It beautifully reminded me that nc⋯⋯ d, especially when it comes to our hu⋯⋯, and fragmented, hearts."
—**BRIAN FRANCIS,** author of *Fruit* and *Missed Connections*

"With masterful use of craft, Peck takes readers on a journey into how devastation draws us together while pulling us apart. With moving imagery and haunting insight into response to trauma, *The Broken Places* highlights the flawed nature of humanity and our ability to move forward and find community after complicated, tragic loss. Above all, Peck gives nuanced, stunning characters who show readers what it means to give ourselves up to our flaws and find love and beauty in the process."
—**KELLY S. THOMPSON,** national bestselling author of *Girls Need Not Apply: Field Notes from the Forces*

"Frances Peck's wonderfully sophisticated and razor-sharp novel takes dead aim at Vancouver's tenuous decadent dreams against an ensemble of mesmerizing characters. *The Broken Places* casts an unwavering eye on a city of glass and its inhabitants who must respond to a savagely cruel event that shatters some families while bringing others closer together. It's Balzacian in its ambition and wit, raising ineluctable questions about family and wealth, love and lust, resignation and resilience, and offers hard-earned truths about the death of dreams and how we'll fight fiercely to keep them intact regardless of the cost. A well-crafted, affecting debut."
—**JOHN VIGNA,** author of *No Man's Land*

"Frances Peck reveals herself a writer with seismic impact as she examines the before, during, and after of crumbling worlds and relationships. *The Broken Places* will scare the living daylights out of you while it yields harsh truths, heartbreak, and hope about the human condition."
—**GLEN HUSER,** author of *Burning the Night*

"*The Broken Places* is a propulsive, terrifying novel about the sudden catastrophic upending of day-to-day life. Hillsides slump, bridges give way, apartment buildings tilt and crumble — while love, desire, greed and devotion are tested, heightened or lost forever. Frances Peck's characters are those we instinctively understand. Beautifully layered and compelling, this novel explores the intricacies of human behaviour — what it is that makes us, and what it is we cherish most."
—**LIBBY CREELMAN,** author of *Split*

"*The Broken Places* is a rare treat that combines high-tension narrative with true literary craft, delivering characters that readers will love to love, hate, pity, and grieve. Set against the backdrop of a devastating earthquake, the story of how a diverse group of people react to their new reality is beautifully delivered, offering many moments of masterful writing and rich, sensory engagement. Layer by layer, Peck reveals the motivations, fears and desires of her characters, doling out clues that culminate in an explosive and heartbreaking climax. Yet the novel ends with hope. Not a sweet-sugary treat, but a hope grounded firmly in believable characters and situations that resonate."
—**RUTH E. WALKER,** author of *Living Underground*

"Frances Peck's dazzling debut novel snatches a cast of vividly realized, multi-faceted characters out of their daily lives in Vancouver and gathers them closer and closer as the book builds toward a dramatic, disturbing macroseismic cataclysm. Peck slides effortlessly in and out of the intimate thoughts and turbulent flux of emotion that individuals experience as they connect, as their destinies interlace, as their lives are irrevocably altered. People disappear; people are transformed. Peck's prose is piercing with precision — here are broken people, and here is what might heal them."
—**CLAIRE WILKSHIRE,** author of *The Love Olympics* and *Maxine*

The

Broken

Places

~

THE BROKEN PLACES

A NOVEL

FRANCES PECK

NeWest Press

Madeleine Thien's essay "Photocopies of Photocopies: On Bao Ninh" appears in *Finding the Words: Writers on Inspiration, Desire, War, Celebrity, Exile, and Breaking the Rules,* edited by Jared Bland. The quotation attributed to a geologist on page 279 is from Andrew Alden, "What Is Geological Strain?," ThoughtCo.com.

Library and Archives Canada Cataloguing in Publication
Title: The broken places : a novel / Frances Peck.
Names: Peck, Frances, author.
Series: Nunatak first fiction series ; no. 57.
Description: Series statement: Nunatak first fiction series ; no. 57
Identifiers: Canadiana (print) 20210212632 | Canadiana (ebook) 20210212640 | ISBN 9781774390450 (softcover) | ISBN 9781774390467 (ebook)
Subjects: LCGFT: Novels.
Classification: LCC PS8631.E355 B76 2022 | DDC C813/.6—DC23

NeWest Press wishes to acknowledge that the land on which we operate is Treaty 6 territory and a traditional meeting ground and home for many Indigenous Peoples, including Cree, Saulteaux, Niitsitapi (Blackfoot), Métis, and Nakota Sioux.

Editor for the Press: Leslie Vermeer
Cover and interior design: Natalie Olsen
Cover image © Kirill Bordon photography / Stocksy.com
Author photo: Rebecca Blissett

NeWest Press acknowledges the support of the Canada Council for the Arts, the Alberta Foundation for the Arts, and the Edmonton Arts Council for support of our publishing program. We acknowledge the financial support of the Government of Canada through the Canada Book Fund for our publishing activities.

 #201, 8540-109 Street
Edmonton, Alberta T6G 1E6
NeWest Press   www.newestpress.com

No bison were harmed in the making of this book.
Printed and bound in Canada   22 23 24 25   5 4 3 2

for Marjorie Watt Peck

The world breaks everyone and afterwards many are strong at the broken places.

ERNEST HEMINGWAY

A Farewell to Arms

∧∨

They create art not for art's sake, but from necessity, to hold together what is beautiful and what was broken …

MADELEINE THIEN

"Photocopies of Photocopies: On Bao Ninh"

PART ONE

Strain

ONE MINUTE you're at your spot in the enormous kitchen, a chrome-and-leather stool at one end of the gleaming granite island. The desert island, you privately call it. You're alone there so often you may as well be marooned.

Down-island: a clamshell. Actually a laptop, slim, silver, screen gone black, the only sign that another human has crossed this strip of land. The human: your mother, who abhors crumbs and unrinsed coffee cups, drips and stains, crusts of toast — all the messes of human life. Your mother, who moves through each day leaving no trace other than some random electronic device. Hurricane Charlotte, Dad calls her, a strange name for someone who glides cold and robot-like through life. Your mother, who never listens, who doesn't understand the first thing about you, who is too oblivious to even know that she doesn't know.

One minute you're sitting there, empty Mountain Dew can at your elbow, the drink having edged you into another reluctant day, along with the fatty-sweet bitsu-bitsu May made fresh this morning. *Breakfast of champions*, Dad said when he strolled in. He swiped a couple of the chewy doughnuts himself, trailed sugar like white sand all the way to the kitchen island. Your mother glared.

One minute you're on your stool. On your phone, scanning Instagram posts from Rebecca Lee, who used to hang out with you. You'd go to the mall, split a frozen yogurt, one topping your choice, one hers, get high, steal nail polish, steal, once, a pair of jeans you shoved under your jacket when Rebecca said no way, you never would. Rebecca, now a stuck-up slut who has quit talking to you.

It's not like she's the only one. Lots of people won't acknowledge you now. You creep along the hallway outside chem lab — which used to be your spot between classes, you *owned* that spot — and your so-called friends fold into a tight whispering knot, no words for you. You angle toward your place in the cafeteria, the table where you've sat for the past two and a half years, and find every chair occupied. In class, it doesn't matter which one, the person in front of you hands papers back without turning all the way. When you enter the washroom you clear the place out.

It's fine. They talked about this in group. *Reintegration*, they called it; also *redrawing*. It's hard for the people in your life to redraw you. They want to see the same you they've always seen. The group counsellor, Drayton, too earnest and granola for your liking though he always gave you respect, would trace a rectangle in the air with his forefinger. For most people, he said, the world is a tidy box. Step outside the box, disturb their sense of order, and they feel profoundly uncomfortable. When that happens, you've got to remember the discomfort is their problem, not yours.

Redrawing. You like that idea.

One minute your earbuds are pulsing Taylor Swift, a not-bad song years ago when it came out, the video with all the ballet dancers, now just lame, an embarrassing scrap of childhood. Like the frilly canopy bed you hung on to until you were fifteen and woke up one day to realize you were no one's princess. Time to make a new playlist. Taylor Swift is so ... yesterday.

One minute you're on your desert island, scrolling, scrolling, looking for a better, more meaningful song, a more mature song, one that suits your mood this boring Tuesday morning, wondering if you should post something about that skanky Rebecca Lee, because you know stuff about her no one else knows, or if you should just let it go, the way you're learning to let things go.

The next minute — *how?* —

You're on your ass, the heavy stool you were sitting on tipped over beside you.

What —?

Pots and pans sail off copper hooks. Crash all around you. Bounce.

Holy shit! Dad?

Instinct kicks in. *Make yourself small.* You curl up like a snail, hold your bandaged hand close to your belly. *Be a snail. Be a snail.* Only you've never had a shell.

The blender flies off the granite island, smashes onto the terracotta floor. Glass sprays. Another barstool falls.

Dad!

You wait. Wire-taut, every nerve screaming *run*. But you don't. It's the one thing you're not supposed to do.

Below the treble of smashing glass and clanging metal, a bass line builds, like no sound you've ever heard before. Deep rolling thunder, but louder. Close. A jumbo jet landing on the roof.

You wait. Terrified.

You wait, like you've waited for so much in life. To be understood. To matter.

You wait. For everything to end. For something else to begin.

ONE

〜

Morning dawned soft grey and still, mother-of-pearl streaking a sky that domed the harbour and embraced the snow-frosted mountains. High overcast, said the forecasters, with sunny breaks. No wind. Warmer than average.

A mid-May day on the laid-back west coast. A day for lingering over morning coffee or chai latte or herbal tea, for beachcombing and dreaming, for tending to tasks and children, to aging parents and spring gardens. A Tuesday. A day for working, but maybe, in deference to the milky mild air, not too hard.

A day like any other. Even better than some. Until it wasn't.

〜

SIX A.M. A little brighter than yesterday, morning light elbowing its way through the gaps in the bedroom blinds, but basically six o'clock today is a lot like six o'clock yesterday. Not too early, not too late. Time to get at it.

Six o'clock has been Joe's time for so long now that he hardly needs to set the alarm. It's not like the old days, when he was fresh off the boat, so to speak, a wide-eyed Newfoundlander in Toronto, with odd jobs and no fixed address, moving from couch to futon, bunking with any co-worker or friend or nighttime acquaintance who'd let him stay in exchange for his handiness around the place, his reliability, his rock-solid good cheer. In those days he might wake at any time, ten in the morning or two in the afternoon, and whenever his eyes cracked open, the day and the city spread before him like a market of unsampled delights.

Here on the west coast, where he's older and settled, a self-employed landscaper in a city of year-round gardening, he follows a stricter rhythm. On any given day, sometime between five fifty and six, he switches from deeply asleep to ready to go. His mind sharpens, as much as it ever does, and his body knows: time to get going.

He is sleepier than usual this morning, but other than that there's nothing different about six o'clock today. Later he will wonder about this. He'll rack his memory looking for the sign he missed in his pre-coffee haze, because there must have been one. Was it in the light or the sky? Carried by the breeze? There must have been something. Some smell or shimmer, a shift so faint as to escape his notice then, but that he could summon up later if he tried hard enough.

Later, when the city has fallen and he has time on his hands, he will think on it. But he will come up empty. There is nothing to account for the great change to come. It's just another morning, quiet, dim, routine. The sheets, which Joe changed yesterday after work, are well known to him. Five hundred thread count, sateen. Pewter, a shade Kiki hunted down obsessively online. The post-sleep smell that hangs in the air is deeply familiar, a mixture of Zest soap from their evening showers and the cleaning lady's orange furniture polish. The bed feels the same, the king-sized Tempur-Pedic boxed into the Shaker-style dark-oak frame, supportive the way only a four-thousand-dollar mattress can be. Joe's cheeks still redden, two years after they put it on their Visa, at the mattress's price tag. Four thousand bucks! That's a lot of landscaping. But Kiki needs the best sleep money can buy, and since Kiki did all the research and is the main breadwinner of the household, Joe shook his head and went along. What would Ma make of such a bed, Ma who slept on the same iron cot, topped with a stained, lumpy grey-ticked pad, her whole adult life? Some mornings Joe wonders, gazing longingly across the vast expanse of sheet, whether it was a good decision. Joe is a compact man. Kiki is also small. The bed is very large, the space between them wide.

Joe lingers a minute, stretches mightily, feels the keg of his chest expand. Tests his knees. A little creaky, but not bad. He's got a long day ahead, a new West Van client with a waterfront property that's gotten out of hand, then another regular, also in West Vancouver, plus a drive out to the nursery if he can fit it in, and already he's flagging. What was he thinking, staying up past midnight to watch that foolish comedy on Netflix? It could've waited. True, he is duty-bound to see every movie that features Melissa McCarthy, because she is fat and has to work harder to be a star. She needs her fans. If you're going to support the underdog, you can't hold back. Joe has seen the entire filmography of the small actor Peter Dinklage, has read all he can get his hands on about the unlikely racehorse Seabiscuit, came to idolize that homely Scottish singer — or was she Welsh? — before she hit it big in North America. Still, it's not like they'd whisk the Melissa McCarthy show off of Netflix overnight. He didn't have to stay up so late.

He hazards a glance across the bed, where Kiki is snoring softly, mouth agape, flecked with — spit? toothpaste? Joe can't tell without his fancy new progressives. For Pete's sake! Can't even see to the other side of your own bed. Gettin old, b'y, he tells himself. One of the countless humiliations ahead. Whatever time Kiki got in, it was long after the credits had rolled and Joe had rinsed the popcorn bowl and stowed it in the dishwasher so the counters would be clear. Long after he'd flipped open his phone again to make sure the ringer was on, after he'd brushed his teeth, pulled out fresh jeans and a tee-shirt for the morning, and crept inside the cool pewter. He vaguely remembers the pipes rumbling in the middle of the night, signalling that the shower was on, but nothing after that. He can't feel it when Kiki climbs into bed, the mattress is that good, designed to hold them together while shielding each from the other's movements. It's a solid, wide bed. Like a tennis court, Joe thinks, still straining to see his lover on the opposite side. Kiki's light snores drone on. No hope of a cuddle.

Joe swings his legs out into the morning air and takes a minute to straighten up. Knees hurt like a bugger when he settles his weight on them, but it'll pass. He just needs to walk around awhile, needs to putter, as Ma used to say. By the time he fires up the truck he'll be fine.

He's leaning against the kitchen counter, on his second mug of milky tea, half-listening to the deejays joshing on the soft-rock station, knees nearly normal, when an elephant-like yawn comes from down the hall. In stumbles Kiki, eyes heavy-lidded, in the earliest stages of awake. Like that, the morning glows and Joe's tea sweetens.

"Would you look at that." He grins. "The miracle of resurrection, in our very own kitchen. On the third day he rose again." Funny how the Catholic liturgy is always there, twisted into the strands of your DNA.

Kiki doesn't crack a smile. Just heads for the gleaming stainless sink.

"He walks!"

"Ha, ha."

"And he talks. At least, in short words."

Kiki fills a glass with water, drinks it down. Gazes out the window over the sink.

For as long as Joe has known him, Doctor Kyle Jespersen — Kiki, to Joe — has never been a morning person. Is this his usual a.m. crustiness? Or something more? Please don't let it be one of the cutting moods that Kiki brings home with him more and more often now.

Joe gentles his voice, hoping to disarm Kiki with sympathy. "Must've been a late one, eh? I'm not even sure I heard you come in. Didn't think you'd roll out this early."

Kiki flashes him a look. "You're not the only one who has to work, you know. Or did you forget? It's Tuesday. Not the weekend or anything."

Sympathy, strike one. Joe absorbs the shot about his memory but not without an inward dig at himself because it's true: he hasn't really registered what day it is. He works weekends when people want him to, especially in the spring. One day may as well be another.

So, it is a mood. Joe sets down his mug, crosses the kitchen, closes in for a hug, and whispers, "I know what you need. A nice cup of tea." When sympathy doesn't work, go for humour. Kiki loathes tea.

Kiki wriggles free and fairly spits. "Jesus Christ. *Tea?* How long have we been together?"

"Oh, Kiki. I'm joking. It's a joke."

Humour, strike two.

Joe feels it advance, stealthy and cold. Not just any mood: the Chill.

Kiki busies himself at the espresso maker, a hulking apparatus the size of a V6 engine that, like their bed, cost a full digit more than Joe would have ever predicted. In the background the deejays' voices give way to the opening piano of an old Elton John song, the one about the yellow brick road. Whether it's the melody or the warm vocals, Joe's not sure, but something about the song makes his throat sting. *You know you can't comb it forever, I didn't sign up for you.* Or something like that. He's never been that sure of the lyrics.

It's getting late, but Joe doesn't want to leave like this, the Chill a clammy fog around their ankles. "How'd it go last night, anyhow? You get lots done?"

Kiki reaches into the cupboard for coffee beans. Doesn't answer.

Direct question, strike three.

"Okey-dokey." Joe rinses his tea mug and stows it in the dishwasher. "I'm off. Got a big day."

"What about the garbage?"

"Huh?"

"The *gar*-bage." Kiki draws out each syllable. "And the recycling. It's Tuesday?"

"Ah, shoot. I totally forgot. Can you look after it?"

Kiki's eyes glitter. "No, I can't *look after* it. It's your job to *look after* it."

"Come on. I'm gonna be late."

"I showered last night and I'm seeing patients all day. I can't afford to get dirty just because you forgot. *Again*."

Joe rubs his forehead, as if to rev up his brain. However hard he tries, certain details — dates, long instructions, people's names — refuse to stay in there. Did he inherit this, descended as he is from a long line of Newfies, supposedly so slow-witted that they merit their own line of jokes? Or did he bump his head one too many times as a boy? He has no idea, just knows that he's been this way as long as he can remember. Kiki, whose finely calibrated mind retains and processes all it is given — an excellent trait in a doctor — used to be more tolerant of Joe's failings, would chuckle and tease him whenever he forgot their cleaning lady's name or a birthday or a dinner date. Not now. Not since the Chill. Every day, it seems, Joe manages to return a dish to the wrong shelf or misremember the chronology of a conversation, and Kiki pounces.

"Kyle." Using Kiki's real name always communicates that it's serious. "I need you to do it this time. I've got a new client, this high-tech guy over in West Van. I can't be late."

"And what? Your time's more valuable than mine?" Kiki turns back to the espresso machine, drops his voice to a mutter, one calculated to carry. "I'd do the math on that if I were you."

When did it start? Joe has traced the timeline back but can never properly work out when the Chill first appeared. They always argued once in a while, the way any couple does, some meltdown over nothing followed by fabulous make-up sex. But never this constant bickering, never this tone, an acid tone, as if Kiki can barely stand to talk to Joe let alone live with him. And Lord knows, there's never any make-up sex. Since the Chill, there's barely any sex at all.

Joe is stymied by this shift, has tried all he can think of to reverse it. Has tried jokes and gifts that all fall flat. Has arranged dinners and brunches with other couples, during which Kiki returns to his old self, funny and gregarious and beaming, only to retreat once they're alone again. Joe has suggested more couple time in hopes that curling up for a series or sharing takeout Chinese will bring on a thaw, but that's been the biggest flop. Without fail Kiki pleads work: the endless paper shuffle, the journal reading, the administrative catch-up that is never, ever over. That's where he was last night, in his office, at his desk until all hours.

You spend so much time catching up but it never makes you happy, Joe wants to say. You're only more irritable. Why keep up with work if there's no relief in it? Just accept that you'll always be a little behind and enjoy life instead. But Joe never says this. Kiki would only ignore him, the way he did when the clinic first took off and Joe urged him to hire an office manager to shoulder the admin at least. Joe offered to take on more clients to help this happen — not that he'd have to, Doctor Jespersen makes scads of money — but it was like talking to a mannequin. Kiki ignored him and went on as always, doing it all alone and wearing himself down, a decision that cost them far more than an extra staff person ever would.

Kiki smacks the coffee grinder, sharp claps meant to loosen any clinging grounds. The whacking goes on longer than usual, and suddenly Joe realizes that Kiki is not moody. He is angry.

Well, screw him. Joe's tired of playing the nice guy, being the patient and understanding one. He grabs his keys from the wicker basket on the counter and jams his ball cap onto his curly head. "Deal with it, Kyle. I'm outta here."

Kiki wheels around. "Deal with it? *Deal* with it?" His voice climbs a ladder at the top of which waits a demon Joe is all too familiar with these days, a raging diva who will have her way, a diva he does not want to meet, not this morning, not when he's late, and especially not brought on by – for Pete's sake! – garbage. So he keeps his mouth shut and heads toward the back door.

"It's your job!" Kiki yells at his back. "You were here all night, for fuck's sake, doing what? Watching movies. Eating popcorn, when you *know* I can't stand the smell of it, you *know* it makes me gag. Sitting on your ass while I'm slaving away at stupid paperwork and going to the gym at midnight. Are you seriously going to tell me to *deal* with it?"

Joe halts in his tracks. What can he say? That he wishes they'd both been home last night watching movies together? That this is Kiki's home too, even though Kiki has been treating it more like a hotel, with Joe just one of the housekeeping staff? That he misses his sweetheart? That in their five years together, the last three in this townhouse, their forever home, Joe has never felt so alone?

He searches for the right words, the ones that will fix it all, that will quiet the raving and make Kiki kind again. But his brain – his weakest muscle, as he likes to joke – gives him nothing.

Meanwhile, Kiki has climbed several rungs closer to diva. "And I'm so tired of it. You hear me? I can't go on like this! It's not a lot to ask, that you just remember garbage day. It's Tuesday, it's one day. The same day every week. Write it down if you can't keep it in your head, or leave yourself a – fuck!" Black liquid sprays and Kiki's ceramic demitasse falls to the floor, but remarkably, given the high drama into which the situation has been whipped, it doesn't break. "Jesus Christ, my hand!

I came that close to burning it. That's the last thing I need, the last goddamned thing! That's it. That's really it. I can't do this anymore."

Slowly Joe turns around, sees Kiki, hand clutched to his chest, hopping around like Rumpelstiltskin even though the espresso has flooded the counter, not the floor. Joe tries to summon up anger. He knows he should fight back, should charge Kiki's mounting hysteria head on, fight fire with fire, stick up for himself like any self-respecting person, but with Kiki he does not and cannot feel angry. He hates this, being a doormat. It's too much like school, when the teacher got after him for not knowing the answer or failing the test or being unable to recite the poem and all he could do was sit there, head hung, silent, humiliated. He gets it from Ma, who never said a harsh word against anyone, whose face was always backlit with kindness, except at the end, when the coma switched off the light. Joe's stomach now flutters with the same black tremors he felt while tending to Ma two years ago, when she shrank and withdrew into some dried-apple-doll version of herself.

That is when he understands: it is grief. It is grief that comes over him as his lover stomps and rages in the kitchen they spent a fortune renovating so that Joe could cook lavish dinners for them while Kiki sat at the counter and opened bills and drank wine, the kitchen where they used to eat breakfast together and compare notes on the day ahead and share one good kiss before parting. Now they snipe and yell and condemn. Something is shifting, their lives slipping sideways. Where it will end Joe can't say, yet already he is mourning the change.

"Kiki, stop. Okay?" He sets his keys back on the counter, crosses the floor, takes Kiki in his arms. "Just stop." Kiki doesn't want to be held, but little by little he quiets until his body finally sags against Joe. Joe puts his nose to Kiki's brush cut and inhales deeply. The warm scalpy smell, the most Kiki part of you, as Joe has always called it, sends a painful rush to his tenderest parts. "I'm sorry I forgot. I'm a lunkhead, okay? I'll put the garbage out when I leave now. The recycling can wait till next week."

Kiki nods against his shoulder.

Joe runs a hand down Kiki's back, smoothing the long, gym-toned muscle straps that bracket his lover's spine. He glances at the clock on the stove. It's so late. No matter how fast he gets the garbage to the curb, he'll never make it to West Van on time. "You okay now?"

Kiki shakes his head, which stays buried in Joe's shoulder, and sniffles.

"Come on, sweetie. Everything's going to be fine." Joe rubs the low indentation in Kiki's back, the part that aches whenever he's over-worked. "Come home after your last appointment tonight. We'll get sushi and open that nice sake Jeremy gave us. Screw the paperwork tonight, okay? It can wait one day."

Kiki shakes his head, peels his face away from Joe's shoulder. His cheeks are wet.

"I can't." He is really crying.

Shit. Kiki never cries.

There is no way Joe can go now. He's going to have to stay and talk and get to the bottom of what's wrong. Except he absolutely has to leave. If it were a regular client, one who knows how punctual Joe is, it would be different. But a new client will just think he's a screw-up, especially a big tycoon like this West Van guy. "Hey, you can come home whenever you want," Joe says. "You're the boss, remember?"

"No, I mean I *can't*. I can't —" Kiki keeps shaking his head. The next thing he says quietly, addressing his slippered feet. "I can't *do* this. This ... I feel like I'm living a lie."

For a second Joe's not sure he heard right. Living a lie? "What's that supposed to mean?" he says. What lie, he wants to ask.

"You know what I mean."

Joe's gut churns. He doesn't know at all, but he wants to know. At the same time, he doesn't. Why does this have to come now? Why this morning, the one time he can't stay? "Kiki, I'm so late. I don't have time for riddles."

"Make the time."

Like that, the match of anger strikes inside Joe. *Make the time?* For months he has had nothing but time, and where is Kiki? Taking appointments after hours, wrestling with files into the night, working out at the gym. When Kiki does manage to check in at home he's moody and distant, at times downright mean, cutting Joe off and ordering him around the way he might an underling. And now, just because it's convenient for Kiki, Joe's supposed to make time for him?

At last Joe is angry. Anyone would be.

"Screw you," he says. And leaves.

∿

Anna has been asleep, properly and deeply out of it, just shy of three hours when the electronic bleat of the alarm clock needles her awake. When she last checked the digital display, vowing after hours of repeated glances that this would be the last, it was 2:58, an awful time, one of the worst. It must have been ten or fifteen minutes later when she finally dropped off.

Drop off — it is one of the most accurate English expressions Anna has learned here in Canada, describing as it does the act of stepping over an edge and hurtling down toward who knows what. Back home, even though the apartment walls were thin and the factories juddered through the night, sleep was more a matter of sinking under. It stole over her the minute she lay down and pulled to her chin Baba's orange-and-red quilt, which, when she was a child, was where she believed sleep lived during the day. But here in the British Properties, on a curved green street as hushed as a graveyard, sleep comes with what Anna might call, if she knew the word, a precipice, a ledge that some self-preserving instinct deep inside her resists as long as possible, urging her to remain on top, where she is safe. For hours she lies in her narrow bed, thoughts whirling like the vegetables she purees for Miss Dodie, whipping up a mental froth that churns and bubbles and keeps sleep at bay. Not even Baba's quilt, which still covers her bed here in Canada, can make sleep come.

Six-oh-three. The time is impossible to ignore when it is displayed in chunky digits two inches high. Perhaps that is why Miss Dodie outfitted the spare room with such an artifact, so that Anna can never fail to see when it is time to get up. The alarm clock, with its wood veneer cabinet that sprouts coordinating brown plastic knobs, is huge. Anna would say it is roughly the size of a microwave except that Miss Dodie's microwave, an original from the early seventies, is immense, bigger even than the backpack that carried all of Anna's worldly belongings to Canada. The clock, which clicks whenever a new digit flips into place, merely amuses Anna, whereas the antique microwave, which she knows will shoot her full of radiation should she ever operate it, terrifies her. She should be brave, she who was born in Ukraine, in the year of Chernobyl, the mother of all radiation releases; she who fled her country when the Russians invaded (*not an invasion*, insisted her neighbour, Oksana); she who made her way here, to the evergreen quiet of this West Vancouver mountainside, on little more than wits; she who soaps Miss Dodie's private parts and the tufted trenches under her crepey arms. But she is not brave. Fortunately the purpose of the giant appliance, like most mechanical and domestic details of this mouldering house, has sunk deep into the bog of her lady's memory, and Anna has made it through nearly three years of employment without ever turning a dial.

Six-oh-five. No longer can she delay. Miss Dodie — Mrs. Dorothy Lydell back when her husband was alive — who cannot recall her own phone number or the names of fruits and vegetables, wakes every morning at precisely six thirty and knows that shortly thereafter will appear, on a silver tray, one soft-boiled egg, one slice of toast (dry), and two cups of coffee. Should these items not materialize, Miss Dodie will say bad words, many of them. Anna, though she is no innocent and is always keen to enrich her vocabulary, nonetheless prefers quiet in the morning and has learned to appear on time. Also, the doctor has said it is important that her lady have a routine. Anna understands routine — she obeys a strict one of her own — and is happy to comply.

Anna has her own closet and chest of drawers here in the small corner bedroom. When the taxi first deposited her and her belongings midway up the British Properties, in front of the sprawling fifties rancher she now calls home, the contents of her backpack filled one quarter of the closet and not quite two drawers. Since then she has added a few castoffs bequeathed by Miss Dodie, most of them shapeless or elasticized – Miss Dodie is both more buxom and scrawnier-hipped than her caregiver – and made of polyester, nylon, or some other discount-store fabric. For Miss Dodie, despite her high-income address and overflowing accounts, the balances of which Anna is required to read aloud on the last day of each month, is confoundingly frugal. She owns wash-and-wear items from the eighties; she refuses to update or even fully repair her mildewed house, which is collapsing around her; she sends Anna to the shops with coupons plucked from bulk-mailed envelopes and snipped from women's magazines; and she checks receipts later – at least when she remembers to – to make sure every item was on sale. This penny-pinching baffles Anna, whose mother *had* to use coupons, *had* to wait for sales. Why, when you could walk into a store and buy anything you wanted, many times over, would you fret over fifty cents here or a dollar there? If she had Miss Dodie's money she would wear silk and wool, grill a T-bone or a lamb chop every night, buy an entire cherry pie from the extravagant bakery down on Marine Drive, use the rich coconut shampoo from the salon where Miss Dodie gets her hair done. Her lady's insistence on deprivation is one more quirk of the wealthy, a tribe that dazzles and puzzles Anna in equal measure, a tribe whose ways remain alien to her though she lives in their midst and whose camouflage she relies on for her underground life in this country.

Anna opens the top drawer of the bureau. *Her* bureau. In it, a neat layer of sensible white underwear and grey cotton socks. Underneath these essentials, well hidden, her small trove of treasures: the discarded utility envelope stuffed with the tens and twenties Miss Dodie pays her every week, the pearl-handled knife from her brother, the solid gold chain that she removed from her dead mother's throat, and the smooth stainless steel flask. Mentally she takes inventory, as she does every morning, but she does not lift up her clothing to actually look at the items. She will allow herself that pleasure later, at the end of the day, when the bulk of her work is done.

From the second drawer, she pulls out one of Miss Dodie's hand-me-downs, a much-washed grey sweatshirt, the origins of which, given its one hundred percent cotton material and faded logo of an electrical workers union, Anna cannot imagine. The only tradespeople to cross into Miss Dodie's world, a world populated by no family and few friends, are the occasional handymen summoned only in the direst of emergencies. They arrive promptly, work fast, and after a dose of the old woman's volatile temper and odd reminiscences, never return. The idea of a worker giving Miss Dodie a souvenir sweatshirt is ludicrous. Perhaps the pullover was left behind, its owner too unsettled by his erratic client to double back for it.

Twenty-five minutes later, clad in the sweatshirt and matching grey cotton pants that she bought with her own money from the local thrift shop, where the brand-name discards from West Vancouver closets can be had for a song, Anna enters the master bedroom. In the scant morning light, muted by the heavy orange-and-avocado drapes, she sees that Miss Dodie is awake and has managed to prop herself up against the pillows. The old woman cranes forward, peering into the gloom. "Annie, is that you?"

Anna smiles. Who else would it be? "Yes, my lady. Is me."

"Is it the silver tray?"

"Yes." Anna settles the bed tray over Miss Dodie's legs, tucks the cloth napkin under the old woman's sparsely whiskered chin, and switches on the bedside lamp. It never occurs to Miss Dodie to say good morning, but Anna does not mind. She cares little for pleasantries. It is possible that the old woman has forgotten the greeting altogether.

"I must have the silver, you know." Miss Dodie runs her gnarled fingers along the edge of the tray. She says the same thing every morning.

"Yes, yes. Always the silver." The tray, along with the sterling cutlery, coffee pot, and cream pitcher that it must hold, is one of Miss Dodie's few luxuries. The woman will accept nothing else, as Anna learned the one morning she substituted a lighter wooden tray along with regular tableware, of the non-tarnishing, dishwasher-safe variety, and was rewarded with an overturned breakfast and two hours of consequences: a sponge bath for her employer, a linen change, a new meal, and repeated promises that the error would never recur. Fortunately Anna has discovered that she enjoys polishing silver, a meditative activity with unfailingly good results that she had never considered the existence of before taking up residence here.

Silver spoon gripped tight, Miss Dodie digs around inside her soft-boiled egg. "It must be silver. You can't fool me, Annie. Don't even try."

Why must the incident of the overturned tray live so stubbornly in Miss Dodie's memory? Why not all the times Anna has brought the right tray and the right dishes? Anna has given up trying to understand the looping of her employer's mind. "No, my lady. Never do I fool you."

"Kelvin always brought the silver. He would never fool me."

Kelvin. Days have passed without the name being uttered, leaving Anna hopeful that Miss Dodie's previous caregiver might have finally fallen through the hatch of the woman's memory. *Saint Kelvin*, Anna inwardly calls him. A strong yet gentle Vietnamese man, so handsome and neat, so quiet and perfectly mannered, with such excellent English, who made the most delicious coffee laced with sweetened condensed milk, who fed Miss Dodie all the red meat and cheese she wanted, who gave the old woman the four best years of her elderly life until he left to marry a strumpet (a word Anna does not fully understand) from the Vietnamese Alliance Church — Kelvin occupies as steadfast a place in Miss Dodie's memory as the incident of the tray. And now here he is again, the brilliant paragon who will forever outshine Anna, she of the plain face, no-nonsense manner, and tasteless food. Anna with her clumsy ways, her halting speech, her grey garments. Perhaps the electrical workers sweatshirt had belonged to Saint Kelvin. Perhaps he could rewire a house as well as care for Miss Dodie like no other human could, at least no one who is still alive.

As if Anna has spoken aloud, Miss Dodie picks up the photo of her deceased husband from the bedside table, smearing egg yolk on the plastic frame. Anna makes a mental note to wipe it off later.

"My Marty, he was no fool. He was a — He was a smart man. He did the … He was a …"

"Scientist," Anna supplies.

"Yes, a scientist. A very smart man. But he didn't fool me." Miss Dodie wags a finger at the photo, in which her husband stands unnaturally erect, frozen in middle age, half-smiling, wearing a suit and tie. "Oh no, he didn't."

This particular line of thinking is one Anna does not like to encourage. "We have hairdresser this morning. Make your hair all neat and pretty."

Miss Dodie is, appropriately enough, not fooled by the distraction. She continues to gaze at her husband. "He was a trickster. Always sniff, sniff, sniffing. But he couldn't fool me."

"Is nice morning. We go for walk before hairdresser, okay? Down by the water."

The minute Miss Dodie looks up, Anna moves to snatch the photo, but the old woman is quicker and clutches it to her large bosom. "Mine! Even with all the dogs. He was mine."

Anna sighs. How to do it? How to get Miss Dodie to finish her breakfast so that they can fit in the daily walk that the doctor insists on, which must happen before they go to the hairdresser's because after that Miss Dodie will be too sleepy to walk. The hardest part of Anna's job here in Canada is moving things along, nudging Miss Dodie from one meal, one room, one appointment, one fixation to another. This is only fitting for one whose workdays at home, in Donetsk, were spent at a factory conveyor belt.

In cases like this, distraction sometimes works. Anna crosses to Miss Dodie's vanity table, picks up a plastic hand mirror from amid the scattered bottles, jewellery, and ornaments, and returns to the bed. "Here. Look at your hair." As she passes the mirror to Miss Dodie, she neatly plucks the framed photo from the old woman's other hand. "Freema will fix it for you. Make it pretty."

Success! Miss Dodie takes one look at her flattened, wispy hair, frowns, puts the mirror down, and returns to her breakfast. Thoughtfully she chews a bite of dry toast. "When did it happen, Annie? When did I get so old?"

"No, my lady. You are not so old."

"I am! I look like that, that ... you know. That *thing* that pulls its neck into its house. Oh, you know."

Every day Anna has fresh reason to berate the English language. Why must there be so many words? How is it possible that her narrow world of Miss Dodie and the house and errands, a world confined to one small quadrant of West Vancouver, leaving aside the rare crossing of the bridge to attend pierogi night *over town*, as Miss Dodie calls central Vancouver, should require such a colossal vocabulary? Especially when the inner world of what matters — shelter, food, drink — is so simple. Anna can picture this thing with the neck that Miss Dodie speaks of, this animal, but what could it possibly be called? It is like a frustrating television comedy when their conversations reach this point, the elderly woman who has lost the words and the nurse who never knew them.

Anna sidesteps the entire guessing game by staying quiet, instead pouring fresh coffee into Miss Dodie's ugly pottery mug, one of the few remaining dishes from a lopsided, dirt-coloured set made by a friend of Miss Dodie's from the previous century.

Miss Dodie sips noisily. Her wet lips make an upside-down U. "Annie, it is beyond terrible, this coffee of yours! The second cup is, is, is ... badder than the first."

Anna has been waiting for this. Nearly every morning, at some point, she hears how she cannot make a tasty cup of coffee. She has tried it all: more water, less water, more coffee, less coffee. Still she cannot get it right. Unlike Kelvin —

"Kelvin," Miss Dodie says on cue, "now he made the most delicious coffee. And he was so handsome. Even though he was" — she leans forward, drops her voice — "Oriental." She settles back, the leak-proof overnight diaper rustling beneath her haunches.

That is all it takes for the urge to kick in, the deep, yearning pull that runs through Anna's body, as if she were a puppet at the end of a master's strings. Kelvin sets it off every time, but to be honest, many things can. A temper tantrum from Miss Dodie. A chicken breast that turns out dry. A relentlessly rainy morning. Too many errands, or too few. Another sleepless night. The puppeteer yanks the string behind Anna's head and makes her look at the doorway. Beyond it lies her room, her bureau, the top drawer, the underwear and socks, and below them, the flask. But — now the master jerks Anna's wrist, the one with the Timex — it is only 7:10. There are the clothes to put Miss Dodie into, the drive, the walk, the hairdresser, then back home for lunch, then the cleaning and tidying while Miss Dodie naps, then the dinner to prepare. Only then.

So much to do, so many hours to count down.

She swallows the longing, spoons the last bit of egg into Miss Dodie's mouth, wipes the woman's lips with a paper napkin, and puts on a smile. "I take care of you now, Miss Dodie. Kelvin, he is gone. He is with the trumpet."

Miss Dodie cackles. "Oh, Annie! *Strumpet*. He is with the strumpet. Oh, you are a funny one. You dress like a hobo and you can't make a cup of coffee to save your life, but you do make me laugh."

Anna cannot help but smile. She pries the empty mug from Miss Dodie's fist, hoists the tray, and leaves the room a little taller than when she entered.

∧∨

At six o'clock, while Joe regards Kiki's sleeping form across the bed and Anna pays out the minutes until she has to get up, Charlotte Stedman is mounting an assault. Head high, chest up, a slight lean from the hips — but not too much. Lift the knees, drive them *off* the hill, not into it. The techniques loop through her mind, an inner soundtrack that instructs her to do it right, do it better.

Her speed in particular needs so much work. Last month's Vancouver Sun Run saw her worst time since she moved up to 10Ks four years ago. There was no reason for such a pathetic showing, no reason at all. Her overall fitness is great. She's forty-five but her body's a decade younger, says her personal trainer. She's injury-free, the intermittent Achilles tendonitis finally calmed by custom orthotics. She prepared for months before the race, rejoining the Running Room group she trained with every year as she built up her distance, going out four times a week and completing every route. Once Sidney came back home, requiring extra time and vigilance before and after school, Charlotte squeezed her outings into the early morning or late night on days when her daughter's neediness ruled out a scheduled run with the group. Charlotte even abandoned her playlist, opting to repeat, mantra-like, the motivational tips from her trainer and the Running Room leader instead of losing herself in the retro grunge of Stone Temple Pilots or Mother Lovebone. "You're shittin' me," laughed Parvat, the beefy paramedic she paired up with sometimes on Running Room evenings, when he asked for her favourite workout tunes. "I had you down as Top 40 all the way. Or some kind of, like, chick power stuff, Lady Gaga or Pink or whatever." Charlotte hadn't known whether to be flattered by the admiration on his sweat-shiny face or insulted by his assumption that she was too fragile for the hard stuff.

Halfway up the hill, she sucks a mouthful of tepid water from her hydration pack. One sip at the midpoint, another at the top. That's the deal. Rewards are the key to success. Run the full 10K route and she gets an extra couple of minutes in the shower, letting the hot water stream over her for the sheer delight of it. Finish the route in less than an hour and she gets a handful of nuts on her yogurt and berries, though this morning she'll forgo that treat, having weighed in, impossibly, three pounds heavier than yesterday. Off to work by seven thirty, a rare achievement now that Sidney's back and has taken to mooning around the kitchen before school, and she earns a half-sweet chai latte from the ground-floor café in her office building. Charlotte has powered through most of her adult life this way, rewarding herself — as she realized one night after finishing a novel that took so long to read that all sense of immersion evaporated — as one would a toddler or a prize horse: for small repeated achievements, with tiny treats at the end.

As she powers uphill, Charlotte reviews her list for today: locate and purchase the Fraser Valley goat cheese so blissfully reviewed on the Vancouver Eats blog, drive back to the office in time to catch up on email and prep for the one o'clock videoconference with headquarters, get progress reports from staff on a couple of nearly due projects, tackle more email, then make it home in time to help May with the food, get changed, and do her evening makeup before the guests arrive. What kind of reward do I get for that, Tayne? she wonders as she attacks the steepest section. She already knows the answer. Once she appears in their great room, cheeks aglow with bronzer, jewels sparkling at her ears and throat, hair up and neckline down, Tayne will squeeze her shoulder a little too firmly, as if testing a cantaloupe, not that he'd know how to tell ripe from green, and graze her ear with his dry lips. "You done good," he'll whisper, the grammar mistake a shared joke, in his view, an amusing backward glance at his rough-edged past.

Charlotte's stride is smooth, but her insides clench as she rehearses the day and rechecks the timing of each chore. Can she do it all? Probably, but it'll be tight. So much hinges on how long it'll take to buy the goddamn cheese. Tayne got it into his head after reading the blog post Sunday morning that they had to lay in a store of the stuff for tonight's party. Some client he's wooing is a vegetarian or a trumpeter of locally sourced foods or just a cheese nut. Or maybe it's the client's wife. Charlotte stopped listening to the particulars after it sank in that she would have to wedge a trip to the Fraser Valley into her already crammed agenda. "No distribution," Tayne said, scrolling on his iPad. "Looks like they only sell their products there, on the farm." There was no question of sending May, who has a full day ahead, cleaning the house and cooking for the party, not to mention taking the cats to the vet, the good vet who's booked up for months so they dare not reschedule.

It's a mental Rubik's Cube, all this rotating, adjusting, grouping tasks together in hopes of getting them to align in one seamless colour. The puzzle has grown only more complex in the three years since Tayne's company went public. Now her husband, hardly a homebody to begin with, is never around to help with domestic matters. When he is home, it's to make calls or entertain. And they entertain *all the time*.

The dinner parties were Tayne's brainchild. As soon as he acquired their spectacular waterfront spread, he wanted to show it off. *Nothing like a home environment to put people at ease*, he said. To get them drunk and turn them into your new best buddy is what he really meant. Some men did deals on the golf course; Tayne did them over martinis and barbecued salmon and, tonight, local dairy. Once GlobalTech went public, the parties grew more lavish and more frequent. Now they're legendary, an indelible part of the company's brand, attended not only by industry insiders but by hangers-on — wannabe inventors, local politicians, society couples, and minor celebrities whose publicists have brokered a little face time with one of Canada's famous families.

The parties are a millstone around Charlotte's neck, already bent low by millstones.

For one thing, she has her own career: a senior position that befits her education and background at Diamond & Day, the international PR firm where two years ago, after leading the wildly successful Lancôme campaign, she was promoted to director of the Pacific region. The job would have been hers years earlier if the fedora-wearing, dapper-suited old fart who held the position for decades hadn't lingered beyond every respectable retirement age. Finally he died, and Charlotte was awarded the job she'd been doing for years. Now, freed from interference, she has surrounded herself with fresh, smart staff, young people with unflagging stamina and a mastery of social media, and she has learned to delegate. Being in the C-suite, or at least the foyer of it, means not only putting in longer hours at her downtown office but also visiting the firm's North American headquarters in Toronto, New York, and Houston. More videoconferencing, she keeps saying. It's efficient; it's environmentally responsible. But no. The head offices are ruled by more dapper old farts, relics long past their expiry dates but still, nonetheless, in charge. Hopefully not for long. Rumour is she's the number-one pick for VP of the whole western division. The rumour has become stale, and the wait agonizing, but the prospect of finally entering the North American boardroom, at last closing in on the top, keeps her going.

It pulls her through twelve-hour days, plus evenings and weekends; it pulls her through the travel, the meetings, the pitches, the crises, and the never-ending river of email.

On top of her more-than-full-time job, Charlotte has her unpaid work — the minimum amount she can get away with for the Stedmans to remain pillars of the community. She advises Tayne on the business, in an informal but vital capacity given her stake in the operations. She sits on boards and volunteers with the local history museum. She oversees May, she runs the house and Tayne's soirees and dinners, she *runs*, she does other workouts to balance her muscle groups, she is mother to a troubled teen and wife to an absent entrepreneur, and twenty-four-hour on-call advisor to both. Her schedule, always packed, contracts further all the time, and with it her insides, which now spend most days cinched into a knot.

The running helps. At the crest of the scenic West Vancouver hill, where the latest hotel-sized mansion is taking shape, grey stucco exterior mostly finished and soon to be blighted, no doubt, with the wrought-iron curlicues of a Mediterranean climate, she turns right onto the high, flat street that is her three-block recovery interval. Glancing at her watch, she picks up the pace. She does not look at the pearling sky, gives no special thought to the pavement under her feet, morning-cool and solid. It is just another day, its horizon inside her head, its minutes fully accounted for.

By the time Charlotte is showered, dressed, and made up, it's nearly seven fifteen. Damn! She clatters down the stairs, her Manolo Blahnik flats ringing in the enormous space. The extra minutes under the hot water have cost her, even though she earned them fair and square. So did the time it took to rethink her outfit. Three extra pounds will not fit comfortably inside the pencil skirt she'd chosen last night.

She smells it before she enters the kitchen, and as she rounds the corner she knows exactly what she will see: a tall pot on the back burner of the ceramic stovetop, and on the counter next to it a rack of sugar-dusted dough balls.

"May!" she yells, though May is nowhere to be seen. Only Sidney is there, slouching over the granite island, shoving a powdered ball into her mouth, with a can of — for chrissakes! — Mountain Dew at her elbow.

"Sidney Stedman!"

The girl pops the dough ball all the way in. Chipmunk-cheeked, she twirls the barstool toward her mother and raises her eyebrows quizzically.

"Come on, Mountain Dew? You know you're not allowed to have that in the morning. And for God's sake, where's May? What's she thinking, making that crap?"

Sidney swivels back and bends down to her phone. She chews mightily, dramatically, jaws pantomiming an oil derrick. This is how she speaks to her mother these days — silently.

Charlotte berates herself. She knows better than to unleash like that. She takes a deep breath. *Try.*

"Sidney, I'm sorry I yelled. Just eat something nutritious, okay?"

Slowly, lingeringly, the girl picks up the can of Mountain Dew and takes a long, drawn-out slurp.

She might as well have raised her middle finger. Like that, deep inside Charlotte, it erupts. Not frustration. Not resentment. Rage. The special brand of searing fury that only her daughter can provoke, that turns Charlotte from cool professional into screeching harpy in a single ruinous moment. She wants to claw the girl's smug face, to yank the shining hair that hides her expression. It is wrong — evil, even — this impulse to harm her own daughter, yet for seconds she wants it. Wants to knock the girl off the stool, hear her head crack on the terracotta tiles.

Seven eighteen. Christ! She cannot, must not, get into it with Sidney when time is this tight. The girl is still fragile, as the counsellor reminds them. Besides, it's May's fault, making the stinking dough balls when Charlotte has told her over and over not to. The kitchen reeks of hot oil, and Charlotte's stomach lurches as she rummages in the fridge for blueberries and plain yogurt. This is no way to start the day. She should probably just skip breakfast and get out of here.

"Bitsu-bitsu! Breakfast of champions."

She peers over her shoulder, the fridge blasting cold air. Filling the kitchen doorway is the great Tayne Stedman. He pauses for a moment as if making a grand entrance, which she supposes he's doing, even in his own home. In several strides he is at the counter, chomping one, then two of the fried balls. He palms three more and crosses to the granite island, a faint trail of sugar in his wake.

"Morning, Sweetpea." He kisses the top of Sidney's head, no doubt depositing sticky remnants there.

"Hey, Daddy. They're yummy, right? May came over early to make them."

Oh, so she speaks. To her father. Charlotte slams the yogurt back down on the fridge shelf and bangs the door shut with one hip.

Tayne turns at the noise. "What's eating you?"

Charlotte glares. For fuck's sake. He knows full well that May's not supposed to deep-fry anything in their kitchen.

"Uh, oh. Mama got a boo-boo?" he says, grinning at Sidney.

Charlotte loathes the little-boy voice he uses whenever he teams up with their daughter, two aggrieved youngsters against one bad mommy. "Cut it out, Stedman." Be a man, not a child, is what she wants to say.

Tayne leans against the stool beside Sidney's, resting a single buttock on the seat. Presumably both cheeks would be too much commitment, as if to say he'll stay awhile in the bosom of the family, which at nearly seven thirty in the morning Charlotte knows will not happen. He eats steadily, scattering sugar and crumbs all over the granite.

She can't stand it. First the stink, now the mess. She grabs the damp dishcloth, crosses to the island, and makes furious circles with the cloth, swiping at the white drifts of sugar. Sidney continues to stare at her phone. Tayne's handsome face breaks into a fake grin and he pumps one fist in the air. "You go, girl!" he tells Charlotte. "Look at your mommy, Sidney. So much energy, so early in the morning. Out running before the sun and still wound up like a clock." Sidney looks halfway up, surveys her mother, says nothing.

"Hurricane Charlotte," Tayne says, easing himself off the stool.

How she despises that nickname! She stomps over to the sink, runs water over the dishcloth, wrings it until the twisted terry bites her hands. "You know full well what's bothering me." She keeps her voice low. Stay in control. Don't yell. "I've told May over and over not to make those goddamn things. They stink up the whole house. We're going to smell like a McDonald's drive-through all day. And they're so bad for you. Just a bunch of empty calories."

"Mmm, empty calories. My favourite." Now back by the stove, Tayne raises his voice to enlist Sidney. "Right, Sweetpea?" He eyes Charlotte as he stuffs another bitsu-bitsu into his mouth. "You should stay away from them, though. Gotta watch those hips."

It takes every shred of her willpower, every goddamn shred, not to hurl the dishcloth at her husband. Fucking asshole! He knows exactly which buttons to push. Exactly. Who ever came up with the bright idea that people should marry and live together, day after day, year after year, learning every characteristic and weakness and phobia of the other, mapping them all into some kind of user manual? Marriage is a hot-flamed forge, Charlotte has learned. It takes all the feelings you have, forms them and beats them and cools them, and produces the most lethal weaponry on earth.

Now Tayne is leaving. That's the Stedman strategy: fire at full power, then retreat. At the doorway he turns toward Sidney. "I'll be down the hall in my office, Sweetpea. Come say goodbye before school."

"Okay, Daddy. Love you."

Then to Charlotte: "Don't forget that cheese, okay? I know Olson's gonna flip over it."

She stands rigid, fists balled. *One, two, three, four …* Counting is one of Sidney's strategies, courtesy of the counsellor.

"And hon – lighten up a little. We'd all get along better if you just eased up. Right, Sidney?" He flashes the high-watt smile that magnetizes investors the world over, the same smile that beguiled her nearly twenty-five years ago. The smile that is now just part of the brand.

"It's going to be a great day," he says as he turns away. "I can feel it."

T W O

$\sim$

The soft air and fair sea that morning beckoned fishermen off the docks. Floatplanes prepared to fly; the ferries would run on time. Soccer games would not be cancelled today, so mothers and the occasional father packed extra apples and granola bars and texted intricate pick-up arrangements. Young lovers stirred on mattresses that had hours earlier been their play-ground; brushed an elbow or a knee not their own; smiled, scratched, fell more deeply asleep. Investment brokers downed espressos in stainless steel kitchens, clacked the tumblers of the solid-wood doors of Coal Harbour con-dos, young stallions let loose into the dusky dawn, taking each block at a canter, the unsaddled freedom of no overcoat foretelling a day of profit. Dogs stood in quivering hope at front doors, back doors, apartment doors, side doors, patio doors, basement suite doors for the thrilling click of the leash. The second batch of baguettes browned; prep cooks chopped and diced and sliced and minced. Babies crooned and sucked their fingers; unloved women entered dull kitchens; baristas beamed at their regulars and some-times meant it. The sick and stinking residents of the Downtown Eastside rustled and stirred, early morning sharp in their noses like nature's smelling salts, then backed farther into the alcoves of mighty banks and once-fine hotels, dreaming of the high that would never end.

The sea held its breath, flat and contained as a saltwater bath.

The sky held its breath, pierced only by the sharp clear song of a spring bird or two.

The earth held its breath, for the moment.

$\sim$

WHAT TRICK OF HISTORY turned a scattering of ramshackle docks, summer cottages, and the odd rough-walled store and clapboard inn, lined like a strip of skin against the dense forest that bearded the mountain face behind, into the mansion-studded enclave that is the North Shore's richest community? The transformation, its speed and its totality, strikes Kyle whenever he views West Vancouver from the water.

He knows the seminal events. The ouster and scattering of the Indigenous people who had lived here since time immemorial, and the gleeful grab of their lands by government and private interests. The purchase of nearly five thousand acres during the Great Depression by the Guinness brewing family, who built the Lions Gate Bridge to downtown. The landscaping by the famous Olmsted brothers, who reshaped the wild and ragged terrain. The lustre of the British Properties, an elite, whites-only suburb that tumbled down the mountain, at its foot the commercial strip on Marine Drive, and below that the waterfront, where summer encampments and slapped-up sheds in time gave way to the sleek compounds of the stupendously rich.

It's something Kyle understands, transformation. Like the Olmsteds he has a knack for it. He makes a living, a considerable one, from his ability to survey the rough and the ugly, to assess angles and contours, light and shadow, to know precisely where to trim, lift, sculpt, and fill to release the beauty that lies in wait. Every tired face he reawakens, every year he subtracts from a patient's appearance, brings the satisfying reminder that you need never accept the deficiencies you are dealt, that with reasonable helpings of desire, will, and talent, and – in the case of his patients – money, you can remake yourself as you please.

The morning is fine. That is to say, the weather is fine. The yellow Kevlar prow slices through Burrard Inlet as if propelling itself, Kyle's slim shoulders barely working. It's the best sort of morning to be out, when the water doesn't fight back but simply gives itself to him. Even though a hard paddle brings its own satisfactions – the deep bellowing of the lungs, arms locked into the stroke, thighs braced against the ribs of the low-sitting craft, abs contracting as he surges forward into a wall of wind, his body as alive and coursing in all its parts as when it batters against a lover – this morning as he parallels the West Vancouver shoreline, more closely than usual to avoid the container ships slipping east into Vancouver Harbour, he's grateful for easy conditions. The day has barely started and already his emotions are at a full boil. There's no need for his body to join them, at least not yet, not when the paddle is a mere prelude to the full castigation he has assigned himself – the short, fast cycle after he beaches the kayak, and the gruelling hike ahead: an easy start along the wide groomed trail that follows the old railway bed; the narrower treed-in path that ascends manageably to Whyte Lake; then the lung-busting climb straight up the Baden-Powell Trail, with a quick stop for the 360-degree views of Eagle Bluffs, before the final leg to the north summit of Black Mountain. After that, following a pause to refuel, the long trudge back. It's a punishing day-long triathlon that he's counting on to purge both his body and his mind. Because both are –

Dirty.

Last night. There are parts he doesn't remember, but there are parts he does. The bleary swirl of lights, beats, sweat, sensation. What was he thinking? Waking up in his fresh-sheeted bed to the splintered memories of it was like nosing a filthy, overflowing ashtray.

He pulls up the paddle, rests it athwart the kayak. Breathes.

You control your situation. It doesn't control you.

He repeats it to himself three times. Says it once, softly, out loud. Scans the horizon and tries to believe.

Above the highrises and few remaining houses that line the Ambleside shore, mansions climb in rows up and up the mountain until abruptly they stop, the Crown land above them an uncrossable border, at least until the coffers of government ring empty and forfeiture appeals. From down here, it's hard to believe that in a matter of hours he'll be up there, overtop the neighbourhoods, gazing down on the inlet, the distance conquered with nothing but the sinew and willpower of his own slight but whipstrong body.

Dirty.

He needs to cleanse, to atone. Not just for last night but for this morning. He lost it in the kitchen, he really did. He is going to leave Joe, that much he knows. But this is not the way to begin. He has to be dignified and respectful about it. He has to be kind.

You control your situation. It doesn't control you.

Change is inevitable. He of all people, a cosmetic surgeon, knows this. As he resumes his side-to-side stroke, he imagines the cottages and tents that dotted this beachfront a century ago, when city folk boated across the inlet for summer holidays and weekends at the seashore. Their camps were primitive, one- and two-room shacks or canvas tents on raised shiplap platforms. The less rugged vacationers – the rose-cheeked Edwardian ladies in white linen, the sort that populate *Downton Abbey*, the TV series all his friends adored – took rooms at the Clachan Hotel, which stood west of here at the Dundarave Pier. Surely they thrilled to the notion of roughing it, their silk shoes stepping daintily through the sandy weeds that passed for lawns, parasols shading unsunned complexions, laughing as the sea breeze lifted their wide-brimmed hats. Then as now, the wealthy dabbled in ordinary life from time to time, with their playhouses and wicker chairs, their tea sets and bathing costumes.

Though he is learning not to judge. West Vancouver, the polished, moneyed twenty-first century version of it, belongs as much to him as anyone. He may live in North Van, six kilometres to the east yet an entire economic stratum away, but his clinic, his clientele, and so many of his daily haunts are right here. The Ambleside Yacht Club is where he stores his kayak, hosing off the seawater after each outing and returning the craft, straightly aligned, to its designated rack. The Shorebird near the Dundarave Pier is his restaurant of choice on the rare days when there's time to buy lunch, its menu fashioned from local ingredients, its dishes high-protein and low-carb, where a forty-dollar bowl of artisanal bouillabaisse is presented with such reverence and mindfulness, as if to honour each mollusc that gave its life, that he is never affronted by the price. His gym is a stone's throw from the clinic, chosen so he cannot dodge a visit first thing before work or last thing before heading home. The neighbours who surround his office, and in some cases covertly visit it, nod hello as they pass to and from their fir-and-glass flats or their fir-and-stone townhouses, their manner easy in the way of those who accept life's bounty, from trust funds to rare art, from hired help to eternal youth, as their great good fortune.

Kyle works and recreates among these residents, he dresses and speaks like them, and he tends them in the most intimate of ways, yet still he does not feel entirely one of them. What they accept as their due has for him been a finish line that you chase, through study and honours, ten- and twelve- and eighteen-hour days, internship and residency and specialization, ramming the obstacles of debt and fatigue, excelling, perfecting, making it at last, exhausted but triumphant, yet still in your deepest recesses unsure whether you have truly arrived.

He lifts his paddle a hair too soon, ruining the rhythm of the stroke and splashing his torso with frigid seawater. His shriek pierces the sky.

Pussy! comes the voice. *What are you, a girlie girl?*

He glances down at the bright orange kayak skirt, the nylon speckled with the beginnings of mildew that he must scrub off when he gets home tonight. The skirt is overkill on this calm-water morning, but it keeps his bare legs warm and shields his backpack, snugged between his shins, from random spray. It holds in his wanton cock.

No. He won't think about that, not yet.

First he will try to calm his nerves and his heart, jangled from this morning's blowup. He will try to enter the spirit of this pearly morning, the sun biding its time above thin, high cloud, awaiting its moment. He'll have hours to think about the hard stuff when he's hiking. The entire day lies ahead of him, a punishment but also, because a day away from the office is so rare, a gift.

Screw you. They may be the two angriest words Joe has ever said to him. Afterwards, Kyle slumped against the kitchen counter, his pounding head in his hands. *You're such a fuck-up,* the voice said. *Weak little shit.* He proved the voice right by crying more. Once he'd pulled himself together, he called Shirin. She was still at home, but she had the appointment calendar on her phone. *Something's come up,* he told her, *a family obligation. Urgent.* The lie is needless, for Shirin is not the type to pry. It's one reason he hired her, that and her flawless complexion. One look at her and his clients prebook for months to come, imagining that each derma-fill session and brow lift will inch them closer to her dewy perfection.

Turns out it is a good day to ditch. A lot of Botox, some laser work, a micro fat graft, an otoplasty. *Easy to reschedule,* Shirin assured him in her softly accented voice. *The ear guy will be upset,* Kyle said. *It's fine,* she said. *Leave it with me. Tell the staff they've got the day off with pay,* he told her.

Kyle has never before missed a day at the clinic, and the ease of the cancellation staggers him. He takes it as an omen, confirmation that this highly irresponsible act is in fact the right thing to do.

Now he has ten hours, maybe more, to call his own. After last night and this morning he needs time to settle and reflect, to get his mind straight, to plan how to end his relationship with Joe, how to perform the most painful cut he will ever make. He will figure it all out today. Just not yet.

He noses the kayak closer to the seawalk, the recreational pathway that hugs the waterfront. Off to one side, on the rocks that separate the paved walkway from the ocean, a movement catches his eye. He angles closer, catching snatches of conversation among the early morning walkers: Farsi, Mandarin, something eastern European, the odd word of English.

What did he just see? A couple of runners wearing bright-hued jerseys streak by. The mounded top of an oversized stroller plows through the slower walkers, steered by an earbudded mother — or is it a nanny? — shouting into her phone. The flash over there on the rocks was something different.

He nears the shoreline, draws the kayak parallel to the land. Drifts a bit, peering closely at the tumbled rocks, but notices nothing out of the ordinary. He is about to head back out when it moves again and this time he sees it, perched on the largest boulder before the point. White and grey, a plump puffball on stick legs. A seagull.

Not just any gull, he realizes as the bird jerks its head again—a deformed gull. The bird's neck bulges grotesquely with giant, pointy growths that make Kyle think of goiters. The gull tosses its head wildly as if to dislodge the horrific swellings and fling them out to sea.

Kyle pulls up closer, drawn to the unnatural sight. The gull's hooked yellow beak gawps open and from it, straining up and out toward the thin overcast, stretches a long, purple appendage. It is roughly textured, like the trunk of an elephant.

What the hell?

Like a sci-fi creature, the scaly purple alien waves and undulates, trying to escape its host. The gull's beady eyes flash terror as it tosses its head again and again, trying to rid itself of its disfigurement.

Then it dawns on him. The gull is not birthing an alien; it has swallowed a sea star. The star's other arms have created the protrusions in the bird's taut neck. He watches, mesmerized, as the gull shakes its head, then shakes again, trying and failing to choke down the last arm. The gull sweeps the landscape with shiny jet eyes, and then, seeing nothing and no one that will steal its breakfast, snaps its head once more. In that final movement the purple arm disappears, completing the perfect hand inside the skin-tight glove of the bird's gullet.

Gross.

Part of Kyle is still a bewildered boy. His own throat constricts as he stares at the bird's distended neck and imagines the hard, wide sea star biting into the soft inner flesh. How is it possible? How can a slim-necked bird accommodate something so huge, so ... so wrong?

Remarkable.

Kyle is also a doctor, and the man of science in him recognizes nature at its weirdest, a birth in reverse—a fully formed creature muscled into, not out of, a tight, dilated canal, the last stiff arm taken in one swallow, carrying energy and life into the feeding bird. Viewed this way, the gull is all hunger, head thrown back, beak cranked as far open as its hinges will allow. A portrait of naked, urgent need.

Cock.

Above all, Kyle is a man. The second he sees the act as sexual, the other thoughts vanish.

∿

"What in heaven's name is that?" Miss Dodie's bejewelled finger points shakily out to sea.

Anna looks where directed. "Is boat. With small man inside."

"No, no, silly!" The woman swats the air with her finger. "What is *that?* That, that ... not dog ... not fish ... that *insect?*"

What Anna sees is a seagull, perched awkwardly atop a grey rock at the base of the seawalk, where she has been tugging her employer along on what is supposed to be a healthful daily stroll. As usual Miss Dodie has her own agenda, which does not involve ending this meandering walk, getting to the hairdresser's on time, driving home, preparing lunch fast enough that it can be served and perhaps eaten before teatime, tidying the kitchen, folding the laundry, or sorting the mail. Nor does it involve unstacking the dishwasher, brewing the tea, taking out the trash, watering the plants, administering the blood thinners, or wiping Miss Dodie's crumb-speckled lips. Unlike Anna's to-do list, Miss Dodie's changes moment to moment. Items are added and erased on a whim, planned activities ignored, accomplished tasks forgotten.

To make matters worse, Miss Dodie employs a vocabulary of her own making, her variations obscuring a language that already baffles Anna in its official form.

"It is seabird," says Anna. "Sea ... gull."

The woman tilts her head. "I know that, Annie. I am not a child or a, a slowster. But look at the — look *there.* Under his face. It's all pokey-outy."

"Is eating starfish. Eating it all up."

Anna has seen this before on their waterfront walks. With its misshapen neck the gull looks freakish if not distressed, but Anna knows that what the bird swallows and how it swallows it are simply matters of nature. We all must eat, and the ways in which we obtain our bread are seldom comfortable — like combing through your employer's garbled speech for a comprehensible word or two; like towing her from appointment to appointment, an eager but distractible purebred on a too-long leash; like wiping the loose flesh between her legs, which even now emits a high ammonia odour. Anna sighs. Now they must make an extra trip home before the hairdresser's.

"Disgusting. Simply disgusting!" Miss Dodie's voice, like the woman herself, is at once tremulously frail and deeply commanding.

"Is normal." Anna takes hold of Miss Dodie's arm and gently pulls her back onto the paved path. With a diaper change on the agenda, they must leave now. "Please, my lady. Come along."

"No." The woman shakes her head vigorously. "I want to watch."

"But we go to hairdresser. Remember? We must not be late. She is making your hair all curly and nice again."

Miss Dodie pats her thin white hair while allowing herself to be steered into the stream of walkers. An appeal to the old woman's vanity works every time. Anna cannot plumb the intricacies of the indefinite and definite articles, or sleep through the night, or make a single pot of coffee to her lady's liking, but this one trick she has mastered.

The equivalent of three city blocks of pathway is all that separates the women from the ancient green Volvo that Anna will steer up the mountain to the falling-down rancher at the top of the British Properties. There, in her bedroom, in the top drawer of the bureau, it waits for her: the smooth, cool flask. As they step, stop, step along the seawalk, Anna counts the hours until the first sip. Seven at a minimum, more likely nine. Once she settles Miss Dodie in front of the evening news with her dinner tray — not the silver tray, but the white plastic one that fits perfectly onto the TV table — Anna can slip into her tiny room and ease open the drawer. The smell, and vodka leaves little, will be masked by her own dinner, which she will eat immediately afterwards. Later, once she has tucked Miss Dodie into one corner of the sagging king-sized bed, she can drink as much and as late as she likes, but not before. Miss Dodie must never see her. If Miss Dodie finds out she will send Anna away, for not only is the old woman a confused rambler, she is also, ever since her husband died of a pickled liver, a strict teetotaller. She requires of Anna complete abstinence from alcohol, and on the first day of Anna's employment made her sign a document to this effect.

They proceed slowly, Miss Dodie halting every few steps to look back at the distorted, jerking gull, Anna pulling at the old woman's jacket to get her moving again. In this way they stutter past several glass-fronted homes, immense residences set off from the seawalk by generous lawns and low retaining walls. In one yard a man in a faded denim shirt is pruning the shrubs that overhang one wall. He nods to Anna, then straightens up and waves. Miss Dodie, whose eyesight comes and goes for no explicable reason, notices immediately.

"Annie! Don't encourage that man."

"I do not en-*cour*-age." Anna keeps her voice low and her eyes fixed ahead. She does not want to upset Miss Dodie, or delay them further by speaking to the man, but she is sorry to ignore him. His greeting was not flirtatious, only friendly. His acknowledgement of her existence was an offering toward which she leapt instinctively, a starved animal smelling food.

"Men only make trouble," the old woman quavers. "They only want one thing. I remember when my Marty — he was a famous, ah ... he did those ... What was he?"

"Scientist," Anna provides.

Miss Dodie nods. "Yes, that. He wanted it all the time, you know."

Anna knows. She has heard about Mr. Dodie, as she thinks of him, and his insatiable needs many times over the nearly three years she has been by Miss Dodie's side. It is dull, listening to the same reminiscences again and again, even with the many variations spun by the old woman's erratic memory. But boredom is a small price to pay for a good job, one that comes with a warm bed in its own room with its own door, and all the food she can eat, and one hundred dollars a week, which is more than enough to buy the bargain bottles of vodka which she hides in her closet and from which she fills her daily flask. Above all the job comes with Miss Dodie, who though batty and periodically outrageous is also kind, and so mired in her own past life that she does not think to ask about Anna's.

$$\wedge$$

Joe will wave at anyone who holds his gaze beyond two seconds. It's an east coast thing, being friendly to strangers, and though he hasn't lived on the Atlantic since bidding farewell to Cupids more than thirty years ago, he carries the Newfoundland ways with him. Being friendly is a west coast thing too. This is not Toronto, after all, or God forbid Ottawa, where he shivered through two frozen, lonely winters before heading toward the sunset. In Ottawa there could be two of you side by side in an echoing, empty lobby and you would take a dump right there on the floor before you'd dream of making eye contact or saying hello. That's not how it is on the west coast. Here you acknowledge people. You might not exchange intimacies with your neighbours or tell them your life story, you might not ask them over for dinner or a beer, or even a handful of peanuts, you might not even let them through your front door if you could help it, but by God you'd look them square in the face and say good morning. Even if they're too snobby to return the greeting, like the pair who just passed by, the old woman leaning heavily on the younger one, probably weighed down with too much jewellery, and the younger one, drably dressed and carrying a giant shoulder bag, sliding her eyes away as if the hired help is not worth the time of day.

I'm not hired help, he wants to shout at the women as they disappear around the point. True, he's been hired by the wealthy man who owns this house, along with two more homes in Canada alone, or so he's heard. And true, he's helping, because the famous businessman is too famous and too involved in his high-profile business to cut his own lawn or prune his own shrubs. But it's not like Joe is some kind of menial labourer or downtrodden servant. It riles him that the younger woman, almost certainly hired help herself, should think such a thing of him, and it's all he can do not to bellow the truth at her. He doesn't have to work. Kiki makes tons of money; they could get by fine without

Joe's paltry income. He *chooses* to work, which sets him apart from most landscapers. Every morning he loads his pickup, every night he sluices off a day's worth of soil and pollen and grass clippings, twice a week he fights traffic out to the Fraser Valley nurseries for the best plants at the best prices, not because he has to, like so many of the undereducated, overmuscled lads who do this for a living, but because he wants to. That's freedom, pure and simple – doing something for love, not pay.

He clips a stray branch, more forcefully than necessary, and the jolt through his arms confirms that he's still upset. Calm down, b'y, he tells himself. Let it go. No need to yell at strangers, no need to take it out on the poor plants. It's alarming, whatever's going on with Kiki, and he can't bear to think where the conversation might have led had he not left when he did. But things will work themselves out. They always do.

At least the shrubs are looking better, more clearly shaped, mostly symmetrical but not perfect, the boxwoods a little fuller on one side, the smoke tree a tad leggy. He likes his gardens to look more like nature and less like art. A little untidiness is a good thing, especially in this part of town where residents demand perfection in all things, from their rare striploins to their fresh-pressed pomegranate juice. Perfection is not what they'll get from Joe. Order with just the right amount of wildness, that's his trademark style. His business cards and the logo on the pickup say it well: Nature's Nurturer. Clever, more than one client has said. He nods modestly, as if he'd coined the name himself. Of course it was Kiki who dreamed it up, Kiki who's behind most of the clever moves in his life.

Joe drops the secateurs, trowel, and long-handled loppers into the wheelbarrow, and the resulting clang bells out toward the ocean. A small dog, possibly spooked by the sound, races across the fresh-mown lawn and dives under one of the neatened boxwoods. A terrier, maybe? The dog scooted by so fast it's hard to tell. The richer the master, the smaller the dog – that's the pet formula these days, judging by his clients. He likes a bigger dog himself, one you can tumble around with and not worry about squashing.

Next up: the rhodos beside the east wing. *Cut them way back*, the businessman barked over the phone yesterday. *They're ruining my view.*

As Joe ambles up the gentle incline to the house, he whistles in a half-hearted attempt to cheer himself up. That song he heard at home on the radio, "Goodbye Yellow Brick Road," has been earworming him. "Where the docks of society hound," he sings under his breath, cocking his head at the rhododendrons to assess their shape. That line makes no sense, though what can you expect from song lyrics? Mind you, he doesn't always get them right. Kiki had howled when Joe sang along with that old Stevie Nicks song, crooning over the hubbub of the bar where they huddled over a flirtatious drink in their early days together. *Just like the one-winged dove*, Joe sang, ogling Kiki, *sings the song just like she's singin'*. Red wine had geysered out of Kiki's nose. *Joe, think about it*, Kiki said, sniffling and wiping at the thin burgundy lather. *It's white-winged dove. White-winged, not one-winged. Otherwise how could it fly? It's not an amputee dove.* Joe flushed and laughed quickly. *For Pete's sake, I know that. I'm just messing around.* It was a long time before he worked up the courage to sing around Kiki again.

The east wing of the immense timberframe is lined with floor-to-ceiling windows that must give a killer view of the Lions Gate Bridge and the forest of Stanley Park. But the businessman is right — the rhodos, planted to screen the lower half of the windows from public view, have brushed out hugely. Joe will need the stepladder to trim them properly.

He doesn't whistle as he trots around back to the truck, the urge kicked by the memory of Kiki laughing at him. It seems he's forever hauling out the ladder. Another five inches taller, even four, and he wouldn't need the danged thing so often. Ma passed along much that he's grateful for — sense of humour, practicality, the Saint Anthony medallion that dangles from his rearview mirror and helps him remember better — but she also gave him his shape.

He slaps the front of his thighs, a habitual rebuke he takes no notice of. Cut it out, he tells himself. You're fine the way you are. Compact but sturdy, thick about the jaw and neck, a barrel chest (which has become more of a barrel torso if he's honest with himself, he'll have to watch that), legs short but powerful, a full head of wiry hair. He hugs the ground, was built for the soil, like a woolly sheep or a garden gnome.

Fine the way you are. Kiki used to say that while nuzzling Joe's matted chest or kneading his round shoulders. Kiki used to say a lot of sweet things before the Chill crept in. Now the loving words are few and far between, and the barely civil exchanges all too regular, though they've never had a teetering-on-the-brink fight as dizzying as the one this morning.

Joe pops the tailgate of his battered Toyota pickup, slides out the aluminum stepladder, and hoists it over one shoulder. Turns around and collides with two soft mounds that squish into his chest.

"Hey!" he yells, steadying the ladder.

The girl regains her footing and scowls at him, as if he's the one out of place. "Hey yourself."

She stands with one hip cocked, eyeing him up and down. She's a youngster, despite the womanly attributes against which he has bounced. Those are advertised by a neon-pink long-sleeved tee-shirt that snugs her torso like plastic wrap. *Riot Grrrl*, say the black letters across her chest.

He lowers the ladder from his shoulder. "You better watch it. I nearly knocked you down."

Her eyes roll skyward, her hip juts further. "Hardly." The word is a spitball hurled from her pink-glossed mouth. Denim cutoffs, snipped short and rolled up shorter, crease a vee into her crotch, even though the morning's barely warm enough for Joe's shirt sleeves.

"Whatever you say." He picks up the ladder again, preparing to give the glaring creature a wide berth.

"This is my house, you know." She juts her chin at him and winds the blond end of her ponytail around a blue-nailed finger. Haughty as a queen at, what? Fourteen? Fifteen? That's how they raise them these days. No respect for their elders anymore, only contempt. He shakes his head ruefully.

Determined not to let the day slide further, he resumes his whistling and strides off purposefully to the east wing. The girl trails him. She watches silently as he sets up the ladder, mounts it carrying the loppers, and starts in on the overgrown branches. The air is hushed and the nearby seawalk for the moment deserted, the metallic shear-slash and the cries of low-swooping gulls the only sounds.

"Hey, you."

He pretends not to hear.

"Hey!"

He stops, takes his time turning around. Man interrupted, he wants her to know.

"I could, like, throw the stuff you cut off into the, you know." He looks at her steadily, waiting for the real words. "Into that." She jerks her head to one side.

"Do you mean throw the *branches?* Into the *wheelbarrow?*" He pronounces each syllable. Yup, this is how they raise them. She can probably name ten shoe designers and the number-one boy band, but not the most basic yard item.

The girl tilts her head, face impassive. She will not accept the lesson, will not repeat the new words. Joe sighs. Fine, he'll let her help. Maybe it will keep her from pestering him. "Okay. Just take out the trowel and the secateurs first."

"The huh?"

"The *tools.* Take the tools out of the wheelbarrow before you start filling it up."

"Well, duh."

This is how it goes, the modern conversation with young people. She is the one who doesn't know the words, yet in an eyeblink he is made out to be the stupid one. He watches as the girl tosses her shining ponytail over one shoulder and bends languidly to the task, a princess gathering petals.

Joe goes back to pruning. At least there will be no sullen teenager sulking around his house; that's something to be thankful for. No kids – Kiki couldn't have been firmer about it five years ago when they realized, soon after meeting, that they were in it for the long haul. Joe was briefly disappointed. He'd had his soft moments of wishing for a little one, a moon-faced baby that would grin at him adoringly, a tousle-headed youngster he could run around the yard with. But life is easier this way, no question.

Really, life is good. He shears off a leggy branch. Things will go back to normal at home. Kiki will snap out of it, they'll both apologize for this morning, they'll steer themselves through whatever phase of the relationship this is. And one evening they'll hug, and the laughs will come easy, and the chilled layer between them will be gone.

Joe works steadily, repositioning the stepladder from time to time, the girl following with the wheelbarrow, which she figures out how to move after scraping the rear metal rest against the lawn a time or two.

Eventually she stops. She stands beside the barrow, hands dangling at her sides. "It's full."

He glances down. "You just have to compact it some."

"Huh?"

"Compact it!" he hollers, before grasping that again the problem is vocabulary, not volume. "Push down on the branches. Press them down so they take up less space."

She pats at the branches as if they were sleeping puppies.

Joe descends the ladder and muscles down on the cuttings to demonstrate.

"But they're all prickly and everything!"

"Here, wear these." He flips a pair of work gloves from the back pocket of his Levi's.

"Eew." She dangles the battered, soil-stained gloves at arm's length.

Joe gulps a generous helping of air and tells himself to be patient. "Look, why don't you go find something to do, go back in the house or whatever. In fact, shouldn't you be in school?" It's Tuesday, for Pete's sake. Garbage and recycling day at his place. Why is the girl even here?

She mumbles something about a day off.

"Uh-huh. How dumb do you think I am? You're skipping. It's not exactly hard to figure out. I did it, your dad did it, we all did it."

"Yeah, right." She toes the ground with her sneaker. "My *dad.*"

"Ask him. I bet he did."

"Uh, like you don't know what you're talking about? My dad is all Mister Perfect Attendance. He never misses work, not even if he's sick, not that that ever happens. He's always working. He doesn't know how to skip anything." She sniffs one of the work gloves and recoils. "Nasty!"

"Really, just go inside. Or to the mall or wherever you go when you're supposed to be in school. Go get your toenails painted." Joe starts back up the ladder.

"No!" she cries. "I want to help."

"Then quit being such a crybaby. Just put on the gloves and make some room in the wheelbarrow. I haven't got all day. I've got an afternoon job too, you know."

He clambers back up the ladder. A few more branches to one side and he'll be done with the rhodos. Then it's just the beds along the driveway to weed and tidy and a little pruning in the western yard.

He leans out toward the overgrown branches and lops off one, then another. Each cut gives him a bigger glimpse into the interior of the east wing: a huge room, off-white walls, exposed timber ceiling, and in the middle, behind a desk that must have been hewn from first-growth fir and skidded out by a dozen lumberjacks, the man of the house himself: Tayne Wilton Stedman, all six-foot-whatever of him, CEO and Chief Innovator, GlobalTech Communications, according to the business card he'd thrust at Joe earlier this morning. It was their first face-to-face meeting, Stedman having hired Joe over the phone, and it wasn't pretty.

"You're late," Stedman had snapped. "Twenty minutes late."

"I know." Joe had spent the entire traffic-clogged drive berating himself: the extra time he'd spent in bed, the stupid fight, his horrible words to Kiki, his inability to remember the most basic weekly act of putting out the garbage. And to top it off, being late. "It won't happen again."

"Huh. We'll see."

Tayne Stedman is a celebrity entrepreneur, one of Vancouver's leading lights, a mover and shaker who shows up in the newspaper and on TV and in those photos from charity galas. His teeth are unnaturally white and he wears a tuxedo like he was born in one. He called Joe last week, in a panic because his regular landscaper had vanished, his phone disconnected, his email sending bounce-backs. Joe had been mentioned by someone on a fundraising committee with Stedman's wife. "Mentioned," Stedman repeated, "not recommended." It was a busy week, he said, and he had no time to check Joe's references, so they'd see how things worked out the first visit. No promises. Joe, usually eager to land a new client, had felt like the last dried-up sandwich on the platter, a feeling that only intensified under Stedman's withering glare this morning.

Now, in his hangar of an office, Stedman somehow manages not to stand by the desk but to tower over it, impossibly dwarfing the mammoth slab. Joe gets a sideways view of the tycoon's face: his hawk-like profile, his lean jaw and twisting mouth issuing what must be orders, though it's impossible to hear the particulars, the triple-pane windows an impervious barrier. What would it be like to run a huge company, to tell thousands of people what to do, to determine their fates? The stock market could soar or plummet today based on what this man is saying right now, twelve feet away.

A long, narrow earpiece protrudes from Stedman's thrust-forward head. It could be the only tool this guy needs in his line of work, Joe marvels. In fact, it could be a *product* of the work. Joe, who owns a flip phone and has yet to feel at home in the twenty-first century, has only the vaguest sense of what telecommunications manufacturing entails. He adjusts his grip on the heavy-duty loppers and slices off another branch.

"Hey!" the girl calls, newly offended. "Watch where you drop stuff! You nearly hit me."

Joe peers over his shoulder. The branch lies on the ground at least two feet away from her.

"Just get out of the way. It's pretty simple."

"Whatever." She crosses her arms over her pillowy chest. "He in there?"

No point pretending he doesn't follow. He leans to the right for another look. "Yup."

"On the phone, right? Like I said, working. Twenty-four seven. He wears his Bluetooth to bed. You could come crashing through that window and he wouldn't quit talking."

Beyond the girl, heaps of twigs and branches litter the ground. "Guess he didn't pass that work ethic down to his child."

"Please." The girl tosses her ponytail, glares up at him in a decent imitation of her father. "I'm not a *child*."

〜

Stedman wishes to God he was working, wishes he was doing anything other than talking to, or more accurately half-listening to and occasionally placating, Charlotte, his lawful wedded wife, mother of his child, hostess of his parties, recipient of half his assets should their peace talks ever break down and the long, sizzling fuse of their marriage finally detonate. As she chatters on, a fraction of some cortex of Stedman's brain registers what she says, while a much greater region previews the presentation his top account managers will deliver in Cincinnati in half an hour. Procter & Gamble is one of the few multinationals missing from GlobalTech's roster and he wants them desperately, with a deep-seated, all-consuming lust he has not felt for years for the trim, long-limbed, and slightly, if he is honest about it, horse-faced woman on the other end of the phone, who has now moved on to — what?

"— shots?"

"What's that, hon?"

"Are you checking email or something? Texting on your other phone? Are you listening to a word I'm saying?"

"Of course I'm listening. I was just distracted. That new landscaper, he's right outside my window and he ... I only missed the last thing you said."

"The shots. Did May take the cats in for their shots?"

"Oh. She could have."

"Well, is the Smart car still in the garage? If it's gone, then she's gone."

"Give me a minute." Reluctantly Stedman turns his back on his office, its multi-million-dollar view being restored to him with every slice of the landscaper's shears, and heads for the mudroom that leads into the garage. He is a wealthy man; it is a long walk. Meanwhile Charlotte issues forth a stream of words, possibly sentences, about the Fraser Valley and traffic and cheese.

Stedman's four-car garage warehouses all manner of vehicles: bicycles, outgrown scooters, the flame-shaped Ducati he rewarded himself with after closing the IBM deal, the hot-pink moped he bought to incentivize Sidney, his-and-hers Segways purchased in some delusion of marital togetherness. In the centre, the Lexus sedan that will soon whisk him to headquarters twenty minutes away in a North Shore technology park. And on the far side, shrouded by a drop cloth whose baby blue precisely matches the machine underneath, his pride and joy, the 1962 racing MGB he had shipped over from Denmark when his company first hit ten million in sales. It's been way too long since he took that little honey out for a run, and now that the winter rains have finally tapered off, the road is calling. He can almost taste the fumes — the little racer has a voracious appetite for oil — can feel the chassis shift and bump under his seat, the steering wheel vibrate beneath his hands, the wind sweep his barbered neck. Why not? Just top up the oil — there are cases of it stacked in one corner — warm her up, then ease her out. Just a quick spin.

Hell, no. What is he thinking? He has to be on call for his guys in Cincinnati, ready to dive into databases, sales projections, next-gen operating systems, and any other instant details they need to support their presentation to the top brass at Procter & Gamble.

Later, then. This afternoon. It'll be dinnertime in Cincinnati, the workday over. Marcus can cover for him for an hour or two. He'll hug the s-curves of Marine Drive, merge onto the Sea to Sky Highway, and let her rip, maybe as far as Squamish —

"Hel-*lo?* Is anybody there? For chrissakes, Tayne, stay with me, would you?"

Stedman snaps to attention. Between the Lexus and the MGB is a slim gap normally occupied by the electric Smart car. "It's gone." His voice reverberates in the cavernous space. "May is gone."

"Damn! I wanted to catch her before she left. We need extra wine for dinner tonight. How many are we expecting again?"

The dinner party. He has completely forgotten. With a forlorn glance at the covered MGB, he shelves his dream and counts up the invitees. "Ten. Twelve if Marcus and his wife can make it."

A beat. "What do you mean, *if?*"

"I know, it's not like him. Babysitter issues, apparently."

Silence on the other end, longer than his stormy wife generally allows. "Charlotte? You there?" He adjusts his Bluetooth earpiece. Did the call get dropped?

"Fine then." Her voice is bell clear, the reception perfect. "I'll pick up a few more bottles while I'm out. Is that new designer – McMillan? That his name? Is he coming?"

"I think so."

"He's the alkie, right? I'll get some sparkling juice too. Anything else?"

"What? No. What you've said sounds just right, hon. Have a fun day."

"*Fun?* Jesus Christ, Tayne. I'm supposed to be at the office putting out fires and here I am driving goddamn *hours* into the middle of farm country to buy some natural unwashed goat cheese that got written up in *Organic Gourmet* just to impress a client of yours who's gone all, all ... locavore. God! If this cheese is so fucking great, how come they don't carry it at Whole Foods? And now I've got to get wine too. I'm not even at the Port Mann Bridge yet, for chrissakes. There's some accident near Abbotsford and the traffic's stopped up like a constipated shit."

He winces. Notwithstanding her cultured upbringing in Montreal's tony Westmount area, a childhood of tennis and house staff, piano and private school, horseback riding and sailing at the summer house in Vermont, his thoroughbred wife has a potty mouth. Fortunately she knows when to sanitize it, sparing him so far the embarrassment of having to smooth over her crassness with clients or staff. No, Charlotte Stedman, née Pettigrew, saves her vulgar words for him, on the assumption, he supposes, that they will remind him of who he is, that despite his high-tone surname he's a Hamilton boy, descended not from the department store empire – the connection people automatically make now that he's a successful entrepreneur – but from the raging, filthy furnace of the steel mill.

Like that, he decides. Life is short. He'll take his drive.

"Listen, hon. I might be late tonight. Some stuff to clear up. You and May will have it all under control, you always do. I'll be back before cocktails are over."

Silence. Strange music – is that a banjo? – trickles faintly from his earpiece.

"Hon?"

"Are you shitting me, Stedman?"

Uh-oh. She only uses his surname when she's really mad. "I promise. I'll be there before anyone even notices –"

"You bastard." Her voice is low and quiet. There's definitely some kind of jangly music in the background. Has he gone too far?

"Listen, Charlotte –"

"No, *you* listen, Stedman. I will say this once. You are a selfish fucking bastard, and I am tired of it. Bone tired. *You're* going to be late? Well, maybe *I'll* be late. Maybe I won't show up at all. How'd you like that, huh? Maybe I won't come home with your fucking *cheese* and your fucking *wine*. I'll just keep on driving and you'll never see me again. No more Hurricane Charlotte. You can host your own fucking dinner parties from now on."

He sucks in his cheeks. Definitely. He has definitely gone too far. "Okay, hon. Calm down."

Abruptly the music cuts out and his wife's words finally, blessedly, end.

∿

The fucker! Charlotte hits the steering wheel of the immobile Porsche Cayenne three times, hard. Late! Late to his own fucking dinner party! A party that is for him, by him, entirely about him, but that *she* has to make happen. It's the story of their marriage. The story of her life.

The traffic has once more come to a standstill. A series of rapid-fire honks sounds somewhere behind her. "Excellent!" she yells. "Really helpful, you yo-yo!" No one can hear, and her words are instantly muted by the SUV's signature virgin wool interior, but still. It feels good to let go.

She takes advantage of the stop to bend down and dig inside her right shoe. From the moment she hit the highway she's had an itchy foot, literally and figuratively. She is dying not only to scratch it but to press it to the floor, to shoot the SUV forward, an icebreaker ramming through sluggish floes. Time to go, already! The morning is leaking away and she's got so much to do.

Sitting up, she adjusts the waistband of her Alexander McQueen trousers, which feel more than three pounds too tight, even after her run, even after skipping breakfast. The faded red Corolla in front of her idles noisily. Up ahead the spans of the Port Mann Bridge appear no closer than before she called Tayne.

Fucking hell! She hits the steering wheel again. After the way he baited her at home, she should have never called him. And what's this shit about Marcus? Babysitter issues? What a gong show this day is turning into.

The cars begin to crawl. Forward a few inches, stop; another few inches, stop. God, she hates driving in this place. Compared to the amphetamine speed of Montreal, where she got her licence, Vancouver traffic drags. No surprise in a city full of sluggish potheads and anemic vegans. Tack on the three-car pile-up ahead, which the traffic station droned on about for so long that she switched over to music, and it's a recipe for out-and-out road rage.

And the music. Jesus! As if the traffic jam and the conversation, if you want to call it that, with Tayne weren't enough, there's the torment of Sidney's playlist, which her daughter regularly uploads to the

Cayenne's audio system so she need not speak to her mother should circumstances compel them to travel together. This new mix is scraping Charlotte's innards. Gone are the frivolous but tolerable dance beats and girl vocals that Sidney favoured before rehab. Today the Bose speakers bleat someone's idea of alt-hillbilly, a rollicking mix of snare drum, washboard, banjo, and earthy male harmonies that irritates Charlotte in a way no scratching will ever relieve. She can just picture them, a clutch of bearded art-school dropouts, their publicity shots staged in a hayloft, their real homes generic highrise condos.

She stabs the digital console, ending the din mid-yowl. Surely the quiet will calm her. Deep breaths, she tells herself. Be in the now.

What if she did it? What if she acted on her threat and ditched her own dinner party? No Tayne, no Marcus, no guests, no cheese. What if she just — didn't go?

As if in sync with her thoughts, the traffic rolls to a halt again.

If it were up to her, not that anyone would ask, there would never be another goddamn dinner party. She was crazy to go along with the idea in the first place. She should have insisted that Tayne throw his parties at the office or in restaurants, not drag them into the only space where there's a remote chance of peace and quiet. How different would their lives be if they'd kept their home to themselves? How different — and how is it she's only thinking of this now? — would Sidney be? Maybe their daughter's behaviour stems from the loud, late gatherings, the free-flowing booze, the constant stream of strangers: new clients, old clients, top-drawer clients, new managers, old managers, up-and-coming sales VPs, newly hired wunderkinds clutching newly minted degrees from MIT. Not to mention the parade of women who accompany the guests. It's always this way: the clients and staff are men, the companions women. There are no male companions, because who would they accompany? In the world of GlobalTech, there are no female bigwigs and only a handful of gay guys.

Sometimes at these parties, in the middle of checking the silver ice buckets or hustling to the kitchen to ask May to grill more shrimp, Charlotte stops and wonders: is this really the twenty-first century?

There she is, in a cocktail dress and heels, serving Manhattans and shellfish to big-jawed men and their streaked-blond conquests as if the decades since the fifties, when her mother the renowned feminist was born, and since the seventies, when that feminism turned radical, never happened. When Charlotte turns the corner into the kitchen, she almost expects to find May in a starched maid's uniform, pulling the aluminum handle of an antique icebox.

She would love to be a no-show tonight, to follow through on her threat to Tayne. If only she had the balls.

She reaches again for her right foot and scratches, grateful for the relief.

It's too much. She has split and split again, like some kind of mutant cell, and now she's nothing but fragments: full-time public relations executive, full-time home manager, part-time advisor to Tayne's business, not to mention part-time volunteer, athlete, and, recently, lover. Add to that motherhood, at long last morphing into a part-time calling now that Sidney is older and, fingers crossed, past the worst of her troubled times. What with the moped Tayne bought her post-rehab, Sidney seldom needs Charlotte or May to drive her to and from school, her friends' houses, or the mall. Her behaviour is under control: she's respecting her curfew, staying sober, keeping out of trouble. She seldom rages at Charlotte anymore. Instead she goes frosty and silent, lobbing gestures and facial expressions instead of word bombs. Let it slide, the group counsellor says, but it's not easy. It stings to be treated like an object, or worse, an enemy. Especially when you try to be calm and then Tayne enters the room and does nothing, *nothing*, and the girl lights up like a beacon because it's her precious father.

At least it's not forever. A couple more years and Sidney will be off at university, and Charlotte can condense the mother job description, file it in a lower drawer, and hopefully not consult it for months at a time.

She knows it's wrong to feel this way, to long for your child to move out. Empty-nest mothers are bereft when their offspring leave, not relieved. They become restless, blue, unmoored. Charlotte knows these feelings intimately, because she experiences them when Sidney's at home. When her daughter was in rehab, and the house, the vehicle, and the text and phone traffic went blessedly quiet, Charlotte understood how much of her daily anxiety stems from her daughter's presence. It is a deep and shameful secret how much she relished the time Sidney was away. Visiting her daughter in a controlled environment, on a strict schedule, felt exactly right.

She shifts in her seat. The SUV's wool interior, supposedly the epitome of luxury, is a ridiculous feature that only makes her itchy. She never wanted this ugly, environmentally irresponsible vehicle, and she fought Tayne on it. But he won. He loves to win. It gives him another reason to flash his cheesy smile and pump his fist in the air.

Breathe, she tells herself, scanning the lanes of cars, wishing for a dose of Nirvana or Soundgarden, a wash of screaming lyrics and thrashing guitar to drown out the world. She keeps meaning to load her own playlist but can never find the time.

There is never any time.

Good thing Mother's not alive to see this. Defender of women's rights and freedoms, she'd be horrified at how much of Charlotte's life is not of her own making. She would peer at her daughter from beneath unplucked brows and lift her upper lip. *Where is the individual in all of this?* she would inquire, in the dry sociologist's voice she donned whenever their conversation danced near personal matters. It was Mother's single pearl of wisdom the few times Charlotte dared approach her for guidance, and it taught Charlotte a lesson she's lost sight of in the maelstrom of life: when it comes to making your way in this world, you're on your own.

On your own. There was never a starker truth, and today Charlotte feels it keenly. From her solo run at dawn to being ostracized in her own kitchen to her pointless attempts to communicate with Tayne, the fact of how utterly alone she is has sat heavily on her all morning.

She reaches across the passenger seat to straighten her Birkin bag, reassured as always by its iconic shape, rounded handles, and soft cowhide. She'd flirted seriously with orange when she ordered the handbag two years ago, a reward for her promotion to director at Diamond &

Day, but in the end she settled for taupe, a more practical shade, not to mention easier to get. Thanks to Tayne's celebrity she waited only three months for the coveted Hermès creation, a blink of an eye in the Birkin world. Much as she hates to admit it, she is grateful to her husband for lifting her public status enough to bump her up the waiting list. The dreaded dinner parties probably helped. She adores the bag, which she has personalized with two dangling charms — a diamond, small enough not to call attention to itself, and a sun, to symbolize day. Still, a tiny part of her (*selfish*, her mother would intone) rues not holding out for the orange. There can be a flattening disappointment in making the sensible choice.

What if she did it, if she ditched the stupid party? She could stay late at work, review the comm plan for their new alternative energy client, which she's been meaning to get to for days, and finally clear her inbox. Not call Tayne or text him. Head home well after dinner has wrapped and the guests have departed. I couldn't help it, she'd tell Tayne, and Marcus too if he was still there talking shop. Some *stuff* to clear up, she'd casually say. Oh, and I've ordered another Birkin, in orange. Not that it's any of your business what I buy.

For one joyous moment the beat-up Corolla ahead of her accelerates. *Go, go, go,* urges an inner voice. They travel three car lengths, then grind to a halt once more.

Charlotte slumps. Daughter of a feminist, university educated, nearing the pinnacle of her career, and what is she doing? Wasting time on menial tasks so that Tayne's house and Tayne's business will run like precision timepieces. Hosting dull parties that eat into the evening hours she needs for email, Twitter, newsfeeds, a run. Allowing vacuous music in the vehicle to keep her daughter from lashing out at her. Driving a fully loaded hundred-thousand-dollar Porsche Cayenne that chugs gas every second it sits here in traffic. And that's not the half of it. Think of all the money she has parted with, millions and millions. For what? The perfect family portrait, her husband's place on the Top 50 CEO list, and a wheel of local cheese.

She didn't use to be this way. The thin vein of recklessness that still runs through Charlotte Stedman was a fat pulsing artery in Charlotte Pettigrew. When she hit university, young Charlotte gave up trying to please her elusive mother, under whose roof she nominally lived. And after her father, whom she barely knew, died in a car accident in Vermont halfway through freshman year, she did whatever she wanted – danced all night, drank with her favourite grunge band, and made out with the sinewy Kurt Cobain–like singer in the bathroom, the alleyway, the band's van, backstage, anywhere furtive and dirty. Diligent even then, she buckled down when she had to and sailed through her communications degree, graduating summa cum laude. But there was more than enough time left over for the wild, messy life she adored, all spontaneity and excess and thumping bass line. She felt, back then, authentic.

The memory of that other Charlotte makes her square her shoulders and pull in her chin. Posture, she tells herself, echoing her personal trainer. No wonder she's prone to injury. Also, attitude. She made her decisions long ago – Tayne, the company, Sidney, her inheritance. No point indulging in regrets.

Tolerance, she vows. And patience. And gratitude. More deep breaths and moments of inner reflection. More being in the present, less worrying about the future. Except –

Goddammit, the wine! She completely forgot. How can she possibly squeeze in another stop?

"Call May," she instructs the dashboard. Two rings, three, four, then May's accented treble saying she cannot take the call just now, please leave a message. Charlotte redials. Again, voicemail.

Goddammit! When she hired May last year, Charlotte gave her the latest iPhone plus an all-inclusive plan. Just as Charlotte has repeatedly asked May not to fill the kitchen with the smell of hot oil, she has reminded her to take the phone whenever she leaves the house. But May, their third and best housekeeper, mild and smiling and wonderful with Sidney, is on certain points unmoveable. No doubt the phone is sitting on the kitchen counter right beside the greasy bitsu-bitsu, May's favourite treat from back home in the Philippines.

Charlotte plays with the GPS, zooming out to gauge where she can find a drinkable grape, a *local* grape, en route to the cheese farm and still make it back to the office for the one o'clock videoconference. Also – shit! She nearly forgot the meeting later with the social media team, which she'll have to wrap up early in time to beat the traffic back to the North Shore to help May set up. And Tayne will be –

Stop it, she tells herself. Just stop it.

The traffic advances another few feet. In the right-hand lane a gleaming black sedan slides alongside her. She appraises the driver. Lightly, so maybe naturally, tanned; handsome profile; bare forearm nicely muscled, not overdone. Chunky titanium diver's watch on the arm that reaches up to adjust the rearview mirror, costly but plain, not the gaudy gold Rolex Tayne insists on wearing.

As long as she has known her husband, appearance has mattered to him. The Rolex, the tailored shirts, bespoke suits in an industry where leaders wear Levi's. Even in the third-year marketing course where they met, Tayne always taking the seat beside hers, he was on a mission to disguise his working-class origins. He carried a worn leather satchel, eschewing the nylon backpacks favoured by the other guys. When he started following her to clubs, he'd sit nursing a beer at a corner table, dressed in ironed khakis and loafers, a preppie in the mosh pit. Not that he ever entered the pit. He simply sat there and watched her dance, disappearing before the band's last set because he had early-morning classes.

She glances again at the man in the car beside her and for a moment imagines his muscled arm flexing, his hefty diver's watch grazing her skin, running up the inside of her thigh. Light waves lap the delta below her waist.

It's hard to believe now, when he's a commander of thousands, but Tayne followed her most everywhere back then. He'd set his sights on her, he announced one blurry Saturday night while pulling Charlotte, adrift on ecstasy, home early from a rave, and he intended to stick around until she saw sense and hitched up with him. The old-fashioned declaration was dorky and irritating, but its determination intrigued

Charlotte. Unlike her grunge boyfriends, Tayne didn't care about being cool. If he wanted something, he said so and went for it. What he wanted then, besides the letters MBA after his name, was her. For a girl who grew up yearning for attention, being the object of someone's desire was irresistible.

Now, of course, she knows better. When Tayne made those declarations, propping up her wasted body on the flagstone steps of her grey stone home, it was the Westmount mansion and the wealth that came with it that he had his sights on, not her.

The man in the black sedan moves his hand, big and square, to his head, smooths the greying hair at his temple – a flattering cut, unfussy, expensive. She imagines the touch of that hand, a stranger's touch, a good-looking stranger. No ties, no questions asked. The way it was for a while with Marcus, straight-on heady pleasure, before he demanded more.

The man moves his hand across his well-cut jaw – classic line, very Marlboro Man – and toward his face. God, he is handsome. Even his ears are perfect. With two fingers he absently wipes his lower lip, as if removing a bead of coffee. The lip is full and sensuous; she would love to bite it. Slowly his fingers travel up, touch his upper lip, very kissable, travel up again. One finger enters his nostril and begins to probe.

Jesus Christ! Charlotte whips her gaze ahead and her anger returns full force. People are disgusting, and endlessly disappointing. It's a fact of which she is offered fresh proof every day, yet by every tomorrow she has filed the insight away and slipped back to believing that most things will be done right.

Not today. Today all the ways that people let you down, all the wasted time and dreams unrealized, all the shades of sour that life can turn – today the buildup seethes inside her, shifting, colliding, gathering power. Years of keeping a lid on it. Years of strict control. Today her right foot itches unbearably. She longs to just *go*.

$\wedge$

SLATE: Did you sense beforehand that something major was going to happen? Were there any signs, any precursors?

SUMMER: You know, you read interviews and talk to people who swear they knew ahead of time. Some saw lights earlier in the day, these weird blue-and-white bands that kind of shimmered in the sky. I didn't see that. There are people who say their pets were acting strange, their cats were running around in circles, dogs barking constantly, stuff like that. Some people say they just knew change was coming. They felt it, like a premonition.

Are they telling the truth? I don't know. They could be. All I know is, none of those things happened to me. It was just another day. This long, boring day you had to get through so it'd finally be over and the next boring day would start.

THREE

∧

The shift began, imperceptibly, a week earlier. The monitors, databases, and research stations that snaked down the west coast, all the protective technology that delineated the risky Cascadia subduction zone, registered nothing.

It also began fifty-five years earlier, when rough-built homes and outbuildings, rows of shops and apartment houses, collapsed within moments in Alaska. The land slid and the roads dropped, taking with them buildings and cars. Parts of the state fell as much as eleven feet; others rose thirty. Latouche Island travelled sixty feet southeast.

It began over three centuries earlier, when the Cascadia fault ruptured massively and the sea hurled salt water inland along North America's west coast, swamping villages and snatching lives. The few who did survive passed along descriptions of the wall of water that rose one winter's night. The Elders' tales were dismissed — the Indigenous peoples of North America, it was felt, being exaggerators at best and outright fabricators at worst — dismissed, that is, until substantiated by the Japanese, those rational thinkers and incontrovertible historians whose written and therefore somehow more authentic records described a mysterious tsunami that had assailed their shores from across the ocean.

It began, too, millennia before that, as the adolescent earth grew into its fitful, changing shape.

It began, if you go back far enough, even earlier. It began when the world was born.

For shift is a constant: this is an axiom not only of life but of earth and sea, of stars and universe. Of people, horses, ferns, rivers, cliffs. Of bacteria, cell phones, faces, sea turtles, fame. Of love. They shift and strain, expand, contract, gallop fiercely ahead or languidly mark time, all the while blindly callous, or perhaps callously blind, to anything or anyone in their path.

∧

KYLE JESPERSEN, honour student, acolyte of science, respected cosmetic surgeon, possessor of a first-rate mind, knows nothing of geology or its shifts. The mountains he will scale today hold no interest beyond their ambitious terrain and cardio challenge. The ground is just the ground, the ocean the ocean. They are surfaces for him to cross, ideally fast, while wearing sports gear.

The surface that Kyle knows intimately is the body. He has never once likened it to the earth's crust, has never drawn parallels between the strains that pummel the flesh and the monumental forces that reshape the earth. The body is simply the body, and to Kyle it is everything. Should anyone ask, he will freely admit that perfecting his own physique is as much his life's work as sculpting the faces and filling the necks of others. It's a stereotype, the appearance-obsessed gay man, but he has successfully dodged enough stereotypes — no effeminate mannerisms, no makeup or stiletto heels, no small white dog, no large black dildo — that he doesn't fret over this one. What distinguishes him from so many of his friends, who work out only to look good, is that he actually uses his strength. Kayaking, hiking, running, cycling, downhill skiing — he does them all and he does them superlatively; *mediocre* is not a word in his vocabulary. Ever since the moment, one afternoon in grade six phys ed, when the magnetism of Stephen McPhail's bare legs, the precise spot where Stephen's shorts ended after swooping roundly over his ass, forced Kyle to admit that he was in one monumental way *different*, he has let the load settle on him, has hefted it and staggered under it, has vowed that the weight will not crush him but only make him stronger. The burden of difference, he decided, can mark him out in good ways, can deepen the imprint he leaves as he forges his way.

So here he is. Uncommonly fit for early middle age, his slight frame as muscled as gym equipment can make it. Career firmly established, practice flourishing, online ratings sky-high. His professional reputation built on discretion, artistry, and enough wit to keep him from sliding into subservience, in both his clients' estimation and his own. But his personal reputation? Technically solid for now, but sure to crumble if he continues this downward spiral. And his relationship with the man who loves him? As drained and lifeless as any med school cadaver.

Stephen McPhail, on the other hand ... The very name makes him shiver.

As the shoreline slips past and Kyle draws closer to the cove where he will beach his kayak, his thoughts run fluid as the current, back to the thrilling, illicit crush, never spoken of and never acted on, all-powerful as a result.

He was a quiet, gentle, eternally puzzled boy, Stephen McPhail, spared from bullying only because he'd been held back a grade and was therefore older than his classmates, and bigger. From the soft shelf of his upper lip sprouted several dark hairs, which he displayed proudly to Kyle, the only one of the smart kids who'd associate with him. Though they had little in common and almost nothing to talk about, Kyle was seldom far from Stephen's side, drawn to the older boy's budding adolescence like a wasp to nectar.

Overhead, a change in the light makes Kyle stop paddling. He looks up, removes his cap to better watch as the sky wavers and unfurls gossamer ribbons of blue and white, striping the shoreline in eerie bands as if the rocks, pedestrians, and buildings lie under water. The sail of a passing catamaran shimmers, at once ghostly and bright.

Then, as fast as it appeared, the strange light is gone.

What was that? The sun burning through cloud? A giant reflection of — what? What could be so huge that it would illuminate the entire shore? Kyle resumes the dip-dip of his paddle. Whatever shook the sky, it has finished. There is no end, he decides, to the strangeness of nature. A gull swallows a sea star whole; the world around you lights up like a movie screen.

Unless he imagined it. Could he have zoned out that much? Could remembering Stephen McPhail, the boy who ruled his own boyhood, trigger a full-scale mental projection? Such is the danger of thinking about the past, and it's why Kyle avoids reflection: it only lures you into the trap of dreams and hallucinations.

Stephen's cock, however: that was no hallucination. He saw it only once, yet the image remains seared into his mind hundreds of cocks later — thousands if you count internet, film, and pictures.

Stephen had gotten the strap. For what, Kyle can't remember, though he ought to. Stephen seldom got into trouble. He never spoke in class; when forced to answer a question he did it with his head hung, mumbling to his desk. Yet that warm spring morning he'd done something serious enough to make Miss Waterford toss her heavy black hair, yank open her desk drawer, and pull out the tongue of rubber, then summon Stephen to the front of the classroom, administer seven stiff slaps to his right palm, her bosom heaving with the effort, and dispatch him to the principal's office.

Moments later Kyle asked permission to go to the washroom. Somehow he knew Stephen would be there, splashing his face, examining his palm, or simply collecting himself before facing the wrath of Mr. Reeves. His friend would be alone and in need of reassurance.

Kyle shouldered open the heavy washroom door. Just as he suspected, there was Stephen. Head hung, the tall boy was leaning against the farthest-away sink, gazing down at his upturned palm and the tube of upright, rigid flesh that filled his hand.

"Wouldja look at that?" He sounded surprisingly conversational for a boy who had just been assaulted, then caught holding his own erect penis. "She gave me a woody."

Kyle did as he was told and looked. Stephen's erection, besides grandly outsizing the pencil-thin hard-ons that woke Kyle weekend mornings, stuck straight out from his body, at a right angle, unlike Kyle's, which pointed to the sky. He looked some more. He looked until the familiar voice cut in — not the voice of his father, who would flee their household once Kyle graduated high school, taking his voice with him, but a mixture of Kyle's Scout leader and church minister, with a little of Mr. Reeves for good measure, a voice that took charge at moments like this and told him to smarten up and think normal thoughts before someone found out.

It took every ounce of Kyle's willpower to tear his gaze away.

He crossed to the urinal, praying for pee. None came. The sight of Stephen had turned him most of the way hard himself. He refocused his prayer accordingly: please God, don't let him see.

"I never got the strap before." Stephen's voice behind Kyle was tinged with wonder. "Not even when I failed grade five. It hurts, specially at the end. But holy shit, who'd've thought it'd give ya wood?"

Who'd have thought? At the time Kyle made no connection between pain and pleasure, and he's not sure he does now. He's never gone in for the whole S & M thing; its overwrought role-playing and elaborate pageantry just make him think of kids' action figures and the WWE. For weeks after the bathroom encounter, he alternated between worrying there was something wrong with him, something immature and under-developed because he stayed soft in the presence of pain, and wondering if his friend was the messed-up one. But nothing in that internal debate diminished the glory of Stephen McPhail's penis pushing thickly outward, seeking the freedom of open air. Throughout Kyle's adolescence the image visited him daily, sometimes hourly, the first real-life cock he had ever seen, belonging to the first boy he had ever loved.

Loved. The breeze picks up slightly and he leans into the kayak. How could a pubescent crush, entirely unrequited – Stephen McPhail was a red-blooded, titty-loving straight boy – count as love? Besides which, love, Kyle has come to understand, develops in inverse proportion to lust. His lust for Stephen was for years immeasurable; it invaded him like a sandstorm. There was no love, only hot, gritty desire. And shame. The two ingredients he to this day requires, the alchemy that transforms the mechanics of sex into the transport of ecstasy.

Last night. Oh, God. And this morning.

Two minutes. He will give himself two minutes to rail at the unfairness of it all and curse his monstrous selfishness, and then he will pack it away until he is on the mountain.

Kyle Jespersen is forty-three, too young for impotence, especially considering that his biological age is twenty-five according to the sports clinic that tested him. He is exceedingly fit, he eats well, he gets a reasonable amount of sleep – never enough, but then what successful person does? – in short, he is in top physical condition. He manages his anxiety, only occasionally resorts to drink or self-medication, not counting the various chemical enhancements to orgasm in which he indulges, which aren't fair to count. He has spent five years in a committed relationship with a man who loves him and who has never denied him physical pleasure. And yet. The problem dogs him, and the more he tries to ignore it the more persistent it gets.

The strangeness of nature.

Viagra, ginseng, L-arginine – he takes them covertly, so his problem remains his secret. But it's just a matter of time before the truth comes out, before it balloons as grotesquely as the sea star in the seagull's craw. This morning he came so close to telling Joe everything. Kyle Jespersen, *Jizz*-person they used to call him in the clubs, wanton and unslakeable, record-holder among his friends for the most orgasms in one night, cannot get it up. Correction: cannot get it up *with his partner.* Goes noodle-limp at the thought of the man he lives with, his forever-after lover, shrimps up at his touch, recoils from his tongue, is turned on by not one part of the man he owns a house and a retirement fund with, whose back he bumps up against under the covers. Yet give Kyle a stranger, some shadowy, stubbled hard-body behind the bushes or in a cubbyhole at the baths, and he springs instantly and nimbly to attention, ready for action, as nature intended, no enhancement required.

So he goes with strangers, many, many strangers, sometimes two a day; and he does it with more strangers, untold numbers of them, online; and he slinks home afterwards, usually late, and hopes Joe will be asleep, and pretends. The logistical troubles are endless, the network of lies and scheduling, the furtive cleaning up, the elaborate fictions and excuses. The deceit and shame have burrowed secret tunnels deep inside him – the secrecy being part of the appeal – but now they are muscling their way into the open. During this day that lies ahead, he has to face the labyrinth he has constructed: not, as he first imagined, some daredevil course with lusty adventures around every corner, but a shameful trap from which he may never escape and into which he must not pull the man he loves – and he *does* love him – Joe.

Last night … God. It's been bad, but now it's worse. Last night he hardly recognized himself.

He has to end it, and end it soon.

He has today to decide how, and he has planned the expedition so there will be no temptations. No wordless bathroom encounters at the gym, no jerking off for the webcam between patients, no furtively checking Grindr on the cheap phone stashed at the office so Joe won't see the app. No horror show like at the club last night. Just a long physical push and a good honest sweat. Today will be scoured clean, not smeared and tawdry, and because the day will be pure, it will show him the light.

The light — the blue-and-white bands in the sky — was it a sign?

Of course it was. He knows it as surely as he knows his own name. One way or another he will work it out. When he gets home tonight, sweat-drenched and spent, it will be with his mind made up. Will he stay for a while or leave immediately? Tell Joe the full story or spare him the details? Place the blame on his heart or his cock?

Cock. If he had any inkling in sixth grade how much trouble the male organ would lead him into, he'd have shut his eyes against Stephen McPhail's erection before the sight of it could hijack his brain. There would be no dirty bathroom scene to replay nightly under his *Star Wars* sheets, no mental image of Stephen's woody to imagine between his lips, against his hip, up his ass — not until he was older and could keep it under control.

Control? You are so full of shit.

For even now, in the grips of a guilty conscience, he feels the blood swell hot and full between his legs. The memory of Stephen's baffled pleasure as he beheld his ramrod hard-on has provoked a desire so urgent Kyle can barely contain it. He wants — no, *needs* — to relieve the pressure. To rip off the kayak skirt, reach for himself, and rub until he spurts into the sky.

No. No temptations. Not today.

You control your situation. It doesn't control you.

Kyle puts his desire into the kayak, points the craft into the wind and paddles furiously, from his torso, legs pressed tight against the boat's inner ribs, hips straining beneath the bright orange skirt, determined to conquer his shame and outrun all he has done.

∿

They are nearly there, just a few blocks north of Marine Drive, where the hairdresser's chair awaits Miss Dodie's freshly diapered bottom. Dutifully slowing, Anna passes the low-slung elementary school, its plate-glass windows dotted with cardboard tulips, daffodils, and hyacinths, the cheery cut-outs of the west coast's wealthiest children. On the right, a row of three-storey fir and riverstone townhouses, with cavernous front entrances and ornate copper downspouts. Along the curb, an exotic parade of parked BMWs, Audis, Porsches, Jaguars. One American compact, *Custom Maid* stencilled in pink on the driver's door. A white van that advertises what looks to be pet insurance, though that cannot be right. Anna's English must be tangled again.

I am truly here, she still marvels when she drives the streets of West Vancouver. The huge houses, only one family in each, the towering trees and tranquil gardens, the sweeping views from the high-up properties, the pure air tinged with sea salt — nothing could be farther from the belching factories and dingy apartment blocks of Donetsk, at least the downtrodden sector of it that she used to call home. There is no grime. No stink of boiled cabbage from open windows. No bombed-out buildings. No soldiers.

They are descending the final block before Marine Drive when Miss Dodie's wail splits the air.

"It's gone!"

Startled, Anna jerks the steering wheel of the 1981 Volvo, a squat green breadbox she is not permitted to nudge above forty kilometres an hour, narrowly missing a spandexed rider streaking past on a racing bike.

"Annie, Annie! A stealer!" Miss Dodie twists against the seatbelt, straining to see the cyclist. "Oh, no. He got away!"

Anna knows the right word is *thief* but she offers no correction, either to the word or to her name, which Miss Dodie insists on rhyming with her own. There is little point. The old woman's mind is in tatters. She does her best to make herself understood, and Anna, for whom English is an inflictor of torment, can hardly criticize. "What is gone?"

"He is! Dirty stealer." She shakes her fist. "He got away. On his wagon. Shall we chase him?"

"No, no. Not him. You were saying, very loud, *it* is gone. What thing is gone?" After a moment or two, Anna hazards a sideways glance. The old woman is slumped forward in the leather seat, full bosom bisected by the shoulder harness, brow drawn with the duelling efforts of trying to remember and trying to hide the fact that she has forgotten.

At the bottom of the hill, as Anna turns onto Marine Drive, another shriek. "My love!"

Here we go, Anna thinks. Another guessing game. What do they call it here, thirty questions? With luck Miss Dodie will lose this train of thought entirely before they arrive at the hair salon, and Anna can sit peacefully with the herbal tea the salon assistant hands her — extra sugar, always — page through celebrity magazines, learn who is pregnant and who is anorexic, who has adopted a refugee baby and who wore it better on the red carpet. But until then she must try to understand or else risk a full-scale meltdown.

"What exactly is gone? Please, describe."

"My love! It's my love!"

Anna stops at the flashing crosswalk lights for two pedestrians, a teenaged boy in a navy school blazer and earbuds, and a snappy old lady with flaming red hair, cradling a tiny dog and a bottle-shaped paper bag. Anna's lips part, a newborn at the sight of a nipple.

When the crosswalk clears, she accelerates. "Where you keep this thing?"

"On my hand, of course. Where it always is. But Annie, it's gone!"

They are making progress. It must be a piece of jewellery. Anna moves past the pastry shop, which sells the most delectable cherry pie she has ever tasted. Once every month or two she stops for a slice when she is running errands. It costs almost half a day's pay. "Is it your watch?"

"Of course not. It's … it's — Look!" Miss Dodie flings out her left arm and Anna draws back just in time to miss a wallop that would have wrenched them off the road. It is a good thing no liquor is coursing through her system and slowing her reflexes. The slow, sweet burn, her private reward, will come eventually. Just not soon. Never soon enough.

"Ring? Is it ring that is gone?"

"Yes, yes! That's what I've been saying. My *love!*"

Understanding dawns. Miss Dodie is missing her engagement ring, the pea-sized diamond she insists on wearing most days, whether they are going somewhere nice or not, the ring her late husband, who even as a young bachelor lived high up the ladder of wealth, slipped onto her finger when he proposed. Anna has heard the story often, though the details differ each time. She used to think dementia erased short-term memories but left the long-ago databank intact. Not so with Miss Dodie. All of the woman's recollections, old and recent alike, are skewed.

"I tell you not to wear it. Is too big now. Too easy to come off."

"But I always wear it. It only falls off because you are starving me." Miss Dodie's voice trembles. "No bacon, no cheese. No more sweeties. I am not in jail, Annie. If I starve to death, you will have my blood on your hands."

It is a well-worn accusation, one Miss Dodie repeats with fresh vigour at least three times a day, whenever Anna produces a bowl or plate of her best attempt at the low-fat, high-fibre fare she is compelled by Miss Dodie's doctor to serve. Now a block from Dairy Queen, a landmark her employer's capricious eye never misses, Anna resorts to distraction to shut down the starvation tantrum.

"When did he give you this ring? Tell the story to me."

Miss Dodie settles back, radiating pleasure. She has no idea how often Anna has heard the tale.

"He kissed me, you know, when he gave it to me. Our first real kiss, a long one, not the dry little peck he gave me after all those movie dates. What took him so long, I'll never know." Miss Dodie gazes out the window while Anna manoeuvres the boxy sedan into the lone parking space on the block. "I was desperate for it in those days. Used to push my face right up close to his so he'd get the hint." She shakes her head. "I'd get a nose full of gin for my trouble, because he was a drinker even then, but never a proper kiss. He wasn't one for hints, my Marty. I had to practically tear my blouse open before he would touch my titties. Silly man. Had to put them right into his hands."

This new detail paints a picture Anna would rather not see. She prefers to view her lady's titties clinically, as large creased sacs to be soaped, rinsed, and towelled dry with the rest of her. When it comes to the body, Anna practises detachment; this is required if she is to manage another's most intimate needs.

Miss Dodie sighs, her patient titties heaving mightily. "And now it's gone." On the last word her voice quavers.

Anna puts the car in park, sets the handbrake, turns off the ignition, and only then assesses Miss Dodie's left ring finger. It is the only unadorned digit apart from the thumb. "Probably it is at the house. You take it off when you wash hands."

Miss Dodie shakes her head. "No. I told you, it's gone. Forever! Just like my Marty." She sighs again, long and with gusto, as if projecting from a proscenium. There is nothing wrong with her respiratory system.

Anna has to end this. It is one minute to ten, the salon is a block away, a five-minute walk in Miss Dodie steps, and the formidable Freema, who presides over the shop like a sitting monarch, does not tolerate lateness. Anna takes Miss Dodie's age-spotted hand and strokes it gently. "We will find your love. Do not worry. We go home after the hair and it will be there, at the bathroom sink."

"No." The old woman's eyes widen and she smiles triumphantly. "I know where it is! It fell off when we were walking. That ... that animal, that sea thing, he has it. He *ate* it."

Anna suppresses a smile. Remembering the distorted neck as the gull worked on the starfish, she can see where the notion might come from. Now, in the interest of time, its preposterousness is not worth arguing. "Okay. After the hair we go back. Do not worry, my lady. We find it."

After the hair, Anna knows, Miss Dodie will remember no part of this conversation. They will drive back up the mountain to the post-and-beam rancher that must have been a jewel of the British Properties — before the paint peeled and moss colonized the roof, before the houses to either side were replaced with view-obliterating three-storey piles the size of country inns, before Mr. Dodie died and the property froze in mourning. Anna will pull into the cracked driveway, go directly to the almond and brass ensuite, which Miss Dodie pretends she can still navigate on her own, and the ring will be there by the sink, its many carets winking under the Hollywood lightbulbs.

As it happens, in the tricky way of Miss Dodie's short-circuit memory, she does not let go the loss. According to Freema, whose regal bearing is by mid-appointment showing signs of strain, Miss Dodie has spoken of nothing else while her hair was washed and the curlers rolled. It is all love, love, love, nothing but lost love. "Ring," Anna tells the towering stylist, who has found her in the waiting area, in the middle of *People* magazine. "She lost her ring."

As Freema strides off, hips twitching under her leopard-print miniskirt, Anna makes a mental note to double the tip today. Miss Dodie is exasperating when she gets stuck, going round and round like a needle caught in a record groove. Does Freema hide a flask for such times, at the back of a drawer behind the hairbrushes and squares of highlight foil? Anna tries to imagine the tall beauty taking a surreptitious slug and blotting her perfectly pencilled lips before plunging into another head of aged hair. No. Not in a billion years. Women like Freema do not depend on vodka to bear them through this world. They have beauty and confidence and inner strength, not to mention, in the case of Persians like Freema, the genetic gifts of an advanced civilization. They are not like Anna. They are not ugly, fearful, Ukrainian.

She returns to *People*, where more impossibly glamorous women strut and pose. Easy times, she thinks. Every one of them, easy times. The celebrity lifestyle holds no appeal for Anna, who values peace and quiet above all, and for whom anonymity is now a requirement. It is not the fame but the effortlessness of these women that she longs for. The basics of life pose no challenges for them. If they need a winter coat, they buy one, brand new and pretty. If they do not wish to cook, they eat at a restaurant. They can select the best brand of vodka and the expensive cherry pie. They do not hoard envelopes of carefully thumbed bills, they cannot count their treasured belongings on one hand. They do not alternate between two brassieres, washing one in the sink each night, hoping it will dry in the rainforest humidity by the day after next. Their hours are spent engaging with life and improving themselves, not inhabiting another person's home and running another person's life. They have the radiant skin and bright eyes of those who sleep through the night. No secrets or terrors keep them awake under their quilts.

There are men in *People* too, handsome men. They hold the elbows of the gleaming women or stride into South Pacific waves or attend basketball games disguised as ordinary citizens. Sometimes they hold babies or the colourful shopping bags of their women. The men all have two hands, unlike Anna's father, whose right one was stolen by the industrial shredder he operated. With it went his job and any prospect of easy times. Before the stump had even healed, they were evicted from their plain but spacious flat, forced into a too-small apartment in the factory district, where her father juggled bills, lost hope, and eventually bonded with the bottle, leaving Anna's mother to take over. Tight-faced and silent, she did. She worked the night shift and kept the house and made the food and raised Anna and her brother and cleaned up after her husband's messes and bore the brunt, the pain, and the scars of his many rages.

Anna's father drank with a mission. When he finally accomplished it — that is to say, died — Anna revelled in the unaccustomed peace. It was short-lived. One Sunday morning her mother looked up from her bowl of oatmeal, forehead creased. "What is my name?" she asked. In three months she was gone, the tumour claiming her brain as completely as the shredder had eaten her husband's hand. Anna was left with an apartment lease and an array of caregiving skills, but few friends and no family nearby, her uncle having moved to Canada years earlier and her brother, Bohdan, having left for Odessa, address unknown. Will I ever have easy times? Anna wondered, folding Baba's quilt, which she had settled over her mother's shivering body in those final weeks, and placing it back on her own bed.

An elegant crimson dress, wrapped around another perfect figure, leaps off the page. Anna sighs.

"Hey. Come on over and I'll trim you up."

She looks up. It is the salon assistant, at the front desk. What is her name?

"Come on, it'll only take a minute."

"I cannot. No money." The name eludes her.

"Pfft." The assistant flicks one hand in the air. "I'll just even up the ends. No charge."

Anna blinks.

"Come on, I need the practice. You'd be doing me a favour."

Reluctantly, Anna heaves herself off the padded bench. *Bridgette*, she sees when she is close enough to read the assistant's name tag. A small bridge? It seems a strange thing to call a woman.

Anna settles into the chair nearest the front desk, mercifully far from the centre of the salon, where Miss Dodie sits on Freema's throne. Deftly, Bridgette fastens a cape beneath Anna's chin, spritzes water from a plastic bottle, combs out her hair in the back. Utters a *tsk-tsk*. "Who cut this last time?"

Anna does not answer. Trimming her bangs is easy, she just has to look in the mirror and snip carefully, but she does a poor job on the back. Usually she hides the mess in a ponytail.

A few snips later Bridgette stands back. "Better. At least it's straight now." She assesses her work in the mirror, cupping the trimmed hair up around Anna's ears. "You ever thought of taking it right up, like this? It'd suit you. Frame your jawline, play up your eyes."

Anna does not look at her reflection. Without understanding all the words, she knows that the woman means *distract from your big nose and miserable face.*

Bridgette nods toward Freema's station, where Miss Dodie's voice rises and falls like a warbling kazoo. "She's nowhere near finished. Come on. It's so slow this morning. I'm bored out of my mind. Let me do a makeover."

This word Anna knows. Late-night TV offers a myriad of makeover shows and she watches them all. Surgery, cosmetics, clothing, Botox, hairstyle, dermabrasion, highlighting, fingernail extensions, teeth whitening, liposuction – she follows every transformation from the funk of Miss Dodie's ancient sofa until her flask is empty and the day is done and the countdown to tomorrow's sips begins.

"What do you say?" Bridgette's eyes sparkle. She seems kind.

"Okay. But I cannot pay."

"No worries. This one's on me."

Twenty minutes is all it takes, the last fifteen of which Anna spends twirled around, back to the mirror.

"Okay." Bridgette gives the bangs a final comb. "The big reveal." She spins the chair around.

Anna gazes at her lap, a tiny bit hopeful, a great deal afraid.

"Come on." Bridgette reaches for Anna's chin and gently lifts it. "Look."

Her reflection. She blinks. It is not her, yet it is.

"You like it?" Bridgette is eager. "It's great, right? Look how it makes your cheekbones stand out, and your eyes."

Anna's hair is brown. Not sun-streaked, not chestnut, no hint of auburn, just bread-crust brown. It has always been long. When she was a girl her mother braided it every morning. Even after she outgrew braids and her face morphed into the marionette visage she endures as an adult, she kept it long. It was the one undeniably feminine part of her. Now her hair lies feathered and teased around her ears; it caps her head so that she resembles a boy. But a handsome boy.

How can it be? With this short cut, so masculine and severe, she looks –

"It's pretty," Bridgette declares.

Not *you're pretty;* she has steered clear of false flattery. Yet Anna has to admit, turning this way and that, seeing on her face shadows and angles that could be described as dramatic, possibly even appealing, that the cut has transformed her. Gone the thin, flyaway strands, replaced by layers of volume. Barely visible the vertical grooves that have begun to bracket her mouth the way they did her mother's.

Here, wonder of wonders, a neck. Her head no longer sits slab-like atop her shoulders — like a weightlifter's, she has always thought. A short but slender curve has emerged.

"I like." A few beats later: "It is good."

Behind her Miss Dodie cackles, wresting her back to reality. What will her lady think of the makeover? What if — oh, she never thought of it! — what if she doesn't recognize Anna? So far Miss Dodie's inability to remember words and events has not extended to people, at least not those she sees regularly, but what if this change is more than her deteriorating mind can process?

Minutes later Miss Dodie clop-clops to the front of the salon, Freema at her elbow. When she reaches Anna, she stops. "You, you — Who?"

Anna feels faint. She has made an unforgivable mistake. Miss Dodie, the only person who cares about her, no longer knows her. She will send Anna away.

"I did her hair," Bridgette smiles at Freema. "It's great, right?"

"Well," says Freema.

"You have — Are you — ?" Miss Dodie's eyes are wide.

Miss Dodie does not know Anna and will never go home with her now. Anna will lose her job. She will be out on the street, no friends, little money, no background she can speak of. Gone her bed, gone the TV, gone the luxuries of a car to drive and a bathroom to herself and a bureau drawer to hold her treasures.

Freema hands Miss Dodie's cracked white purse to Anna so that she can pay. Miss Dodie shakes her head. "I don't know," she says.

Anna ducks her head. Everything, lost. For a ridiculous haircut on a homely woman.

Miss Dodie's trembling hand reaches out to touch the newly feathered hair. Anna flinches.

"I didn't. I didn't know." The old woman struggles. "You could ... Oh, Annie. You are beautiful."

FOUR

⌃⌄

The morning wind never blew above a breath that played against the cheeks of boys at recess and friends in Stanley Park, that lifted the downy hair of toddlers and old women, then eased off entirely. Thin clouds roofed the ocean; above them, seagulls turned. More clouds ringed the coastal mountains, where ravens swooped and called.

It is nature's way that the earth should draw its breath, imperceptibly, stealthily, holding, holding. Building and shifting, tiny dislocations that alone change nothing but that over time will push anyone, anything – a family, a city, a world – to a single teetering moment.

⌃⌄

THERE'S A LOT of blood.

A moment ago, as Joe climbed down the ladder, the girl's whimpering a steady, irritating riff, he had silently cursed her, and himself for letting her help. What, did she break a nail? Snag her hair on a branch? Now, standing beside her, all he can think is: how can there be so much blood?

From her right hand, which she's cradling in her left, fall coin-sized drops that polka-dot the grass.

"It's cut!"

No kidding. "What happened?"

"The stupid branches! I was pressing them down like you said. I pushed down really fast and really hard with, like, my whole body and my hands slid, and one of the branches must've had a sharp end like a razor because it hurt, and when I pulled up my hand it was cut." She snuffles wetly.

"Where are the gloves I gave you? I told you to wear them."

"I told you, they're gross! They're all stained and … and disgusting. *Now* look." She thrusts out her hand. A line zigzags from the top of her baby finger into the meat of the palm, oozing red.

"Hang on." Joe reaches toward her face.

"Asshole!" She ducks, quick as a boxer.

"Relax, okay? I'm just getting this." He removes from her ponytail a wide, cloth-coated elastic. "Here. It'll close up some of the cut until we get you in the house." He loops the elastic around the base of her finger, then doubles it. He waits for her to flinch but she doesn't, just sniffs.

A blur of white shoots out from the rhododendrons. The frenzied terrier again. It dashes underneath Joe's ladder and out onto the grass, where it executes a series of tight three-sixties, as if trying to bite its own tail, then streaks brainlessly across the lawn toward the front of the house. Wired little thing, thinks Joe. As uptight as its owners.

"Is it okay for your dog to just race around like that?"

"He's not mine. He belongs to the neighbour, over there." She nods to the west side of the property. "He's been around our place a couple of days now, going crazy like that."

The girl's hand is still dripping red, though more slowly.

"Let's find your dad. He can take it from here."

"Yeah, right. He'll be on the phone. Doing some *deal*."

"Trust me, he'll hang up."

"Why would I trust you? You're, like, a total stranger." Even so, the girl lets herself be steered toward the back door.

Amazingly, she is right. The girl — Sidney, she tells him when he presses for her name — leads Joe to her father's office after a quick stop in the kitchen for a dishtowel to wrap her hand in. Stedman is not there. In a bored, I-know-what-will-happen voice, she instructs Joe to pick up the cell phone on the desk and call her father's other cell.

"Stedman here."

"Hello? It's Joe, the landscaper. I'm in your office with your daughter. She cut her hand pretty bad."

In the background Joe hears Stedman talking to someone else. Is he on another call? He's got three cell phones? Stedman's voice booms. "Look, I'm in the garage. Something I can't get out of. I'll wind it up soon, meet you in the powder room off the kitchen. There's iodine and bandages there. Cupboard under the sink."

The line goes dead.

Joe stares at the thin phone that has spit out Stedman's telegraphic sentences. *Are you kidding me?*

Sidney leans against the other side of the desk, holding the towel around her hand. She looks tiny. Joe takes a deep breath. "Show me where the powder room is."

The girl shrugs. "See? I told you."

Joe sizes up the massive slab of furniture beside him. Desks make him uncomfortable, remind him of school and homework and confinement. Lined up carefully along the edge of Stedman's desk, near one corner, is a big blue-and-yellow hardcover, maybe some kind of textbook. Next to it, a framed photo of Stedman shaking hands with the former prime minister, the robotic one with the die-cast hair. Well, Joe thinks, that says it all.

"Come on, kid." He gives the girl what he hopes is a reassuring smile. "Lead the way."

The powder room holds enough supplies to clean the cut and wrap it tightly with gauze, all of which Joe does. Still not a twitch from the girl. "I don't know, it may need stitches," he says. "It's pretty jagged. It could open up as soon as you take the bandage off. You want to keep an eye on it, okay? You and your dad."

Joe speaks to Sidney in the bevelled mirror that spans the wall above a square stone trough, brushed steel spigot positioned over it, that serves as a sink. Someone's idea of field-hand chic, he guesses. The room has no shower or tub, yet it's bigger than both of his bathrooms combined. At one end is a sitting area, complete with a scuffed-up leather armchair—distressed, he suspects, not actually well worn. Plus there's a rough-hewn side table and a wicker basket filled with magazines.

For Pete's sake. Is someone supposed to sit there reading and nursing a beer while someone else takes a dump across the way? He's worked for and around them for years, but Joe is still puzzled by the super-rich. They're always after stuff they don't need, while the stuff that should matter, they're blind to.

Sidney is bowed over her wrapped hand, face curtained by straight blond hair now that there's no elastic to hold it back.

They wait.

When Stedman doesn't come, Joe suggests a cold drink. Sidney knits her brow at him.

"Enough with the drama," he says. "You need to stay hydrated."

The kitchen, like every other room he's seen so far, is vast, its scale unrelated to its function. Joe loves to cook and fixes all the meals at home. It suits him fine, and Kiki too, who works too much and would live on takeout otherwise. But he cannot imagine preparing food in this gleaming industrial space the size of a TV studio. Cannot imagine rummaging for lettuce in the bowels of the double stainless steel fridge he's now searching for a beverage, carrying the leaves to the sink on the other side of the room, pulling dishes from cupboards twelve feet away, gathering seasonings from the spice rack that's practically in the neighbour's yard. The foolishness of it.

He shoves aside bottles of salad dressing and jars of pickles and pesto. "Is there anything in here to drink?" he shouts to Sidney, who's perched on a barstool at the faraway granite island. "Juice? Pop?"

"In the beverage fridge." He looks up at her, questioning. She jerks her head. "Over there."

On the opposite side of the kitchen, tucked under a counter that holds a small flat-screen TV and an artfully arranged pile of cookbooks, is a built-in cooler, its glass door revealing rows of bottles and cans arranged by colour.

"How many brothers and sisters do you have?" he asks, eyeing the dozens of drinks. He takes out a can of Mountain Dew.

"None."

It figures. A convenience store cooler full of drinks for one girl and, maybe, her friends. And the hired help. The parents will be covered by the dozens of bottles peeping out of the built-in wine unit over by the main fridge.

He flips open the tab. "Where do you keep the glasses?"

"Doesn't matter. The can's fine." She picks at the taped-up gauze on her hand.

"Leave that alone." Joe places the Mountain Dew in front of her on the granite-topped island. "Next thing you know it'll come undone and you'll get dirt in there."

"Don't tell me what to do." She works a nail under the tape, starts peeling it back.

"Hey, are you deaf or something? I said leave it." Joe reaches for her good hand to pull it away when suddenly, slap! His forearm stings. Not as mightily as when she open-hands him again in the exact same spot.

"Ow! What the —"

She leans in, eyes on fire. "Don't you *dare* touch me."

"What do you mean, don't touch you? I just bandaged your hand."

"I mean don't *touch* me." She swings her hair, sits up straighter. "I know how this works. You're nice to me, you fix up my cut — which, FYI, is your fault in the first place — you give me my favourite drink, and I'm supposed to be all grateful and everything. Let some old perv feel me up."

Joe slaps his thighs. "Ha! That's a good one."

She tilts her head. "What's so funny? I'm not some little kid. I know how guys like you operate."

"Guys like me? What's that supposed to mean?"

"Guys that ..." She searches for the right words. "Sweaty guys that work outside. That whistle when you walk by and look you up and down and stuff. It's gross!"

"Uh-huh, right." He longs to tell her off for her high-handedness, but part of him is enjoying this. "Guys who work with their hands, is what you're saying. Guys who do manual labour and get paid by the hour. Who aren't rich and famous and glued to a cell phone all day."

She lowers her head a fraction, possibly having gotten the message. "Whatever. You touch me again and I'm telling my dad. You'll lose your job."

Her threat is all but swallowed by the roar of an engine kicking to life outside. Sidney scoots over to the window. The engine revs twice, three times, a deafening growl that announces many horses under the hood. As the sound rises the girl's face falls, and like that, Joe's testiness evaporates. A guy who won't get off the phone to tend to his bleeding daughter and then starts fooling around with a friggin car isn't going to give two hoots whether some stranger's in the kitchen touching her hand, and the girl must know it. Slowly she returns to her stool.

Joe reaches for her good hand and this time holds it firm in both of his. "Hey, kid. Don't pick at the bandage is all I'm saying. Plus, you got nothing to worry about. I'm not into girls."

She flicks him a quick look. "Oh."

He waits for a glimmer of judgement or disgust to cross her face, but then he remembers: her generation doesn't care. One thing you can say for network TV — it transformed his people into kooky but loveable sitcom characters, still a dumb stereotype as far as he's concerned but a lot better than the dirty pervert and pedophile labels that ruled when he was young. Sidney, who probably wears pink shirts to protest bullying and rattles off *LGBTQ* more smoothly than he can, is supremely unfazed by his orientation. She sits beside him, a girl of her time, simultaneously inclusive and achingly alone, damaged hand on the granite countertop, unhurt one resting quietly in his.

Under his haunches the MGB chassis vibrates richly, awaiting release, straining to perform as it was designed to. The racing engine clears its throat, releasing three loud coughs into the hushed neighbourhood air outside the garage. Stedman can almost feel the wind that will scream past his ears when he pushes the convertible up to speed on the Sea to Sky Highway.

Keeping time with the revs, the zing of success buzzes through him. He's still digesting what his two best guys reported, laughing and jostling each other for the phone: Procter & Gamble, the giant multinational, the biggest account they've gone after this year, landed in under fifteen minutes. Landed without a fight, a magnificent bluefin gone docile on the line, happy – no, grateful! – to be flipped onboard. *Why waste everyone's time with a boring presentation, they said, just sign us up.* The young account manager spoke so fast that Stedman struggled to keep up. *Then they said, it's a beautiful day, let's spend the rest of it golfing.*

He won! He pumps a fist in the air just thinking about it. Life is good. The MGB cups his large body; the vibrations massage his lower back. With P&G signed, GlobalTech has met its target for the entire fiscal year and it's only second quarter. They can relax now and coast through to December, though of course they won't. Already he's running scenarios for leveraging the cachet of P&G to lure an even bigger target, the last hurrah before his final bold move. Maybe they should go for Nestlé. Or … hell, why stick with the consumer sector when they could be knocking on the golden doors of oil and gas? Exxon, BP, Chevron – the natural resource titans deserve better telecom products too. When they see how GlobalTech can revolutionize their networks, can help them communicate faster, more efficiently, and at the same time – and this is the real selling point – more simply, how can they refuse? All businesses, established or upstart, know that time is money, so Stedman has always, from the earliest years of building his company, recruited the brightest engineers and designers and the most charismatic sales team to back them up, and has concentrated on speed. Speed, in today's world, is all that matters. Whatever you're offering, people want it now, no waiting, no processing, just immediate, visible results. Speed is what GlobalTech promises, and speed is what it delivers.

Stedman adjusts the rearview mirror a centimetre or two, taking in the wide garage behind him. Yes, life is excellent. Now that the guys in Cincinnati no longer need him, the hours before tonight's dinner party spread lavishly ahead. He has earned this break. He'll run the MGB all the way up to Whistler, grab a late lunch in the village, enjoy the quiet of shoulder season, the ski and snowboard crowd gone wherever they go when the snow retreats, the hikers and mountain bikers not yet arrived. Marcus has checked in from the North Van office, where everything is running smoothly as everything does under Marcus's command. Charlotte is occupied, off buying supplies for tonight, and then ... back to her office? He can never keep track of her whirling schedule, but fortunately there's no need. She is always where she's supposed to be, when she's supposed to be there. There's also the gardener, but he must be nearly finished.

The gardener — hell! It all comes back to him. Sidney hurt her hand and that hired man, the new one who showed up late, is looking after it. Stedman is supposed to do something. Follow up with the guy? Check on Sidney himself? He can't remember; he was too wrapped up in the call from Cincinnati.

He glances at his gold Rolex President, one of his earliest investments in the company. When you look successful you attract success, he told Charlotte, who quietly paid for the acquisition from her family funds. That thing with Sidney was ages ago. Whatever the details were, they'll be taken care of by now. Even a gardener who can't be bothered to be on time would be capable enough to rinse the girl's hand and dig out a bandaid to cover her scrape.

Sidney is Stedman's only daughter, and naturally he is concerned for her welfare, but he knows her and her exaggerated dramas. She has many admirable qualities — fends for herself, doesn't fill the house with giggling girls as he feared when she went teenage, seldom interrupts him while he's working — but accurate reporting is not among them. Like her mother she's given to overstatement, to pronouncing, for example, while sprawled on the immense sectional in the family room, that humans have made the world their garbage dump, that consumerism is running rampant, and that corporations lack conscience, conveniently overlooking the fact that the sofa cushioning her butt comes courtesy of her father's corporation, as do the designer jeans that hug said butt, and the allowance with which she herself, most weekends at the mall, participates in the consumerism she so passionately condemns.

Still, he has promised to put in an appearance. "I am a man who does what he promises," he says aloud. The drive will have to wait awhile. He hits the steering wheel, annoyed at the emergence of one more pesky detail.

As he swings himself out of the MGB and plants his Italian loafers on the driveway, an off-side movement catches his eye. There, low to the ground. What the hell? A mob of tiny frogs – or are they toads? – hop-hop-hopping, making their stuttering way from the shrubs into the faint sun that splashes across the driveway. He's never before seen a single frog on the property, of any type, let alone a cluster. They head in rapid formation for the street, fortunately a quiet cul-de-sac where no vehicular disaster awaits them.

Where are they going in such a hurry? Is it mating season for toads? Is there a predator nearby? One of the neighbourhood raccoons, or even a bear come down from the forest?

"Sidney," he mutters as the leaping mass disappears up the street. Her mother is not here and neither is May. It's down to him. He will go inside, look at her bandaid, murmur words of consolation, and then – *then* he will begin.

$\wedge$

On eastbound Highway 1 the phalanx of vehicles surrounding the Porsche Cayenne has at last crossed the Port Mann Bridge, and Charlotte, in a rare instance of marital harmony, unknowingly mimics her husband. Enveloped in another powerful, costly vehicle, this one meant for the suburban boulevard, not the international racetrack, she too is pounding the steering wheel, to the point where her hand throbs. She too is talking to herself. Quietly, under her breath, not in some nutty-lady way, just tiny lines here and there to vent her anxiety, like slits in a pie.

"Babysitter issues, my ass. What a crock."

The handsome, disgusting nose-picker in the car beside her has inched out of sight, leaving Charlotte to ruminate about sex, and therefore Marcus. Marcus, who with his silent, pallid wife may or may not be at tonight's dinner party, depending on the child-care situation. Marcus, who is Tayne's right-hand man, who runs GlobalTech's North Van headquarters, who after seven years with the company, years of fourteen-hour days and weekend meetings and taking Tayne's calls and emails twenty-four seven, has earned his boss's undying trust. Efficient Marcus, who according to Tayne has productivity hardwired into his body. Handsome Marcus, who pushes floppy black hair off his high forehead; who disarms clients, colleagues, and middle-aged women with his goofy grin; whose untucked button-down shirts conceal a tiny paunch, the price a thirty-something man pays for an efficient, round-the-clock career. Naughty Marcus, who has been sleeping with her for the past four months, never actually sleeping of course, but being with her long enough to do the deed, which they manage, aptly enough, with efficiency — in hotels, motels, the backseat of this very SUV, and once, thrillingly, in Marcus's office, next door to Tayne's CEO suite, when everyone else had gone home after an evening meeting.

"Yeah, right." Charlotte is muttering about Marcus and also Marcus's mother, who has practically regrown her umbilical cord she's so eager to look after the bawling grandson who has bestowed on Marcus two years of proud fatherhood and two and a half years of zero conjugal sex. So no. There are no babysitter issues.

It was supposed to be fun, the thing with Marcus. Until then Charlotte had been faithful to Tayne, though Lord knows there were temptations. The occasional client interested in more than a PR strategy. Guys from the Running Room, pumped and sweaty, with a patina of sex that had worn off her husband years earlier. Marcus was her first affair, and she set the rules early: it was for sex, full stop. She had neither the desire nor the time for more.

Like so much in life, Marcus happened as a consequence of timing — Charlotte overcommitted yet understimulated, Tayne off building his empire, Sidney away at rehab. Marcus sleep-deprived, shell-shocked by how parenting had derailed his clockwork life, and so desperately, unrelievedly horny that during yet another dinner party, when his hip brushed Charlotte's in the kitchen, where she'd come looking for May and he'd come for more Prosecco, he turned toward her instead of away. Charlotte, throat afire, skin suddenly alive, stayed right where she was. The air between them burned; they later joked that had a piece of paper fluttered by, it would have ignited and singed them both.

Marcus grasped her sleek ponytail, pulled her head back, and kissed her, sloppily and with too much tongue — all that bubbly — but with no hesitation, as if in his efficiency he had planned it all along.

In a way he had. For months he'd imagined them together, he told her three days later in a motel room at the foot of Capilano Road, his floppy hair tickling her abdomen which, thank God and her new Pilates class, didn't jiggle when he touched it. "I watch you at all those parties, and when I'm at the house to see Tayne. You get this look, like you're staring at something no one else can see. I know you're lonely. I know you need something. You need *this*." He placed a warm palm on her mound, freshly waxed for their rendezvous, the booking squeezed in between conference calls the day before.

Studded as it is with clichés and assumptions, Marcus's image of her as the dreamy, pining wife is an amusing reminder of how clueless he is. The faraway look she gets in the middle of others' conversations comes not from unfulfilled yearning but from her schedule, jammed with tasks from the moment her eyes open until the moment her head hits the eiderdown. At dinner parties she falls into a trance calculating how soon she can signal that the evening is over, and in what order she should tackle the many tasks ahead. The night Marcus had kissed her, she'd gone looking for May to beg her to clean up in exchange for an extra day off. As soon as the guests left, Charlotte had to retreat to her office, a small, square den off the family room, and review a client proposal due the next day. Then she'd sift through the email that had come in since she left work at five. Once that was done, by eleven if she was lucky, she'd finally deal with the flyer her friend Alice had drafted for next month's silent auction, a fundraiser for the West Vancouver Museum. The document needed heavy lifting and Charlotte had been putting it off, dreading the mangled prose of her friend, a sweet soul, popular professor, and tireless promoter of local history but a prisoner of the snaking, weedy syntax of academia. The flyer was what Charlotte was contemplating when Marcus's hip grazed hers in the kitchen: the excess verbiage she had to cut and all the time it would take, and whether she shouldn't have just written the goddamn thing in the first place instead of delegating the job to Alice, and whether she'd make it to bed before one o'clock and get the minimum five hours she needed to log a halfway decent time on her morning 10K run.

"See? You're doing it now," Marcus had said that afternoon in the motel, low light sneaking under the too-short curtain and playing on his boyish smile. "Does that mean you need more?" He slipped a finger between her legs and wiggled it – efficiently – until Charlotte's mind emptied.

It was supposed to be fun, the thing with Marcus. The fun came at a price – staying up later and getting up earlier to recapture the hour or two stolen from the day – but it was worth it for the sweet, timeless moments of escaping her life, for Marcus's greedy wanting of her, for the satisfaction of doing something not because she had to, because it was expected of her or was good for her, but because she wanted to. Stealing time with Marcus was like buying the obscenely expensive Birkin bag. It was about desire and its gratification. It was about doing something – as Mother always reminded her – selfish.

The thing with Marcus was fun until one day it wasn't, and then it became work, like everything else. The change crept up gradually but the realization hit her at once, two weeks ago, while having her teeth cleaned. Reclining in the padded dentist's chair, eyes closed, only slightly offended by the background Muzak, she savoured the twice-a-year weightlessness of having nowhere else to be and nothing else to do but submit to the hygienist's ministrations. Like it used to be with Marcus, she thought, and that single truth jabbed the air out of her buoyant fun.

Like it used to be. Because now, four months after that first stolen sloppy kiss, Marcus is a burden.

"I want to see you more," he announced one morning not long before the dental appointment. It was one of their furtive calls, placed from Charlotte's office so it wouldn't show on her cell phone log, the purpose limited to setting the next sweaty encounter. "Let's go away somewhere, spend the night."

"Get real." She scrolled through her inbox. Ten new emails.

"Come on. Some nice B & B in the Okanagan, or maybe an inn on Salt Spring Island. I want us to sleep together, have breakfast in bed."

"You know I can't do that. I'm swamped." Four new emails appeared. "Anyhow, you can't get away. You going to tell your wife you need some quality time alone, a little getaway from her and the squalling baby?"

"I want to spend time with you, Charlotte. *Real* time. It's like we're teenagers, doing it in the car and the bathroom. I want to be a grown-up with you."

Six more emails sailed in, including one from head office with an urgent flag. "Gotta go," she said and hung up.

I want. Marcus says it so easily, and in full expectation that he will receive. It's a presumptuous trait, and a selfish one, but it makes him invaluable to Tayne. Whether to find it charming or irritating, Charlotte can't decide. Increasingly, she wishes she could master it herself.

After that, a torrent of the same: Marcus wanting more time together, Charlotte saying no. Her refusals only made Marcus try harder, demand more. Let's meet for lunch, go for an afternoon drive, see a weekday matinee, walk along the Richmond dikes. Impossible requests, all of them. Yesterday during a strategy session with the two young women who head her social media team, he texted her, a practice she'd forbidden for fear she'd forget to delete the evidence. *Need to see u. Today. Where and when?* She trashed the text and carried on with the brainstorming, never missing a beat.

Now, it seems, it's payback time. Marcus is jamming out of the dinner party, something he has never done, not once, and he's doing it because of, air quotes, babysitter issues. It's a lie, pure and simple, one that he knew would find its way to her.

Message delivered, Marcus. Loud and clear.

The kilometres fall away, the Porsche now at full highway speed. Charlotte turns on the radio, trying one station after another until she finds an old Radiohead tune. The melody seeps into her, the soaring vocals calm her some.

So what if Marcus snubs her? Why should she care? The pleasure of being with him has all but evaporated anyhow, leaving the dry dregs of scheduling and negotiation and mechanical sex. It's become a routine: they waste no time kissing or fondling, shed as little clothing as possible, just enough to rub each other in the necessary places, and he pushes into her and gets off in a frenzy while she fingers herself to orgasm. Speed-fucking, that's their thing—a dizzying, muscular high when they were first together, now just another series of steps to execute, swiftly and diligently, as she ticks her way down the to-do list.

Well, it's time to end the Marcus project. Let him pressure her and send her second-hand messages. She's done. "It's over," she says out loud, trying it on for size. The relief is as sweet and pure as the Radiohead song.

To either side farms and fields sweep past, the city far behind. Her Abbotsford exit is just ahead. Abbotsford! A place no one would ever go except to buy local. It's like another country out here in the Fraser Valley, nothing to do with Vancouver. A weird mix of rural rednecks and Sikh farmers.

Charlotte can pick up British Columbia wine at any liquor store back in the city, but getting it straight from the winery will give her a story to amuse the small but earnest cadre of Tayne's clients who care about such things. "It's a local grape," she'll say. "Bottled within a morning's drive of home, recommended by the vintner himself." She knows it will be mediocre swill at best, the Fraser Valley fighting several weight classes below the Okanagan in the wine ring, but from what she can tell, quality is not what these locavores are after. Serve them any wilted green or pulpy tomato—if it grew within a hundred-mile radius they'll gush over it in that superior, *caring* way. Not for the first time she probes the logic. It can't be about saving the environment. She's used up a quarter tank of gas, much of it idling in locked-up traffic, just to get here. Supporting the local economy? Being nice to your neighbours? All she knows is that it's not about the food; it's about the *idea* of the food.

She leaves the highway and turns north, cruising deep into the farmland. Soon signs for the Janes Winery appear. So do billboards for Christ. Lurid images of black-bound prayer books and fires of hell, of weeping mothers and ultrasound fetuses – she forgot about this feature of Abbotsford, part of the southern BC bible belt. As she rounds a curve, a row of leafed-out trees on one side and silent fields on the other, she comes face to face with a huge-eyed diapered baby. "Take my hand, not my life," says the sign. Charlotte wants to shed a tear all right, but for the uneducated, not the unborn; for the gullible masses hoodwinked by fundamentalist propaganda. Religion is yet another prison, her mother used to say before heading to pro-choice rallies with her braless, unshaven acolytes. Supporter of many causes, Mother fought for abortion rights above all. "Women will never be free," she advised pigtailed Charlotte, "if we cannot choose whether and when to have a child. Until then we're no better than servants shackled to the home."

One thing you could say for Mother: she eluded all shackles, leaving aside the thirteen hours it took to drop her only spawn from the womb, a home birth guided by a sister protestor and midwife. Mrs. Pettigrew – who eschewed her married name; she was Ms. Riordan all her life – attended so little to Mr. Pettigrew that Charlotte's father lingered more and more months at their Vermont summer house, where life was simple and free of bombast. Charlotte's girlhood featured the briefest of maternal sightings, mostly when the paths of mother and daughter accidentally intersected in the corridors and landings of the stone Westmount mansion in which Charlotte was raised. When they did find themselves in a room together, stationary, Charlotte became her mother's mute audience, was delivered long, impassioned lectures about women's rights, universal equality, the need for solidarity, the importance of agitation. What about the rights of girls? Charlotte longed to ask during these performances. The importance of daughters? Do they get a chance to be heard?

At least Charlotte, herself a mother and shackle-wearer now, makes a point of asking about Sidney's day, and she always stays put for the answer, or she did back when her daughter still spoke to her. There's no need to listen closely. As with Tayne when he launches into a soliloquy about the business, pretending he wants to share but really just savouring his own mellifluence, listening is not the point. Being there is.

Charlotte does her best with the wife and mother roles but is grateful every day to have a career, demanding as it is, to remind her that she can do something besides serve children and men. Though PR is hardly a passion, she relishes being in charge and can't wait for the next rung with Diamond & Day. She's a shoo-in for VP Western Division; she's heard this repeatedly from Toronto and Houston. But it's taking forever. Well over a year now and still no announcement.

Far ahead, on the crest of a hill, appear the white stucco walls and red tile roof of what must be the winery, an incongruous patch of Mediterranean in this landscape of cottonwood, alder, and farm buildings. Jesus! She was crazy to agree to this, adding an eternally long side trip to an overflowing day. She'll have to hightail it from here to the cheese shop and then speed back to the city to make her one o'clock video call. The video call which — it suddenly hits her — has no agenda, about which her boss was oddly cagey when she pressed for details.

Could it be, finally? It has to be. It makes total sense. At long last, she's going to make VP.

She cannot, must not, be late. It's nearly eleven. The videoconference is at one. It'll be close. Worst case, she can always pull over and do the call from the highway, but then she'll be late for the social media meeting back at the office, which will make it tight to get home for the dinner party prep —

The urge kicks in, spreading from the basement of her stomach up and out, flaming through her fingers and toes. *Keep going.*

It's weak but insistent, a current that will not be ignored.

Keep going. Don't go home. Just keep driving.

It's not the first time the impulse has visited her. Usually it comes on at times like this, when she's alone on a stretch of highway, her responsibilities heavy and her mind awhirl. The idea is as arousing as an orgasm, and for one thrilling moment, as she winds along the country road, she pretends. Checks the gas gauge: full. Glances at her Birkin bag: she's got cash. It would be easy. Do a U-turn, loop back to the highway, drive east until the sun sets in the rearview mirror. When her eyes grow heavy, pull over at a roadside motel, nothing fancy, so long as it's clean and doesn't smell too awful. Slide between hospital-cornered sheets and sleep until she's ready to get up. Do it again the next day. Continue east to the Prairies, let their vast horizon swallow her. Or go all the way to Montreal. The destination doesn't matter. What matters is shucking it all off: distant husband, angry daughter, pouting lover, demanding career, the appointments, the tasks, the lists, the pressure. The life that's grown so unbearably heavy.

The winery nears, its entrance at the base of the hill flanked by weeping willows.

It was in Chicago where she first felt the urge, a snowy night years ago when her flight kept getting delayed. She was killing time in the business lounge, on her third mini-bottle of wine and dying for distraction, when she spied an abandoned paperback on a table. What was it called? It was a book she'd never choose, one of those hard-boiled detective stories where the hero's a tortured misogynist, the women are either harpies or bimbos, and everyone speaks in macho witticisms. Yet for the next three hours she raced through it. The part she remembers is not the mystery but a tale embedded in the main story. The detective tells the femme fatale about a case he once worked where a man up and vanishes, misses a golf game one afternoon and is never heard from again. The man leaves behind a wife and kids, a house, money, affairs all in order, no sign of unhappiness or trouble, by all accounts a successful life. Years later he's spotted in another town. The detective tracks him down and the man explains what happened. The day he disappeared, a heavy beam fell at a construction site he was passing and narrowly missed him. Though he was only scratched by a piece of debris, inside he was jolted, and his world fell out of step. A moment's disruption and he could no longer bear the life he had, so he went in search of a new one.

The notion enveloped Charlotte that night at O'Hare, as the snow blanketed Chicago: the idea that a successful, settled person might walk away from their life without a thought. It'd be easy, she realized that night in the centre of the continent. Exchange her ticket to Vancouver for one to – anywhere. Montreal, which still feels like home. Vermont, where she summered as a girl in the rare company of her father while he was still alive. Or New Orleans: she'd never seen the French Quarter, never heard blues in the sultry air. Why stop at North America? Her passport and platinum card would take her anywhere she wanted – Lisbon, Geneva, Sydney – and the trust fund she inherited when she turned twenty-five, a fund to which she has sole access, would keep her there in style and anonymity. It would be simple to disappear for a while.

She doesn't want this wine, doesn't want the party it's destined for. Doesn't want the people who will be there or the script she will have to follow.

Pass by. Keep going.

The driveway is just ahead. She holds her breath and imagines not turning in. Feels the wonder, the excitement. The uncertainty, the fear.

No. Her thoughts drop back into their familiar track. She will do nothing of the sort. She will do the responsible thing, not the alluring, fuck-it-all thing. Responsibility is her specialty, along with follow-through and attention to detail. It's why she's going to be VP. She is known company-wide as an overachiever and a taskmaster – *I mean that in the best way,* the president has assured her.

As the Cayenne's tires crunch on the white-gravel drive, lined with barrels of pansies and late tulips, the cheery hues of spring, Charlotte releases a sigh. As quickly as the fantasy visited her, it is gone. Wine, then cheese, then back to the office and let the real day begin.

She steps out of the SUV and wrinkles her nose. The acrid stench of manure reminds her how far she has driven. *Janes Winery: Home-Grown,* says the green-and-black oval over the front porch. Gilt lettering curls into vines that trail from an ornately carved bunch of grapes. As signs go it's generic winery, not the slightest attempt at creative or quirky. Like so much in life.

It wearies her, the mediocrity of it all, the predictability. A world full of people doing the least they can get away with, taking the easy route instead of putting in the time, satisfied with just getting things done instead of doing them well. It's the locavore way, settling for unexceptional food so you can feel virtuous and forgoing the real measures like, say, trading your gas-guzzler for a hybrid or boycotting the dry cleaner.

As she reaches the heavy wooden doors of the tasting room, she feels a kick. From deep in her gut, near the part that wanted to keep driving.

Marcus. She plucked him from her own backyard, from her husband's domestic stock. Just like a locavore, she did it not for his quality—he was never a great lover, barely an adequate one—but because he was, pure and simple, nearby.

And Tayne. It doesn't bear thinking about. She never picked Tayne Stedman; he picked her. He singled her out, wore her down, and the minute she weakened snapped her up. And Charlotte let him. She held out her wrists and let the shackles slide on.

$$\wedge$$

TALK 910: In San Francisco we've got a long history of being prepared, but it's intensified since Vancouver ten years ago. Tell us, Summer, did you think about earthquakes or worry about them? Were you prepared?

SUMMER: I was oblivious back then, to pretty much everything. It's amazing how you can sleepwalk through life. You're barely equipped to make a bowl of cereal let alone deal with a disaster. It's not like we discussed it at home, talked about being prepared or what to do. We were all supposed to call my uncle if something happened and we were separated, that was our only plan. My parents weren't exactly on top of things. They worked, like, all the time. At that point in my life I was alone a lot, unless I went to school, which wasn't that often. When I did go ... well, that's where I learned duck and cover. When the house started shaking, I did that automatically.

TALK 910: You were a very brave young woman.

SUMMER: No. I wasn't brave.

TALK 910: We're getting the signal. Before we go, what message would you leave with listeners in the Bay area?

SUMMER: That it can happen to you, it really can, so do everything they tell you. Get your home and your office ready, make sure you've got a plan worked out with your family, get all your supplies, water, bandages. And pay attention. Because you know, crazy stuff can happen anytime. You can be sitting there, listening to some song or just staring into space, and then bam! In one second your world turns upside down. And your life, it's never the same again.

FIVE

∿

Eleven twenty-two a.m. The city: a sweeping tableau.

Some kept to their assigned places in the montage. Youths too old for school drifted within the confines of the Gap, seeking freedom through denim. Shut-ins and screw-ups stayed indoors, gaped at reality shows, nursed grudges, wept over life lost, surfed the net for bargains and porn. Bureaucrats nestled in ergonomic chairs, building networks of words on gently curved keyboards. Mechanics stood, feet planted, necks craned, beneath hoisted undercarriages. Panhandlers and proselytizers held fast to staked-out alcoves and inter-sections. New mothers stared at stained tablecloths, praying the silence from the crib would continue.

Others moved against the backdrop. Swooping birds, agitated pets, and fleeing frogs and toads were spotted far and wide. Runners and cyclists hur-tled along recreational trails, threaded their way among ambling pedestrians. Newly rehabbed men, hair shorn bristle-short above tender necks, delivered flyers door to door. Medical couriers in compact cars, awash in reggae and techno beats, sped to labs with cool-packed specimens. A tattooed trio hoofed it eighteen blocks to rehearsal, cursing the dead weight of guitars and amps, missed the fucking bus again. Sailors and water-taxi drivers navigated False Creek, alert to the aimless paths of stand-up paddle boarders.

The city at 11:22 a.m. Stasis and motion; stress and strain.

∿

KYLE IS IN MOTION, though not on the water. Two hours ago he beached his kayak between the salty rocks of Sandy Cove, on the West Van shoreline, a small pebbled stretch visited only by wealthy locals with no interest in stealing watercraft. He wheeled his bicycle from the nearby trees where he'd hidden it earlier, after the blowup with Joe, transporting the bike there in his Subaru hatchback and driving back to the Ambleside Yacht Club to begin his self-styled triathlon. The cycling segment was short, a furious pedal northwest along Marine Drive, past gated properties, past Eagle Harbour, to the soaring Gleneagles Community Centre, where he locked his bike to a storage rack and refilled his water bottles at the drinking fountain. From there he struck out on foot: first an easy jog along the former railway bed turned walking path, past youthful retirees walking standard poodles, past clutches of middle-aged women in yoga pants and fitted hoodies; then a gradually slowing trot as the trail angled up to Whyte Lake and beyond on the Baden-Powell Trail. Now, hair slick with sweat, lungs searing, Kyle is half an hour from his first rest stop, the panoramic flat-top of Eagle Bluffs, where he will catch his breath before the last gruelling leg to the summit of Black Mountain. The damp earth and fir needles have replaced the nightclub smells, but the guilt — the guilt will not be scoured. The guilt has gathered like the forest, closing in around him, dense and claustrophobic. No matter which way he looks at his problem, no matter how he dissects it and rationalizes his methods, there is one constant. He has wronged Joe. Sweet, loyal Joe, who has done nothing. Who has only loved him.

Anna, too, is in motion. Freshly coiffed but her spirit beginning to droop, she steadies Miss Dodie as they retrace their steps along the oceanfront pathway in a fruitless search for the missing ring. The beloved diamond did not materialize in Miss Dodie's ensuite bathroom, nor on her bureau, nor anywhere else in the tired old house. Now, to placate her lady, Anna half-heartedly scans the paved seawalk, resigned to the impossibility of finding the piece, a large specimen by ring standards but a speck in these vast surroundings. It must have slipped between the boulders that line the ocean side of the path, or been spirited away by an eagle-eyed walker or a curious crow. Yet Anna continues to search, her employer's patter washing over her to join the lap of waves against the seawalk. Occasionally Anna stoops and inspects the ground. Then she moves on, pulling Miss Dodie behind her. Mostly she waits — for the hunt to end, for the clock to advance, for evening to come so she can open the drawer, push aside the sensible underwear, and with the first long, sweet pull, quiet the keening edge of her eternal yearning.

Joe is also in motion, still at the waterfront mansion, behind schedule thanks to the late start and the girl's mishap. He is working his way through Stedman's backyard, where weeds flourish resolutely between the heather and ornamental grasses that line the driveway, its interlocking bricks pocked with moss, which he'll have to clear next time. Halfway down the drive sits a powder blue sports car, the source of all the roaring revs earlier. It's a two-seater convertible, a ludicrous vehicle if you've got friends to drive with and you live in a rainforest. But it's an eye-catcher, no question, a far cry, not to mention tens of thousands of dollars, from his own dented pickup. Joe can imagine Kiki in the driver's seat, elbow out the window, mint-green cashmere sweater and classic Ray-Bans completing the picture. Kiki of all people could pull it off. Joe tries to put himself in the passenger's seat, his unruly hair, damp pits, and soil-stained jeans a joke beside his neat and polished partner — tries, fails, and stoops back to the weeds, a sinking worry gathering force.

The Stedmans do not move. They are in stasis, locked in their respective positions. Stuck.

Tayne has returned to his domain, his office, where he stands rigid over the great wooden slab of desk. His headset, a long, narrow noise-cancelling prototype fresh from GlobalTech's innovation lab, juts from his jawline. He is six foot three and a hundred ninety-five pounds of contained rage. Before him spreads the newly cleared view of the Lions Gate Bridge, Vancouver Harbour slipping beneath it, a panorama of ocean and sailboats and container ships and barges of which he takes no notice. The fist-pumping thrill of this morning's Procter & Gamble win has fizzled. Marcus has called with potentially game-changing news: their three-year contract with Merck has expired, this morning's renewal deadline come and gone, the pharmaceutical giant suddenly impossible to contact. If the contract is dead — and it may not be, Marcus keeps saying; there could be a simple explanation for the delay — the fallout will mean hard decisions. P&G, though high-profile, will in no way fill the gap. Who will go and who will stay? Will they run satellite offices with reduced staff or shut them down altogether? How will they spin the news so the shockwaves don't rattle markets, so their shareholders stay confident? As CEO, leader, and innovator extraordinaire, all the big decisions will be his. They will come easy, as they always do, in a snap of insight. He has people to manage the niggling details. No, it's not the prospect of layoffs and closures that has him seething, nor even the potential scuttling of his bigger plans. It's the loss. Tayne Stedman, titan of tech, is a man who competes to win. He does not do loss. He never has. And here he is, fresh from this morning's victory, on the brink of losing — titanically.

Sidney too is in her usual spot, alone at the kitchen island. That's where she was when the gardener patted the wrist of her good hand and disappeared out the back door, taking his stained work gloves and pitying eyes with him. That's where she was when her father strolled in a lot later, glanced at her bandage, ruffled her hair enough to push it into her eyes, and left. Back to his office, no doubt, not that she'd ever follow him there to confirm. They exchanged two sentences, hers a question — could she take a painkiller? — and his a distracted reply: ask your mother. But she isn't here and you are, Sidney wanted to say but didn't, because he was already gone. Since then she's been on her phone, scrolling through Instagram, a bit clumsily because of being suddenly left-handed. It's all school selfies today. *Algebra: most boring subject EVER! Mr. Dentons got hot new jeans. Amandas empty seat, she never came back from the bathroom, prolly in there puking.* Sidney posts nothing. What is there to say? So it's another boring school day. Good thing she skipped. It's another boring day at home too. Cutting yourself on a stupid branch hardly counts as excitement. It's just a different kind of boring. Ever since rehab, boring has become her equilibrium state. That's a term she learned in chemistry, back when she used to show up: any forward reaction in her life is countered by a reverse reaction that balances it out, so in the end everything stays the same. Time passes, events too, but nothing actually *happens*.

Charlotte is likewise confined, not to a desk or an island, but to a farm shop in Agassiz, closing in on the coveted cheese. The lineup — because naturally even in the middle of Butthole BC there's a lineup — is finally down to one person. None of the four customers ahead of her were satisfied to buy and leave; all required that the purchase of local goat products provide a well-rounded educational experience to boot. She has endured endless questions: Where do the animals graze? How and when are they groomed? Is their temperament generally agreeable? (Seriously, *temperament?*) Details have been offered as to what the creatures eat, and how often; how and when they are milked; how far they range; how curious they are about the world (at which Charlotte snorted audibly). Even the birthing process has been described and discussed. To quell her hysterical urge to call a halt to the caprine documentary, Charlotte has endlessly circled the tiny shop, sniffing wax-wrapped bundles from the cooler, handling bottles of goat's milk lotion, eyeing the repulsive bouquet of goat's hair makeup brushes, feeling her nerves fray further and her foot continue to itch. Finally, just as she is steeling herself to barge in, the last fervent shopper shuts her trap and gathers her bags. Finally, it is Charlotte's turn.

S I X

∿

Eleven thirty-five. High noon approached.

Stomachs rumbled for the tuna sandwich, the takeout salad, the Tupperware of stir-fry left over from last night. Dieters longed for one forkful of creamy pasta, a single swirl of butterscotch. Ragged lines started to form outside the Downtown Eastside soup kitchens. A dentist in Burnaby began a root canal, running late, no lunch again today. In a Surrey parking lot a major deal closed: fentanyl-laced heroin whose victims would not, this day, make the headlines. In highrises people stepped into elevators, arms filled with briefcases and handbags and hotel linens, infants and grocery bags, confident of reaching their chosen floor. Motorists buckled up, fished out ticket stubs, prepared to exit eroded concrete parkades. Students eyed clocks in unretrofitted schools and cheap portable classrooms, willing the digits to advance. Soon they would be released, an exhalation of children, running and skipping, kicking balls, drawing houses in the dirt, shoving the weak. Soon they would be free.

Some did not eye the time. Single mothers and landed immigrants, dancers pulling down day jobs, recent grads working retail — to them noontime was another hour's pay in the long, dull labour of getting by in the country's most expensive city. If their minds wandered beyond work, it was to bills and debt, trips they would not take, lunches they could not afford. If they dreamed, it was of a day when an hour would be simply a measure of time, when time slipped free from money.

Stomachs rumbled.

The earth rumbled.

Faintly at first, a negligible displacement that registered nowhere. Midway across the Georgia Strait, some twenty kilometres off Vancouver's renowned shoreline, just below the sea floor, the pressure of centuries gathered, unstoppable. Like children, addicts, and dreamers, the earth's crust ached for the release of movement, the rush of freedom.

Now it was ready. Beneath the strait, the sea floor groaned, another movement in a series of infinitesimal slips along the patient fault line. Two shallow blocks of crust butted up against one another; two blocks that could not, would not, yield.

Motion and stasis. Stress and strain.

Three phones rang.

$$\wedge\!\!\!\vee$$

JOE STRAIGHTENS, drops the trowel, and reaches for his hip. The flip phone's "Benny and the Jets" ringtone says who it is. All the worry, the not-rightness of things, that he's been pushing down since breakfast rises like vomit.

"Hey, Kiki."

On the other end, hard breathing. No words.

So it's like that. All morning he's been trying to forget the fight. Danged if he'll get pulled back into it now. He struggles to keep his voice neutral. "Where are you?"

A couple more breaths. "Hiking. I'm nearly at Eagle Bluffs."

"Hiking? What the heck?"

"I know. But after this morning — God, I just couldn't do it. I couldn't face a day at the clinic." More panting. "I'm heading up to Black Mountain. It's a bitch. I'd kill for a switchback."

Joe's heart lifts. The raging diva is gone. Is Kiki calling to apologize? "C'mon, switchbacks are for pussies. That's what you always say."

A small cough but no sign of the chuckle Joe hoped to tease out. So it's still there, at least a little. The Chill. Will he ever make his lover laugh again?

More fast breathing. Joe pictures Kiki: muscles straining, legs pumping, elbows swinging in an unbreakable rhythm. Doctor Kyle Jespersen is the most determined person he knows. *Say you're sorry.*

Finally Kiki speaks. "So how's the new client?"

"Taking longer than I thought. The property's huge. But I should be done soon." The girl, her cut, that snobby Stedman — he knows better than to test Kiki's patience with all that. He wills Kiki to say it: *I'm sorry.*

"Listen, Joe. When I get off the mountain later, could you pick me up at Sandy Cove? I'll have the bike and the kayak."

Unbelievable. He's not calling to apologize at all. The nerve, after being so nasty this morning. "Fine," Joe says. "Phone me when you're down."

"You'll have room for the bike *and* the kayak?"

Joe fights his mounting anger. Why does Kiki do this? After five years together he still doesn't trust Joe to get it right. It's like he has to supervise every detail. I'm reliable, Joe wants to say. I may not be the smartest guy in the room but I follow through. I'm self-employed, for Pete's sake.

"I'll have room. I'll dump the clippings. Don't worry." But Kiki does worry. It's like living with a foreman.

"Do you have the blanket? I don't want the bike getting scratched up."

"I've got the blanket."

"Listen, Joe —" Kiki is breathing hard.

Say it. Say you're sorry and everything will be okay.

But Kiki only says, "Okay, see you later. Love you."

It's the last straw. "Why do you do that?" The words spill out before Joe can stop them.

Panting. "What?"

Joe curses himself. *Shut it. Now's not the time.*

"What? What did I do?"

Just hang up. Say goodbye and hang up. Don't — "Love you. Why do you always say that?"

"What do you mean?"

"You used to say it all, Kiki. The *I* and everything. You never do now. You never say the *I*."

Silence, no breathing even.

He should have kept his mouth shut. But he hates it so much, the way Kiki tosses off this most intimate statement the way he'd say *see ya* or *bye-bye*. It's like Joe is a child or a small pet.

"It's like it doesn't mean anything anymore."

Still no response.

Come on! He wills Kiki to say something, anything.

Then the line goes dead.

Joe stares at his phone. Just like that they're back to square one, the fight that started the day. An iceberg fight, where so much of what's dangerous is right there, under the surface.

He's an idiot. He should have waited until they were face to face to tell Kiki something like that. Should he call back? Say he didn't mean it? Grovel?

Except he can't. It would be a lie. He does mean it.

He flips the phone closed. Considers going back to the weeding but decides to cool off first.

He circles around to the front of the house, which faces the placid sea, so different from the fierce blue Atlantic where he grew up. What has happened to them? It's as if Kiki has gone dark, has flipped off the breaker to his thoughts and feelings. This morning's meltdown only clinched it: Joe has no clue anymore what's going on inside his partner's head.

He stands, legs astride, solidly planted yet shaking inside. Gazes past the lawn, past the rich folk on the seawalk, past Burrard Inlet, to the wide Strait of Georgia, Vancouver Island a mountainous silhouette on the other side, as far off and mysterious as the future he once thought he knew.

◢◣

"It's gone. Dead in the water."

It's Marcus calling and this time it's definitive. It is the worst news Stedman has ever received in the decade-long ascent of his business.

"What the fuck?" Stedman paces the familiar track alongside his desk, his body ramrod straight. Control. It's all about control.

"I've tried everyone I know at Merck," says Marcus. "They're not talking. Confidentiality and all. But I've put out some feelers. Word is it's Millitech."

A piece clicks into place. Until now the two companies have had an unspoken agreement: GlobalTech, the pioneer with the pedigree, owns the best clients, the cream of the corporate crop; Millitech, the second-rate knock-off, takes the dregs.

"Damn it all." Stedman's angular jaw clenches. "They've been planning this, I bet. Just waiting for the right minute to invade our territory. I didn't expect them to start at the top."

"I know."

Far off, the sound of dogs barking, many dogs. Stedman stops pacing and, as if for inspiration, touches the blue-and-yellow cover of *The Innovator's Dilemma*. His MBA buddy Steve had pushed the book on him back when GlobalTech was little more than a name scrawled on an index card. Since then Stedman has become a champion of disruptive innovation, the book's theme. Invade a market at the low end with a poor-quality invention that offers a benefit no one thought of. Gain ground. Improve your quality. Gain more ground. Conquer the market. The mobile phone was disruptive innovation: crappy reception but, more than making up for it, portable. Netflix was disruptive innovation: low-quality images but available on demand. Disruption is the MO that has kept Stedman ahead of the curve and propelled him into the stratosphere, but now, dammit, he needs to re-evaluate. Has he let GlobalTech get fat and complacent? Let success curb the leaps that make for true innovation? Let a wild child come from behind and disrupt his market?

The book's cover, as familiar as his own face, mocks him. He looks away. "How do we spin this, Marcus?"

"Damned if I know. There's just one media bite so far, some blogger from *BCBusiness* who caught wind of it from who knows where. I've got a call in to Epstein & Wilson. Should hear back from them anytime."

Stedman laps the desk once more, processing. "Okay. But do not give those shit-eating PR guys anything without talking to me first. You hear me? This is big. I don't want them micromanaging our every move."

Marcus is quiet a moment. Then clears his throat. "Where is Charlotte?"

"Charlotte? You know we can't use her." They never work with his wife's firm. Conflict of interest.

"I was wondering — you know, the dinner party tonight. Will she want to go ahead with it? Under the circumstances."

"Christ, how should I know? I'll worry about that later, after we've talked to E&W. Look, do not deal with that crew on the phone. Get them out to the office. Give them the tour, show them what's at stake. It'd do them good to be around some real work for a change. If I leave now I'll get there around the same time."

"Okay. And if there's a change of plan, you know, on dinner, I can call Charlotte. I don't mind."

"Whatever. Right now some damned dinner party's the least of my worries."

After the call Stedman continues to pace. It's a question of timing. If he can get word out right away on the Procter & Gamble win, flood the media channels, maybe it will offset the bad news about Merck. For that matter, what about Merck itself? Didn't the company land in trouble a while back? A flurry of bad publicity, something about patenting a gene test. Maybe he can revive all that, make it look like it was GlobalTech's choice to dump Merck, part of their commitment to socially responsible clients, yada yada yada. It'll take time, late days and long strategy sessions. The MGB won't be going out for a run anytime soon. And his ultimate plans for the company — well, he'll have to rethink them now. Will have to rethink everything. Disappointment is bitter on his tongue.

Outside, unheard by Stedman, the barking and yipping of neighbourhood dogs, which has escalated during his call, swells to a chorus. The white terrier halts his frenetic race around the newly clipped property to join in with his tribe. Together they yowl, for reasons they do not understand. All they know is: something is not right.

The inlet is becalmed, also unnoticed by Stedman, even though the expensive ocean view is one reason he labours incessantly. The sky has pearled over; high, thin clouds trail silver above the flat sea.

The calm might console Stedman were he a man to draw strength from nature. He is not. He continues to prowl, as if confined to a cage, unaware of the soundscape or the stillness or the forces gathering beneath him. The only forces in his world are the ones inside his head.

Phone call number three shatters the silence of the farm shop, where the shopkeeper is out back wrapping an entire wheel of cheese, enough to justify the odyssey east. Charlotte answers immediately.

"Oh. I didn't think you'd pick up. Where are you?"

Amazing how her daughter can turn hello into an accusation. "In Agassiz. Buying cheese."

"Where's Agassiz again?"

Do they teach them nothing in school? Not even local geography? "The Fraser Valley, east of Chilliwack. Remember that weekend we spent with Uncle Tim at Harrison Hot Springs? Out that way."

"God! Why would you go there?" A beat, and Sidney's voice softens. "I mean, is it nice?"

Charlotte's radar pings. It's strange enough that Sidney would call. Now her daughter is working her.

"It stinks. Like manure." The shopkeeper chooses that moment to reappear, glowering over her spectacles.

Charlotte retreats to the shop entrance and lowers her voice. "Look, I don't have time for the whole story. Ask your father to explain. I've gotta go. I'm late."

A small sniff on the other end. "My hand got cut."

"What do you mean, cut?"

"The yard guy put iodine on it and wrapped it up." Another snuffle. "He says I might need stitches. It's all jagged and everything."

Yard guy? She must mean the new landscaper Tayne hired. Why would he wrap up Sidney's hand? "Where is this cut?"

"My hand. Like, the little finger. It really hurts!"

Charlotte breathes – in, out, in, out – to curb her mounting anger. She should be glad Sidney is talking to her at all, yet she knows she's about to be played. She knows better than anyone the unique blend of helpless and manipulative her daughter has perfected over the years. They talked about it in family sessions at rehab, tense conversations that resolved nothing and that, between the angsting and the commuting, consumed hours of Charlotte's precious time. They talked about

Sidney's neediness and pleas for attention, which led her to drugs and alcohol in the first place. They talked about her hunger for reassurance and her so-called acting out. Or rather Charlotte talked and the counsellor talked. Tayne kept excusing himself to take urgent calls and Sidney sat there like a lump, eyes down, mouth buttoned. "Speak kindly to one another," the counsellor kept saying. "Kind words will unlock an iron door."

Charlotte has tried hard to understand her daughter, and to some degree she does. She was a teenager herself after all, and she remembers full well the self-involvement of those years. Still, there are days she wants to jerk Sidney out of her sullenness, grab her by the shoulders and shake her until her orthodontically adjusted teeth rattle and her twenty-twenty eyes tear up, until the girl understands how easy she has it. Look around, Charlotte would tell her. So many people with real trouble, people who endure chronic pain, who can't afford a night out or a cell phone plan or a new pair of shoes, people who have no one in their lives. A cut finger, for chrissakes? Suck it up, princess.

"I need a painkiller, Mom. Just one."

Fucking hell. She should have known. It's about drugs. Always it comes back to the drugs.

"Absolutely not."

"Come on! It really hurts." A few more sniffles and the conniving begins in earnest. Charlotte knows it for what it is, has been here countless times. "Dad said I could. If you said yes too."

Goddamn Tayne! He knows better. "Where is your father?"

"Where do you think? In his office. On the *phone*."

"No painkillers." Charlotte glances at the woman behind the counter, who's craning her neck, not even trying to hide her eavesdropping, the goat-loving cow. "Listen, do something to take your mind off the pain. Make an ice cream sundae, watch something silly on TV." What's on at this time of day? Those vapid women's talk shows? Wait — "Sidney, it's Tuesday. Why aren't you at school?"

In lieu of answering, the girl begins to mewl, tiny fake sobs meant · to deflect Charlotte's attention from the fact that her only daughter, whose truancy last fall and whose rehab through the winter have kept her behind in class, is skipping school. *Again*. And Tayne! Why hasn't he done something about it?

"What did your father say?"

"That I could have a pill if you —"

"No, no, not about that. About you not being in school. You've been warned about that, young lady."

"Nothing! He didn't say anything. He's busy with *work*. Plus he's got the sports car out in the driveway, he was gunning it like he's going off somewhere. Mom, I just need one. I know you've got a bunch stashed. Just tell me where and I swear I'll only take one."

Anger boils inside Charlotte so violently that she's amazed she doesn't spontaneously combust. How does Sidney know about her prescription? Charlotte has never mentioned it and she rarely takes the pills, only when her hip speaks to her after a hilly run. And what the fuck is up with Tayne? The sports car? What is he thinking? Why didn't he send Sidney to school? Why isn't he dealing with her? It's a mystery how her husband can run a multinational company when he is blind to all of life's details unfolding around him. As always, it falls on her to discipline Sidney and she is sick of it, sick to death of being the bad cop and enduring the lifelong wrath of their sulky daughter. Why can't Tayne man up for once and do his part?

"Sidney, listen to me. If the pain gets really bad, you can take two Aspirin. There's a bottle in the downstairs powder room."

"Mom, Aspirin? It hurts so much —"

"Those are the only painkillers we have. There are no prescription drugs in the house."

"*Liar!* You're lying!"

"Sidney Stedman! You stop right there." With a glance at the nosy shopkeeper, Charlotte steps out onto the building's wide verandah, where pots of annuals flower gaily. It's not possible that Sidney has found the pills. Ever since her daughter's Christmas meltdown, when Charlotte, pushed to the edge, called in multiple favours to get Sidney into rehab pronto, screw the cost, she's kept her prescriptions in a locked file drawer in her home office. The liquor cabinet in the dining room is also locked, though if you jiggle the door a certain way the lock pops open, something she's been meaning to get repaired. Of course it's pointless to lock up the alcohol when Tayne insists on keeping the kitchen wine rack filled, all those bottles just lying there for the taking. Thank God Sidney has never cared for wine.

"Listen to me, for—" Charlotte stops, breathes, forces herself into mommy mode. "Use your fu— Use your strategies, okay? Breathe deep and think about this. Okay? Think about all the time you spent in rehab. Remember how sick you were, all the work we did to get you better and get you out of there."

God, it was a relief when Sidney was away. The peace and quiet of the house. No emergency texts, no tantrums, no time-sucking meetings with the guidance counsellor. Charlotte felt like herself again. Not a mom or a supervisor or a jailor; just a woman. Maybe that's why she took up with Marcus.

"If it hurts, accept the hurt," she tells Sidney, reciting what they learned in family sessions. "Then put your mind somewhere else. Just take it minute by minute, day by day."

A loud wail on the other end, like a baby. A big, overgrown infant. Charlotte hates this about her daughter. Hates it! Hates every minute of it, the patrolling, the lecturing, the hurting, the being hurt. Hates being a mother, has always hated it. If only she'd listened, when she had the chance, and ended it. She remembers Mother, fresh off the flight from Montreal, red in the face, talking to Charlotte for once—*to* her, not *at* her—pleading. *You are throwing away your freedom, Charlotte. Where is the individual in this?*

"Go get your father. I don't care if he's in the office. Go get him and put him on the phone."

Silence, except for faint sniffles.

"Sidney, listen to me. Put me on with your father."

Still nothing.

"Now! For chrissakes, just do it!"

Prolonged silence, then a click. The line goes dead.

No fucking way! The little brat!

Charlotte pitches the phone. It bounces once, twice, three times down the wide-planked verandah steps, comes to rest against a pot of purple-and-yellow pansies.

She stares at the fucking flowers and counts to ten. She borrows Sidney's strategy whenever stress and anger overwhelm her, which is practically all the time now. Nearly every goddamn day.

The phone is toast, she realizes when she picks it up. Not one icon on the splintered screen responds to her jabs. "No service" runs along the top under the spiderwebbed glass. The tiny triumphant banner makes her want to hurl the goddamn thing all over again.

$$\sim$$

No phone rings for Anna. She doesn't own a mobile. There is no money for one, no need either. Who would call her? She has only a few acquaintances here, all of them from the Ukrainian hall *over town,* as Miss Dodie calls it, across the Lions Gate Bridge. Once every few months Anna takes the long bus ride to the hall for pierogi night and the relief of conversing in her own language, but she does not encourage friendships. Only rarely does she use Miss Dodie's phone to reach her uncle, who is the reason she chose Canada, not realizing until she landed in Vancouver that he had moved years earlier to Ottawa, half a continent away. Only twice has she called home, or what is left of it, their part of Donetsk more damaged than ever according to Oksana, the family's next-door neighbour until the shelling drove her to live with her sister. During both calls the once-irrepressible Oksana, a supervisor at the garment factory where Anna's mother had worked, sounded so beaten and desolate that Anna could not bring herself to phone again. Miss Dodie allows her two long-distance calls per month. She has never used them all.

No phone rings for Anna, but a cry cuts the air. "Over there! My love!"

Her face lit up like a child's, Miss Dodie points at the sprawling waterfront house.

"You see ring? Truly and really?" Anna cannot help her skepticism. Miss Dodie inhabits a universe that crosses into reality but once in a while.

"Yes! Yes! It's over there, on that ... that fence thing."

There is no fence, but Anna grasps her meaning: the stone retaining wall that divides the public seawalk from the private property. For once Miss Dodie leads the way, pulling Anna. The woman's discount pumps, which she wears everywhere — running shoes are for athletes and children, she insists — click unsteadily across the pavement. "Here!" She halts.

The top of the stone wall, roughly shoulder-high, is flat and clean. Not even a fir needle marks its surface. "No," says Anna. "Not here."

"Don't be silly. Not on that thing. I know that. It's on the ... over *there*, in the, the green."

Impossible. No one, especially not Miss Dodie, could see a ring in the grass from this vantage point. The turf is too thick and the lawn too high, held back by the retaining wall, for them to peer into it properly. Anna's weariness deepens. It is midday, hours before she can drink. "No. No ring is there."

"It is! I see it." Wriggling mightily, Miss Dodie wrenches herself from Anna's grasp and hurls her body against the retaining wall.

Horrified, Anna realizes her employer is trying to scale the smooth stones to reach the lawn. She darts behind the woman and embraces her soft torso, holding her firm. "No, my lady! No! You must not."

"If you won't get it, then I will. I am not a child, you know!"

"You cannot go up. Is too tall."

Miss Dodie writhes, her strength surprising. "Let me go! It's mine and I need it. Don't be such a, a, such a *fuckster!*" The word ricochets off the wall. Anna glances over her shoulder. Miraculously there are no walkers within earshot.

"Miss Dodie, please. No swears, remember?"

"Don't tell me! I will do what I want, and I. Want. My. Love!"

"What's the problem?" The voice above them is pleasant and calm. The voice of a saviour.

"Please, sir." Anna looks up. The man on the lawn is short and sturdy, with kind, crinkly eyes. Also vaguely familiar. "My lady is trying to go on your grass. She is thinking her ring is there."

"Ring? Like, on-her-finger ring?"

After a moment of parsing, Anna nods. "Is not possible, but she will not understand."

An ear-splitting wail from Miss Dodie, who continues to struggle against Anna's hold. "Don't tell me. Don't you *tell* me!" Her cries are joined, and soon overtaken, by the barking of dogs.

The man removes his ball cap and scratches his head. "Why don't we do this the easy way. There's some steps over there, to your right. I'll open the gate. She may's well come up and take a look."

Anna curses silently. The man is not supposed to go along with this senile fantasy. He is supposed to confirm that there is no ring, not on his property, and send them home. But already he has unlatched the gate.

Anna steers Miss Dodie toward the steps. "Fuckster," the old woman says under her breath. "I am not a child, you know. You, you *Russian*."

Anna bites her lower lip, hard, to keep from yelling the white-hot words that want out: that Miss *Dodie* is the fuckster and that Russians are pigs. The old woman knows nothing, nothing! Every fibre of Anna wants to shout that she may speak Russian, but she is not and never will be *Russian*.

Roughly she jostles the old woman up the stone steps and onto the man's lawn. There is a metallic taste. Her lip. Bleeding, of course. That is what they leave behind wherever they go, the violent Russian bullies: blood and ruin and humiliation.

Calm down and shut up, she tells herself. Miss Dodie will soon forget the outburst. Already the woman is smiling faintly.

Anna is getting better at swallowing her feelings. She cannot risk angering the old woman, who gives her the kind of life she needs: anonymous. Besides, underneath Miss Dodie's tantrums and fantasies and off-colour stories, she is a good person. And she is sporadically kind, for which Anna is grateful. Anna may be tethered to her employer's schedule and diet, to the shoulder bag filled with diapers and tissues and juice that bumps against her hip wherever they go, but it is a fair bargain for one who requires invisibility. There is only one freedom that matters, and she will taste it soon enough, in the golden evening when she slides open the bureau drawer.

If evening ever comes.

As Anna stands on the thick green grass of the property, on the line that divides private from public, the famed from the ordinary, her present from her future, she believes for one eerie moment that this day will never end.

∿

PRINCIPAL JAMIESON: People, we've heard the most remarkable story this morning. We can take so much away from it, and from you, Summer. You're an inspiration – all you've suffered through and all you've done with your life since then. Before you leave, we have a final question, this one submitted by the girls' hockey team. If you could do one thing different, what would it be?

SUMMER: There are so many things. [*Pause*] I guess the main one is, disconnect.

PRINCIPAL JAMIESON: Disconnect? From what?

SUMMER: Well, I was seventeen, just a little older than all of you. And when it happened I was plugged in. You know how it is, you're on social media, kind of zoned out, music up loud, away from it all. If I could do it over again I'd be offline, just ... in the world. No earbuds blocking it out. Sometimes I wonder – this may not be true, but sometimes I think that if I was in the moment and paying attention, you know? Just paying attention to all the details and signs around me, I might have been ready.

PART
TWO

Rupture

YOU'RE ALONE, as usual. You're alone most of the time.

You're at the kitchen island on your usual stool, resentment churning in your stomach. That slut Rebecca's stupid Instagram posts, the irritating Taylor Swift song, your stinging hand, your cold-hearted mother's failure to understand even the most basic things about you.

You're trying not to let it get to you. You're trying to accept the feelings for what they are, feelings. They're not right or wrong and you're allowed to have them. You are not going to give in. You will not look for the pills. You're breathing deep, reaching for your strategies.

One minute you're a lonely figure in the echoing kitchen. It could be any day, any time. But it isn't. It is today, 11:44 a.m.

Later you will never be sure: did this minute mark the end of your past or the beginning of your future?

Like that, it happens.

You're on your ass. Floor tiles cold on your bare legs. Stool overturned beside you. Pots and dishes raining down. *Slam! Crash!* Empty Mountain Dew can bounces away. Toaster smacks the floor, just misses your left foot. Then your mother's silver MacBook.

Years of school drills kick in and muscle memory pulls your body in close to the island. You open the door of the cupboard below the counter. Grab the doorframe tight, both hands, to hell with the bandaged one. Huddle in, hug yourself to the cupboard. Hang on for all you're worth, the countertop a granite overhang that you hope will deflect the worst.

Shaking, shaking. Your body, alone in the clanging kitchen, shaking. A kernel of popcorn in a vast heated pan.

The roar is deafening. A deep, insistent vibration, like a jumbo jet on top of the house. It goes on and on, all around you, closing in.

Then a hole. Later you'll say you blanked out. Not blacked out, like the old days—you're convinced you stayed conscious—but however hard you try, you will never summon up that lost time. You stay where you are, that much you know, because when you come back to yourself, you're still clutching the doorframe. Your bandaged right hand throbs. The shaking has stopped, and with it the all-encompassing roar. You wait, resting your head on a pile of dish towels inside the cupboard.

Only not really resting. In fact, not even close. Your neck is taut, your limbs tense. Your whole body, strung like wire, screams *Run! Get out!*

You try not to listen, because leaving is the one thing you're not supposed to. *Drop, cover, hold on.* The teachers said that over and over again.

You stay put. The world stays still.

Minutes pass. How many?

Gradually you register the noise. Not the jet-engine roar from before or the crashing of dishes in the kitchen, but a high-pitched wail.

God, it's so loud! How did you not hear it before?

The screeching goes on and on. *Stop!* Your head hammers. You want to cover your ears, but the teachers say no, do not let go of the cupboard frame, not until someone says you can. Hang on tight, stay where you are. It's the only thing keeping you safe.

Your ears ring, your right hand burns, your brain is a pan of scrambled eggs. Strategies, you think. Breathe. You count to twenty.

Who's going to come? Your mother's not home. She's not even in the city. She's ... where? Someplace out in the country, buying something. Then it comes back: the phone call, her clipped voice, which freezes over whenever you disturb her, which is basically any time you speak. *No, Sidney. No. No painkillers. No.* No, no, no. Always no.

Dad? You try to remember. He was outside in his sports car. Did he leave? Or is he still here? In his office, on the stupid *phone?* No way can he be doing deals, not after this.

God, the screeching! It won't stop. Like a siren or —

Wait. It's the house alarm. The shaking must have set it off.

As you clutch the cabinet frame, pain arrows through your right hand. There is a bandage, spotted with blood at the base of the baby finger, the stains mere pinpricks and fairly dry. You cut yourself? There's broken glass everywhere, but you have no memory of it happening, of wrapping up the wound.

Images flash: a curly head, a bunch of branches, sharp. Then in a rush the whole memory. That yard guy, you were helping him when the branches cut you up. He cleaned your hand and bandaged it.

As best you can from your hiding place, you look around.

Everywhere you can see, wreckage. The rest of the kitchen must be trashed too. And the rest of the house.

Your room! No.

It's so cold. You curl tighter, hoping to trap some warmth. God. Why did you put on stupid shorts this morning? Your knees are scraped, and a small crescent-shaped cut on your calf oozes blood, though slowly. You look yourself over, oddly detached. Is it really you?

You have to get up, get going. Find Dad, he'll know what to do.

But you're not supposed to move. What if the shaking starts again? Aftershocks, you know about them, they follow the main earthquake. How soon do they come? You replay years of classroom lectures, the Great ShakeOut talk you get every fall, but it's all a blur.

The alarm sirens on and your temples pound. God, will it ever stop? There's a control panel not far away, in the mudroom off the kitchen. If you move fast maybe you can shut off the alarm and dive back under the island before the ground heaves again.

You can't. It's too much.

All you want is someone to take care of you.

You might cry a little then, squeeze out a drop or two. Enough to make you sick of yourself. Then you quit thinking. Stand up.

The kitchen is a war zone. Broken dishes, fallen cookware, squashed houseplants, recipe books and bills and receipts and magazines that have tipped off the shelves and the desk in the little alcove near the stove. The stovetop gleams slick and shiny, something spilled all over it. Not the oil from the bitsu-bitsu; the tall deep-fryer hasn't moved from the back of the stove. The doughnuts themselves, which May set on the counter to cool just hours ago — hours? a lifetime — are scattered all over the floor. On the other side of the kitchen the terracotta tiles are stained burgundy. You sniff, your insides go *zang!* No. You don't do that anymore. You don't even like wine. Nearly all the contents of Dad's wine rack, built into the wall over by the beverage cooler, have tipped onto the floor and smashed. Shards of glass and perfectly aged rivers spread over the floor.

You take one step from your hiding spot, then—holy shit! A black-handled butcher knife is sticking straight out of the island's dark wood, barely a foot away from the cupboard you've been clinging to. You hug yourself.

Across the kitchen, half blocking the doorway to the mudroom, a giant stainless steel box which you realize with a sick thud is the refrigerator, toppled over on its side. What does it take to tip something that big? The fridge doors are still shut but the pantry yawns open, a mess of cans, boxes, and broken bottles puked onto the floor. The floor tiles bloom with petals from your mother's twice-weekly bouquet, the glass vase in smithereens.

Glass—God, it's everywhere. So much glass. You glance at your feet: both sneakers still on. That's something.

You pick your way through the wreckage, sidle past the fallen fridge. In the mudroom the deacon's bench, on its side, spills hats and scarves out of its hinged seat. On the floor a jumble of raincoats and boots, umbrellas, reusable shopping bags.

There it is—the alarm panel. You step over mounds of clothing and with your uninjured left hand clumsily enter the code: your birthdate, chosen by Lily, the first helper in this house, so it would be easy to remember.

The nerve-fraying wail continues.

Shit! Both hands are shaking. You must've hit a wrong number. You gather yourself. Focus.

You re-enter the code, this time pausing on every digit.

Yes.

The after-silence settles over you like the first sweetness of an oxy high, after you wash the pill down with whiskey, the warmth closing over you like a puffy sleeping bag—

No! Your heart races. You don't do that anymore. Focus. Breathe.

You count all the way to eight before your breathing slows.

Go back where it's safe.

Stepping over coats and scarves, kicking an umbrella out of the way, you're nearly in the kitchen again when something catches your eye. You hesitate, turn slowly toward the door from the mudroom out to the side patio and driveway.

What is it?

Forget it. Whatever it is, you don't need to see it. There's enough chaos in here. You're not ready for what's out there.

Yet your feet move, as if in a dream. Horizontal blinds partially shutter the window set into the top panel of the mudroom door. You reach up, stop. Reach up more and turn the rod. The blinds open. You see —

What?

Still you can't tell. You stretch up on tiptoes.

Normally what you'd see from this window is the driveway and one flank of the garage. Instead the window is filled with blue. The sky? Only it can't be, not from this angle. This … *thing* isn't sky-blue anyway. It's lighter, more like powder blue.

Your stomach kicks.

What you're seeing is wrong, really wrong. Like that night you were so high and lying on the school roof and that guy Dustin, who was Rebecca's Lee's boyfriend for a week or something, fell onto the concrete walkway below. You can still see his lower leg, angled out from his knee the way no leg ever should be.

What's out there, right up against the window and blocking your view of the world, is your dad's sports car, which he was revving up in the driveway earlier. Which you saw from the kitchen, with your own eyes, which he had moved out of the garage and parked *halfway down the driveway.*

Oh my God, is he still inside it? He quit gunning the engine ages ago, even before the yard guy went back outside. Did he ever come back in the house? You struggle to remember.

The car should not be there, outside the door, so far from where it was parked.

Your feet and hands are like ice. Where is he? What just happened? What kind of earthquake makes something as heavy as a car not just shake but *travel?*

SEVEN

The fishermen were long off the docks, safely out at sea, except for the laggards who, dallying wharfside or stepping aboard at precisely 11:44 were jolted into the frigid Pacific. Those who could not swim, which was an unexpectedly large number, thrashed helplessly, begged onlookers struck deaf by terror, took one and then two last breaths, and succumbed to the sea they loved.

Soccer moms who hours earlier had bagged snacks felt sudden panic. The kids were at school; they themselves were not. A few mothers shrieked and ran into the street, into the path of falling trees and utility poles. Some staggered up from office floors and began frantic, fruitless attempts to reach schools not yet seismically fitted. Some did nothing: the stay-at-home moms pinned under china cabinets and caved-in roofs, the fast-food moms disfigured by deep fryers, the health-care moms beneath mounds of brick that had yesterday been the oldest wing of St. Paul's Hospital, the moms on the SkyTrain, trapped underground, silently screaming.

Lovers in bed, more than you'd think on a Tuesday near noon, clung tight to one another. Prayed, murmured tender words, said sorry, sorry for everything. A ceiling fan fell and opened one woman's temple; her wife pinched the skin closed with sex-scented fingers till the world stilled and she could tend the wound. A futon in a ratty East Van apartment skated across hardwood, its occupants agape as the ceiling collapsed where moments ago they had lain entwined.

Investment brokers, if not trapped in elevators, swayed in their sky-high offices, swore as their screens smashed and systems went down, yelled at phones that would not complete the calls they'd begun the second the shaking stopped. Fortunes were lost — and made — in the frenzy they could not direct.

At the door of a Vancouver Special a border collie pawed, smelling death on the other side. Bakers cracked their heads on counters amid showers of bagels and spatulas and sugar sacks. Baristas ordered customers to duck and hold, or else wailed hysterically, instinct overriding mandatory safety training. Lonesome women hugged themselves tight, recited regrets in private whispers. A white-haired, arthritic sales rep knew, in that last second, that he could finally stop working. Babies smothered in cribs, crashed headlong when strollers flew from careful hands, survived unscathed in unsurvivable buildings, died before their first hello.

The homeless and the junkies did what they always do: backed into lonely dark corners, snatched the new kid's white sneakers, called loudly upon their Lord or their pimp, finished injecting just as soon as arm and needle had steadied. For them life was always this way, nasty and brutish. They got on with it.

∿

STEDMAN IS ON THE FLOOR, is all he knows, white ceiling above him. He tries to turn his head. A creak and then his jaw pops — damn, that hurts! The pain needles him toward consciousness.

He gropes the hardwood to either side. Feels books and papers, something boxy and wooden — a bookcase? Then remembers: he's in his home office. He moves his head through a trajectory of pain, the right side of his face screaming. Sees a shadow looming over him. Squints at —

An alien.

So he is dreaming. A nonsensical dream, because the alien looks like Sidney if Sidney had a metal head.

"Dad? Are you okay?"

Sounds like Sidney too. They're clever, these beings, even when they're part of your bizarre dream.

He shuts his eyes and retreats into his mind, where all is fuzzy and muted. Small fingers dig into his shoulder. Alien fingers.

"Dad? Dad! Wake up."

Gradually she comes into focus. She is kneeling beside him, hand on his shoulder.

"Sidney?"

"I'm okay. I'm fine." Her voice is tiny, as if coming from the end of a corridor.

His throat feels like a gravel road. "What happened? To your head?" Every word hurts.

She reaches up and raps with her knuckles. A bright metallic ping. "It's a bowl. One of those stainless steel ones from the kitchen. In case" — she looks around — "you know, if things start falling again."

Falling? This *is* a dream. He closes his eyes and settles back in.

"Dad, stay with me, okay? You've got to wake up. You've got to figure out what to do."

Sleep. The only thing he wants to do is sleep.

"Dad!"

The voice booms in his ear. His head splits, his eyes fly open. "Sidney?"

"Yes. Jeez, Dad. It's me. You've got to get up. We have to call Uncle Tim. The family plan, remember?" She pulls at his shoulder. Her other hand slides beneath his neck and lifts his head.

He roars with the pain.

Her hands go away. "What?" she wails.

"It fucking hurts!" He hears a sharp intake of breath beside him. "Sorry, Sweetpea. I didn't mean to use the *f* word."

Time passes and the explosive pain dulls, but his face still aches like a bastard. Eventually he reaches up and with spider fingers touches his right cheek. Feels something decidedly unskin-like.

"It's your Bluetooth," she says, leaning over him. "God! It's like, jammed into your face."

"Take it out, okay?"

"No! It's all bloody and gross. There's like a ... a hole. It's stuck right in!"

He traces his face below the cheekbone. The pain is excruciating. Finds the horrifying place where the long, narrow device has punctured the fold of his cheek. Something must have hit him hard to drive it in like that. The bookcase, did it clip him when it fell down?

The device, supposed to be their next and greatest prototype, is wedged in solid. Dammit! What the hell were the lab guys thinking? Clearly safety wasn't on their mind. He tries to grasp the hard plastic edge, but he's too weak. Not to mention chickenshit.

"Sidney, I can't do it. You have to."

"No."

"Sidney!" This is no time for her to go soft on him. He pretends he is chairing a meeting. "I am not asking you, I'm telling you. Pull it out. Now!"

She sniffles loudly. He squints and tries to focus, but all he sees is her bowed head, an expanse of stainless steel. She's nearly an adult, almost the same age he was when he left Hamilton for good, yet so much of her remains a child.

Briefly he relents. "Sweetpea," he whispers, hoping to lure her close. Nothing.

"Where's your mother?" He is racking his brain for memories but can only recall Charlotte's voice, raised, angry. That in no way narrows it down. Plus he keeps picturing a goat, which makes about as much sense as an alien.

"Out at some *farm*. Buying *cheese*."

Yes, the goat cheese. They're having a dinner party tonight. But why does Sidney sound so angry? "Honey, are you okay?"

She looks up, scowling beneath her protective dome. "I *told* you I was. Thanks for listening."

He touches his cheek and winces. "What exactly happened here? I'm a little unclear."

"Duh. An *earth*quake. Look around."

"I can't with this thing in my face. It hurts to move. Hurts to talk."

She picks at her hand. There's something on it. A bandage?

"You sure you're okay? Did you get cut?"

"That happened before, remember? When I was outside helping the yard guy."

Yard guy? Stedman tries but remembers nothing.

"He's the one who fixed it up. You didn't even come, not until way

later. You were too busy with your precious *phone*, and your *sports* car."
A sharp snort. "Look what that got you."

He rolls his eyes. At least that doesn't hurt. She has to be difficult,
even in an earthquake. *Saucy brat.* That's what his own mother hissed
at him when he gave her lip. After years of the same from Sidney, he
understands where the impatience comes from. But this is not the time
to call out his daughter's attitude.

Why can't he remember anything? *Your sports car*, she said. Yes,
he did have the MGB out. Did he drive it somewhere?

He changes tack, goes for plaintive. "Sweetpea, I'm sorry. I'm
asking you now, okay? Asking properly. Please, just pull it out. Then I
can get up and we'll figure out what to do."

The mixing bowl tilts, the rim a steel unibrow over his daughter's
flat eyes.

"I know you can do it," he says. "I believe in you." So much of life
comes down to sales, to knowing the right technique. "You're so strong."

Her chest heaves and she spews a great sigh. Removes the bowl
from her head, pushes her long hair behind her ears, and leans so close
he can smell faint citrus on her breath.

Her cold fingers touch his ear, tiptoe down his cheekbone.

"Just do it, honey. One big pull. Don't worry, you won't hurt me."
He can't feel her breath anymore, then realizes it's because she is
holding it.

After that there is only pain. *Jesus fucking cocksucking mother-
fucker!* his mind screams. An all-consuming galaxy of pain, himself a
tiny star in its midst. *Sonofabitch motherfucking fucker!*

Did he say that out loud?

Keep it shut or she won't finish, cries a woman's voice. His mother?
Impossible; she's been dead ten years. He listens anyway and lies rigid,
deep in pain, swallowed by pain, a minnow in the jaws of the killer
whale that is pain.

The air above him cools; in it, an absence. When he hears Sidney
scuffling off to one side, he understands the deed is done. Then her
sobs begin, huge snotty ones, and suddenly he is deeply sorry.

"It's okay, Sweetpea. I'm okay." When he moves his mouth, there is new pain.

"You're not! There's so much blood."

He opens his eyes. His daughter is hunched over, heaving. She is also, he registers through his haze, pulling off her long-sleeved tee-shirt. She kneels, shivering in a blue bra, wipes her nose on her bandaged hand. Clumsily she tears one sleeve off the top, balls it up, and bends over him again. He shuts his eyes, not wanting to see his daughter's breasts so close.

"It's going to hurt," she sobs.

"That's okay, honey." Feels the warmth of her above him again. Feels the wad of cloth press into his face. Feels the pain explode. Then feels nothing.

∿

Minutes pass before Kyle dares leave the boulder he's been crouched beside, forehead to knees, arms crossed over top his ball cap, for ... how long? When he unfolds himself his legs cramp, the lactic acid pooled from the steady grind uphill.

As he straightens and shakes out his legs, one then the other, he surveys the scene. All around him rocks have tremored loose. Some have come to rest in piles, like impromptu cairns. Others — big ones, furniture-sized — have fallen far below his hiding place. He heard them rocket past as the earth shook and he prayed, reciting the Lord's Prayer over and over, the words tumbling effortlessly from some rarely accessed part of his memory.

My lucky day, he decides, scanning the boulder-covered slide that stretches steeply above him. An exposed rock slope has to be the worst part of a trail to be on when an earthquake hits.

Exposed. Just like last night.

No, not now. The earth just moved, for God's sake. And he's okay.

Was it really an earthquake? the skeptic in him asks. Rockfall triggered higher up is a more likely explanation. Yet what would set that off? The ground isn't waterlogged; the worst of the spring runoff finished weeks ago. It felt like more than falling rock. The ground moved under his trail shoes, after all, enough to unbalance him and throw him against the boulder, where he stayed – praying, of all things, so it must have been serious – for who knows how long.

Of course it was an earthquake.

God, did you get lucky.

Maybe. But who's to say the danger's over? Unstable rock teeters in loose piles everywhere. A car-sized slab fifty feet upslope tilts precariously. How long before gravity gives it a nudge? He'll have to listen for any sound, be ready to take cover, walk carefully so as not to unsettle any dangerous rocks. But – walk down? Or up?

Below Kyle stretches the bottom third of the rock slope, which he ascended a short time ago. Below that, where the boulders start, the dark fringe of forest appears unchanged. No big trees have come down, or so it seems. That's good, right? Yet rocks big and small litter the base of the slope, and some have pushed into the forest, blocking the trail from which he emerged.

Down or up?

Bottom or top?

Shut up! he tells the voice, which resides in his pants. Or perhaps in his gut. Some low part of him that is unacquainted with his brain.

He's felt earthquakes before. Vancouver gets minor tremors on occasion, and this is probably another. Still, he'd like to know. If he continues up, at least as far as Eagle Bluffs, the panorama of the downtown core, Burrard Inlet, and Howe Sound will tell him something.

Or he could google it. If it's really an earthquake there will be headlines already. There will be tweets.

Or – Joe will know what's going on. If it was an earthquake and not a rock slide, Joe will have felt it too.

The idea of asking Joe comes automatically; it's a reflex after five years together. Kyle's backpack is halfway off before he realizes that right now, contacting his partner might not be the wisest idea. How can he ask Joe what's happening down there without getting into the whole "love you" thing? Honestly, it scared the shit out of him when

Joe said that. Joe must sense that something is off, but Kyle is not ready to have that conversation. They veered too close to it already, in the kitchen this morning. There's still so much to think about, so much of this punishing day to work through.

Then again, if it was an earthquake, he needs to know that Joe is okay. He decides to risk it.

He pulls the cell phone from the zippered compartment inside his backpack. Hits Joe's number and gets a busy signal.

Is Joe still at the waterfront house in West Van? When they talked he hadn't finished there yet. That was what? Kyle glances at the time on the screen. Only fifteen minutes ago?

He waits a moment and tries again. Still busy. Who would he be talking to? Joe hates the phone.

Kyle checks the screen. As he expected, he's still in cell range; he's got three bars. One reason he chose the Black Mountain hike is that he'd have service the whole way. Even though Shirin has rescheduled his appointments, she's at the clinic all day and has to be able to reach him if anything urgent comes up.

The clinic is the next number he calls. Like Joe's line, it's busy. He waits a minute, tries again. This time hears nothing. No ringing, no connection.

He tries Shirin's cell. On the other end, silence. Dead.

Not good, Doctor Jespersen. Prognosis poor.

Worry ripples through him. Has the shaking interfered with the cell towers? Or, more likely, are the networks jammed? That can happen in an emergency, he knows. Too many people making too many calls at the same time and the system gets overloaded, nothing goes through.

That would mean this is an emergency.

His stomach flops. No cell service. What exactly is going on down there?

As a last resort a call to 911 will go through, won't it? But if this really is an emergency — the possibility settles a little deeper — the last thing he wants is to take up the dispatchers' time. He's not injured or lost. You don't call 911 because you're worried.

Texting Joe, that's a good option. A message is more likely to go through than a call. Less bandwidth or something.

He keeps it short and basic: *On the mountain. Everything fine. You ok?* Sends the message, checks that the sound is on for notifications. Eyes the battery level: eighty-three percent. Good thing he charged it up this morning.

Come on, limp-dick. Quit wasting time. Up.

Up it is, to Eagle Bluffs. He'll scope out the city below, see if anything unusual is going on, and plan from there.

A couple of deep breaths as he steels himself. The thin tee-shirt he chose knowing he'd be hot most of the day clings to his torso, clammy and cold now that he's been still for so long. In fact, all of him is chilled, right down to his toes. Maybe a few jumping jacks to get the blood going. He sets down his pack, pulls off a few.

Joe. Is he cold right now?

Unlikely. Whatever Joe is up to in town, he won't be cold. He is never cold. Joe is like a puppy — warm, playful, easy. Easy to fall for, which Kyle did the minute he saw that crinkly-eyed smile and curly hair. Five long years ago. Kyle was still at the downtown Vancouver clinic, one of six doctors in what was starting to feel like a rejuvenation factory. He was thinking seriously about starting his own practice when along came Joe. The timing seemed right. If you're headed toward something permanent in your professional life, why not in your personal life too?

Five years ago. Back then Kyle thought he wanted a puppy for a lover. Now he wants a dog. A full-grown, hard-bodied, junkyard dog.

He does ten more jumping jacks, looks back down the slope. Towering cedar, fir, and hemlock stand shoulder to shoulder, edging the base of the rock slide. He'll be back in that forest soon enough, heading home. To what? That's the question of the day. All he knows is that when he breaks up with Joe, nothing will be the same. He will throw off this stale, settled life he's gotten stuck in, like he's some hidebound middle-aged suburbanite, and clear his future for something new. What the new version will be, he has no clue.

Five years. An eternity. How do you do let someone down after that long?

As Kyle hoists his pack, he vows that no matter how things turn out, he will continue to love Joe, even though it's just platonic love. None of the Grindr hookups or bathroom blow jobs or porn sites, none of the nights he's supposedly doing paperwork but is really at the park or the sauna, none of the mornings Joe turns to him with those warm doggy eyes and he feels zero desire, not even a stirring — none of it has fully rubbed out the love. Even last night, in the middle of disowning Joe in the most public, most conclusive way, the love was there.

Liar.

It was there. It *is* there. It's just separate from sex now.

Liar. You say, "Love you."

Yes, because I love him.

Like the man said, you are not in that sentence. You left it a long time ago.

〰

The place is a disaster. Complete and total chaos.

The sea-facing living room, which they entered minutes ago from the covered patio, has fared the best. Ornaments have smashed, spilled from the mantel over the low fireplace; prints and paintings have flown, and potted plants too — soil dots the thick cream area rug. But the low leather sofas, the coffee table the size of a trampoline, the side tables, and the other furnishings are still neatly grouped, as if everything's normal. Far worse is the wide corridor-slash-sitting-area that leads from the living room to the kitchen, once home, evidently, to an assortment of knickknacks, books, framed photos, ceramics, and other collectibles, all of them swept to the floor, broken pottery and glass everywhere, books tented open, the one armoire that's not built in pitched over face-first.

Inside-out, Joe thinks as they pick their way around the debris. Everything that should be tucked away in the background has spilled out in the open.

He guides the old woman around a broken pot, the tall ficus plant it once held tipped like a drunk into the corner. What about his own place? Will the antique highboy in the foyer have done a face-plant like the armoire they just passed? Because buffing out the scratches will take forever. Then there's the tall blue-and-white vase in the corner, the one filled with dried hydrangeas. And — oh, God! — the Fiestaware, every bit of it displayed on open shelves in the dining room. Dust magnets, the cleaning lady muttered the first time she sized up the collection. If the state of this house is any indication, there won't be a dish left intact. Eighteen years of his life he trawled through antique shops, estate sales, and eBay, pleaded with friends who owned a piece or two to part with them — eighteen years gone, just like that, turned into orange, green, and yellow shards on the hardwood floor. And what about the books and papers in Kiki's office, where none of the bookcases, which are stuffed full and then some, are built in or anchored?

Kiki! cries a soft inner place in Joe, the aching place where he's keeping all that's gone wrong today. Did he make it to the peak of Black Mountain? Will he be okay? You wouldn't feel an earthquake up there, would you? The old lady leans into him, unsteady on her feet. Joe knows nothing about the physics of earthquakes, he realizes, has no idea whether they're felt up high, on mountain tops. Kiki would know. He knows about most things. He's got to be safe up there.

In the kitchen, cupboards gape open, broken dishes are strewn everywhere, liquids have spilled over the stove and counters. Cans and packages and cookbooks and papers and flowers and glass, so much glass, litter the floor. The granite island is surrounded by pots and pans and topped by the heavy oblong rack that once suspended them overhead. Jutting out from a wooden cupboard below the island countertop, as if this were a slasher movie, is a gleaming butcher knife.

The woman called Anna looks at it and shudders. "Where is all the people?"

"Far's I know it's just a girl and her father. I left the girl right here, sitting on a stool. But that was a while back, before ... before this." Joe scans the area around the island for blood and sees none.

"We must find her. And the father. Is big house."

"I have a big house," the old woman says, peering at a can she has plucked from the mess. "Artichoke hearts. Would you look at that? You can make a nice dip from this. Just smush it up and mix in ... some kind of ... you know. The white stuff?" She looks to Anna for help.

"Hush, my lady. Not now. We must find the people." Anna turns to Joe. "You go upstairs. We stay down here, search them here."

"No," he says. "We stay together."

Joe doesn't know why, but he is certain they shouldn't separate. After leading the two women earlier to the covered patio, which entailed picking up and hauling the old one, who had pitched to the lawn in the first violent tremor; and after huddling with them there, hoping no tree or utility pole would crush the sloped glass panes over their heads, hoping the outdoor furniture, which skidded and tipped, wouldn't vault into the air and smack them; and after ordering the women, once the shaking stopped, to stay put until they were sure it was over; and worst of all, after hearing screams from the seawalk below, seeing the terrified face of the younger woman, and feeling her fear echo deep inside himself, he knows they must not part ways.

"What's your name?" he'd asked the younger one when the shaking was finally over. Noting the electrical union logo on her shapeless grey sweatshirt, he felt an instant connection. "I am Anna," she said. Then he understood why she looked familiar. He had seen these two on the seawalk earlier, the stuck-up snobs who wouldn't wave to him. The younger one's hair is different now, so he didn't recognize her at first. And up close, it's clear she is no snob.

Anna nods, accepting his decision, and Joe draws himself straighter. These strangers have fallen into his care, and he must do what he can to protect them.

"Pee-you. It smells in here." The old woman's head swivels. "Wine! Look, it's everywhere. Like a common tavern." Her watery blue eyes come to rest on Joe and her voice drops. "This is unacceptable, sir. Alcohol is the enemy. It killed my husband, you know. And B, you mustn't leave spills on the floor. It will bring the … it can … you know, those black ones that carry the heavy loads."

Slaves? Joe thinks wildly. No, wait. She means ants.

From the minute he overheard these two below the lawn, the old woman's voice sure but her words garbled, the other one responding as if nothing were amiss, he grasped the situation — the old lady is batty, the caregiver's playing along, and together they've arrived at some kind of harmony. Can you imagine? If he had to spend every day interpreting and bowing to someone like that, he'd be a friggin puddle on the floor in no time.

He glances at Anna, but she's not even trying to understand. She is staring at the floor, where wine has indeed splashed liberally. She inhales deeply, then places a hand on the old woman's shoulder. "Miss Dodie. Listen, please. This is a very bad thing. We have … the ground, it moved." She looks uncertainly at Joe.

"It was an earthquake. A strong one." Actually he has no idea how strong the quake was. He's not even sure how long it lasted. The screams from the seawalk and the roar that went on and on — was it minutes? seconds? The Stedman house seems fine structurally, at least the parts he's seen. Maybe the quake wasn't that bad, not the Big One or anything. Maybe Kiki, up in the mountains, doesn't even know it happened. Joe relaxes slightly. "That's why the house is such a mess," he says. "The earthquake shook everything up."

Miss Dodie nods and her papery jowls wobble. "Earthquake," she repeats. She turns to Anna. "You look different. Your head."

Anna pats her hair. "The girl changed it. This morning, remember? The hairdresser." Her accent is thick. Russian? Eastern European? She sounds like Elena from the hardware store in Lynn Valley.

"Of course I remember." Miss Dodie gives Anna the once-over, from her feathered brown hair down to her black-sneakered feet, then touches her cheek. "You are such a good girl, Annie. I remember. But you look so different. You used to have more … You were more … hairy."

Joe snickers, then inhales sharply, hammered by memory.

It was Saturday morning. Just three days ago. They'd both slept in. Joe had been at a friend's watching movies until eleven, and Kiki had tiptoed in sometime later than that, after a paperwork blitz at the clinic. Saturday night has become one of his favourite catch-up times; there are never any interruptions. Kiki was awake and shifting around on his side of the bed, so Joe scootched over the tennis court line and curled up against Kiki's back, spooning. Also hoping for more, and pressing his hard hope against Kiki's warm skin. But Kiki pulled away. The question hung there, so Joe foolishly asked it: *Can't I even hold you?* Kiki sighed. What that meant, Joe was afraid to ask. *Fine,* was all he said. Delicately, Kiki inched over to the edge of the bed. Like Joe was a pile of vomit or shit. *You're so hairy,* he eventually said. What do you expect, Joe wanted to yell. I'm a man, for Pete's sake! Kiki used to rub his cheek against that chest hair, used to kiss it and tug at it. Now it's one more strike against Joe, one more thing he can't get right.

Where is he? Joe takes out his phone, flips it open.

"Come," Anna says. "No phone now. We must find the people."

"In a minute." He tries Kiki's number but nothing happens. He steps farther into the kitchen, over by the island, and tries again. A busy signal this time, and the next two times. He tries a text instead: *Shook up but ok. Hope ur2.* There's no time to punch in more; texting takes so long on his old-school flip phone. He hits send and hopes for the best.

The butcher knife protrudes menacingly from the cupboard below the island. Joe pulls the knife out and places it on the granite countertop. Then thinks better of it and pushes the blade into a honeydew he scoops off the floor.

"Oh, look!" says Miss Dodie. "I could eat. Shall we share it?"

"Not now," says Anna. "We eat later." She turns to Joe. "Why you do that?"

"Aftershocks."

She shakes her head, does not follow.

"The mini-earthquakes that happen after the main one. If the knife's on the counter it's only going to fly around again and hurt someone. It's safer here." He pats the honeydew, pleased with his elegant solution.

"The ... aftershocks. The earth will shake more?"

"They're not as strong as the main earthquake, but if they come we'll feel them for sure."

Anna's eyes widen. She knows even less about earthquakes than he does, he realizes. He decides to keep the threat of tsunami to himself for now. Most of all they need to stay calm. He will keep them calm.

Anna shakes her head. "I cannot imagine more —"

"My Marty would not put up with this mess, not for one minute," Miss Dodie chimes in. "He would put a stop to all this nonsense."

"Marty is husband," Anna tells Joe. "Dead."

Miss Dodie wrings her hands. "The things people get away with nowadays. Such a mess! Where is the woman of the house? She's not doing her job." Her hands stop mid-fidget and a loud cry escapes her. "My love!" She holds out her left hand. "It's gone!"

"Is ring we look for outside, on the grass," Anna explains to Joe. She raises her voice. "We come here to find your love ring, my lady. Remember? Now there is earthquake. We will find later. Do not worry."

Miss Dodie rocks back and forth, her low pumps grinding something crunchy into the kitchen floor. Joe spots a trail of cereal along the tiles. Rice Krispies?

God, what a mess. *Inside-out.*

"What do you think you're doing?" The shout from behind makes him jump. In the doorway opposite stands the girl, a shiny bowl on her head, one sleeve missing from her long-sleeved tee-shirt. She doesn't look injured apart from her cut hand. "Oh, it's you," she says. "Who are they?"

Other than their names he has no idea. "This is Anna. This is — uh, Miss Dodie." He feels foolish speaking the name. "They were outside."

These essentials seem to satisfy the girl and she enters the kitchen, stepping around a toaster oven that lies in a backspray of crumbs. She looks less defiant now, hair limp under its strange helmet, the Riot Grrrl logo on her torn tee-shirt drooping.

"Sidney." Joe is glad he remembers her name. "Where's your father?"

She thumbs behind her. "His office."

No way! Stedman can't still be in there, ignoring his daughter, ignoring his house, doing deals like nothing's happened. This is an emergency, for Pete's sake! It'll take all of them to figure out what to do next.

"I'm going to get him." Joe heads toward the girl. "We need him out here, now."

"He can't come."

"Oh yes he can."

"No, I mean he *can't*. He's on the floor. He's — he's unconscious." Sidney's voice catches. "He's got this hole. In his face! I tried to fix it but I don't know what to do. I posted on Facebook that we're okay but I don't know if he is. I don't even know if the post, like, took. The wifi went down when I was doing it."

Joe's guts stir. Again he wonders: how serious is this?

The girl cradles her injured hand, the one he bandaged what feels like hours ago. Something kindles inside him, a kind of purpose alongside the fear. Whatever's going on outside, however bad it is, there's nothing he can do about it. But here, in this house, he can help.

"Come on. Let's take a look at him." He turns to Anna, then to Miss Dodie, who is reaching for the honeydew. "All of us. We stay together. Sidney, show us the way."

∿

The goat lady, as Charlotte has come to think of the bony white-haired woman who runs the cheese shop, stares at the telephone receiver in her hand. "It's not going through. There must be damage to the system."

Charlotte, who fled outside the moment the ground began to move, has just re-entered the shop, shaken but determined to get to the bottom of this strange occurrence. Using the phone at the counter, the goat lady has tried and failed to reach the goat man, her husband, at the warehouse down the road. Now her call to a neighbour won't go through either.

"Don't you have a cell phone?" Charlotte asks.

"They are useless in a disaster." The woman speaks with the loftiness of one who knows. "The networks get overloaded in no time. Too many calls. I'll see if I can get online." She disappears into the back room.

Land lines are of little interest to Charlotte. There's one at work she could try calling at some point, but the Stedmans haven't had a home phone for years. Charlotte's cell is tucked away at the bottom of her purse, useless as balls on a priest ever since she flung it onto the porch steps.

Why did she have to throw her phone, of all things? Her lifeline. How is it that her only daughter, her own flesh and blood — or so they assume, because Charlotte occasionally wonders if she was the victim of some hospital nursery swap — can drive her to such acts?

"Definitely an earthquake." The woman has reappeared. "There's only one sentence about it on the CBC site for now. Thank goodness the internet's working. And texting should be fine. It doesn't use much bandwidth."

"Was it big or small or what? Are they saying?"

"The line on CBC is 'Major earthquake hits Vancouver. More to come.' That's it."

"Major?"

"Well, think about it." The woman peers at Charlotte as she might a dim-witted child. "If we felt it this much out here, a hundred and twenty-five clicks away, it was major. I mean, look at the place."

Charlotte looks and her stomach lurches. How did she not notice? Cracker boxes have fallen from the shelves, a pyramid of goat's milk soap bars has collapsed on the corner table, the display of hairy makeup brushes has tipped over. At the counter the woman is wiping up liquid from a tub of feta that has fallen off a display pedestal. Charlotte swallows. Goat this, goat that, everywhere you look. All goat, all the time! Hysteria wells inside her.

"Best thing is to stay put." The woman sprays the counter with cleanser. "Ride out the aftershocks."

"I'm not staying anywhere. I'm getting the hell out of here."

The woman shrugs. "Suit yourself. But when there's an earthquake it's best to shelter in place. Especially during the main quake. Running outside, like you did, that's the worst thing you can do." She gives the counter a final swipe. "Drop, cover, and hold on — that's what they tell you. Don't go outside where things can fall on you."

"Things? What things?"

"Trees, telephone poles, power lines. Glass, if any windows break. Out there you've got no protection. You stay inside and hide under something strong, you can at least protect your body."

"From what I can see the only things that fell were in here, inside the shop. Where *you* were."

A breath puffs from the woman's nose. "We were lucky. This was nothing, what we just felt. I used to teach English in Japan. You live there, you learn a thing or two about earthquakes. I was there for the Kobe quake in ninety-five — now, that was a disaster. I lived in Osaka. We didn't get it nearly so bad there, but let me tell you, life was not the same for a long time. Trains, highways, completely messed up. Office buildings, schools, hospitals — there was damage everywhere. It was like a war zone."

"Thanks for all that, but it's not exactly reassuring, you know? Listen, my phone's broken. I can't text anyone. I've got to get hold of my family."

"They're in Vancouver, I assume." The woman assesses Charlotte. "That is where you're from, right? The city?" She makes the word sound smutty.

There is little Charlotte wants more right now than to smack this know-it-all farm lady across one ruddy country cheek. Fine for you, she wants to say. You're here at home, with your cheese and your livestock. Where am I? In the middle of fucking Hicksville, with no phone, no human being I know, no way to find out what's happening. I may as well be in outer space.

"Let me use your laptop, then. If I can check email or my daughter's Facebook page ..."

The woman's mouth turns down. "Facebook? Well, I don't know. I'd have to—"

"Look, I'll pay you." Charlotte opens her handbag. "I promise, I'll be on and off in a flash. You don't need to download any special software to get on Facebook."

The woman puts a hand on her hip. "You think I don't know that? I own a business. We've had a Facebook page for years." She waves her fingers. "I don't want your money. Don't insult me. Wait here."

When the woman brings the laptop out to the counter, the first thing Charlotte does is check webmail. Leaning toward the screen, her nostrils clogged with feta fumes, she's beset by the usual mix of despair and stress as dozens of unread messages load. It's been what? She checks her watch. Four and a half hours since she last logged on, in the kitchen with her MacBook Air, Tayne down the hall in his office and Sidney scowling at the end of the granite island. It was a quick check then, she was so pressed for time. It feels like an eternity ago. Now emails pour in from Marcus, head office — is it finally? damn, no, nothing about the promotion — from clients, Marcus, the Running Room, a local art gallery, Marcus, Alice from the museum board, the new hire at the office, two more from Marcus — what the fuck, is he stalking her now? On and on they go. Once this is over and she's home again, she will finally look into separate work and personal accounts. This is too much. Way too much.

Then they stop. The last email is from Sarah, one of her two social media advisors, sent at 11:42. Subject: *Instagram ideas for LexisCo.* Nothing from Tayne. Nothing from Sidney, not that her daughter would ever email her. Nothing more from the office. Not a word about the earthquake.

She composes a bare-bones email to Tayne: *Felt the earthquake out here. You and Sidney okay?* Is about to hit send when she decides to wait. It makes more sense to check Sidney's Facebook page first. She has promised to stay off it — *it's like you're reading my diary!* her daughter whined — but it's the most likely place for news. Sidney is always looking at Instagram, but she does most of her posting on Facebook.

Nothing. Sidney's last post was Sunday, two days ago. It's a selfie she took in her room. Her long hair hangs like drapes drawn partway across her face, which is slack and expressionless but in an overdone way, a caricature of boredom that Charlotte has seen all too often. *Another thrill-filled day*, says the accompanying text. That's the entire post, apart from two frowning emojis at the end.

Oh for chrissakes. It's so typical. When was the last time Sidney was excited about anything? Or pleased? Or merely satisfied? Apart from limply hugging Tayne two months ago when he pulled the cover off her new moped, a rehab graduation gift, it's been years since the girl displayed any emotion other than anger or resentment — unless you count boredom, which Charlotte doesn't consider an emotion. Gone is the toddler who chuckled at everything and followed her mother everywhere — around the house, into the bathroom, out to the car when it was time to leave for work, so close on her heels that Charlotte used to joke to their daily helper that if she suddenly halted, Sidney would pile into her. Gone is the girl of four, five, six who spent hours drawing; who went nowhere without markers, glue stick, glitter; who tugged at Charlotte's arm — *look, Mommy, look what I made!*

She was a sunny girl back then, and an obedient one. When Charlotte said, *no, Mommy's busy, go play on your own*, Sidney did as she was told and would amuse herself for hours until her father came home. That was back when Tayne showed up before bedtime. Sidney would wait at the front window of their old North Van split-level for his car to appear, then dive into a closet or under a table, where Tayne would find her after a lengthy search and loud inquiries about where Daddy's little girl could possibly be. Then, for a while, Charlotte could come unclenched, knowing the girl was in her father's care. She could breathe from her secret pocket of air, the one you're supposed to create if an avalanche sweeps over you. She could be alone, herself, just Charlotte, for a precious fleeting time.

The goat lady is busy tidying her displays, so Charlotte quickly scrolls back through Sidney's Facebook posts, a stream of angst and sarcasm with generous helpings of incoherence from the drug and booze years. Posts about the boredom of school, home, life. A poem that alternates between swearing and gibberish. A photo of Sidney with a tangle of tank-topped girls, all legs and bosoms and shoulders, eyes unfocused and ringed with black. A photo of Sidney in a black toque, head thrown back, bottle of Jack Daniels to her lips. There is nothing of the cheery, creative little girl here, nothing remotely recognizable.

Puberty did it. One touch of that evil wand and Sidney went from sweet and placid to brazen and deceitful. She stole money from Charlotte's purse and pills from her bathroom. Guzzled liquor from the cabinet and topped up the bottles, as if no one would notice that the gin tasted like tap water. Took the Smart car out joyriding once, unlicensed and high as a kite, waking the whole family at her friend Rebecca's house, where she parked in the driveway at two in the morning and laid on the horn. Got thrown out of the cineplex for shrieking drunkenly through a movie. Got caught stealing jeans from The Loft. Got caught buying opioids on school property. And always, after every fuck-up, an excuse or a lie: *I never took your money, I meant to pay for them, I was buying it for Rebecca, I wasn't drunk.*

Those were the times Charlotte bitterly regretted her decision. Why hadn't she listened to reason? Was her need to upset Mother really so fierce back then that she was willing to pay for it for the rest of her life?

It was a cliché from the beginning. Charlotte couldn't be pregnant, it was impossible. She'd quit taking the pill because it made her gain weight, but she used her diaphragm faithfully. Yet her doctor confirmed what the home kit said. Equally clichéd was Tayne's reaction: *I'll stand by you no matter what.* All she could think was: what the fuck have I gotten myself into? She'd moved to Vancouver with Tayne on a lark, not sure if she'd stay there or even stay with him, and here she was, knocked up. *Get rid of it* was all Mother said on the phone, before launching into a forty-five-minute account of the women in poverty conference she had attended and the talk she had given. That was when Charlotte Pettigrew, daughter of a superstar feminist, made an extraordinary choice: to have the baby and marry the father.

For once she had the undivided attention of Mother, who took the unprecedented step of flying to Vancouver to change her daughter's mind. But no amount of maternal pleading, cajoling, railing, or bribery – and money *was* offered – could dissuade Charlotte. She would accept the jobs of wife and mother and would fulfill them perfectly, having learned at the maternal knee precisely what not to do. In the process she'd deliver a permanent FU to the woman who bore her but could not be bothered with her.

Charlotte stops scrolling, drawn to a post from a few months ago, a selfie in which Sidney holds under her chin a family photo from the GlobalTech picnic two summers ago. Charlotte knows the photo well, for it sits on her desk at work: the three Stedmans sprawled on a blanket, roast chicken and bottle of lemonade beside them, Charlotte and Tayne facing the camera, Sidney in profile, watching something offside. In Charlotte's version she and Tayne sport wide manufactured smiles – they'd just been bickering about how soon they could go home – but Sidney's photo is different. A huge angry mouth, drawn in thick black marker, covers the lower half of Charlotte's face, turning her into a leering, glowering jack-o-lantern. *My mother the liar*, reads the single-line post.

In the selfie Sidney smirks triumphantly.

Liar?

Anger explodes inside Charlotte.

I'm the liar?

Her heart races and her temple pounds. Breathe, she tells herself. Be in the present. But she is trembling with rage.

Liar? Who the fuck is Sidney to accuse anyone of lying when the most blatant falsehoods in the household fall from that girl's mouth? They've had years of lies – where Sidney spends her days, where she goes after school, why her clothes smell like pot, who dropped her off at three a.m. in a belching Camaro, when and why she quit her after-school art class, where Charlotte's bottle of Vicodin went, why the hundred bucks for new jeans did not result in new jeans. Years of it, lie after lie, and now Charlotte can believe nothing, not one single word, that leaves her daughter's mouth. *A painkiller, I cut myself, just one painkiller.* Sure. And here on her Facebook page, this most public of public forums, which Sidney has forbidden her to view – as if; *all* parents look at their kids' Facebook pages – the truth is twisted yet again to brand Charlotte the liar.

Be kind to one another, the counsellor told them. Kind words will unlock an iron door. Uh-huh.

Liar? Tayne was the liar at that fucking picnic. His lie was the reason they were fighting in the first place. He'd promised Charlotte they would stay only two hours at the stupid event but they'd been there three, and Charlotte had work to do and her running meet-up that evening and was growing impatient. Tayne was the goddamn liar, so why is *she* the one her daughter disfigures and plasters all over Facebook for her hundreds of followers to see and judge and laugh at?

Luckily the goat lady is still cleaning up because Charlotte cannot tear her eyes from the post: Sidney's smirk, the thick angry lines of black marker.

More than that, the ingratitude. All Charlotte has ever done is bail her daughter out. Written notes to cover her absences, made her espresso on hangover mornings, picked her up that time the boys left her under the Lions Gate Bridge and drove off into the night. She has kept the worst of the girl's transgressions from her precious, beloved father, who never has to get *his* hands dirty, never has to be the bad guy, never has to be around for all the shit. Because Charlotte is the goddamn mother. Which means *she* is the bad one, the one who says no, the one who asks why, the one the girl blames and yells at and scratches and once, in a drunken rage, kicks in the stomach. Charlotte is the one who finally intervenes and gets Sidney into the best rehab on the coast, because otherwise it would never happen. It's not like Tayne would do anything. He's too busy with work and besides, he thinks Sidney's fine, she's just going through a stage. He doesn't accept words like *addict* and *alcoholic*. To him they're fancy words for *loser*, and Tayne Stedman is not a man who loses, as he all too frequently reminds her. No, it's been Charlotte all along, Charlotte who has done everything. And this is her thanks for taking it, taking it for years, the lies and temper and cruelty, taking it because it's her job to take it and she's never done a half-assed job of anything and she will succeed at being a fucking mother even if she fucking kills herself in the process.

The goat lady, finished rearranging her stock, hovers at one end of the counter. Clearly Charlotte's time is up. She almost closes Facebook but at the last minute decides to scroll back to the top, just in case. And there it is, a brand-new post: "Earthquake! Me and dad at home. He hit head but we're ok. Mom out shopping somewhere ... Valley?"

Out shopping? As if she's enjoying a carefree morning, indulging in a little retail therapy out here in the boonies. Jesus fucking Christ! They have no idea, none whatsoever, how much time and work she sinks into keeping their lives running. How much of her money is behind the lifestyle they take for granted. *You done good* is the biggest thanks she ever gets from Tayne. And from her daughter? *My mother the liar.*

Well, fine. They want to take her for granted? Let them.

She closes Facebook without posting anything, either on Sidney's page or her own. She trashes her draft email to Tayne too. To hell with them. They're so okay together at the house, they're such pals, let them wonder where she is and whether she's alive. How long before they even notice that she hasn't checked in?

The goat lady has edged her way behind the counter and stands across from Charlotte. "You done?" She nods at the laptop. "I need to get on email too."

"I'm done." Charlotte picks up her bag, fishes out the keys, and turns away. She is dying to get out of this smelly, claustrophobic shop.

"Wait!"

She stops.

"You forgot this."

The woman holds out a large, weighted-down plastic bag.

"Your cheese."

∿

AESTHETICA: Your first show, *Ghosts*, catapulted you to fame. Suddenly everyone knew Summer Rain. Can you talk about the title?

SUMMER: Well, back in the eighties scientists were looking for proof that the Pacific Northwest is on a live subduction zone. Before that there was a lot of debate. So these scientists are exploring tidal marshes, looking at the layers of soil that built up there, and they find these forests of red cedar that are all dead. Going by the growth rings they can tell the trees died around 1700, and died fast. The shoreline the trees were on suddenly dropped into the tidal zone, and the salt water killed them. The scientists called them ghost forests. It was physical proof that a mega-earthquake hit the Pacific Northwest back then. The ghost forests proved that the whole region is on a fault, and that this huge area which everyone thought was basically stable was going to break again.

AESTHETICA: So how does *Ghosts* tie in? The show wasn't about scientists or forests.

SUMMER: You've got all this evidence of what happened, right? Physical evidence, trees and soil layers, things the scientists could see and measure. And later you've got all the photos and videos and news coverage of the Vancouver quake. And there's also me. [*Laughs*] I'm part of the physical evidence. But what about the non-physical? You know, the spiritual or emotional evidence that something huge happened? Your feelings, the relationships you have, what you believe in – that's all shaken as much as your actual surroundings. Maybe more. Where is the evidence of that, except in people's memories and minds? I tried with *Ghosts*, I try with all my art, to give shape to those invisible effects. Because you can build new houses, you know? New trees are going to grow. But the traces that are inside you, that's what you're always going to be haunted by.

EIGHT

$\wedge\!\!\!\vee$

Ships out at sea suffered little, cushioned by their mattress of ocean, but anything docked got slammed. In Vancouver Island's eastern ports and in Gulf Island harbours, ferries and water taxis pitched and rocked. Passengers screamed, took hits from backpacks, souvenirs, cafeteria crockery. The Bowen Island vessel, in the midst of offloading when the shaking began, lost its ramp. Two vehicles plunged into the sea. A third, half ashore when the ramp jolted free, tipped and teetered before backflipping into the drink. For the rest of his life the driver, a high-school nobody vaulted to fame by his miraculous survival, remembered nothing after the call to disembark.

At the floatplane terminal on Vancouver Harbour, a politician boarding a Twin Otter lost her footing, tumbled backward down the steps, hit concrete, snapped her neck. The pilot, who had been handing her up the stairs, was concussed by a hard-shell suitcase that flew from another passenger's grip.

YVR was worse. The concrete of runway 26R buckled just as a loaded Airbus 320 touched down, inbound from Toronto. The plane lurched, the landing gear crumpled, the aircraft skidded nine hundred feet along the grassy infield. Forty passengers fled before the fuselage erupted in flame. The other hundred and ten, plus full flight crew, were incinerated inside. There was no one to save them. Two of the airport's fire trucks were pinned beneath a support beam in their storage shed. The others had raced to the two-hundred-foot control tower, the nervous system without which pandemonium would rule the skies, built to withstand a 7.2 quake yet leaning perilously, on the verge of collapse.

$\wedge\!\!\!\vee$

THE LAST PUSH UP to Eagle Bluffs is short, but it tests Kyle's stamina. All the time he spent cowering beside the boulder — five minutes? ten? two? — then deliberating whether to go up or down has leached heat from his body. His legs and ankles still feel stiff and cramped; not even the jumping jacks loosened them completely. His backpack pulls at him though its contents are meagre: an empty half-litre water bottle, another one two-thirds full, two power bars, one partially eaten package of beef jerky, a tube of sunscreen, extra socks, pocket knife, headlamp. His windbreaker is no longer in there; he pulled it on as soon as he set off up the mountain. The jacket is failing its chief job, maybe because the worst drafts are the ones chilling him inside. It'll take more than lightweight nylon to stop those.

It's shock, you don't need a medical degree plus cosmetic surgery specialty to figure that out, and it has only intensified since the breeze picked up and began tickling his nostrils. Brought with it —

Smoke. Ash. Something's burning. Not good.

His heart is pumping, yet his feet are clammy and he can barely feel his toes. He will not look down the mountain, not yet. No point frustrating himself with partial views. He'll wait until he can see it all, and see it clearly.

Above him a granite face rises stoutly from the dwarf evergreens that pass for trees in the subalpine. Eagle Bluffs. The trail will lead him around and onto the bluffs and then he'll have all the view he needs: the western half of West Vancouver, sloping up toward him from the shoreline; glimpses of the coastal highway directly below; the waters of Howe Sound spreading into the distance, the swell of Bowen Island in their foreground; the long channel of Burrard Inlet that forms the West Van coastline; and across the inlet, far in the distance, the treed finger of land that is Point Grey, in the city.

Those are the landmarks, but what will he see? A city unscathed, an ocean unruffled? An ordinary tableau that says all is well? Or smashed roofs, snarled traffic, fire? The smoke has to be coming from somewhere. A giant wave, God forbid, heading in? Images of the tsunami that swept Indonesia, swallowing hotels and beaches, buses and families, play at the edges of his mind. That can't happen here, can it? Sure, there are all those blue-and-white tsunami evacuation signs along the coastal routes, even warning systems — sirens, or is it horns? But aren't they over-the-top precautions? Surely they're not ... for real.

The questions spike his fear, which in turn dials up his adrenaline. Up he pushes, up and up, through the thinning trees, nearer the open bluffs, closer to the answers he is not sure he wants.

∧

"I live with a doctor. I know a little about wounds." Joe scratches his curly head and assesses the great man lying unconscious on the floor, balled-up cloth stuck to his cheek, blood oozing thickly around it.

A gentle push staggers Joe aside. "I do it." Anna kneels beside the man. "I am nurse in my country."

"She is," Miss Dodie says. "That's why I hired her. She has the papers somewhere, don't you, Annie? They won't let her work here without taking a bunch of tests first. It's silly."

It's the first fully with-it comment the old woman has made. Maybe she's not a complete deadweight, Joe thinks, then scolds himself. She's old. She can't help it if she's losing her marbles.

"She's a good girl," Miss Dodie continues. "But she can't make a decent pot of coffee, and she is starving me. No cheese, no cake, no bacon. I ask and ask and I get that green ... those — leaves! A pile of leaves. What am I, that ... that pretend fellow?" She looks hopefully at Joe. "You know, with the baseballs over his, up in his sleeves — Oh! He smokes a midget pipe."

"Um — Popeye?"

"Yes! He loves that skinny woman, the oily one." The woman's eyes gleam. "They have sex."

"You, girl." Oblivious to her employer's ramblings, Anna is addressing Sidney. "Get me those things you use for your hand, the ... the liquid you paint on it, and the bandage. Get me also the grey-coloured tape, the ... what it is? The chicken — no, the duck tape. Go fast."

Neither one of them knows the right word for anything. Joe is exhausted trying to keep up. Miss Dodie sidles closer, bringing the cloying scent of baby powder and, not far beneath it, the tang of urine. "Your restaurant is very big, very nice," she tells him. "You must be proud. Only the spills are bad. You clean them up and you will get more people, I guarantee it. But I'm getting tired now. Can you give me my dinner? Something simple, maybe a rare hamburger. Blue cheese would be nice. Then I'll be going home."

It's not worth setting her straight about who owns the house, or that it is a house and not a restaurant. Nor is it worth even guessing when any of them will get to go home.

He's got to try Kiki again. He feels unanchored not knowing where his partner is. Somewhere up in the mountains, that's all he knows. And alone, which doesn't bear thinking of. What kind of shape is he in? Is he hurt? Unconscious?

If he could hear Kiki's smart, take-charge voice, even for a minute, it would be such a relief. Kiki would assess this situation in seconds. He'd know exactly what to do with these strange women and these uppity Stedmans, and Joe would gladly listen, because he doesn't have a clue.

The old woman leans closer. Several short bristles quiver on her chin. With a bejewelled forefinger she tap-taps his chest.

"Excuse me, sir. Do you smell smoke?"

∧

Back on the Trans-Canada Charlotte is struck by how few drivers besides her are heading east. She's well over the speed limit, no traffic holding her back. In the westbound lanes, however, any number of fire trucks, ambulances, and tow trucks zoom past, no lights or sirens but in a hurry. A bunch of pickups and utility vehicles too: Shaw, Telus, BC Hydro, FortisBC. Helicopters pass overhead, a few floatplanes too. All bound for the city.

Major, the goat lady said. What exactly does that mean? Will the power be out at home? Will things have fallen off shelves like in the cheese shop? Sidney already cut herself today — could she do it again? At least Tayne's at home. Surely he'll emerge from his office long enough to check on his precious daughter. And May should be back from the vet any time now. Sidney will be fine. She'll have loads of attention, as usual.

That fucking Facebook post! Charlotte is still furious — livid — at the ugliness and pure spitefulness of the defaced photo. She cannot believe, after all the time she's devoted to Sidney, precious time that she will never get back, listening to her, ferrying her around, propping her up, bailing her out of trouble, that the girl would smear her so viciously and so publicly. And for Sidney to single her out and leave her absentee father's halo intact? There's a grim lesson there, one Charlotte would have done well to learn years ago: neglecting your child scores you way more points than raising her.

At least she's moving, unlike earlier this morning. She's doing one forty now. The Porsche Cayenne takes no notice. A straight stretch, divided highway, no one to pass — why not? One forty-five, one fifty. Giant boat that it is, the Cayenne practically steers itself.

Keep going. Just keep driving.

If ever there was a day to keep going, this is it. Except Charlotte has things to do. She has a plan. Drive far enough east to find a working phone. Contact head office, see if they can reschedule the one o'clock video call. Shit! It's already twelve-twenty. She cannot be late for the call, not when her promotion's in the offing. Earthquake or not, she needs to prove her reliability. Next, call the office land line. If that doesn't work — the goat lady's line was dead, after all — she'll find internet somewhere and post to Facebook that she's all right. Texting, of course, is out. Why, *why* did she have to smash her cell phone today of all days? Texting is the most likely way anyone, especially Tayne or Sidney, would reach her in a crisis.

Crisis . . .

The family plan! In a flash she remembers. Sidney, for homework once, asked them to choose a person outside the Lower Mainland they'd all report to if they were separated in an emergency. They decided on

Tim, Tayne's deadbeat brother in Toronto, a serial entrepreneur who has nursed at the teat of her inheritance for years. It's a decision Charlotte hasn't thought about since then.

She revises her to-do list. After head office, call Tim. Brief him on her situation. Get news about Tayne and Sidney, both of them probably scarfing down dough balls and congratulating themselves on some quality time together without Hurricane Charlotte or My Mother the Liar there to ruin the party.

And the dinner party — how could she have lost sight of that? It's the only reason she's out here in the middle of nowhere, with a reeking mound of cheese. She mustn't drive too far east or she'll be pushing it to get home in time to help May. Then she has to put on a designer dress, redo her makeup, and greet people, including Marcus if he shows. Smile and think of charming things to say and generally act like she gives a shit.

So many emergency vehicles headed toward Vancouver — what kind of traffic will she have to fight on the way home? She inches the Cayenne up to one fifty-five.

There is nothing she wants less than to host Tayne's posse of hangers-on tonight. *Major.* Is that a good enough reason to cancel? If she manages to reach him, she'll suggest it. Whether he'll listen is anyone's guess.

The town of Hope is a few minutes ahead. She'll stop there, find a payphone, and get online at a library or internet café. Then sit somewhere with a latte and calm down.

So there was an earthquake. She will deal with it. Just another to-do on a long, long list.

∿

Almost there. High enough now for a clear sight line over the city if he were to turn and face it.

But he keeps going. He won't look, not until he's all the way up.

Goal-oriented — every school evaluation, every personality test, every supervising doctor, every lover has described him that way.

When Kyle sets his mind to something get the heck out of his way, his mother used to brag. But that's not what keeps him pushing now. He no longer cares about reaching the bluffs. He is spooked and needs to see what's going on below, and he's putting it off.

He is scared. So much is not right. Smoke, thicker by the minute. Sirens, a lot of them, far off in the city as well as closer to him, on the roads beneath the mountain. Helicopters, one of them beating the sky right now, search-and-rescue judging by the yellow paint. The engines of other aircraft he can't see.

Do it. Turn around.

Maybe it won't be that bad. Maybe the city will look more or less normal. If it doesn't, what choice does he have but to accept what's there and assess what to do next? A methodical series of procedures lies ahead, like the surgical checklists he relies on at work, and the comfort of this thought eases his mind. Complete the first step and the rest will follow.

So he climbs. Climbs and feels his thighs strain with each tall step. Climbs and looks straight ahead, ignoring all else. Climbs and tries not to hear the mayhem or smell the worry. Climbs until the climbing ends and he is there, on the long, wide floor of boulder-strewn granite that is the top of Eagle Bluffs. He is there and he is utterly alone – no hikers eating sandwiches, no chipmunks skittering out from hiding, no ravens calling overhead, no whisky jacks angling for crumbs.

Through the cloud-threaded sky seep weak patches of blue. He faces northeast, away from the city, toward the fir and cedar that choke the backside of the bluffs. The other way, if only he would turn, lies his city, maybe his whole future.

Do it.

I can't.

Face it. Come on.

Joe is down there. Where? Doing what? What if he's hurt?

It's done. You can't change it. Just look.

No.

Limp-dick. Pussy.

He breathes in all the air his lungs can hold, tells himself he must.

Turns around and looks. And from this day forward knows exactly how much of a pussy he is. He sweeps the horizon once, slowly. Turns away. Squats, then drops to the rock, his legs unable to hold him. Hangs his head, covers his eyes.

It was only seconds, but it was enough. Enough that he will spend the rest of his life struggling to unsee.

Oily black smoke. Columns of flame licking skyward from the treed streets of West Vancouver. The two framed highrises on the Dundarave shore, construction halted a month ago amid protests, reduced to heaps of concrete and steel. The giant crane that marks the controversial site toppled, its red arm now pinning half a block. The mint green fifties apartment building, icon and eyesore of the West Van shoreline, tipped backward, a dinosaur resting on its haunches. In the sky a swarm of helicopters, floatplanes too, more aircraft than he's ever seen at one time, circling, waiting to land. To the east, the skyscraper-choked downtown hidden from sight, but the air above it black with smoke. No wonder he could smell it. So much fire! Below him – God! so close – the snaking curve of the Sea to Sky Highway, a cantilevered section that juts out over the ocean, tilted at a sick-making slant, four lanes plus median buried beneath a hill of earth and boulders and trees that this morning made up the roadside cliff. From the landslide protrude six, maybe seven vehicles. Coming from them, the faintest of far-off screams.

There are people in there. Inside the cars. Inside the earth.

God. Oh God.

Vomit rises in his throat. He swallows, lowers his head onto his arms, starts to rock.

It's happened. It wasn't supposed to, not in his lifetime. At least that's what he always believed. But it's here, now.

Today.

NINE

∿

The Big One, they call it. The major subduction earthquake dreaded up and down North America's west coast, across the Pacific, all around the Ring of Fire. The twice-a-millennium ripping of the Cascadia fault, the offshore zipper that hugs a thousand kilometres of coastline, from Vancouver Island down to northern California, that has for centuries been locked tight, waiting to give. The magnitude 9 apocalypse that will reduce coastal towns to matchsticks, ravage every major city in the Pacific Northwest, smash the entire coastal system of rail lines and highways, shake skyscrapers till they drop glass and balconies, acorns of debris. And the vast wall of water that within half an hour will eradicate every outer shoreline in the zone.

It will be Sumatra in 2004, Japan in 2011. Only worse. An orgy of annihilation the likes of which modern North America has never seen.

∿

THE HOUSE IS FILLED with images. She noticed the minute she left the bright, salt-air, rumbling world outside. Colour-splashed abstract paintings, askew on the wall or slipped to the floor. Dark prints behind spiderwebbed glass. Carvings and figures pitched over on tables and shelves, framed photos dashed onto corridor floors. Everywhere she looks are decorations, broken.

Anna visited an art gallery once. She was sixteen, on a school trip to Kiev, her first time outside the Donbass region. The Podol Fortuna was renowned for its socialist realism, as their teacher called it, creations that depict life in an ideal socialist state. *Art by the people, for the people*, he said. *Don't touch.* Afterwards Anna returned to her family's cramped apartment, its one nod to ornamentation the faded rose wallpaper that smelled of boiled cabbage, with her appreciation for art still at zero but with an eye-catching yellow-and-green tee-shirt that she loved beyond reason. Each time she pulled it on, the gallery name and logo spirited her off, for an afternoon or a day, from her shift-work family and industrial neighbourhood. That tee-shirt made her happy. It made her brother, Bohdan, bend double with laughter.

Here in Stedman's office Miss Dodie is an appreciative gallery visitor, picking up every photo, object, and book within reach, examining the walls and the furniture. The hired man, whom Anna initially took to be the homeowner, is concerned with practicalities and has left to track down the source of the smoke. The true owner lies passed out on the floor beside her, surrounded by fallen books and papers once held by the large wooden bookcase that lies facedown on the floor, his wound closed and bandaged as best she can manage with limited supplies. That leaves the girl, who after gathering first-aid items is without tasks and has retreated to the oversized desk chair where she sits, face bloodless and blank, thumbing her cell phone. Scrolling, scrolling, never stopping to register anything.

Anna understands shock. She needs to reach the girl, keep her here.

"You, girl. What is your name?"

"Sidney." Her eyes stay on the screen.

"Oh, like Australia."

"No! It's the name of a person. Just like *Anna*."

So she is angry. Anger Anna can deal with. It is born of fear, and fear means the girl understands what is happening. Also she remembers Anna's name, a good sign.

"I am tired of this restaurant," calls Miss Dodie. "When are we going home?"

Anna gets to her feet and joins Miss Dodie at the floor-to-ceiling windows, all of them miraculously intact. It's her first glimpse, since it happened, at the world beyond this house. Little of the city is visible through the windows, which instead overlook the property's sloping side yard, the waters of Burrard Inlet just beyond, and the Lions Gate Bridge and Stanley Park in the background. From this vantage, all appears normal. She takes heart. Maybe the tremors, for all that they knocked Miss Dodie off her feet and upended the contents of this house, haven't affected the rest of Vancouver.

The inlet is quiet. A couple of sailboats are heading in toward the harbour and one supertanker is plowing full steam out to sea. Is it *too* quiet? Where are the usual clusters of container ships, barges, and pleasure boats? The kayaks and catamarans near shore? A single stand-up paddle boarder, stroking fast for the beach, is the only other movement in sight.

The Lions Gate Bridge, too, looks quiet. Except — wait.

Anna looks longer, taking in the details. No. Something is off.

A breeze blows and she sees it, the vertical cables that dangle over the water, half-detached, like skipping ropes held at one end. Apart from the swaying cables, nothing is moving — not a single car is crossing this major artery between Vancouver and the North Shore. Yet the bridge, she realizes with a stab of unease, is by no means empty. The north end of the span, where traffic is delivered into North and West Vancouver, is hidden from sight. But at the south end, where the suspension bridge rises from the trees of Stanley Park, vehicles jam the bridge deck, motionless. She didn't see them at first; the side railings obscure the view. Is it an accident? A multi-car pile-up? Or has traffic stopped because of damage ahead? She cannot tell.

The world is still, eerily so. Except —

She hears the throaty thrum, then in moments sees them: two, three, now four helicopters, arriving one after the other from the west. And from behind the Lions Gate Bridge, where the inlet squeezes into Vancouver Harbour and the downtown core sits out of view, plumes of smoke billow higher and higher. No wonder the whole house smells of it.

The stand-up paddler has reached the stretch of foreshore that's visible through the window. He leaves his board, drops the paddle beside it, and dashes inland, a frantic blur.

It is not good. What is happening on the other side of the window signals trouble. Yet what looms in Anna's mind, more immediate than this framed view and far more compelling, is the wine.

So many smashed bottles, but one or two must have survived. When can she go back to the kitchen, alone?

She turns to the girl. "Your father, he is okay, I think. No more blood. His head is hit hard, but he wake up soon maybe."

Sidney has put her phone away and hugs her knees, which Anna realizes are bare. The girl is wearing shorts.

"You go, have more clothes. Pants, jeans, blouse. Maybe jumper."

"Jumper?"

"*Chort*," Anna says under her breath. English. You learn it in Europe only to find out they change the words here. "Sweater. Go find sweater. You must be warm. Is important, okay?"

With a great sigh, as if she has been asked to scrub hearths or cart boulders, the girl heaves out of the chair and stalks off.

Miss Dodie, who has tottered over to the desk, holds a framed photograph with a smashed glass front. "Be careful please, my lady. Put it down. Is danger." Anna berates herself for her inattention to the woman. She has one job. She cannot be distracted by the world outside or even, as much as it draws her, the wine. A single careless moment is all it would take to capsize Miss Dodie's precarious life, and with it, her own.

"Danger. I'll say." Miss Dodie holds out the photo of two men shaking hands. "This one, this one here —" she stabs a finger at the cracked glass "— he used to run this whole place. In charge of everything. You know, in the capital city. Oh, he was a fuckster. He put the muzzle on all the scientists, that's what Kelvin told me. The ladies in the book club said so too. That was back when I went to the seniors centre."

Saint Kelvin. He has left Miss Dodie's employment but he is never far, the companion Anna will never be, knowledgeable and good at everything. Broken glass would never come near Miss Dodie under his care.

"This one —" Miss Dodie is still on about the starched politician. "I was glad my Marty wasn't around for this one. He'd have been so angry! He was a scientist, you know."

Anna knows. She has heard many times about the pioneering research done by the late Mr. Dodie. Fish, that's all she can extract from Miss Dodie's rambling accounts. He did something with fish. Anna knows all she needs to about fish. Give her one and she can scale it, gut it, bone it, shake it in flour, fry it in a pan, and eat the whole thing, crispy tail and all. If you are Ukrainian, and you find yourself in the Donbass region when the Russians invade and stir up all the crazy separatists, and the dirty *soldaty* from all sides start blasting your city, and the food shipments stop and the stores and restaurants close and you're grateful for any fresh morsel smuggled in from the countryside, that is all you need to know about fish. That and maybe how to move like one, quick and agile and darting, when you escape your homeland and its sour, downtrodden citizens, who have let themselves be passed around like a football, again and again, throughout history.

Not Anna. Never again will she be anyone's football. She is made of stronger stuff and now her home is Canada, where strong stuff is valued. In time, when it is safe, she will throw off her invisible life and do something that matters. She has it in her, she knows she does. She will not be in *People* magazine; it is not fame that she seeks. It is accomplishment. In some way, she will make her mark and be rewarded and the yearning and the fear will stop. At last her life will make sense, and she will be quiet inside. She will live in easy times.

"Please, put it down," she says again. In the minute she has been daydreaming, Miss Dodie has wobbled back over to the windows, where she stands, gazing out and clutching the broken photo. As Anna approaches to confiscate the hazard, a pungent smell overtakes the pervasive smoke.

She sighs. There is never a good time. "Come." She reaches for the woman's shoulder. "We go to the bathroom." Maybe while Miss Dodie is on the toilet she can nip into the kitchen and see what the wine cabinet holds. Maybe there is more than just wine. Her ears tingle as she imagines the burn of vodka — vodka! — slipping down her throat. A warmer, truer friend she has never had.

But Miss Dodie grips the windowsill and will not be budged. Anna prepares to do battle. Through her employer's failing body runs a girder of steel will.

"Come." Anna grasps her elbow. "Just a little walk. We make you clean now, okay? Clean your bum."

The photo crashes against the wall, glass tinkles to the floor.

"Annie! Don't say *bum!*" Miss Dodie's eyes snap. "How many times must I tell you? It is *rude.*"

"Okay, yes. Rude. I am sorry." Anna grasps Miss Dodie's arm to steer her down the hall but the woman shakes her off, stamps one low-heeled pump on the hardwood floor.

"I am not a child! I can do it myself!"

"What is going on here?" A deep, clear voice rises from behind the massive desk. "Why am I on the floor?"

Slava bogu, thinks Anna, the man is awake. At last, another reasonable adult on the premises, someone who will make sense of what is going on. An ally.

"Hello," she calls. "I am Anna. With me is Miss Dodie."

"There is no money on the property," the voice booms. "I repeat, no money. Whoever you are, I'm going to count to ten, slowly. While I do, you will get the hell out of my house or I call the cops."

∧

Hope is a shithole. Charlotte cruised the centre of town for almost half an hour, long enough to learn that A, there are no payphones anymore, not even in this backwater; B, the tiny library is closed on Tuesdays; C, there is no internet café and no Starbucks; and D, the people are rude, nasty lowlifes.

It'd be nice to cut the place some slack, really it would, but the trio of young mothers she faced off with was the last straw. Sprawled on a bench beside the town square, they were chatting and smoking up a storm, keeping half an eye on their youngsters in the sandpit, when Charlotte pulled up and asked through the lowered window of her idling SUV where a person could get a decent latte.

"Whaddya mean decent?" rasped the fat platinum blonde. Pack a day minimum was Charlotte's bet.

"I don't know. Someplace with good espresso. Maybe independently owned?"

The blonde pursed her lips, her pencil-thin eyebrows sharp vees, and drew deeply on her cigarette.

What? Too many syllables? Charlotte brought it down a notch. "As long as it's not Tim Hortons, I'm easy."

Three sets of eyes hardened. The blonde elbowed the skinny one beside her, who flicked her butt to the ground and withdrew into the hood of her black sweatshirt. "Hey, why you driving around looking for lattes?" Platinum asked. "Like, don't ya know there was an earthquake?"

For the life of her Charlotte couldn't connect the two comments, so she chose to ignore them. "If you could just tell me where the nearest café is."

Again Platinum jabbed her friend's bony side. "Back the way you came, lady, right beside the gas station off the highway. Unless you want McDonald's, you'll hafta drink Tims like the rest of us." Her eyes widened innocently, but her mouth twisted into a smirk. Just like Sidney's in that fucking Facebook selfie. The third girl, a mousy thing with glasses and a stringy ponytail, collapsed into giggles.

Now Charlotte is at the last available table in the harshly lit Tim Hortons, metal chairback ramrodding her shoulder blades, an unspeakably bad latte before her, cooling in a mud-brown paper cup. Beside it a chocolate-smeared napkin, evidence of the Boston cream doughnut she ordered in a fit of — what? Pique? Fury? Frustration at this hick town with its substandard amenities and insolent teen mothers? Surprisingly the doughnut wasn't bad, not bad at all, but now her waistband feels even tighter and remorse has set in. A doughnut? She knows better than to eat junk like that, especially when she's stressed.

Around her the restaurant's abuzz about the earthquake. She heard the basics from the acne-scarred youth at the counter who, after telling her they had no payphone, took her order. "It's a big one," he said. "Lower Mainland's a mess. There's not a lot of details because the city's literally cut off, no phone calls or texts getting through. Everyone on Twitter is saying it's a disaster. Highway's closed somewhere around Chilliwack and it's gonna stay that way for a long time."

"*Closed?* What do you mean, closed?"

"The Trans-Canada's heaved up in places, they say. Like, literally no one can drive on it. The other routes are all blocked off. That's why it's so busy in here. No one can get home."

Heaved up? Charlotte spent the first part of the morning on that stretch of highway, the long shoot through the Fraser Valley. She thinks back to the Port Mann Bridge. Was traffic still jammed up there when the earthquake struck? The new Port Mann is designed to sway in a quake; there was a lot of publicity about that when the bridge was built. Supposedly swaying is a good thing, though if you're on the bridge sandwiched between vehicles at the time – that doesn't sound ideal to her.

Snatches of conversation drift by, the occasional sentence drowning out the others. "Felt it as far east as Calgary," says a hearty female voice near the front. "I'm sure as shit glad I left when I did," booms a barrel-chested guy in a safety vest. An old man, quavering, says something about the Pattullo Bridge being gone.

Gone?

Panic is knocking on Charlotte's door, but she refuses to let it in. Numb is all she feels. Numb from the earthquake, from anger at her family, from the myriad of obligations and unknowns. The morning's events have turned her gradually and uncharacteristically apathetic.

She has let go of the need to connect to the videoconference or phone head office to beg off. From all she's heard, the earthquake was big enough that everyone will know why she missed the meeting. Tonight's dinner party is almost certainly off, not that she could make it home in time anyway, with every westbound route either damaged or closed.

The list-making part of her knows that priority number one should be to head to the nearest hotel. With Vancouver off-limits, hordes of stranded motorists will be looking for rooms. Priority two: a phone so she can call Tim in Toronto and try the land line at work. Will her team still be there? Will they have left for home? Number three: internet. Surely to God wherever she stays will have a business centre, though Hope has thus far, ironically, delivered nothing but disappointment. If need be she can use the hotel staff's computer long enough to check email and post a Facebook update. Four: gather information. Once she finds herself a room, she should park herself in front of the TV news and absorb.

She knows all this, has itemized the tasks as if drafting a publicity checklist, yet here she sits in this noisy, offensive place, toying with her napkin, in no rush to leave, thinking semi-seriously about ordering another doughnut. In a weird way, not that she could explain it to anyone, there's a kind of freedom in being stuck. She can't go home or to the office. She can't call or text anyone. She can't check email. Whatever happened in Vancouver, however it has affected her family and staff, she can't change it, nor can she influence the outcomes. It's as if she is outside time: around her the world is moving, but she inhabits a stationary universe where her role is curiously undefined.

The fantasy steals over her, the one that leapt out of that mystery novel in the Chicago airport, the one where she up and walks away, leaving behind every burden, errand, and emotional cesspool, of which today there are so many. The idea pulls her like a magnet. But it's ludicrous. What is she, lazy? Some useless fuck-up who disappears when life gets tough? That's not her. Besides, she's got so much skin in the game. All of her inheritance is tied up in GlobalTech, everything but her personal trust fund. Like it or not, she's locked in.

At the next table two grey-haired women share a box of Timbits — a whole box! — and swap accounts of when they first felt the vibrations. "I was just starting on the pots," one says. "From yesterday, eh? My shows were on so I left them overnight. So I'm at the sink, I'm up to the elbows in dishwater, when they start rattling on the counter. Like a frickin' machine gun. Scared the life outta me." "It was the wineglasses I heard," says the other. "You know how I got them all pushed together in the china cabinet? Because we're still saving up for a bigger one? Oh my God was I glad when that stopped. I thought they'd break for sure. Here, you have the jam-filled one."

What would it be like? Spending your day in your own home, washing dishes, doing the pots when the spirit moved you, no housekeeper to create daily schedules for. Meeting a friend in the afternoon over a box of Timbits to shoot the breeze, not to discuss work or plan an event. No ticking off tasks, one after the other after the other. No counting every minute, every email, every calorie, every client. Just *being*. The irresponsibility of it is distasteful yet at the same time compelling, like a smelly sock you have to sniff.

"Mind if I sit here?"

It takes a moment to realize that the question, in an Australian-accented baritone, is directed at her. She looks up.

"There's nowhere to sit. Place's hopping. You mind?"

A beat passes, then another, while she takes him in.

Holy shit.

Her mouth dries up as she realizes he's waiting for an answer. "Sure" is all she can manage. She pulls the nearly full latte toward her to make room on the table, folds her napkin into tiny squares to hide the chocolate smudge.

The Australian slides into the chair, graceful as a cat, swings long blue-jeaned legs under the table, sets down a bottle of iced tea. He smiles and something gives way inside her. The youngest Bee Gee, the one who wasn't part of the group — that's who he looks like.

"Everyone's coming off the highway because of the quake." He unscrews the cap of his iced tea and drinks, head back, muscles in his tanned neck taut above the white vee of his tee-shirt.

Charlotte also tries to swallow but her throat catches; tries to answer but cannot form a word. She uses the folded square of napkin to brush a few crumbs off the table and sucks in her abdomen so her waistband loosens. Across from her the god from Down Under tosses his shaggy blond hair and sprawls sideways, one arm thrown behind the chairback, settled in and grinning like he's known her forever.

She drops her gaze to her brown paper cup.

"How's your coffee?"

"Bad. It's a latte. In theory."

His laugh falls lightly. "How about I get you something else? Hard to go wrong with Lipton." He tips the bottle of iced tea toward her. "It's classic."

Andy Gibb, that was his name. The impossibly gorgeous singer was plastered all over the walls of older girls' bedrooms when Charlotte was a kid. He died, didn't he?

She looks up, meets his pale-blue expectant gaze. "Thanks anyway. I'm fine."

He leans farther back and she tries not to stare. There aren't many guys above forty, about where she'd put him age-wise, a few years younger than she is, who can get away with a skin-tight white tee-shirt. The Australian is one them. The way he stretches, easy and at one with the material, it's as if he's wearing nothing. Charlotte folds her napkin smaller and tries to block the animal waves emanating from this man who has materialized in Hope, of all places, the armpit of southwestern BC.

"Bryan," he says, extending his right hand. "With a *y*."

"Charlotte." She hesitates, then reaches over. Their fingers touch, their palms slide together, and she is done for.

"Pretty name." He holds on a fraction longer than courtesy requires. His hand is warm, his fingers rough. "You from here, Charlotte? Or just passing through?"

She withdraws her hand and resists the urge to shake it loose to disperse the lightning jolt. "Passing through. Definitely."

"Oh? Why definitely?"

She hears the teasing and decides not to sugarcoat it. "I'm more of a city girl. This" – she waves her hand weakly – "it's not really my scene."

More silver laughter. "From Vancouver then, Miss Charlotte." He doesn't wait for confirmation. "That was my guess. Nice clothes, expensive car."

Suddenly she's wary. "What do you know about my car?"

"I pulled in behind you. Saw you get out." He looks out the window at the choked parking lot. "Stayed in the truck a bit to check my phone, but when I came in here I saw you straight away." He leans forward and she catches an earthy scent. "No worries, Miss Charlotte. I'm not hassling you. There really is no place else to sit."

She lifts her shoulders, then drops them. A trickle of disappointment. It would be okay to be hassled by this man, just a little.

"How about you?" she asks. "Passing through too?"

"Yeah. Took off from Whistler early this morning."

"A lot of Australians in Whistler."

"God, yeah. Half the bloody country's there. I worked at the resort over the winter, ski patrol. Lessons too, mostly the little kids. Now I'm off to Banff. Summer in the Rockies — I always wanted to try that."

"Is it your first year in Canada?"

"God, yeah. Definitely."

"Oh?" She crinkles her eyes. "Why definitely?"

"Right, good one. I just mean Canada's not home. At least not yet." He takes another swig and backhands his lips dry. His hand is work-lined, strong. "I miss the summer. Nothing can touch summer back home. The beaches go on forever, the water's like taking a bath. Not like here. They keep saying it's the Pacific, but no way's it the same ocean." It sounds like *why* when he says *way*. His eyes dance. "You ever been to Australia, Charlotte?" Her name is candy on his tongue.

She shakes her head. "I haven't had time. I'd like to, though. It's on the list."

"What is it making you so busy, then?"

"The usual. You know, work. More work."

"Career woman. Makes sense, the Porsche and all. Let me guess. You're a lawyer."

He radiates confidence. Why not?

"Bingo." Instantly she wants to take it back, but then decides what the hell. It's not like he can check up on her.

"You married, then? Got a family? Or at least a husband, looks like." He peers at her left hand.

"No." She holds out her ring finger. "I just got divorced. I haven't gotten around to taking this off. Guess I should." She eases off the platinum band and drops it into her Birkin bag. "No kids."

A great force is gathering in her. She can tell this man anything she wants to, be anyone she wants to be. Single, childless, unencumbered.

Who'll know the difference? The possibilities make her giddy.

"So you're a free woman?" His teeth when he grins are pure white, the front one slightly chipped. How would it feel to run your tongue over that snag? Would it be rough or smooth? Would it catch on your lip if he kissed you? Her cheeks flame.

"Yeah, I know." He has misinterpreted her flush. "None of my bloody business." He leans back again, runs a hand through his chin-length hair. "That's an Aussie for you, coming on too strong. I get no end of shit for it. But it's hard when there's so many amazing ladies around. It's hard ... you know, to hold yourself back."

Holding back. She's had a lifetime of it. Delaying a little more and a little more, until she finishes this project or picks up Tayne's wine or Sidney's new phone. Denying herself food, sleep, concerts, movies, anything frivolous. Delaying all gratification.

She is in Hope, BC, in a shitty Tim Hortons, the last place in the universe she would choose to be. She is out of contact, out of range. Outside her real life, outside time. What if this once she didn't hold back? Who would know? She's been working so hard for so long. She's done everything she's supposed to, and then some. She has parted with her money, her advice, her attention, her time. When did she last do something not because it was expected of her, or because it was good for her, or to bail out Sidney or prop up Tayne, but because, simply put, she wanted it?

She glances at her naked ring finger and the words come out. "I am a free woman. I don't mind you asking."

"Well then." He toys with his iced tea bottle. "That's good."

"I was on my way home to Vancouver when I heard about the earthquake. I was in Kelowna the past few days, on business. A convention — a lawyers' convention. Looks like I'm not getting home anytime soon." The story arrives so easily it takes her breath away.

"What're you gonna do?"

"Stay here, I guess. Find a hotel room if there are any left." She swallows, out of her depth yet not frightened. "Or what passes for a hotel room around here."

"Come on, city girl, it's not such a bad place. It's just a small town."

She shrugs. "What about you? You have to be in Banff right away?"

"Nah, not really. I get there when I get there. Figure I'll take my time, see the sights."

"And you …?" She hesitates. *Don't hold back.* "Are you a free man?" She tries out his name. "Bryan?"

Her pulse skips from adrenaline. What if she's misread him? She has forgotten how to do this. With Marcus there were no moments of doubt, just one flaming kiss and they were off.

Bryan leans in close. Mere inches away, eyes blue like the Australian Pacific. Skin browned and traced with faint lines, like an endless summer beach. Says: "I am free in every way."

$$\wedge$$

Where the hell is the gardener? He was late showing up this morning and now he's missing.

Fighting down his panic, Stedman has sent Sidney to check the yard, porches, patio, and garage while he covers the main floor and upstairs. His daughter protested, cradling one raggedly wrapped hand as if he'd demanded that she walk around on it. *But it hurts!* she said.

This is not the time to start whining, he wanted to say. Not the time to act like your arm's broken and you're some poor orphan who got a raw deal in life. But he said nothing. He doesn't understand this need of Sidney's to enlist sympathy at all times. She lives in a stable household, has everything a girl could want and then some. It's not like her scrape or bruise or whatever it is — the specifics are hazy — is the source of real pain. Not like, say, your father's steel-toed work boot landing square on your nine-year-old ass, or his rough-knuckled fist smashing your nose, shooting constellations through your tender brain. Months of therapy at the priciest hideaway on the west coast and the girl still feels every touch, every slight. She started soft and has gone softer.

The minute he forms the thought, he is sorry. He leans against the fir stair rail, handmade by the master woodworker from the Squamish Nation down the shore, and rubs the unhurt side of his head. He's not being fair. He has to be more patient. Sidney is still so young, and she's had a rough time of it, the drugs and the rehab and all. Hell, he should have raised her better. He's been too hands-off. He left the child rearing to Charlotte, the privileged perfectionist who resisted motherhood in the first place, and Charlotte has done what Charlotte always does: picked and picked and picked at the girl, fussing over her and correcting her as if she's a spreadsheet instead of a human. No wonder the girl turned wild. All she needed was a little freedom.

It's going to hurt no matter what, he told Sidney minutes ago. *Just find the gardener and do it fast. We don't have much time. And no pills. Stay the hell out of the pills.*

Tough love, that's what she needs. Tough love and a little independence. He will work on that going forward.

Right now there are more urgent concerns. They need to find the gardener, pronto, and get the hell out of here, get to higher ground before the big wave hits. If it were up to him the ocean would already be at his back; he'd be jogging uphill with Sidney in tow, the two castaway women trailing at whatever pace they could manage. But Sidney won't go without the gardener. *We have to find him!* she wailed when Stedman told her they were leaving. *I'm not going anywhere until we do.* Stedman knows that within the paradoxical mix of inertia and melodrama that fuels his daughter lies a core of resolve that is pointless to resist. So here he is, scouring his home for an intruder, jeopardizing his safety and that of his only offspring for some random labourer. The world has indeed turned upside down.

Upside down.

This is really happening. It's not a dream. He has to keep reminding himself.

At first he wasn't sure. When he finally came to, it was to memories of Sidney hovering over him, the unaccustomed view from his office floor, the overlapping voices of strangers he thought were burglars, the searing pain in his face. Now, though his head is still thumping, his mind is clearer. He knows the real disaster will be on them soon — not the quake itself or the aftershocks but the giant wall of water that will this minute be rolling toward them, ready to sweep ashore and engulf his house and grounds, every building and property and person at sea level. The most desirable, most expensive oceanfront in the country is also, at this moment, the most deadly.

Tsunami. The word's smooth vowels horrify him. It was his topmost worry when he bought the house in 2005, the news media still running apocalyptic images of Sumatra, its seacoast devoured by a monstrous wave several months before. He had quizzed the real estate agent and instructed his assistant to repeatedly email North Shore emergency management about the risks of living on the West Van shore. The response was bemused reassurance. *Sure, we're on a subduction zone*, the real estate agent said; *so is every inch of coastline from northern California to Haida Gwaii. If you live in earthquake country you know there's gonna be shakeups, including, yeah, the Big One someday. But we're talking in the next century or two.* The agent smiled as he said this, indulging the fantasies of scientists and emergency planners while he, man of commerce, remained in the real world.

But a tsunami? Stedman's information told him that even if the Big One hit, even if it raised a column of ocean that gathered and swept landward, it was the west coast of Vancouver Island that would bear the brunt. Metro Vancouver, buffered by the protective width of the Island and the Strait of Georgia, might see above-average surf but nothing that would threaten life or property. The real danger, said the emergency managers, and this Stedman confirmed through his assistant's internet research, is a local quake — not out in the subduction zone, offshore beyond Vancouver Island, but somewhere close by, say under the strait. A quake like that could trigger a real water wall, maybe ten feet, maybe more, depending how shallow the rupture is. Possible? They shrugged. Sure. Likely? Not very.

Stedman's house, like most in this little enclave along the seawalk, is built on a seam of rock that runs just far enough below ground to allow for a crawl space under the western wing. The bottom of that crawl space is seven feet four inches above the high-tide mark. He knows the precise height, having insisted that it be measured before he signed a purchase agreement. He'd run the scenarios and got one of his guys to crunch the numbers, same as he'd do with any business deal.

Seven feet four inches. He could live with that, he decided back then. No matter how you slice it, the rewards of an oceanfront address outweigh the risks, especially when the address is this timberframe jewel, built in 2001, a mere four years before he bought it, and constructed to meet all seismic standards. With its soaring ceilings and jutting porches (*outdoor living spaces*, the agent called them), its hewn beams held together with solid wood pegs the traditional way, the house was a far cry from the plain two-storey knockdown that, judging by the photos, had blighted the lot before. A few of those sixties and seventies shoeboxes are still kicking around, ancient artifacts in this part of town, where task number one after buying a house is to book a bulldozer.

As he heads upstairs to scour the bedrooms for the damned gardener, who has disappeared off the face of the earth — unreliable, clearly; he won't be hired again — Stedman mentally surveys his local pocket of waterfront, one of the last along this eastern stretch of West Vancouver to feature single-family homes, the shoreline largely given over to highrises. Which neighbouring houses have withstood the shaking and which have collapsed? He tries to line up the few dwellings around his, a couple of weather-beaten oldsters and a few splashy new mansions, but it's no good. He can't picture anything beyond the house to either side of his. Who the hell are the neighbours? He never sees anyone, apart from a suited man three driveways down who occasionally sets out garbage bins. There's the Chinese guy one house over to the west; Stedman met him once. But he doesn't actually live there, does he? Charlotte is always railing about how most houses on their tiny block sit unoccupied, the offshore owners present on the deed but seldom in the flesh. Absentee homeowners are a hot-button issue now, guaranteed to rile up all the bleeding hearts who need a cause. What's the big deal? Their house is always quiet and he doesn't have to contend with the neighbours, both big pluses in his book. The simple fact is that his stormy wife will never be happy. He could set her up at the most exclusive Point Grey address, hire an entourage of staff, throw in a genie to grant her every wish and a chef who never put fat in anything, and still she'd have a file full of faults and demands.

The window for a tsunami depends, Stedman knows, on the cause. With a big subduction quake it could take a couple of hours for any water to hit Vancouver; a more local rupture and the timeline shrinks to half an hour or less. Who the hell knows what kind of event they've had, but he's not taking any chances. It's been what — twenty minutes since the tremors stopped? Thirty? More? He glances at his watch. The hands are frozen at 11:45. Damn it all! So much for the bulletproof Rolex. He has no idea how long he was out, no reliable sense of how long ago the quake was. They've got to get out of here this minute.

That is when, with a stroke of his renowned perfect timing, Stedman locates the gardener — in the last place the man ought to be, the master bathroom. What the hell? With five bathrooms to choose from, why this one? Why go upstairs, cross Stedman's bedroom in outdoor boots, leaving smears of soil and grass on the white area rug, and use the farthest-away, most private facilities in the house?

"Hey!" Stedman calls as he crosses the bedroom. His face howls with every step. "You! What the hell are you doing in there?"

No answer. Just the sound of running water. Lots of water.

In the bathroom he finds Joe filling the double sinks. Over in the corner, the faucet of the jetted tub spills a loud, continuous gout.

"Dammit, what is with you? This is no time to wash! We've got to get out of here. Now!"

Joe responds with what can only be described as the stink-eye. "Uh, you're joking, right?" He shuts off the sink faucets and turns around to check the tub. It's half full.

Stedman touches his bandaged cheek. The right side of his face is on fire; the three Aspirin the nurse gave him have not kicked in. "Listen to me. There could be a tsunami headed here right this second. We've got to get out of here. There's no time to clean up or whatever —"

"You think I'm an idiot? We need water, as much as we can get. It could get cut off anytime."

Water? Who the hell cares about water? And what's with this *we*? Does this jackass think he's part of the household now? Stedman pulls back his shoulders, clears his throat, and summons his CEO voice. "Look, we are heading for high ground, right now. And you are coming with us. It's almost half an hour since the quake. It may already be too late." Again the panic lifts off in him. Time to take charge. Time to go!

He moves to grab the gardener's arm, but Joe steps neatly aside, crosses to the tub, turns off the faucet. Faces Stedman and folds his arms over his small keg of a chest. "Relax, okay? There's no tsunami. There's no warning out and no evacuation order. Your neighbour's monitoring the CB channels and they say the danger period's passed. Everyone on the West Van waterfront is advised to stay put until further notice."

"Neighbour?"

"On the other side of your boxwood hedge. Vincent."

The Chinese guy? His name is Vincent? "I thought he didn't live there."

Joe eyes him quizzically.

"There's a lot of houses like that around here. Investments. The only people you see are property managers. Plus the hired men, like yourself."

The gardener's face darkens. "Well, he's there now. I talked to him fifteen minutes ago, after I walked your property."

No tsunami. Stedman lets the idea sink in. "You're sure? About the tsunami?"

"Positive. Direct from emergency management, Vincent says."

No tsunami. No need to run.

The coils of Stedman's body loosen marginally and he takes a deep breath. He's got things under control. They're going to be okay.

The gardener is still frowning. "Your other tubs and sinks are full, except for the sink in the powder room off the kitchen. That one should stay free for drainage. I looked inside the crawl space and did a full walk-around outside. No rotten egg smell, so your gas line's not leaking, but you'll want to shut it off just the same. There's fires everywhere.

Not on your street so far, but a few blocks away. Smoke's strong when you step outside."

"I'll think about that." Stedman considers. "There must be a main shutoff somewhere."

A small noise escapes Joe. "It's out back, by the kitchen door. And look, the driveway out there is heaved up pretty —" He stops. "Forget it. I'll take care of the gas. There's still power, technically, but I turned off your main breaker. Everyone has to. Orders from emergency management. There's too many lines down and the crews don't want the power on until they've got the fires under control."

"There are crews out there?"

"Barely." Joe removes his cap and wipes his brow. "A fire truck over at 15th and Marine, at least that's what Vincent heard on the radio. Just the one truck, even though the whole block's on fire and there's an old highrise on the shore ready to fall over. The fire department's dispatching, apparently. Their comms are working, but they're having trouble figuring out which trucks should go where. There's too many streets blocked by debris and they can't get through. Whole buildings are gone, they're saying, just a bunch of piles on the road. Vincent's gonna walk up to Marine Drive to see if he can help out, run garden hoses or fill buckets or something. We should do that too."

It figures this guy wants to play fireman. Stedman has no time for macho bullshit from some know-it-all hired man. Priorities, stick with the priorities. "I'm not going anywhere. My daughter's here and I need to stay with her. And we need to track down her mother. My daughter's been trying to reach her, but the calls won't go through. She's not sure about texts either. Then there's work. I have to get hold of my people, make sure everything's okay there."

"Suit yourself. But they need all hands on deck against the fires. You're lucky here so far, but it might not stay that way. Say a house nearby has a busted gas line. A fire gets close enough to it, it's gonna blow. Where's that leave your place?"

"I'll deal with that if and when it happens. Right now my responsibility is to this house and the people in it."

Joe pulls his hat back on. "You're not responsible for me, buddy. I'm outta here. I'll do my bit to help with the fires" — he pauses for a second, presumably to let Stedman marvel at his heroism — "then head home. My truck, though, it's gotta stay here for now. Vincent says the roads are closed to traffic. Only emergency vehicles allowed."

"You say he has a radio?"

"A CB. He's been picking up chatter ever since the earthquake."

A CB? Stedman has no interest in this Vincent or his legacy technology. There must be a radio here that'll run on batteries, or maybe one of those wind-up models. Where do they keep things like that, emergency supplies such as they are? The pantry? The mudroom? A walk-in closet? Honestly, he has no idea. Except for his office and the garage — and the wine unit, which, he recalls with a fresh pang, lost most of its contents to the kitchen floor — he has no clue where Charlotte stores anything.

Charlotte. Why isn't she here? Or, since it's a weekday, at her office? Why is she gallivanting around the Fraser Valley — shopping, of all things? It's some kind of food she's after, isn't it? Certain details before the quake are fuzzy. Then he remembers: cheese! Leave it to Charlotte to obsess over a detail like cheese. Sidney checked Facebook a while ago, but her mother hasn't posted anything. "She was in full-on hurricane mode when I called her earlier," Sidney told him. What else is new?

No point asking Sidney where there's a radio. She'll have no idea. A radio is like a telegraph in her world, a pointless relic from an ancient past. No, only Charlotte would know whether there's a workable unit in the place. Or May.

May! Damn it all, he forgot about their daily helper. Didn't she go out somewhere? For groceries or to some appointment? She took the Smart car; he remembers confirming that for Charlotte earlier. He shudders to think how that tuna can of a vehicle might hold up under a fallen tree or utility pole. He opposed the ridiculous purchase from the get-go, but Charlotte was adamant, said they owed it to society to balance their gas-guzzlers with something environmentally friendly. Society! Who the hell outside their own household notices let alone cares what the Stedmans drive? Who cares whether they go to the dry cleaner, which Charlotte put a stop to a couple of years ago, mainly he suspects to placate Sidney, who was dragging home from school every day in a funk about chemicals? Charlotte gets like that once in a while, dredges up one or two of those big liberal ideas bred into her when she was a kid, when that man-hating mother of hers marched at the head of every protest. Well, here's where socialist thinking has landed them: their maid likely the filling in a Smart car sandwich.

It's beginning to dawn on Stedman all that he must do: track down Charlotte, get through to his office, try to locate May. Possibly approach the neighbour for updates or an extra radio, though hopefully it won't come to that. He is not a man who enjoys neighbours. You get chummy with them and before you can properly recollect their name they're wandering into your yard and showing up at your dinner parties and asking if you have a job for their oldest son who's just earned some third-rate diploma in programming.

What else? Keep an eye on Sidney, obviously, make sure she doesn't get into the pills or the liquor cabinet. Deal with the old woman and her nurse, the strange human jetsam the earthquake has flung onto his property. Keep them calm until the situation settles, then figure out how to get them out of his house and his life.

"I'll shut off the gas on the way out," the gardener says, brushing past Stedman. Then he stops and turns. "Your daughter, I saw her in the living room —"

"The great room."

Joe snorts. "Whatever. The huge room. The big-shot room. She should've gotten that cut stitched up. Don't forget to check it, okay? Keep it clean, change the bandage."

Cut? Bandage? The only bandaged wound he can think of is his own.

The gardener looks at him a bit longer, then turns away. He mutters something as he leaves. It sounds like "You're welcome."

∿

VUE.COM: You say people were shaken, emotionally. Yet in your work you seem quite the opposite. You are frozen, unmoved. As if none of it touches you. Your name is Summer Rain and yet you are like ice.

SUMMER: [*Pause*] Is that a question?

VUE.COM: What I mean is, in all your performances you are rooted to the stage. You stay immobile while the chaos swirls all around you. Think of *Idols*. The booming percussion, the strings of glass that smash everywhere, the heavy objects, the idols themselves that topple over. There you are in the middle, still and silent. What are you saying with your silence?

SUMMER: It's not about the silence. I'm not saying anything with that. It's more about the contrast.

VUE.COM: Contrast between ...?

SUMMER: So whenever you have some huge event that rocks an entire region, not just an earthquake but say a storm or war or what have you, it's supposed to be about everyone, right? About society. The big picture. But in the end it's always about you, yourself. How the individual is affected. I don't think that's selfishness, exactly, or narcissism. It's that the only thing you carry around afterwards is yourself. The event is recorded on you and absorbed by you. You are the walking artifact of what happened. And the question is: what do you do with all that? Do you let it collapse you? Or do you stand strong?

PART THREE

Shockwaves

WHEN IT HAPPENS, you're not where you're supposed to be.

When are you, anyway? It's like your whole life is lived on the verge — of adulthood, of the group who used to be your friends, of expressing something true, of your mother's affection, of sobriety. All of them places you should be, places you *want* to be, but you never quite make it there. You're always off to one side, someplace like here — the wrong place — and doing something like this — the wrong thing.

You were shivering before so you went upstairs and put on warm clothes, the purple hoodie and jeans you wore all through the winter in that stupid place where you never felt like getting dressed at all. Is that why you're here, on the edge of danger, about to ruin everything? You put on the clothes and they took you back to that time, that mind-space? That need?

So much of what you do is bad. You used to be proud of that, being a bad girl, drinking and swallowing and snorting everything in sight, having sex with all the boys and even a couple of the girls, staying out late, stealing stuff. Now you mostly feel adrift. If you're not a bad girl anymore, what are you?

What you need is a meeting, or to contact your sponsor. You need to reach out, you know you do. But how are you supposed to find a meeting now? How are you supposed to track down your sponsor when you can't even find your family?

You tried calling your uncle. It's what you're all supposed to do in an emergency. It didn't work. You tried texting too but you're not sure it's going through because he hasn't answered. He's not on Instagram or Facebook. He's weird that way. You can only hope he sees your Facebook post and doesn't worry.

You phoned her too, even though you knew it wouldn't work, even though you're mad at her and she is disgusted by you. You've sent her five texts and checked her Facebook page a dozen times. Now your phone is dead.

Your good hand grips the latch. The other one hurts way more than you'd think. Luckily it won't take much to open the glass door because the lock is toast. You've done it a hundred times. All it takes is one good pull.

One pull, a single moment, and everything will change. Five months sober. Then, just like that, not.

Behind you, heels click on the hardwood. You turn. The old woman wanders in, kind of staring into space, like she doesn't see you. Probably she doesn't. She's crazy.

It's not going to stop you. You need it too much and you don't care anymore. You've tried breathing and counting, but none of it works. You need to dial everything down — all the sirens out there, the smoke, the helicopters, the military ships arriving one after the other, the screams you heard earlier from the seawalk, the screams you closed your ears to. The whole world is completely fucked, so what difference does it make? You need it so much your hand is shaking on the latch.

Your hand is shaking and then the cabinet is shaking and all the bottles in it and the whole room and the floor under your feet and you drop and curl up in a tight ball because it's happening again.

No earbuds. No Instagram. You're awake, unplugged, every sense working. You're a ball of nervous alertness, but it doesn't matter. You are no more ready than you were the first time.

TEN

⌵

The Big One, the megathrust subduction earthquake along the undersea Cascadia fault, will rip through the Pacific Northwest coastline and smash every big city to dust. Though Vancouver will be pummelled, its bodyguards to the west, Vancouver Island and the Strait of Georgia, will take the bulk of the Big One's fist and will shield the city from the tsunami. The Big One, when it reaches Vancouver, will flail like a spent heavyweight in its final round.

The earthquake that struck at 11:44 that mild May morning was not the Big One. Up and down the coast seismologists and geologists, emergency planners and insurers, mayors and business leaders and preachers and paramedics drew breath and wiped their foreheads and clapped each other's backs.

Spared, at least for now. Not the Big One. Not this time.

In Vancouver and the southern Gulf Islands, on the east coast of Vancouver Island and the northern tip of Washington, there was no back slapping. The event was not the Big One. It was far, far worse.

⌵

KYLE IS QUICK-STEPPING down the trail. His knees howl at the impact, his body is tense with fright. Although he has left the view behind at Eagle Bluffs, the images stay with him: the city in chaos and on fire. Surely not his home, though. People trapped, people injured. Dead? Of course some must be dead. No one he knows, though. Not Shirin, none of his staff. Certainly not Joe.

The thoughts of work and home, the image of Joe somewhere in the upheaval — *where?* — spur him on and dull his twinging knees as effectively as any pharmaceutical.

There's a strong correlation between positive thinking and positive outcomes; he has seen evidence of this throughout his medical career. To offset the terror that is fighting for a toehold he adds up all he can be grateful for. One, the text from Joe: *Shook up but ok. Hope ur2.* He's not sure where Joe is or why he hasn't replied to Kyle's texts. Maybe he's still mad. The whole *love you* thing was disturbing, not like Joe at all. Same with his *screw you* comment this morning. He obviously knows something's up. But he's not injured; that's what matters now. Two, Shirin has texted that she's safe and the office, though a mess, is fine. Three, he's heading downhill and he's going fast. A couple more hours and he'll be at the community centre where he left his bicycle. Four, his bicycle. Without it he'd have to walk home, an hours-long trudge along Marine Drive to North Van, then up and over through a maze of residential streets. On his bike, possibly the best way to travel if the roads are clogged with people trying to get somewhere, he'll be home in a fraction of the time. Five, if the roads aren't open at all, he has his kayak. He'll have to walk the extra seven kilometres from the community centre to Sandy Cove, where he stowed the craft up on the rocks, but after that he can zip along the water to North Van and cut his walking distance in half.

The kayak. On the *rocks.*

The realization arrests his list-making. What if the rocks at Sandy Cove have shifted and tumbled like the boulders where he waited out the quake? His kayak might be useless, squashed like a banana. For that matter what about his bicycle? It could have been clipped by a projectile or flattened by a power pole.

You control your situation. It doesn't control you.

At the moment, that is one hundred percent bullshit.

As his anxiety mounts, he isolates it and wills it aside. No point dwelling on all the variables now. If he has to walk the whole way, he'll walk. He's strong and full of energy, a second — third? — wind having kicked in once he came to his senses on Eagle Bluffs above, after an over-long attempt to process the disaster below.

Disaster. There's no other word for it. The city is coming apart. Sirens scream, the sky vibrates with aircraft, the highway is buried. West Vancouver is on fire, downtown too. Who knows what's happening in all the neighbourhoods he couldn't see?

Thank God Joe's not hurt. But where is he? Is he alone? Scared?

Like you care. You're going to dump the guy.

He makes himself concentrate. Five things to be grateful for. He needs more to shush the panic.

Six, his phone is still at seventy-four percent. No calls are going through — he tried Joe again before heading down, checked voicemail too and got nothing — and the wifi is somewhere between slow and nonexistent, but there's comfort in knowing he's partially connected. Maybe Joe, the North Shore's last owner of a flip phone, will get online somewhere and find Kyle's Facebook update, posted from Eagle Bluffs; it says he's fine and on his way home. Except that Joe avoids using the interweb, as he calls it, and professes not to understand Facebook, as if there's anything to understand. *Old school* is how Joe describes his aversion to the digital world. Stubborn and afraid of change is how Kyle would put it. It's another sign of how mismatched they've become.

At least he is making fantastic time. Already he's at the boulder slide where he took cover during the earthquake, and the descent has taken half as long as the climb up. At this rate he'll be off the mountain in an hour and a half, maybe less if his knees, now twanging nonstop, can stand the jog.

As he jumps from boulder to boulder he's thankful for, seven, his agility work in the gym. The balance board routine his personal trainer puts him through — standing two-legged, one-legged, stepping off, stepping on, a variety of squats and footings — has always felt like a wasted part of the workout, the mincing dance of a fag instead of the mighty slam of weights. The balance sequence has embarrassed him since January, when he signed on with the trainer as a New Year's resolution to push himself to the next —

Liar. You booked him because you knew that in three sessions, four max, he'd jump the fence.

Kyle keeps to one corner of the equipment room during his balance routine so the weightlifters, heaving through real workouts, can't see him. Now it turns out his personal trainer was right —

And you were wrong. He let you blow him on day two.

— and Kyle is more quick-footed than ever. As long as he always looks ahead a step or two, he can keep up a steady speed. He's practically running on the rocks, a rising tide of optimism bearing him along. Feeling good, feeling strong; the panic is at bay. Just a matter of time and sweat and he'll be home.

He is nearly at the end of the boulder slope, scanning the tight line of trees for the orange ribbon that marks the trail entrance, when it happens.

For a second he doubts. The vibrations in his feet feel real enough and the landscape appears to sway, yet he's certain it's a flashback. For one second the doctor in him is impressed by the power of the mind, how it can control the body so absolutely as to conjure up a moving horizon and thunderous rockfall.

A second later he understands. By then it's too late.

$$\wedge$$

Miss Dodie will be fine in the powder room, alone, for a few minutes. Anna tells her employer that she is going to find something to clean the woman's bottom with — she does not say *bum*; she does not want another tantrum.

It is not the truth. This bathroom, into which would fit the entire living room of Anna's childhood apartment, holds every cleaning supply she could want.

Perched on the toilet, polyester slacks pooled around her ankles, urine-soaked diaper still fastened around her (to air out, as Anna puts it), Miss Dodie is morose. "Annie, when did I get so old?" She shifts her haunches, their leak-proof wrapper rustling squeakily. "Whatever you do, don't let that man come in and see me like this."

Which man she means, the gardener or the homeowner, Anna isn't sure, but it makes little difference. She has no intention of letting anyone in the bathroom. Gently she closes the door, shielding Miss Dodie from view. She will go straight to the wine cabinet in the kitchen, grab a bottle, hide it somewhere for later, and come right back.

Carefully she picks her way around upturned furniture and smashed knickknacks. No noise, she must not make noise. If she is discovered stealing wine, the result will be worse than any earthquake. The rich man will throw her on the street for theft, and Miss Dodie will fire her for drinking. She will have nowhere to go.

The breakage is extensive but hardly alarming to one born in 1986, the year nuclear destruction rained over northern Ukraine. Who in this clean, orderly country of Canada could comprehend the Chernobyl Exclusion Zone? The deserted, rotting city of Pripyat, whose fifty thousand citizens were herded onto buses, leaving behind their apartments and toys, dishes and vehicles, to fester forever? Who could imagine the more recent heartbreak of the Donetsk airport, the gem of modern Ukraine, reduced by warring forces to rubble, dust, and corpses? This tossed-around house, the disorder outside, the beat of helicopters, the distant sirens, the ashy smell that leaks through the windows, the occasional yell that carries across the water — none of it compares to the destruction of Anna's homeland.

The kitchen. At last. Silently she steps over a spill of long-stemmed flowers mixed with glass shards and comes face to face with the wine storage unit. Spies two unbroken bottles, one red and one white, grabs both. Retreats to the more enclosed mudroom, a good hiding place for now.

Now that she has the wine, she cannot wait. Just a little, that's all she needs. Just enough so that she can manage.

Back home she managed until late September, when in the midst of a ceasefire the Russian insurgents resumed their assault on the airport. She had gone about her business those final turbulent months, clocking in at the factory, returning to the apartment straight after work, venturing out only when the cupboards held nothing. She told herself the conflict was temporary, the damage limited, the civilian casualties rare. She held herself in check as the blocks around her were pounded by shelling. She stood firm and silent while neighbours either ran away or disappeared or were brainwashed by the Kremlin into thinking the invasion was for their benefit. Until the Russian invaders unleashed their wrath once more on the airport, gleaming symbol of all that was new and hopeful in her country. That, for Anna, marked the end.

Ears alert to any sound, cheeks flushed with nerves and longing, she unscrews the cap of the white. Thanks to God, that fictional trickster, for the demise of the cork. Takes a long, slow swallow. *Slava bogu!* A Riesling. Her throat opens wide, like a woman's legs for a lover, her body tingles and blooms and awakens, and for a moment she glimpses all the joys life might hold. Quiet. No questions or nightmares. Nothing to hide. Easy times.

Her head is still tilted back when she hears footsteps. In the kitchen, coming her way. She caps the wine and shoves it, along with the unopened bottle, into the soft pile of scarves and toques that have spilled out of the fallen-over deacon's bench.

No sooner does she stand, piecing together an excuse for why she is here instead of in the powder room with her half-dressed employer, than it hits. Without thinking, she drops to the floor, arms crossed over her head. The tiles beneath her rumble and the house tosses, a ship on an angry sea.

Oh, my lady! Stay on the toilet. Hold tight!

From elsewhere in the house an erratic percussion rings – crash! smash! bang! Anna curls into a fetal position. She is a bad woman, a terrible woman. She has done unspeakable things and must pay by living with this eternal need, which has now blinded her in the worst possible way. She has left Miss Dodie alone. Poor, trusting Miss Dodie. Please, please, let her be all right.

The second it stops, Anna moves as fast as the objects in her path allow. If her lady is frightened, or worse, hurt, Anna will never forgive herself. And Miss Dodie may never forgive her. She may scream and call Anna a Russian and sack her on the spot, and Anna will lose it all – the roof over her head, the squat old Volvo, the bureau drawer that contains the flask she depends on and the knife her brother gave her and the slowly fattening envelope of money – every item she has scraped together to call a life. Of all the times to be jobless, homeless, and friendless, in the midst of a natural disaster is surely the worst.

Rounding the corner to the powder room, she entreats deities she knows do not exist. *Spasi Gospodi*, let her be all right. It was a colossal error, leaving the woman alone with her pants literally down.

The bathroom door, when Anna gets there, is ajar. Jiggled open by the aftershock? She flings it wide to find the toilet lid down and the room empty.

Gone? No. Not possible.

At her doddering pace Miss Dodie cannot have gone far. She did not pass the mudroom where Anna hid the wine, which leaves only the corridor in the other direction, toward the dining room.

Anna jogs the short distance. Curses herself for neglecting the woman in her care. And burns with shame, because underneath her fear for Miss Dodie's safety have sprouted tendrils of desire. The single watering of Riesling, that one deep swallow, now demands another, and another, until the bottle is done and the next one beckons, and the vine of yearning binds her tighter.

∧

Joe is crossing the kitchen when it happens. He's headed for the side door off the mudroom, which was until recently blocked by Stedman's sports car. Fortunately Joe was able to shoulder the small vehicle away enough to clear the doorway, because guess what? The big guy had left his spendy collector's item out there in neutral without setting the parking brake. As soon as the driveway heaved up, the car rolled back and clobbered the house. The body damage would make you weep.

Joe is nearly free. He has made sure everyone is safe. He has shut off the gas and switched off the main breaker. He has stockpiled water, cleared all the exits, and put away obvious hazards. Whether out of superstition or sentimentality, he has unlooped his mother's Saint Anthony medallion from the rearview mirror of his truck and pocketed it. Now he can leave this nuthouse and go to where the fires are raging, where a *maintenance man* — Stedman's jab made him want to slug the friggin arsehole right in the bandaged face — will be appreciated. A few hours of good hard labour might help him make sense of this crazy day, not to mention fill the time it'll take Kiki to walk – or cycle? – home. Then what? Joe has no clue what will happen then. What shape will their townhouse be in? What shape will Kiki be in? What the hell is going on with Kiki?

Just yesterday Joe's future looked comfortable, predictable. Now he can't begin to guess what it has in store.

He avoids a gory spill of wine, gone dark red and sticky, and a small TV lying screen-down beside it. He's almost across the kitchen, nearly out, when it hits.

Instinct pushes him under the first covered space he sees, a built-in desk that once supported the flat-screen he just stepped over. Glass rains down, objects crash, something big falls with a sickening thud as he hugs his body tight and shuts his eyes tighter. If the aftershock is any less intense than the main event, you'd never know it. The floor tiles shake, his teeth rattle, the smashing continues. He clutches the medallion in his pocket and prays the built-in shelves overhead will hold.

They do.

The tremors end as abruptly as they struck. One moment the kitchen is all movement, the next deathly still. He stays where he is, not ready to leave his bunker yet to assess the new damage. Even if it's minimal, he's going to have to stay in this inhospitable house a while longer, at least until he's checked the motley crew of occupants.

Cocooned awkwardly under the desk, he pulls out his phone. Still nothing from Kiki. Not one text, not one voice message. Is Kiki avoiding him? But there's nothing from neighbours or friends either, no one back east, where an earthquake of this magnitude must surely have made the news. He tries Kiki again for – what – the tenth time? Nothing. Cell service must be completely down.

Did he make it to the peak of Black Mountain? Is he on his way down? Or – God. What if he can't head down? What if he's injured, lying somewhere unconscious? Or worse?

No way, not a chance. Doctor Kyle Jespersen will be fine. He's always fine. He's the smartest person Joe knows, and the most determined.

Winning is programmed into the guy's genes. He'll be fine, he will get down the mountain, he will make his way back to Joe.

Won't he?

Joe hugs his knees tighter, makes himself small. That his man will always come back to him is something he's never questioned before. Now he doesn't know what to think. *I feel like I'm living a lie*, Kiki said this morning. What lie? Joe didn't know then and he doesn't know now. He doesn't want to know. Maybe if he stays huddled in this safe cave, it will all vanish: the fear and instability and ruin this day has brought.

"Hey." A hand taps his shoulder. "You okay?"

He uncurls himself and looks up. Sidney, in a purple hoodie and jeans, her hair in a ponytail again, kneels down beside him. The Riot Grrrl is gone, leaving simply the girl — young, fragile, drained.

"You okay?" she asks again.

Of course he can't stay here, cowering. The girl is scared, and not one person in the house knows how to cope with practical matters, except maybe the nurse. He'll get them squared away, make sure they've got what they need for a few days on their own, then strike out into the real world.

"I'm all right," he tells Sidney. "How about you?" He glances at her hand. The bandage, fresh and clean a few hours ago, blooms with stains, the edges unravelled like the wrapping on an ancient mummy. Such a short time since he looked after the girl's cut — an outing to the movies, brunch with friends — and yet it feels like an eternity has gone by. "I can change that for you. Does it hurt?"

Sidney stares at him, eyes huge and unblinking. "It's not me," she says. "It's the old lady."

⌄

Charlotte is not one to waffle. Her career is built on decisiveness. Her title at Diamond & Day is Director, Pacific Region, but it might as well be CEO, Decision Management. From the first email check of the day until the last before bed, she is at it: yes, no, no, next week, okay, ninety grand, the small conference room, Sarah can do it, yes, two news spots, give it to head office, Toronto, needs a better key message, send it now, please revise. Plus there are all the non-work decisions that punctuate every day. Will she run her 10K in the morning or at night? Can Sidney stay late at the mall? Should they hire May's cousin for the extra laundry now that they're boycotting the dry cleaner? Better to invite the Schwartzes over for brunch or meet them at the Four Seasons? Did the window washers leave so many streaks that she should demand a redo? Should Tayne bring in the latest tech wizard on contract or hire him full-time? Send May to Whole Foods or Costco today, or is there time for both? Discipline Sidney for skipping school or let it slide? Switch to dry food for the cats, and is there a decent organic brand? On and on it goes. Wrestle one question to the ground and two more rise up.

Yet now, in a matter of hours, a tide of indecision has swamped Charlotte, and it bobs her up and down: yes, no, yes, no. Her daily responsibilities suspended, and her identity stowed away with her wedding ring, she is for once simply riding it out.

Whether to sleep with Bryan — that was easy. They sealed the deal across the Tim Hortons table, no need to put into words what their eyes and bodies already agreed to. Hastened by the sudden rattling of ceramic plates and napkin holders, and the word *aftershock* which rippled through the doughnut shop, she drove off, Bryan following in his truck, to the Comfort Inn, the biggest hotel in Hope according to the pimply guy behind the counter. Hotel, my ass, she thought as Bryan, who insisted on putting down his credit card, led them to the tiny ground-floor suite: two floral beds and a beige kitchenette, complete with a two-burner hotplate, the epitome of tacky but the only room left. She shut out the ill decor, slid off her jacket, pulled off her top, unfastened her bra. Allowed Bryan to admire her toned torso and pert nipples before removing the rest. Let him take the lead from then on, knowing a cocksure Australian would want it that way, would want to push her onto the bed, pin her arms over her head, run his tongue down her body, flash her his Andy Gibb grin, then flip her over and shove himself in. They went at it hard, from zero to sweat-soaked in seconds, and that was fine. After the suddenness of this morning's shockwave, the jolt of fright, and the discovery that whatever the hell had happened it was major, a frenzied fuck seemed like the right response.

It was easy, too, to let herself doze afterwards. It's been weeks since she clocked more than five, six hours a night. Even though she never, ever naps, Bryan's warm arms, the reassuringly bleached linens, and the soft pillow beneath her head made sleep impossible to resist.

Just as effortless was the decision to eat eggs at four in the afternoon. Bryan had kissed her awake, then straddled her, the shaggy tousle of hair over his face mirroring the tangle around his cock, the latter soft and friendly but beginning to stir. His sea-blue eyes pinned her as firmly as his thighs. "I'm starving," he said. It came out *stahving*. "Let's eat." Charlotte had calls to make, had to get on the guest computer and check email, Facebook, newsfeeds. Had to – dammit! she'd forgotten – call Tim in Toronto. But it would all be easier after food. She was starving too, her stomach rumbling as they entered the hotel restaurant, a small, plain room off the small, plain lobby, both filled with knots of people trading stories about the disaster. Scanning the all-day breakfast menu, she ignored the fruit and yogurt she'd ordinarily choose and ordered the lumberjack special. She finished it all, pancakes, bacon, sausage, scrambled eggs, and three cups of weak, bitter coffee, the worst swill imaginable yet she drank it greedily.

Now, licking the last bead of syrup off her fork, she considers feeling guilty. Her waistband will bite into her tomorrow and she'll have to run another half hour to compensate. Then thinks: fuck it. In times of trouble it's natural to stockpile. The calories and caffeine will come in handy for the long night's drive back to Vancouver.

Those were the easy decisions. Ahead are the tough ones. Stomach full, crotch damp, mind teeming with all that has happened, she knows she has to part from this studly man, thank him for the escape, and send him on his way. Has to tackle the checklist that pours out of her every hour of every day, only now it's oozing like heavy cement, miring instead of motivating her.

"This has been great." She rummages in her bag for her phone until she remembers: it's broken. "More than great. But I've got to get going."

He is grinning again. Has she ever met a man who smiles so easily, for whom happy is a default setting? Imagine letting life buoy you along, content with whatever random shore you wash up on.

"Nah, you don't." His eyes twinkle. "What's the rush?"

"I've got to check on –" Damn. In the life she has fabricated she is divorced, childless, a lawyer. "I've got to get hold of the office. Make sure everyone's all right, let them know where I am."

"Come on." He leans in. There it is: the warm salt musk of sex. "It can wait till tomorrow. The phone lines are down, remember? You won't get through. No one's expecting you to check in at work today." He lightly traces her jawline and she shudders. "I'll tell you what can't wait," he says. "This."

His other hand, under the table, moves up her thigh, up and up to the fork in her close-fitting pants, which he presses gently.

God. So many things to do and only one thing she *wants* to do – head straight back to the tacky beige room and let this man have his way with her. As his fingers rub, her checklist takes flight; tasks float into the air where they will stay – won't they? – until later. Then she will tug them down and deal with them. They'll be fine up there for a while.

Bryan removes his hand and signals the waitress.

As they wait for the bill, uncertainty nags at her. She can't ignore her obligations, especially to her family, at a time like this. How can she be so selfish?

Bryan drops a few crumpled bills onto the table and winks. He can tell she's wavering.

Charlotte Pettigrew, you are the most self-centred creature to walk the earth. It was the criticism her mother most often levelled on those infrequent occasions when their paths crossed, and it was true. At age twelve, thirteen, fourteen, Charlotte thought about herself constantly; she obsessed over details like her birthday, and would her mother remember this year. Like school, and would she ever find a best friend to giggle with. Like her room, and how long could she stay there before anyone noticed (answer: a day and a half). Like her report card, no mark below ninety-five, and would anyone congratulate her. Like hoping, while her mother recounted every minute of some council meeting or sit-in, for a pause when she could talk about *her* day or *her* week. Like waiting for her mother to ask, even once, how she felt or if she needed anything. She flushes when she remembers how desperately she wanted attention, to be told or shown that she mattered.

Bryan feels again for the seam of her pants under the table. "Come on, Miss Charlotte. Stay the night with me. You want to."

His finger twists and her breath catches. Oh God, she *is* selfish. "What are you, the devil from Down Under?"

"Whatever you want me to be. Whatever it takes to get you back in that room." He scoots his chair in, reaches under the table for her hand and places it on his crotch. The bulge of him, wanting – wanting *her* – does her in. She matters to someone, if only for another hour or two. And so Charlotte falls, in some gravity-defying way that's more like flying. Lets desire propel her back to their rumpled room. Lets herself be shoved by this antipodean force of nature into the beige armchair, where she ignores the press of her handbag and his jacket and the car keys, where she fucks and is fucked, wants and is wanted, where her mind empties and her body fills.

$$\wedge$$

Stedman prods the bandage on his right cheek. The gauze is moist but thank God still in place. He brings his fingers away and assesses the blood: pale, thready, not worth worrying about.

His face throbs; in fact, now his whole head hurts courtesy of the soapstone polar bear that sailed off Charlotte's bureau and dinged the good side of his skull. Useless doodad! He kicks at it, lying there on the hardwood, and misses. Dammit, his coordination is off. He connects on the second try.

Downstairs, the murmur of voices, the house coming alive again. *The aftermath of the aftershock.*

The words seem strange, like a foreign language. He has never strung these particular words together before.

Sidney's girlish treble rises above the mix. Good, she's up and about. He won't have to go downstairs and check, won't have to mingle with the strange crew making themselves at home down there.

Stedman resumes his analysis, totting up pros and cons. He's been at it awhile, since before the aftershock. It's going slowly. So many variables, and his brain is so foggy after all the knocks to the head. He's never been a man for details. Big ideas are his thing; they're the reason he is where he is today. He is an innovator, a risk taker, a man of action. This business of making lists, taking stock — he has staff for that. And Charlotte.

Damn it all, where is she?

No one knows. Sidney has called her mother any number of times, texted her, emailed her, checked her Facebook page. Not a word, and now Sidney's phone is dead.

The cons are piling up. He has no idea what's happening at work. One cryptic text from Marcus — *Damage but sheltering in place* — and a "technical difficulties" message on the company's homepage have left him none the wiser. He's tried phoning Marcus, the headquarters reception number, and of course Charlotte, but he gets silence every time. Sidney said something about cell towers being down — the gardener told her that. It hardly matters, since Stedman won't have a working phone much longer. His main mobile is in smithereens, thanks to the bookcase that struck him in his office. Of his two backups, one has died. Between the P&G celebration earlier and the Merck melodrama, he never got around to recharging it. The other phone is down to fifteen percent. That one's recharging from his laptop, but it won't make it far before the laptop battery conks out. All because the hired man insisted on turning off the power. Not only can Stedman not recharge his devices, but the home wifi doesn't work either. He had to use data on his phone, which he stopped doing once the battery got dangerously low.

What a mess. He touches the skin around his eyes, his jutting cheekbones. His scalp, under closely razored hair, is tender with fresh cuts. On the wall in front of him is the grimy outline of the mirror he'd approached to give himself a pep talk. Now its gilt frame lies at his feet, as does the glass that sprayed him when the aftershock dashed the mirror onto the bureau. Why didn't he run for cover when the tremors began? What held him here, as if nothing serious was happening, just wind shaking the house as it whistled past? It was a bad decision, and he's lucky to have escaped with just a few nicks to the head.

Continuing his inspection, he touches the collar of his bespoke cotton shirt, surprised to find it still buttoned to the top, the Robert Talbott herringbone tie loosely knotted. Glances down to see a surprisingly ordinary sight given all that's happened — shirt, tie, and trousers, a look he adopted years ago to stand out from the denimed, black-tee-shirted tech crowd. It could be any weekday, except that his cuffs are grey and blood smears his white shirt front.

Maybe he should change. Maybe fresh clothes will smarten him up. He has a dozen shirts identical to this one, ordered from the Hong Kong guy who operates from an upper-floor office at the Park Royal mall. Hong Kong tailors are simply the best, an impeccable silver-haired gentleman told him once years ago, apropos of nothing, as they waited at the bar of the Vancouver Club for their respective lunch companions. The comment ate at Stedman until he ducked into the men's room, where he scrutinized his reflection for some sign that he needed sartorial advice. The truth is, everything he knows about taste, style, and quality he has learned this way, haphazardly, overwriting his thrift-store programming with bytes of real-money intelligence — real money being, paradoxically, the kind that's handed down to you unearned. The kind that came with Charlotte, via her bleeding-heart mother, the aging hippie who dispensed a string of tight-lipped lessons his first weekends in Westmount about which fork to use, which glass holds red wine and which white, when to wear a dinner jacket and when a sport coat will suffice. She delivered it all wearily, in her overeducated Katherine Hepburn voice, in an attempt, the reluctance of which she couldn't hide and the hypocrisy of which she couldn't see, to spruce up the unpedigreed clod her rebellious daughter had dragged home. Charlotte's mother, descended from early Montreal industrialists, the ones who gathered money in piles like autumn leaves, who owned the Victorian mansions that used to loom over Sherbrooke Street. Charlotte's mother, the feminist imperialist.

He surveys the dishevelled room, pondering whether to change. What a mess. Magazines have slid off night tables, reading lamps have tipped onto the floor, framed photos too. The delicate white orchid on the table near the balcony door is crushed beneath a squat stone Buddha.

Crap. Multiple years' and untold dollars' worth of crap, gathered and curated by his genetically tasteful wife.

This is his bedroom too; they still share a room and even a bed, though the idea of crossing the mattress has become ridiculous. Yet what in this space, where he spends six or seven hours a day, eight on weekends, is his? In a monetary sense, zero. Charlotte has paid for it all. She has bankrolled him from the beginning, dipping into the bottomless Pettigrew investments. The plan was to repay her once GlobalTech went public, but then the Indonesian factory came up for sale, and he had first dibs on that e-commerce company the MIT kids started in Cambridge. There's always something to buy. That's how you grow.

Now she wants it back. She made the announcement out of nowhere a few days ago, in this very bedroom, as he was peeling off his socks.

He was gobsmacked. "For what?"

She didn't answer, because the answer would be: nothing. She doesn't need her money, this wife who has everything.

He shook his head. "You know it's tied up in the business."

"Then we sell the properties."

What the hell? "Charlotte, we have to hold on to them. They're investments." It's true. The ski chalet in Whistler, the apartment in Paris, the house on Oahu — they belong to the Stedmans but are not their homes. The Stedmans are too busy for recreational travel.

"You owe me, Tayne. The family money is gone. There's nothing left. I want it back."

Hurricane Charlotte. Everything's a drama with her. He knows his wife: when she says there's nothing left, she means they're down to the last few million. Well, she'll have her capital back soon because soon it will be time for his big plan: tap the Chinese investors who've been sniffing around, cash in his stock, accept the under-the-table bonus they've offered for smoothing out the deal — and it's a *gigantic* bonus — repay Charlotte, and use the rest to seed a new venture. What that venture will be he hasn't decided, but he knows it will be brilliant and disruptive and big. He could have told her about the plan days ago, here in the bedroom, but he's been waiting for the last pieces to fall into place. Getting Procter & Gamble on board was one piece. Now there's the Merck setback to stickhandle, but that won't take long; he has faith in his people. Then he will tell her.

What could Charlotte possibly want that she doesn't already have? He takes in the biscuit-coloured walls, the muted designer drapes, the white area rug now soiled by the gardener's muddy boots, the king-sized memory foam bed with its bazillion-thread-count sheets. The slightly curved white sofa — *it's a Ruhlmann*, Charlotte had breathed, flushed after winning the piece on auction. There's not a damn thing in here he cares about. Not one thing he would save in a fire. Correction: an *earthquake*.

The word echoes in his mind. He tries to fix on it.

What happened, exactly? Aside from the smoke, the world outside seems curiously tranquil. Sure, they've heard sirens and air traffic. Sidney's watched Coast Guard boats and military ships disgorge soldiers into dinghies. The gardener has brought stories of mayhem from the Chinese neighbour. But here at home, apart from the breakage and disarray — he could sob when he thinks of his wine collection, gone — and apart from the strangers in his midst, life is much the same. Could he have dreamed the past hour and a half, or misremembered? Entirely possible, because truth be told, his mind is not firing on all cylinders. If he had any battery power to spare, he'd google concussion symptoms.

As for the gardener's updates, how reliable are they anyway? A few fires and emergency crews, sure. He can smell the smoke. Power lines down, he'll believe that. But highrises collapsed, roads blocked, telecommunications knocked out? The neighbourhood, even the entire city, incapacitated? It seems farfetched. The gnomish man is not the brightest bulb in the pack, and Stedman suspects that he, like Charlotte, is prone to exaggeration. No tsunami has materialized, the house has not shifted, no one's beating down the door for help. It can't be that bad. This is the twenty-first century, after all. Severe weather events, as the media calls them, are commonplace. There are news stories practically every day: people housebound, huddled in outerwear and duvets, sandbagging against encroaching waters, rowing down suburban streets, stuck in the ditch beside some snow-choked highway. Sometimes they refuse to go, waiting on roofs or barricaded in basements; sometimes they evacuate, leaving their tree-crushed bungalows to moulder and their possessions to float down cul-de-sacs.

He crosses to the white art deco sofa and perches on its stiff, expensive edge. It made Charlotte drool, but it's the most hideous piece of furniture he's ever laid eyes on. Not to mention the least comfortable. It's little more than a white vinyl church pew. Reminds him of those tall boots girls used to dance in back in the sixties — what were they called?

The sofa's unyielding leather is smooth, unmarked, a field after first snow. Not a shred of damage. Built to withstand up to ... what? on the Richter scale.

How big was this supposed event, anyway? What did the gardener say again?

Hell. He can't afford to be so forgetful going forward. He needs facts, as many as he can marshal — real facts, not fake viral news from God knows what kind of person next door — so that he can assess how and when to move. He is not a detail man, but this much he knows: facts are essential for control, and control matters more than anything.

He strokes the arm of the shiny white sofa.

Where the hell is she?

Enough. Time to do something. Change his shirt. Check on Sidney. He heard her voice, but who's to say she wasn't clobbered by some piece of flying bric-a-brac? Though she's fine, he knows. His daughter's a tough cookie. Just like her mother. Charlotte is many things – beautiful, foul-mouthed, a dramatizer, and a sterling minted bitch when she's riled – but above all a survivor. There's no need to worry about either of them.

He stares at the hardwood, mesmerized by the line where it borders the area rug, sharp and fuzzy at the same time.

He needs to inspect the house, secure things, do something prudent – what exactly? – with the utilities. Or did the gardener do all that? He shut off something besides the power, some ... service. Stedman tries to remember.

Damned gardener, thinks he's knows it all. Typical blue-collar arrogance. Stedman got more than enough of that growing up in Hamilton, still a steel town back then. He got a bellyful of it in his boyhood kitchen, at least when his father bothered to come home.

A low mood pins him to the unforgiving sofa. He will count to ten, like Sidney does when life starts to spiral out of control. They learned about it at rehab, in the family sessions. When he hits ten he'll stand up and take the first step, and then the next ones will come.

One, two, three ...

What is that, by the low bookcase under the window? On the floor.

... four, five ...

He squints. Various items lie scattered there, mostly decorative objects that have departed the shelves, but his eyes are drawn to one thing.

... six, seven ...

A book. Except not a book. Lying face up, open to the middle.

Dammit!

Stedman leaps up from the stiff sofa and in three strides is holding the book. Or rather the thing that looks like a book. *That's how it works, Daddy,* Sidney said when she gave him the volume many Father's Days ago. She was so proud of the gift. *If anyone breaks in they just think it's a book. They don't know there's stuff hidden in it.*

Not stuff. Money. Twenty thousand dollars.

Twenty thousand in cash, because you never know when you might need it. Folded away in the hollowed-out book which is a secret storage space. Which is now empty.

ELEVEN

⋀

Not the Big One. A shallow crustal quake, the media reported. The rarest type in the region.

Just under the Strait of Georgia, that marine highway joining Vancouver and the Island, plied daily by ferries and boaters, commuters and tourists, an active fault – a fault known to no one, never mapped, never LIDAR-sensed, never monitored thanks to a decade of federal disregard for science – had slipped. It slipped and unleashed a 7.4 contender, a weakling next to the magnitude 9 expected from the Big One. Weak but shallow. Weak but nearby, local.

In the argot of earthquakes, shallow and local equal deadly.

The mainshock lasted forty-five seconds. In less time than it takes to boil an egg or sing the national anthem, the world's third most livable city, the brightest and richest of urban centres, model of green living and racial tolerance, plum of the global investment portfolio, heart of Canada's cannabis culture, home to farmers markets and organic cuisine and the country's largest open-air drug trade and one of its most destitute neighbourhoods, was knocked to the mat. It toppled hard and went down for the count, a count that went past ten. Past twenty. More punches, injuries, aftershocks. Past a hundred. A count with no end in sight.

⋀

AFTERNOON LIGHT SEEPS FAINTLY into the dining room. Some enters through the long, narrow windows set into the far wall; some spills over from the family room to which the dining room is attached, in an open, high-ceilinged L, by a mammoth riverstone fireplace. Whatever pale rays make it into the dining area are absorbed by the room's dark green walls, mahogany wainscoting, and heavy furniture, a decor that in another house might suggest intimacy but that here conjures the opposite.

Longer than it is wide, the echoing space puts Anna in mind of a castle hallway or a gallery, a miniature Podol Fortuna whose artworks teeter on sideboards and litter the floor. Superimposed on the largest of the fallen canvases, outlined with drops of crystal, spread like this morning's starfish inside the gull's craw, the body of Miss Dodie is almost art. Not so much a still life as a performance work, since — *slava bogu* — the old woman occasionally moans and flops her head.

Anna kneels by her employer's side, chafes her wrists, and lightly slaps her cheeks, willing the woman to regain consciousness. No blood haloes out from Miss Dodie's freshly set hairdo. That is a good sign. So is the twitching and head movement, which mean no broken neck, no spinal cord injury. Anna issues a silent thank-you to the gods or the universe — to whoever or whatever watches over senile old women and closet alcoholics.

"My lady," she says fervently, continuing to pat Miss Dodie's cheeks. "You must wake up. No sleeping now. Is not correct time."

The instant Anna burst into the dining room and saw Miss Dodie on the floor, she knew the old woman had not collapsed but been felled, as surely as the elk hunted down in the Polissyan forests she had crossed on the long walk to Poland — only not by any firearm but by the restaurant-size chandelier which, judging by the ragged hole in the ceiling, had originally hung over the dining table.

What in the world was Miss Dodie doing in here? What could have made her slide her diapered bum off the toilet, pull up her slacks, for they are indeed fully zipped, and totter off to the dining room? Once here, why would she lean over the table, as she must have done to be in the path of the falling fixture? It is pointless to wonder. Miss Dodie will never remember, and Anna is in no position to guess the intentions of her lady's moth-eaten mind.

Like that, the girl's blue-jeaned legs are there. Startled, Anna looks up. Sidney seems younger now, barely a teen, oversized hoodie hanging off her rail-thin body and camouflaging her chest, the girl's only ample part.

"Is she dead?" Sidney asks.

"No. She is, how you say? Sleeping."

"Unconscious."

"*Da*. That."

The girl kneels beside them. Pouches of flesh pool back from Miss Dodie's face. "She's so old."

"Yes. Very old."

The girl sniffs. "She stinks!"

"Is diaper. She needs new one."

"She's not all there, is she?"

Anna puzzles a moment. "She is here. She *is*. She is alive."

The girl shakes her head. "No, I mean she's not, like, with it. Her brain — her memory's gone. She's out of it."

"Out of it." Anna repeats the words slowly. Pictures the *it* Miss Dodie is out of — the world, in all its teeming detail, Miss Dodie floating on the periphery, beyond. It would be a state, Anna decides, of near perfection, to be removed at last from the chaos of life.

"Yes." She nods. "Out of it."

Sidney places her unbandaged palm on Miss Dodie's bosom and they watch the barely perceptible rise and fall.

Anna leans in and the girl's nose twitches. "You've been drinking."

Anna does not meet the girl's eyes, just shakes her head no.

"You have! Wine. I can smell it."

She is a child, and a child is owed no explanations. Even if it is a rich child, even if you are in the child's home.

The girl continues undeterred. "Where'd you get it? You stole it, didn't you? From the kitchen. That's why you weren't here when this happened." She gestures at the mess beside them. "You were out there drinking instead of in here looking after her."

This child thinks she is so smart; her voice is full of it. Anna trembles with anger, also with fear, but she will not give the satisfaction of a reply. Instead she places two fingers on Miss Dodie's papery neck and counts. "Slow. Her heart goes slow."

Miss Dodie moans.

"Please, my lady. Wake up." She touches the woman's shoulder. "Wake up for Annie."

The girl stands. "I'm going to find the gardener. He'll know what to do about this."

Anna's stomach flips. It is not enough that the girl knows she has been drinking. Now she will tell the man who helped them, Joe, and he will tell Miss Dodie, who is lying here injured, maybe seriously, because of her and who forbids alcohol and abhors drinkers, and Anna will be fired.

As the girl thumps off, Anna tries to control her panic. The gardener is the one in charge in this house. Will he throw her out?

A noise like a soft snore escapes Miss Dodie's purplish lips. Anna closes her eyes. The old woman needs full care at the best of times, and now that she is hurt she will need more. There is no one else here to look after her. As long as Miss Dodie remains in the house, surely Anna will be allowed to stay.

She stands up to stretch her legs, and for the first time spies the wooden sideboard along the back wall of the dining room, its upper glassed-in cupboards filled with crystal bar glasses on one side and—

She cranes her neck. *Vot eto da.* The motherload.

—on the other side, bottles and decanters of clear, honey, and amber liquids, a whole cupboard of them just sitting there, waiting to be drunk. Unlike the kitchen wine collection, the sideboard's trove is intact; the cupboard door has miraculously stayed latched through two rounds of intense shaking.

Now that Anna has spied them, it takes all her resolve not to rush to the bottles and upend them, one after the other. So close! Her cheeks and extremities kindle.

Wine helps her function, but liquor will make her fly.

She crouches again beside Miss Dodie and feels a square press into her upper thigh. A packet of gum, and it reminds her what is happening. She is already in trouble for the wine. She cannot drink more. What is she thinking? Look what her drinking has done to Miss Dodie, the one person in the world who needs her, and at random moments even cares for her. Anna pops a white-shelled square of gum into her mouth. Maybe she will choke on it. It would be a quick resolution, a fitting punishment for her guilt.

When the curly-haired gardener arrives, Miss Dodie's fingers are fluttering. He looms over the two women, hands on his hips. Anna tries not to tremble.

"How is she?"

"She is not — She is un-conscious." The new word falls clumsily from Anna's mouth. *I am innocent*, she rehearses silently.

Joe glances at the ripped-out ceiling. "The chandelier fell on her."

"Yes." Anna's voice sounds hoarse despite the gum. Now he will accuse her of stealing the wine, and drinking on the job, and negligence. Her heart thumps wildly as the room draws in and the already faint light dims. The ever-present smell of smoke threatens to gag her.

I am innocent, I have done nothing wrong. They are the same lines she practised as she fled Donetsk, hopeful that innocence, if she could convey it convincingly, would protect her. She used the words only once.

Her hands shake as they run down Miss Dodie's body, assessing. Joe watches closely. Does he think she is drunk? Steady, she tells her body. When she touches Miss Dodie's right knee, the woman flinches. The knee is so swollen that it stretches the polyester pant leg.

"Where is the girl?" Anna asks.

"Gone to get her father. What did you do?"

"I have done nothing!"

I am innocent, I have done nothing wrong. In four languages she had practised it: Russian, Ukrainian, Polish, and English. She googled the Polish and English translations before leaving, and googled how to pronounce them. Recited the lines over and over, all four versions, as she packed.

"I have done nothing wrong," she says. She keeps her voice even.

Joe peers down at her. "What do you mean, nothing wrong?"

"I tell you, I do nothing." She must convince him, and oh God she needs a drink. The bottles are just over there.

She took vodka with her that day she locked the apartment door forever. The day was splendid, an unusually warm afternoon for late September. Brilliant sun, blue sky, light breeze shaving the edge off the heat. The day after skirmishes turned into fierce battle at the Donetsk airport. A perfect day to be outside, a perfect day to escape.

"What the hell is going on?" It is the father, striding toward them, Sidney trailing behind. As cavernous as the room is, his voice manages to fill it.

"I need scissors," Anna says. "Sidney, can you bring?" If she directs the attention to Miss Dodie, maybe they will ignore her.

The girl runs off, but Joe will not be distracted. "What do you mean, you didn't do anything wrong?"

It was a gorgeous day. She made it as far as the park near the blown-out hospital, an off-limits building that the rebels and their Russian comrades had nonetheless shelled. Patients, doctors, and other civilians matter not to such thugs when weighed against political conviction. Her vague plan was to walk to the city centre and find a ride north to Kharkiv, where the refugee camps were rough but reportedly livable.

Anna stands up, looks Joe straight in the eyes. "I am innocent. I have done nothing wrong."

A hand clamps her shoulder and spins her around. Stedman's bandage is a stark white patch on his beef-red face. "I knew it was you!"

The aftertaste of wine sours on her tongue. She wills herself not to vomit.

"My money," the tall man growls. "Give it back."

Money? Anna is confused, but she knows this is how they corner you. She stands straighter, tugs down her grey cotton sweatshirt. *I am innocent.*

She pictures the tee-shirt she wore that day, her favourite one.

"Hold on." Joe shakes his head. "What money? We're talking about what's going on here." He waves at Miss Dodie and the broken chandelier.

Sidney runs into the room, pair of scissors in one hand.

Anna nods at the girl. "That one, she is lying. I am innocent. I have done nothing wrong. I steal nothing."

"Sidney?" Stedman sounds surprised. "You knew my money was gone?"

The girl's face is blank. "I don't know what you're talking about. Her either. I'm not lying about anything."

Sweat beads Anna's brow. She cannot, must not, lose this job. Miss Dodie needs her, and God knows she needs Miss Dodie. "She is lying! She is, I tell you."

It was so mild on that beautiful day that she decided to wear her favourite tee-shirt — tighter than when she bought it, and faded, but with the magic yellow-and-green Podol Fortuna logo intact. *Art by the people, for the people.* Bohdan used to tease her mercilessly whenever she wore it. Fair enough. What did she know about art? No more than when she was a schoolgirl on that long-ago trip to Kiev. Yet the idea of it, the possibility of human-made beauty in the midst of human-orchestrated terror, was a comfort she clung to.

Now she knows better. Knows that what comforts you can also bury you.

Joe kneels beside Miss Dodie, then looks up at Anna. "Sidney said you took her pulse. That's not true?"

"Yes, is true." Sweating profusely now, Anna turns her head so that no one can smell her breath. "I check her like this." She presses two fingers to her own neck. Right where the soldier put his huge, rough hand, cupping her jaw, testing before buying. He was alone, the park empty, people cowering indoors following the airport attacks.

"Has she been unconscious the whole time?"

"Yes. Un-conscious."

A soldier alone, no comrades in sight. Barely distinguishable from the trees in his olive camouflage, face swathed in a balaclava despite the warm day. Only his eyes showed, burning, rabid.

Stedman leans in close, says fiercely, "I know what you did. You took my money. Give it back now and I won't press charges."

He stared at her chest. *Art*, he grunted. *Artists are subversives.*

He was a rebel, not a Russian; she knew it the minute he spoke. Her own countryman. He could have been a neighbour. I am not an artist, she wanted to say, I am a Ukrainian, like you, but her mouth had frozen. Her body too. *I am innocent. I have done nothing wrong.* If she knew it and believed it, surely her face would show her innocence.

Vigorously she chews her gum. Her breath must not smell, her mouth must not tremble. "I tell you, the girl is lying."

Stedman eyes his daughter. "Sidney, I know you wouldn't lie to me. Tell me now. What do you know about the money?"

"Let's see if she'll wake up," Joe says from the floor. Lightly he slaps Miss Dodie's cheeks. The old woman sighs; her eyelids flutter but stay shut.

Anna's mind races. *Unconscious.* Silently she repeats the word, making it her own. Please let her stay unconscious. As long as Miss Dodie is helpless they will not force Anna to leave, no matter what they suspect her of. She is sure of it. Besides, it is better for Miss Dodie this way, better that she sleep through all the horrors. Anna knows. She has been conscious – acutely so – for every fear, every probe, every scream and grunt and thump and slice. No oblivion, no easy times, only the foul truth, breathed into her face and pressed into her body so that she understands personally what her people have collectively known forever: the unspeakable bargains you strike in the pursuit of freedom.

"Listen to me! It is my money and by God I will get it back. Whatever it takes." Stedman's words bring Anna back.

Joe is still trying to rouse Miss Dodie. Sidney is picking a fingernail on her bandaged hand, deaf to her father, seemingly bored.

Please, thinks Anna. *Please nothing happens this time. Please you will leave me alone.*

All around her, confetti made of crystal, paintings in a tumble, china in shards. Yet the table has not budged. The upholstered chairs have not broken. The bowl of fruit on the table has slid only a little off centre, spilling a few grapes and a lone green apple.

How do you know what you are, fragile china or a solid chair?

Until a soldier grips your face in his calloused hand, until the world takes you in its fist and shakes you, how do you know?

Joe slaps Miss Dodie sharply and the woman kicks out with one leg. Anna flinches, feeling the pain. But it works. Miss Dodie opens her eyes.

"Where? My ... Where is my ...?"

Joe's voice is reassuring. "She's right here." He points at Anna. "Right beside you."

"No!" The woman tosses her head. "Not her, you stupid man! Where is my, my —"

"We look for ring later," Anna says. "Is lost."

"*No!*" The old woman's mouth works and her face flashes impatience. "Where is my — my *ball?* My food? Apple!" The word hurtles from her, free at last. "The apple, I found it. It's mine." She turns her head. "She never feeds me." A finger trembles in Anna's direction. "I would starve if it was up to her."

Anna shakes her head, weary but relieved. Miss Dodie is back. The woman has lived eighty-six years, cannot say what day or season it is, cannot clear the mucus from her own nose or the poop from her own bottom, yet she will not be kept down. She can wander off, reach for an apple, be brained by a chandelier, and lose not an ounce of her unquenchable will.

Miss Dodie turns to Joe, who has stood up. "My apple! This is your restaurant. You stole it, didn't you? You can't fool me. Don't just stand there, give it back! You stupid stealer. Stupid *thief!*"

The gardener, until now the calmest one of them by far, is rattled. Anna sees thunderclouds inside him, bunched and ready to burst. But they will not, it appears, explode onto her. Joe is preoccupied with Miss Dodie, cannot take his eyes off her. He is not upset about Anna drinking wine and neglecting her employer, at least not now.

"Shut up, you old witch." His voice is low and his eyes burn. Like the soldier's. "Don't you ever, *ever* call me that again. You hear me? Never."

Thief? Anna wonders as Joe stalks out of the room. Joe stole the businessman's money? *Joe?*

⌃

When Kyle comes to, he has no idea how much time has passed. The sky is flat grey with hints of blue, wispy with high cloud, same as it's been all day. What's not the same: the air traffic. The distant thrum of turbine engines and rotor blades tell him that aircraft are converging on the city en masse. As he takes in his surroundings, three helicopters pass directly overhead, the distinctive red of the Canadian Coast Guard streaking the sky.

He is in a boulder field, an empty moonscape over which hovers the faint smell of lit matches that's released when rocks smash into rocks. It's the same slide area where he sheltered during the main quake, only his time he's out in the open, wedged between slabs of granite, his upper body draped backward over a midsized rock.

He doesn't move, afraid of what might hurt. Whatever happened, it won't be good.

A few minutes, that's all he needs. A few minutes to rest in ignorance. How long since the aftershock? And since the main quake before that? It's got to be the same day. No way a night has passed; surely he'd know that. He'd be a lot colder. Then it hits him: *look at your watch.*

The first bubble of worry rises. *Why didn't you think of that right away?*

He lifts his right arm in front of his face. Pain-free. Good.

The numbers on his watch are clear, in focus. Vision not blurred. Also good.

It's 1:32. The aftershock hit when—1:30, 1:15? He's not sure. He starts from the main quake, which he knows was around 11:45. Adds on the time it took to scramble up to Eagle Bluffs, do his gruesome surveillance of the world below, recover, then descend to this point.

It's no use. Every time he tries to add another increment of time, he loses count. The numbers arrive then float away, like an internet signal dropping in and out.

Not good.

He runs his right hand lightly over his face and forehead. A tender spot on one cheekbone, definitely a contusion, but his fingers come away clean. He lifts his head off the rock behind him, manages only an inch or two before a pounding timpani line assaults his skull. He probes his scalp, feels a patch of sticky wet hair. Looks at his fingers. Blood.

Shit.

Shutting out the pain, he tries to sit up, the mother of all abdominal crunches. His brain sloshes forward, not wanting to stop, and his back — oh God his back won't straighten. Pain rips through him. He reaches behind with his right hand and massages his lower spine, as much of it as he can reach below the light daypack still strapped to his back. The muscles give slightly and the pain eases enough that he risks shouldering off the pack. It works. He places the pack on the ground, relieved that he has the use of both arms.

From his semi-upright position, he takes in the rockspill dislodged by the aftershock, a tumble that ranges from granite monoliths to walnut-sized stones. One of the smaller rocks likely made the dent in his cheek. Another, he sees now, dinged his left forearm, leaving a red welt that's bound to bruise.

When his back is loose enough, he pulls himself the rest of the way up to a seated position. Does a gentle head roll to unkink his neck, looks down —

Oh, Jesus.

He makes himself exhale slowly. Makes himself detach and evaluate rationally, an MD just arrived on the scene.

His left leg is extended straight out in front of him, knee swollen into a softball below the hem of his shorts.

But the right —

No, stay with the left. He tests the left foot: point, flex, a slow, creaky ankle rotation. Tries to bend the distorted knee and winces. A lot of soft tissue damage there, but at least the joint responds.

The right leg.

Overhead a raven unleashes an ordinary throaty caw as if circling the same old world as yesterday. Kyle fixes on the sound, nearer than the distant thrum of aircraft, and tries desperately to focus. He fists the wet out of his eyes.

What's curious is that in the right leg, he feels nothing. He knows it's not paralysis. His back prangs sharply and that's a good sign. He has movement in his torso and hips. Is it because he can't *see* the damage that he can't feel it? He can't remember any connection between sight and sensation in the medical literature.

He stares at his legs but his brain refuses to compute. Instead it skates away to his living room, miles below, a lifetime ago, to the tan leather ottoman that commands all attention, comically large in the modest space. The giant footrest was Joe's idea; he wanted something big enough for them to use at the same time. *Watching the telly like two old nellies*, he'd said in the store, elbowing Kyle in hopes of dislodging a laugh. Kyle hadn't even smiled, embarrassed by the joke's broadness, its *gayness*, and the image of neutered, passionless coupledom it evoked. He assessed all the other footstools, their colour and shape, durability and feel, while Joe guarded his pick. He had bonded with the grotesque thing and Kyle knew there'd be no swaying him – Joe the Capricorn, the steady goat, hard-working, occasionally morose, above all loyal. Not that Kyle believes in that ludicrous mythology, the sun signs more bits of hokum passed down by his mother, along with how colour affects mood and how personality is reflected in the shape of the hand. How did such a parent ever produce a man of science?

Man of science? You're a plastic surgeon. Not the good kind either. No cleft palates or burn victims for you.

In the end Kyle relented and they bought the ottoman. In time the broad leather mesa became a shared joke, Joe loudly praising its beauty each time they used it, their feet knocking together as they talked about their day or watched a series.

What Kyle wouldn't give to be sitting beside Joe in their living room right now, sock feet resting on that ottoman. The image no longer seems kitschy or claustrophobic; it seems like the most appealing situation imaginable. Instead, his right leg, below the knee, is pinned by a boulder almost exactly the size of that giant piece of furniture but weighing multiples more.

Shock crests over him. He needs to deal with the facts, a faraway part of him knows, but he cannot make himself focus.

Where is Joe? How come you're not with him?

The thought of Joe down there, possibly alone and unsure, keeps Kyle from tipping into unconsciousness. He is responsible for Joe. It has always been that way. The instinct to oversee his partner, almost paternal even though Kyle is younger by seven years, is as woven into the fabric of their lives as their domestic routines, jokes, and nicknames. Give Joe a backyard and a greenhouse and he knows exactly what to do, but don't ask him to recall a deadline or shop with a list. Don't expect him, when you take a rare holiday, to remember his passport or even know what day you're leaving. Don't ask him to weigh in on current events or to take life seriously. Kyle is the conscientious one, the one who reminds and supervises, informs and teaches.

"You sure you know what you're doing?" Kyle's older brother, Bradley, had asked when Kyle called to announce they were moving in together. "I mean, you're obviously not with him for his mind."

Kyle snubbed his brother for months after that remark even though deep down, in some pinched, uncharitable part of himself, he saw in it the germ of truth.

Right, and you're such an intellectual. You tighten sags and inflate lips. You may as well be a landscaper.

"I'm with him for love" was what Kyle told Bradley on the phone. "I love him." And he did love Joe. Still does, though in a much different way. Even after last night.

Last night. What you did —

No.

The knee of the unpinned left leg aches mightily. He leans forward, gently palpates the swollen joint, winces. It's painful but okay.

But the right leg. He can scarcely look at it let alone touch it. He leans forward and places one palm against the rough boulder. It's so big, so heavy.

Fatigue closes in and he draws his hand back.

Look at the big doctor. Nothing but a candy-ass sissy.

Who does it belong to, that voice, coarse and male, that goads him whenever he's weak or afraid? His father? Ronald Jespersen, a suit-and-tie insurance man who worked ten-hour days until he doubled over at a meeting, dead of a heart attack at fifty-six — classic — never knew his son was gay, had probably never uttered the word *gay* in his life, yet instinctively zeroed in on any softness in the boy, fine-tuned his aim, and fired. Bradley, a ruddy-cheeked bruiser, needed no such correction. He plunged eagerly into baseball and rugby and, in time, anyone with a moist opening between her legs. Kyle, though, was an ongoing source of exasperation. He never acted like a girl, wasn't drawn to dolls or flowers like some of his friends when they were young. There was no experimenting with his mother's lipstick or, God help him, dressing in her clothes. His weaknesses betrayed him more subtly than that: in the precise way he lifted a fork, with a just-so curve as it neared his mouth; the way he tilted his head down but cast his eyes up, through the fringe of long lashes; the mild impediment that made him swallow his *r*'s and *l*'s until his father dragged him, at age eight, to a speech therapist; the delicacy of his dumpling cheeks and his baby-fat belly; how swiftly he crumpled under criticism; how he couldn't dam his tears when the big boys emptied his bookbag and played catch with his lunch or the smart-mouthed girls called him *Flubber* or *Princess* on the bus. Each one of these defects, somehow, Kyle's father isolated and attacked. *Arm straight, wrist strong*, he'd command at the dinner table. *Shoulders square, like your brother. Look a person in the eye when you're talking to him. Put down that brownie before you turn into a tub of lard. For God's sake, don't cry. Whatever you do, fight back.*

Easy for his father to say. There was no fight in Kyle back then. There was drive to succeed, in due course, but never fight. If you've lived your short life under siege, if you've suffered the self-loathing of victimization, how can you knowingly swipe at someone else?

Liar. This morning with Joe. What would you call that?

No, not his father's voice. The sentiments are his father's, some of them, but not the voice. The voice is part coach, part preacher, part drill sergeant. It berates him, it hectors him, it reminds him of every weakness, and there are many. It shouts and cajoles; it also threatens in whispers; and at times when it might save him, like last night, it goes silent.

$$\wedge$$

Stupid? Joe paces the small patio outside the mudroom door and gulps fresh air, though it's not very fresh, more like charred and cindery. The fires must be close now. Time to pitch in and fight the flames with the other volunteers, the way Vincent is. Time to leave this house full of nutcases.

That rich old bag—how dare she call him stupid? He's the only one here with the sense to circle the house, eyes open to danger. He's the only one who knows to shut off the utilities so the house doesn't go up in flames if the fires get close. He's the one who goes next door, checks that the neighbour's all right, gets the news. Not the nutty old lady with her heavy jewels and her paid companion. Not the famous businessman either, with his architect-designed house and his *powder* room with a sitting room inside it and his megabucks sports car that he was stupid enough to park in neutral.

Joe has just come from next door where he was lucky to catch Vincent stuffing a pack with water, food, and gloves, about to walk up to Marine Drive to join the fire crews. Even Vincent's update, which is more than a little disturbing, because basically they are screwed, the whole Lower Mainland shut down, wasn't enough to shake Joe's anger.

She's the one who's stupid, the dried-up old bat, with her royal voice and her toilet smell. Mrs. Thurston Howell III is who she reminds him of, with a few decades added on, like she got left out in the sun on Gilligan's Island to roast and wrinkle. *She's* the one who ended up flat on her back, for Pete's sake, knocked out by a chandelier. A friggin light fixture! He was smart enough to take cover as soon as the aftershock started. How is *he* the stupid one?

They're nut jobs, every one of them. It's just his luck to end up with a crew like this one. All the more reason to leave. People are still supposed to stay where they are, Vincent said, that's the word from emergency management, but Joe's had enough of the strange behaviour and loopy conversations around here. Miss Dodie and her nurse can't string a sentence together between the two of them. The old woman thinks she's in a restaurant and it's all about food. The nurse keeps saying she's innocent when it's obvious she's hiding something, but what? Not the stolen money that Stedman keeps raving about, Joe's sure about that. And him, Mister Big Shot, he may be crazy rich but he doesn't have two clues to rub together. How the heck does he run a business, let alone a money-making global one? The girl is the only one in her right mind, and she's doing the only sensible thing you can do when you're surrounded by nutbars: keeping her head down and staying quiet.

As he walks, he fingers Ma's Saint Anthony medallion in his pocket. *Put all the initials you want after your name and you won't have an ounce of sense if the Good Lord didn't see fit to grant it to you,* she'd say whenever he dawdled home with another straight-c report card. There was always some consolation note inked on it — *A happy, helpful boy who works hard* — in the teacher's perfect cursive. *You're smart in a different way,* Ma would say, tapping his chest. *Smart in here. You get into the big city, off the Rock, and you'll see. Tests and grades and teachers — that foolishness don't matter one bit when you're older. You got real-life smarts from growing up here, where people are sensible, and that's what counts.*

Apple-cheeked, his mother was, her face pink from vats of jam she made from the fallen plums that littered the neighbour's field, or from the laundry and ironing that were never finished, or from the fat molasses cookies she slid out of the oven, cheaper and more filling than store-bought, she always said. Kind, no-nonsense Ma, who raised him on her own, who met his carefully rehearsed coming-out announcement when he was sixteen with a chuckle and three words, *I know that,* before asking if he wanted another tea biscuit. There's not a single person in this fancy mansion fit to scrub his Ma's toilet. The two months he spent back in Cupids watching her dwindle before his eyes was the hardest time in his life, the most daunting test he'd ever taken.

Until today.

A blur of movement yanks Joe back to the here and now. Rounding the corner of the house at warp speed and hurtling toward him is the white fur bundle he's sighted several times today. It's the neighbour's, Sidney said.

The dog skids to a halt, roadrunner style, at Joe's feet and cocks his head, stumpy tail frantically wagging. Joe crouches down and scratches the little terrier behind the ears. The animal's whole body quivers. With pleasure? Or anxiety, after the day's unreal events? A tiny pink tongue appears.

They talked about getting a dog, back in the early days. It'd be nice to have another life in the place, Joe said, someone to dote on and buy treats for. "Our baby," he said.

Kiki rolled his eyes. "Spare me. It'd have to be some tiny shirt-pocket thing, right? Like a rat. What a cliché."

Still, Kiki had gone along with the idea for a while, stopping with Joe whenever they passed the dog park, crouching to pet every grinning retriever and soul-eyed mutt tethered outside the local Starbucks. It was easy then because it was hypothetical, them in their seven-hundred-square-foot apartment in the West End that didn't allow pets.

Three years ago, when they bought the North Van townhouse with the little hedged yard, Joe figured it was time. Not Kiki. New house, new clinic — he couldn't take any more change, he said. Maybe when the practice was up and running and he could help out properly. Time went by and the clinic took off, claiming more, not less, of Kiki's time, and they talked about it rarely, then finally not at all.

It's like Kiki has forgotten. Not just about the dog, about *them*. Has forgotten who they are, Joe and Kiki, a duo. Has forgotten their love. Joe feels the press of his mother's medallion on his upper thigh. Can Saint Anthony, patron saint of lost things, find something for you that someone *else* has lost?

"Thirsty, boy?" Joe scratches deeper and the dog vibrates. "That's a boy. I bet you're thirsty."

He stands up, his knees creaking, one step behind the rest of his legs as they usually are these days. Gettin old, b'y, no doubt about it. But not stupid.

He crosses to the faucet next to the mudroom door and scans the yard for a dish or container.

"What are you looking for?" Only Sidney's nose is pushed through the door, as if the rest of her is afraid to come outside.

"Something to put water in. For the dog. Is it Vincent's?"

She nods and hands him the stainless steel bowl she's been carrying around.

"You sure?"

She nods again. "I can get another one in the kitchen. There's a whole set of them. May uses them all the time." Her face screws up as if she's about to sneeze, and suddenly there are tears on her cheeks.

Joe opens the door all the way and pulls her outside. The girl has sliced her hand, been through a major earthquake and an aftershock that was almost as bad, seen her father's bloody face and an old woman lying unconscious in front of her, and it's the first time he's seen her cry. He pats her forearm, uncertain how to comfort her in this era when a man risks arrest for making physical contact. He ducks his head so he can peer through her curtain of hair. He doesn't have to move much; they're nearly the same height. "Is May your housekeeper?"

She nods.

"And she's ... missing? I mean, you don't know where she is?"

A huge wet sniff. She shakes her head.

"Don't you worry, now." He rubs light circles on her arm. "She'll be fine. She's just waiting it out somewhere like the rest of us. She'll be along before you know it."

Sidney wipes one cheek with the thumb of her bandaged hand. "Thanks for fixing my cut before." She looks up at him. "Joe."

He can feel his face pink up. "Go on, it was nothing. You need a new bandage, though. That one's all grimy. I asked your —" No, don't mention her father. "Let's go inside and fix it up."

"In a minute." She turns her face to the mild sky. "It's actually nice out. How crazy is that? You'd think it'd be … I don't know. Not."

Joe fills the stainless steel bowl from the faucet. The terrier, at his side the second the water starts flowing, laps furiously. Joe squats again, to heck with his knees, and buries his hands in the dog's warm coat. "How old are you, boy? Eh?"

"He's three. Vincent got him as a puppy right when my dad's company went public. That's how I know."

"Three?" Joe rubs the dog's throat, right on the sweet spot. "Well, I'm almost fifty. Whaddya think about that, boy?" His fiftieth is in August. He's been wondering how to celebrate the big day.

"What's that in dog years, eh? In gay years it's like sixty-five, maybe seventy."

A siren splits the air, another ambulance or fire truck rushing into the fray, and that's when it dawns on him. Not a revelation or a bolt of awareness, more like the fated arrival of a visitor long expected.

He will be fifty. Five-zero. Half a century.

Old.

Kiki is seven years younger, forty-three, still on the good side of the final decade that can possibly be called youth. And Joe's coming up on fifty.

Suddenly Joe sees how it must be. Every morning Kiki wakes up, youthful, fit, bursting with energy, opens his eyes to a stocky, greying garden gnome on the cusp of *fifty*. A man with stiff knees and reading glasses and wiry ear hairs. A man about to be old, already old in their circle of thirty- and forty-something friends.

How has Joe not realized this before now? Once he crosses over to fifty, that'll be it. He'll be some taxidermist's version of a man. He may as well be dead as be fifty.

⌄

Stedman is at a loss and he doesn't like it, not one bit. He is a man accustomed to being in charge, to controlling his life, his surroundings, and yes, he'll admit it, his people. He is not from the C-suite; he *is* the C-suite. He belongs in the driver's seat and yet here he is, in his own home no less, crouching in the back. His money is missing, twenty thousand dollars snatched from the privacy of his bedroom, and he doesn't know who took it or how to get it back. Not one necessity of life is working, not his phones or his laptop, not even his damn fridge. He cannot find a battery-operated radio. He cannot contact anyone — Marcus, his housekeeper, or his wife. He's cooped up with a bunch of strangers, under orders to shelter in place, required to keep the utilities off — or so says the know-it-all gardener.

Tayne Stedman is not a man who does others' orders, and he's less sure all the time whether to believe a word the hired man says. *Thief*, the old woman called the guy. From deep in the grips of dementia, she may have nailed it.

At first he thought it was the nurse. There's something secretive about her, something false. Also, she is poor. Also Russian, which any businessman knows means three degrees of separation from the mafia. But Sidney says that's impossible: the woman hasn't set foot upstairs. He has to believe his little girl. There was one breathless moment in the dining room when the nurse accused Sidney of lying and aroused Stedman's old suspicions — his daughter the addict, the screw-up, the shoplifter for God's sake — and he wondered, though only for a second or two, did Sidney take it? Does she need it to buy drugs? Then he remembered: she's cured, she's better now. He believes her.

That leaves the hired man, whom Stedman caught red-handed in the master bedroom soon after the quake — why didn't he make that connection earlier? — and whose muddy boot prints still stain the area rug. Of course that smug little prick took his money. It's obvious. Stedman will confront him. Soon. As soon as he collects himself.

The truth is, he doesn't feel right. He's emotional, his face and head ache like a mother, and he can't concentrate. He's queasy too. He nearly lost his breakfast when the nurse knelt beside the old woman in the dining room and, quick as a flash, sliced open a pant leg to reveal a mottled knee the size of a grapefruit. "Holy shit," he muttered, bitsu-bitsu reflux burning his throat. Then he caught sight of Sidney, clutching the ridiculous metal mixing bowl. "Sorry, Sweetpea. I didn't mean to curse."

"Fuckster!" the old woman yelled, fully awake, when the nurse — Anne? Hannah? — touched her knee.

"Can I get you a brandy?" he asked the woman. "For the pain, I mean? There are no decent pills in the house." He peered sideways at Sidney.

"I do not need your help, sir," the injured woman said. "I am a guest in this untidy restaurant, as are you. And alcohol is evil." It was another bad idea, the only kind he seems capable of today. He leaned into Sidney and the two of them stood transfixed while the nurse examined the woman's contusions and bandaged up the knee.

Afterwards he came here, to his office, the room where he thinks best, to make a plan. He spent the first fifteen minutes gathering not his thoughts but the remnants of his eighteenth-century ormolu mantel clock, which must have toppled from its shelf during the aftershock. This apotheosis of French craftsmanship has survived famine, revolution, epidemics, and wars; has crossed the ocean in disease-ridden ships and lurched across continents in jouncing stagecoaches; has adorned the mansion of one wealthy collector after the next; and now, in the home of Tayne Stedman, has met a brutal end, the porcelain elephant inset smashed to bits on the hardwood floor. It took time to mourn the loss, the unfairness of which moved Stedman to tears. His beloved floor, the Brazilian cherry he paid an astronomical sum to have properly installed — the strips running vertically the length of the room so the eye follows the lines to the windows and their panoramic view — has shattered the only household object he cares about. His lustrous dark floor, so beautiful, so hard. Charlotte, herself no stranger to exacting specifications, had nonetheless mocked his choice and the price tag it carried. Go with regular hardwood, she said, and a nice Persian rug.

Where is Charlotte? When will he hear from her?

His office is grand, no question, its magnificent wood and its wall of harbour a world away from the scuffed pine floors and dumpster view of their first apartment, in Montreal. He'd proposed it casually – they spent most of their days and nights together anyway, so why not save money by sharing a place? He made it sound like yet another lark, knowing an earnest declaration would scare her off. He'd already found the apartment, a third-storey railway flat on a ripe-smelling, low-rent street in the immigrant sector of Montreal North, guaranteed to piss off Charlotte's mother. It was amusing and more than a little hypo-critical: the renowned champion of women, migrant workers, and the downtrodden demanding that they take her money and rent a decent apartment in a safe white neighbourhood. He knew full well that her protests would cement Charlotte's decision to move there with him.

That long-ago apartment was the smallest he'd ever lived in, more cramped even than the rattraps his father scrounged up in Hamilton. One long corridor, lit by a single bulb, stretched like a spine from one end of the flat to the other. Radiating off the hallway like ribs were a tiny kitchen with a battered white stove and a noisy green fridge; a box of a living room in which they installed other boxes – milk crates for shelves, wooden fruit boxes pushed together for a coffee table, and a rickety pallet that held a second-hand futon; a bathroom so small that the toilet kissed the bathtub; and at the end of the hallway the dark bedroom, where they turned to each other most nights despite the exhaustion of studies and work, where they were for a time, in the shabby surroundings, their best and happiest selves. Two more fruit boxes, one on each side of the mattress, held clock radios, tis-sues, textbooks, and, always, candles. The power went out often in Montreal, for no reason other than the quirky Quebec hydro system, said Charlotte. She kept a flashlight at her side of the bed, another in the kitchen, and a tiny silver penlight in the bathroom medicine cabinet. At the back of the kitchen cupboard they stashed a few days' worth of canned sardines, peanuts, peaches, anything that was cheap and could be eaten cold.

Stedman hated those outages. It's unsettling how in an instant you can be left powerless, in all respects. No wonder he's uneasy now.

Where is she?

It's not that he's worried about Charlotte, exactly. She's in the Fraser Valley, a safe distance from the damage. She's a woman who can look after herself along with micromanaging everyone else. But you'd think she would at least do a Facebook update. Sidney wrote a quick post to say all is well in the house, but there hasn't been a word from Charlotte.

Seated at his prized desk, Stedman surveys his office. He'll be in for a bitter dose of contempt when his wife comes home to this mess. If anyone can hold an individual responsible for a natural disaster, it is Charlotte Stedman. It will be his fault the house is trashed, his and Sidney's, and Charlotte will be the wronged party. Such are the interlocking roles of the Stedmans as they rub against one another in the flux of family life. Would it be different if they'd had another child, if he had pulled off the achievement he always dreamed of — a son? No point thinking about it now. That window has closed, or just about. Charlotte must be what? Forty-five? Forty-four? Something like that. And they'd have to have sex, about as likely as gluing back together every broken object in this place.

He has to call her. Except — right, no cell service. Sidney tried earlier. She hasn't been able to reach May either, or Tim, though why the hell would she want to do that? Stedman phones his brother once a year, on Christmas Eve, and they exchange three or four facts before Tim starts rattling off the hockey scores, a signal their time is up. That's more than enough visiting as far as Stedman is concerned.

Why didn't Charlotte text or email right away, while they still had service? There could be a perfectly reasonable explanation. Yet something doesn't ring right. Something feels ... off.

∿

It must be shock preventing Charlotte from concentrating on the proper things, like contacting Tim in Toronto, trying to reach Tayne and Sidney, and figuring out how to get home. It must be shock at the root of this mad idea that has bloomed out of nowhere, a desert flower unfurled by sudden rain. True, it could be the massive joint Bryan has sparked up, high-grade and instantly mellowing, but she's going with shock. One minute they're listening to the tinny newscast from the clock radio – only one story today, the earthquake – and the next Bryan upends her plans.

"Come with me," he says after a lengthy exhale. "Leave your car in long-term parking and ride with me to Banff, spend a few days in the mountains. Then you can head home if you feel like it. If things're getting back to normal."

She hasn't said no, which means – what? That she might actually be open to such an unhinged proposition?

Right now there's a lot she *is* open to: the pot, which she never smokes because she can't afford to slow down; Bryan's warm palm smoothing her hair, his laid-back voice, his randy penis; the idea that this detour to another province is no big deal, just a spontaneous road trip with benefits. It's like a parallel universe here in Bryan's arms, being watched over by her sun-kissed protector, his blue eyes never off her, his smile for her alone. The attention intoxicates her far more than the marijuana. She imagines days of only the two of them, the rest of the world suspended.

"It's tempting."

"Come on, Lottie, what've you got to lose?" He came up with the nickname after their tussle in the armchair and has been teasing her with it ever since. Silly and old-fashioned, it suggests a frivolous girl. Charlotte doesn't mind. This woman she's impersonating could use a new name.

Bryan crushes the last speck of joint into a bottle cap on the night table. "Change your mind along the way and I'll drive you back. Promise. I'll bring you right back here. You can pick up your car and go home and that'll be the end of it."

"What if I don't want to drive with you? What if we're fighting?" She makes a face. "What if you go psycho and start threatening me?"

His laugh rumbles through his chest and into her cheek, which is resting on his ribcage. "Oh, I'm *planning* to threaten you. I've got this pile of demands, very bad demands, and if you don't go along with every one of them I'm dropping you on the Trans-Canada and you can bloody well hitch a lift home." He kisses her hair. It needs washing but she doesn't want to shower, doesn't want to move.

All day long she's felt the lure of the road. What if she did it? Didn't fantasize about it but actually *did* it? Jumped in the truck with this sexy stranger and rode as far as Banff. Said fuck it, made the irresponsible choice, the self-centred choice, for once in her life.

A shiver darts through her, shoulders to toes. She is cold — the sliding door is open to clear the fragrant haze — and also worried about being busted in this non-smoking hotel.

Bryan pulls her close. "Come on, Lottie. Everyone knows you were at that conference. They're not gonna expect you back for a while. You heard the news, only emergency crews allowed through. The way I see it, you got yourself a free pass for a few days. You got nothing holding you back."

A free pass. The idea is candy. And yet —

She can hardly confess that there is a great deal holding her back: that she is not divorced but married, in a high-profile way, to a tech legend who hasn't had a real conversation with her in years; that she's the reluctant mother of a sullen teen who spreads misery wherever she goes; that she's a PR specialist in line for a promotion she should have landed so long ago that she wonders if it'll ever come through.

What if things really were different? She glances at her naked ring finger. She's masquerading as a divorced and childless woman — what if, for a few days, it were true? What if she had no Tayne, no Sidney, just herself and a life of her own making?

The idea caresses her, fills her with excitement and fear in equal measure.

You are the most self-centred creature, Mother would say.

"A free pass, Lottie. You think about it."

Bryan untangles himself from the sheets and pads into the bathroom. As a long stream unleashes in there, Charlotte surveys the disorder. Usually she'd feel compelled to straighten the sheets, fold the cast-off clothes, and pick up her handbag, which fell to the floor earlier as they rocked in the armchair. Not now.

A free pass.

The Birkin bag lies on its side on the ugly beige carpet. To anyone in the know, the accessory announces that she's an extraordinarily wealthy woman. Except that it lies. The Pettigrew money is gone, every penny. She will get it all back plus interest, Tayne keeps saying, but she knows better. Her so-called investment is lost to her. She still has her salary at Diamond & Day, and her trust fund, which is hers alone, protectively swaddled in the complex paperwork it arrived in on her twenty-fifth birthday, but these modest assets aside, Charlotte is for the first time without serious capital.

For the first time this realization, rather than panicking her, unburdens her.

TWELVE

∧

Everywhere there were people.

Unsecured cabinets pitched forward, monitors shot off desktops, windows imploded, dishes sailed. Everywhere there was glass. And everywhere, in the path of falling objects, underneath all the fragments, were people.

Parking garages caved in, masonry buildings juddered into piles, day-care ceilings collapsed, construction equipment tipped. Pinned beneath it all, people.

In homes and on sidewalks they lay, inside crashed buses, behind dumpsters, on massage tables and under car hoists, in bubble-tea shops, old age homes, alleyways, school portables, emergency rooms, jewellery shops, chem labs, in the path of all destruction, in all the broken places, trapped, dead, in pain, terrified, crammed together, desperately alone.

The earth had moved; nature had struck. Yet who could fault nature for following its laws? What happened was cyclical, foreordained, a matter of time and force, an event as unstoppable, as inevitable, as sunrise. And the price was paid by people.

∧

GINGERLY, BREATH HELD, Kyle reaches down his right leg to the exposed stretch between where his shorts stop and the ottoman-sized boulder starts. Touches the skin with trembling fingers. It is cold and waxy.

It's going to be bad. Fractured for sure. In how many places? Closed fracture or open?

Calling 911 is warranted now. He needs help and he needs it soon. He rummages in his flattened-out backpack, on the ground where he laid it, hoping mightily that his phone has survived the crush against the rock. His stomach falls when he sees the screen, a starburst of cracks, but when he thumbs it on, thank God, the phone works.

He touches the numbers, waits. Waits some more.

Something, anything. *Please.*

There is only silence.

He tries again. Nothing.

On your own, pussy.

With a wallop, the graveness of his situation hits home. He slumps back against the rock, his spine protesting. Fight the shock, he tells himself. Concentrate.

What about Joe? Last night —

No.

Kyle swallows. His throat is dry but he can't be bothered to fish a water bottle out of his pack.

There is so much to do. He has to roll the boulder off his leg, assess what kind of break he's dealing with, set the bone, then splint it, then ...

Exhaustion takes over. The treeline down the hill blurs, and he can no longer see the boulder on his leg. Can't see, can't feel ... numb.

It can't go on like this, he's known it for months. Finally, this morning, he said it out loud. To Joe.

This morning. When the world was itself. When he walked on two legs.

He goes under.

∿

"Joe?" says Sidney, turning back to the house. "I'm going in. Meet you in the downstairs bathroom, okay? I'll get the gauze."

"Okay." Joe gives the terrier a final pat, stands up, rubs his doggy hands on the front of his thighs.

Fifty.

The old lady was right. He *is* stupid. It's so obvious. It explains everything about the Chill — Kiki so distant and moody, hardly speaking to him anymore, never touching him; the little blue pills Kiki's been hiding in his shaving kit; the awful fight this morning, where for every word Kiki spoke, whole sentences waited unsaid.

I'm living a lie.

In Kiki's eyes Joe must be — what? — some kind of aging relative, some old guy kicking around the place, a baggy old cardigan you wore everywhere until it started to unravel at the seams.

The little dog, who has lapped up every drop of water Joe gave him, twists his head, devoted eyes fastened on his provider. Joe is surprised by how it moves him.

He bends over again and scratches the warm spot behind the dog's pointy ears. Maybe he should go ahead and do it, get a pup of his own and see what happens. Kiki's home so little as it is. How long before he'd even notice? And if he keeps pulling away, if he means what he said this morning — *I can't do this* — if . . .

Oh God, what if he ends it?

Joe can't think beyond this. Can't imagine a future without Kiki after all this time. Can't bear the idea of being fifty and, dog or no dog, living without his one true love.

"Who's a good boy?" Joe bends closer. His eyes shine as wet as the terrier's. "Eh? Who is? Who's the best boy?"

$$\sim$$

When did it begin, this needling suspicion that his wife is up to something? She's so remote these days, so easily riled. Is it because Sidney's back home? For reasons Stedman can't fathom, Charlotte seemed happier with their daughter in rehab. Or is it the money? Her sudden demand to be repaid took Stedman by surprise the other day. Charlotte knows her inheritance is safe. GlobalTech stock is at a historic high, which is why he is poised to sell.

Try as he might, Stedman can't pinpoint when his wife began to drift. What he can recall, as keenly as if it were yesterday and not twenty-five years ago, is the first time, in university, he gazed on Charlotte Pettigrew's milky skin, perfect posture, and thoroughbred poise, fruitlessly disguised by dirty hair and Doc Martens, and knew he had to have her. She was beyond compare. Flawless appearance, fine mind, unquestionable lineage, and the right amount of spark to keep things lively. And the money. Of course, there was the money.

But her wealth was a bonus; it was never the real reason he wanted her.

He recalls how his throat tightened at the sight of her, how his limbs flooded with certainty. She was the one. The famous Stedman intuition was at work even then, a quarter of a century ago. He recalls the inevitability of it, the jolt of confidence and lust and acquisition, as plainly as he recalls the morning several years ago when he gazed at her, in the kitchen of this very house, over the head of a toast-munching younger Sidney, saw his wife's lipsticked mouth purse as she swiped at crumbs from their daughter's plate, and realized he could no longer spend ten minutes in her presence without being vexed by every tic and gesture.

How did it happen, such a monumental dislocation, without his noticing? How did he go from coveting Charlotte so keenly that he plotted every step of their merger — including steps she'll never know about — to at times almost loathing her, and yet through it all needing her so much he cannot let her go?

His spirits plunge. They were low to begin with.

He rests his head, bandaged side up, on the great slab of desk. Quit thinking, he tells himself. *Do* something.

∿

From the maw of Charlotte's Birkin bag, on the dingy motel carpet, peeks a splintered screen. The glass catches the lamplight, a wink of complicity. Her phone.

A free pass.

Bryan is right. As long as her phone is broken no one can reach her, and as long as cell service in Vancouver is jammed or down or whatever is preventing calls, she can't connect with anyone there either. She is officially off the grid.

There's Tim in Toronto, whom she should call from the hotel phone or Bryan's cell. Only it's so easy not to. What are the chances that her husband the oblivious workaholic and her daughter the recovering addict will even remember the so-called family plan, which they discussed exactly one time, years ago? If by some miracle they do, Charlotte can claim that she forgot. Same goes for contacting head office. She was disoriented by the disaster, she'll say, or distracted with worry. She wasn't thinking straight.

A free pass.

Bryan comes out of the bathroom, muscled thighs scissoring gracefully, penis swinging heavily enough to suggest he's getting ideas again. She imagines this scene unfolding in other settings, a motel on the way to Banff, a suite once they're there. A day or two, maybe three. No lists, no planning, no meetings, no work. No mute pyjama-clad husband hugging the far edge of the bed when she crawls in past midnight. No scowling daughter who pretends not to hear her, then tells the Facebook world that her mother is a liar. Days filled with none of that, filled only with pleasure and sleep and talking and touch.

A free pass.

The idea holds her tight, swings her in a dizzying do-si-do, dips her frighteningly deep.

She wants it.

〜

The aftershock is over and Miss Dodie will recover. Anna, however, is in trouble.

If she is to face the accusations against her, the true one about drinking and the false one about stealing money, she needs strength. Just one sip. Then she will find Joe, who has wandered off, and ask him to help settle her lady somewhere more comfortable than the dining room floor, where Miss Dodie lies, uncomplaining but not for long. Then she will square her shoulders against the punishment to come.

The house is quiet, no hum of furnace or appliances to compete with the song of the sideboard, a low, steady tone meant for Anna's ears alone.

She cannot.

Across the dining room, inside the glass-fronted cupboard, the bottles gleam and the crystal decanters beckon. There was an earthquake, they seem to say. This is no time to resist temptation. Just a sip or two and everything will look better.

No. Not possible. Miss Dodie is right here, dazed but awake.

Yet the bottles sing their song, and Anna cannot stop up her ears. From her scalp to her toes, she is rocked by longing.

∧

J.L. HUMPHRIES: Let me reiterate, Summer Rain, how delighted we are that you have agreed to be part of *New York Minute's* ten-year retrospective of the Great Vancouver Earthquake. You are so widely known and respected for such a young woman. Your work is everywhere, and your face is of course instantly recognizable even though it's so – Oh, I'm ... ah – [*Shuffling*] Just a moment.

SUMMER: [*Inaudible*]

J.L. HUMPHRIES: I'm ... Ms. Rain, forgive me. I'm deeply – Let's move on, shall we? [*Clears throat*] One notion that strikes me in researching your work is how vivid and sensory are your representations of that catastrophic time. So many people have, it would seem, blocked certain details. That is to say, they might recollect how they spent the day of the earthquake, and the two or three days afterwards, but their recall is often muddy, lacking in, shall we say, concreteness. You, on the other hand, seem to have retained many details. Is that the, quote, artist's eye, unquote?

SUMMER: I wasn't an artist then. Just a girl.

J.L. HUMPHRIES: Granted, granted. But a talent like yours does not come out of the blue.

SUMMER: Oh?

J.L. HUMPHRIES: I mean, that is to say, you dabbled in art as a girl, did you not? You filled books with pretty drawings, little butterflies and so on?

SUMMER: [*Inaudible*]

J.L. HUMPHRIES: Oh? Well. [*Shuffling*] Fine, fine. So, while you're being so ... so candid about that time, I wonder if you might tell us more about yourself. You are always silent in your performances, yet one has the sense there is something you need to say, something that, perhaps, you are not aware of *having* to say. An untold story. Perhaps about your family?

JESSE STERNE: No questions about the family.

J.L. HUMPHRIES: In other interviews you have mentioned your father, how he was injured in the initial quake, and you have alluded to the tragic outcome. What about, shall we say, your mother? What can you tell us about her?

JESSE STERNE: Next question.

J.L. HUMPHRIES: I ask only in the most general sense, to establish context for our readers.

JESSE STERNE: The mother is not — the family is not part of this interview. We made that clear. Read the terms and conditions, okay?

J.L. HUMPHRIES: Summer, Ms. Rain, when people read your story they will wonder about your mother.

JESSE STERNE: Enough. Drop it or this interview ends —

SUMMER: Love waves.

J.L. HUMPHRIES: I beg your pardon?

JESSE STERNE: Look, you don't have to ... [*Inaudible*]

SUMMER: Love waves. You've heard of them, I presume.

J.L. HUMPHRIES: I don't believe I have.

SUMMER: Really? And you did all that *research*? So ... in an earthquake, the shaking and the damage come from two kinds of waves, body waves and surface waves. Surface waves are waves that move along the surface of the earth. I'm sure you know all about them. Love waves – they're named after the guy who discovered them – they're a type of surface wave. Love waves are special, see? They travel real slow, and horizontal, with this sideways motion, and they're the ones that destroy the most buildings. It's hard to believe because they're so slow, but they can yank a foundation out from under a structure. And then guess what? The whole thing, the whole fucking thing, just collapses. Love waves. Ironic, right? Can you see the irony in that, you pompous asshole?

THIRTEEN

∿

It unfolded and the world watched, the way it watches disasters now, in the age of global media. People in every time zone viewed the devastation on monitors, scrolled through the debris on tablets, sampled the tragedies in blog bites, tweets, and emojis. They forked up steak, folded over pizza, slurped ramen, scooped basmati, crunched celery, and chopsticked dumplings in living rooms and dorm rooms and takeout joints, riveted to iPhones and high-def TVs, drinking ale and sake, tea and Red Bull, checking personal texts and work emails before switching back to the earthquake, flooded with horror, awash in compassion, stuffing money into relief-fund jars and hitting the donate button on GoFundMe pages, stabbed with gratitude because someone else got hit, not them.

∿

THE SOW WAS MASSIVE, and she reigned over her corner of the farm, a stout, confident dowager. One Sunday a month the regional bus carried Anna and her family along the thirty bumpy kilometres that separated the land of steel mills and factories from her uncle's place in the country. Once there, Anna would head straight for the sow, eager to see the animal's flesh-coloured hide stubbly with bristles, her waddle wide and rolling, her eyes as bright and alert as a human's. Despite being surrounded by muck, straw, and stench, and confined to a too-small pen, the pig always struck Anna as cheerful. Every scrap you threw at her she gobbled, her mouth slit into a smile just for you, her food-bearing friend. It was the easiest, most contented relationship Anna had ever had. Her mere presence made another creature happy.

The same lusty noise the sow made as she crunched carrot ends and turnip tops comes from Miss Dodie, propped up on a dining chair, her back to the dining space and all the bad memories there, gnawing a hard green apple.

The woman can barely walk. After Joe stomped out, angered by Miss Dodie's raving, and Stedman and the girl left, sickened by the unsightly knee, Anna concluded it was up to her to move her lady. She braced herself against the dining room table and hoisted for all she was worth while the woman's legs found, then lost, then found their balance. At least Miss Dodie's upper body still works. As they shuffled past the long table, the woman neatly snatched the green apple that had rolled from the fruit bowl, holding it close until she was installed in the chair Anna had readied for her. "Thank you, Annie," she said, polishing the apple against her blouse, smiling as broadly as that contented pig long ago. "I knew you would let me eat this ball."

Anna takes heart. The enthusiastic crunching, surprising in view of Miss Dodie's partial plate and professed distrust of uncooked fruits and vegetables, suggests that underneath the swelling and the bruising she is basically healthy. As she eats, she appears mesmerized by a wind-blown, tree-fringed meadow in dark oils on the floor in front of her, a painting that Anna moved from the rear of the dining room and placed strategically in front of the chair. She did this, at the same time positioning the chair to face away from the dining room, so that Miss Dodie will pay no attention to her.

Stealthily, while Miss Dodie is occupied, Anna glides across the floor, a few steps and a few steps more, until she is there. She turns and checks the rounded shoulders of Miss Dodie, who is still chewing and staring down at the painting. Her lady will not see her now; the woman lacks the mobility to twist around.

Inside the glass-fronted cupboard, the magic bottles wait. She must do this fast, and silently.

She reaches for the door, the burn already in her throat, and pulls. Nothing happens.

No! It cannot be locked! Yet that explains why the bottles did not fall out during the shaking.

Anna stifles a sob. She cannot stand it. She is so tired, so alone. She must have a drink.

In the small bevelled mirror set between the glassed-in cupboards, a glimpse of motion. Anna freezes. Not Miss Dodie. The woman cannot walk. Who? Wildly she tries to concoct an explanation for why she is standing here, at the liquor cabinet, instead of tending her injured employer. Then she realizes: it is her own image staring back at her, her own face made foreign by the new haircut.

Slava bogu. She tells her pulse to slow.

Was it really this morning that she sat in the young stylist's chair? What was her name? Like a tiny bridge. Was it this morning she saw herself in the mirror and thought, *so it is possible I am not hideous always*, this morning that Miss Dodie said she was beautiful? It is more than Anna has ever been told. *Durnukha*, the rebel soldier had growled afterwards, her chin in his filthy rough hand. Ugly woman. Confirming what she already knew, that she is a zero, a blank that does not register on any scale.

Not even a full day, just part of a day. A few hours, a few minutes, one second, and your whole world can change.

The thrum begins to build, a distant train approaching. It came so close to mowing her down earlier, when the others were here, inflamed as she was with guilt and shame.

"Miss Dodie!" she calls. "I make noise for one minute. Do not be afraid. I clean away the bad mess." She grasps the cupboard's handle with both hands, braces herself, and yanks. Again. The sideboard shudders violently enough to knock glass against glass, and like that, the lock pops.

Zatknis, he had muttered, shut up. Then clapped his hand over her mouth, making the instruction redundant.

"Annie? Is that you?"

"Is fine, my lady. Do not worry. I finish soon."

The train gathers speed. She grabs the first clear liquid she touches. Please let it be vodka. Unscrews the cap, tips it up, wets her lips and tongue. *Da.* No cheap firewater either. It is sweet, premium stuff.

But it was only a taste, too small to count as a sip. After so much upheaval she is owed a true sip.

She tilts the bottle and swallows deep and her insides flare as bright and hot as if she has flipped a switch and all that is good and true and fiery is entering her, and she is letting it in, way in. As she gulps, the train-like thrum forms a word. *Blood.* The syllable pulses in her head, its own insistent heartbeat.

She will not count the swallows. The drink will not be over until she takes her mouth away. As long as her lips stay on the bottle, it is a single sip. That is fair.

There was blood.

She stops only when she needs to breathe. Eyes the bottle, a brand she does not know. Licks the neck, tonguing a stray drop. It does not count.

It was not Anna's first time, that afternoon in September in the leafy park. She had had men before, five men who made her acquaintance in bars back when she could still stop at tipsy.

But there was blood. Blood and then —

She places the vodka bottle exactly where she found it so that no one will notice it has been disturbed. It is unnecessary when every item in the house has shifted and nothing is where it is supposed to be, but it is the habit of a practised sneak.

She went to the bars on Fridays, with two girls from work. She had been offered her mother's old factory job and was earning enough to keep the apartment and pay the bills. In those days she permitted herself vodka at home on alternate evenings only, but on Fridays there was no limit; she drank as she pleased with whomever she pleased. She did not have easy times, but on Fridays she had less lonely ones.

Already the vodka's taste has vanished, its heat dissipated. Gone too soon.

One more sip, then. Under these extraordinary circumstances she is allowed one more, to help her focus, to make her a better helper to Miss Dodie. To make her better.

She snatches the bottle fast, even though Miss Dodie is still in her own world, doggedly crunching. As Anna swallows, she shuts her eyes. The fire spreads through her, dissolving the fear and guilt and thoughts of blood. Smoothes comforting fingers along her forehead and down her spine and into her toes, fingers of heat that massage her gently until suddenly they grip her, dig into her arm, pull the bottle away so abruptly that she chokes —

Her eyes fly open. She is not alone in the mirror.

"*Nyet!*" she shrieks, sputtering and choking.

"Annie? Annie, what is it?" Miss Dodie calls.

She cannot answer. It is all she can do to breathe.

There is so much in this world Anna does not understand, a fact that has declared itself on many occasions. When one Sunday she saw the contented, smiling sow hanging from her uncle's barn door, upside down, cut open, dripping blood into a bucket for headcheese, the staple of their afternoon sandwiches. When years later her purse contained a single ten-dollar bill and the word *nurse* was accepted by Miss Dodie, who forgot to ask for papers or references. When the soldier pulled himself off her and rolled to his side, on top of her art tee-shirt, the sight of which must have re-inflamed him because he rolled back, inhaled deep, and launched a fat, viscous gob onto her cheek. When she stood on the rich man's lawn, beside a mansion she never dreamed of entering, and felt this unfathomable earth jolt, pitching off its very axis.

Joe speaks for her. "It's fine, Miss Dodie. Anna is fine."

So much she does not understand, but this she knows for sure: she is done for.

Fog has dulled the usually dextrous mind of Doctor Kyle Jespersen. When he comes to, still sprawled against the rock-throne that has propped him up for — how long? — he leaves an ominous, sweat-inducing dream, something about thunder and a dog, spooked, tearing at its own flesh, in exchange for a far worse nightmare: the boulder field, echoing and bleak; the tall evergreens below closing rank, dark and impenetrable now that clouds choke out the light; and for miles in every direction nothingness, no one, only the occasional whine of far-off planes and helicopters.

He shakes off the black images as best he can.

He will get out of here. Will crawl down the mountain if he has to. Will do whatever it takes.

His right leg is on fire. How the hell did he sleep through that?

He forces himself to look. What he sees is no dream. The leg is appalling, scraped and gouged by the rough boulder, purplish and black and grotesquely swollen, the ankle barely distinguishable as a joint. The saving grace is that the breaks, at least two tibial fractures from what he can tell, are closed. No gaping wounds to contend with on top of everything else. The blood, and there's more of it than he'd have thought, is mostly superficial.

Doctor Jespersen's field requires precise surgical handiwork, and even among his overachieving peers he is renowned for his perfection-ism. This so-called procedure, however, is a botched job in all respects. He hasn't set a major bone since the sleepless shifts of his residency twenty years ago in London, Ontario. Then he paid little attention to such routine interventions, certain that the scattershot life of the family physician or emergency doctor, knowing a little about every-thing, heart attacks to stitches, measles to menopause, was not for him. He wanted depth, not breadth; he longed to immerse himself in one area and master its every intricacy.

He is out of practice but has done his best with what's at hand. He has no medical storage closet, or basic supplies, or even – thanks to his bone-headed decision to travel ultralight – the baggie full of bandages and antibacterial ointment he'd normally pack for a full-day hike. The meagre contents of his backpack are all he's had to work with, which in terms of useful items for setting a crushed leg have yielded exactly nothing.

Then there's the small matter of his brain. It's a mess of crossed circuitry up there. Whole sections have grown slippery, unwilling to reconnect and transmit, making an already difficult task nearly impossible.

Shortly after he pushed the boulder off his leg, a herculean feat given his fatigue and the poor leverage of a seated position, he spied at the bottom of the rock field some thirty feet away a straight branch two and a half feet long, a couple inches around, clear of needles at one end. Thirty feet away. Nothing. A tiny distance that equals a marathon of agony when you're dragging yourself around and between and over rocks, your left knee tender and fluid-filled, your right leg a useless, pulverized encumbrance that zaps you with volts of torment for every inch you gain. By the time he finally grasped the branch, the bracing scent of pitch tickling his nose, sweat had soaked the band of his cap and pooled at the base of his spine. He savoured a moment of pure gratitude. Then swore out loud. The backpack! He'd left it behind at the boulder, thinking only that his crawl downhill would go easier if he was unburdened. Now – God, it was too much to bear! – he would have to retrace the same torturous ground, the broken leg jolting and the good leg – the one with the softball knee – panging, both arms trembling from exhaustion, this time uphill, *and* dragging the branch with him. Only to come back down again to where the trail enters the woods.

Weak-ass pussy. You deserve it.

He cried then, much as he hates to admit it. It caved him in, the unfairness of it all, the unrelenting pain, his sheer brainlessness. As he wept a raven joined in, its mournful caw echoing off the boulders.

Calm down, Kiki.

That was a different voice, and it steadied him slightly to hear Joe's name for him. No one else uses it; in fact, hardly anyone knows about it. The endearment mostly embarrasses Kyle – *it's girly, like I should be wearing a kimono*, he told Joe once – so he has insisted they keep the name to themselves.

Joe pouted at first. "You ashamed of us or something?"

Kyle laughed and said no, but the truth is he was uptight about a lot of things when they first met: holding hands in public, kissing in front of their families, even grocery shopping together. Joe was his first serious boyfriend. No one Kyle had hooked up with before had ever accompanied him into daily life. It's impossible to have a relationship, he'd told himself, when you're a student until age thirty and work all the day's hours after that.

"It's like being with a straight guy," Joe would say. "Like you're in the closet. Is Kiki ever coming out to play?"

Kyle is not ashamed of being gay. Granted, he has never advertised the fact — he's not that fag who wears feathers and makeup and sashays down Davie in the Pride Parade — but he doesn't hide it either. Any reticence he feels has less to do with being beside a man than with being half of a couple. It's unsettling how easily some people give themselves over to a lover. He has toiled all his life to become successful and accepted — as a boy, a student, a doctor — so to exchange being a complete version of himself for being half of something else feels wrong, unnatural. Who would gain from it? He could never love or respect a diminished facsimile of himself. Nor, surely, could Joe.

No one will respect you after last night.

No. Not now.

Kyle lay on the hard ground, readying himself for the anguishing push uphill to his pack. The raven's cry disappeared into the mountains. Make the first move, he told himself. Do it.

He lay on his stomach, head resting on one arm, willing himself to go.

What is with you?

It was a rhetorical question, he realized. Concussion. He's got all the signs. After another minute or two, he clenched his teeth and set off.

Now, an hour and a half later — no, an hour and twenty-one minutes; he must not lose track of time, must not forget how to *tell* time — he has bellied his way back to the boulder and has, with the clumsy hands of a thick-headed oaf, not the trained fingers of a fine surgeon, cleared the branch of its remaining branchlets using his old pocket knife, which he has sharpened — *ha, ha!* he actually barked out loud, startling a bird into sudden flight — precisely never. The next bit is unclear, the pain so agonizing that it overrode the details, but he did what he could to position and set the leg, the grinding of bone on bone beneath his own skin nearly severing his last attachment to consciousness. Then he lashed the branch, from his foot to just below his hip — *good thing you can reach your own ankle; that personal trainer helped you in so many ways* — using the nylon side straps and front straps of his backpack, which he'd sawed off with the rapidly dulling knife. To think he'd once cursed those straps, extra tie-downs that he never made use of on his day hikes.

Once the leg was as secure as he could make it, strapped in four places, one of his spare wool socks tucked around the knee to fill the gap between it and the splint, he let himself sleep. He vowed as he went under to keep it short. Not for any medical reason — sleep would only heal his brain — but because it was already past three thirty and he couldn't waste the remaining daylight. He still needed to locate a second branch for the other half of the splint, attach it, then find a walking stick to support his weight, then get to water … and then, finally, start.

Now it's nearly four o'clock. Awake but groggy, he inventories his supplies a final time before setting out.

Tube of sunscreen.

Right, because it's all about the skin.

Phone, still at sixty-two percent. Excellent.

Useless. Even 911 doesn't work.

An extra sock, which he'll use for padding once the second branch of the splint is attached.

How long's it going to take you to find a decent branch? Then you've got to hack the needles off. And undo the straps you just tied and attach the new branch and redo all the lashing.

Headlamp, thank God. He can't do without that. It'll be dark by nine, earlier under the dense tree cover.

When did you last change the batteries? Around the time you sharpened your knife?

The pocket knife, now so dull it could double as a spoon.

Great, if you had anything to eat with a spoon.

To eat: two power bars and half a package of beef jerky.

Look ma, no utensils necessary!

Finally, water, the most essential supply. He has two half-litre plastic bottles. One is empty, the other half full. He can keep both filled at the creeks he'll pass on his way down the mountain.

Creeks? You stupid-ass moron.

Oh, God. He covers his mouth with one pitch-sticky hand. Creeks.

On the hike up he paralleled a couple of midsized streams and crossed several more, leaping nimbly from rock to rock to avoid dunking a foot in the shallow, fast-moving water. There's also a long stretch of trail that's a creek bed, mostly dry but choked with rocks – big, small, the ones near water slick with moss, some tippy and treacherous.

He will never get through that creek bed. Not in a million years. *You are fucked.*

What was he thinking? It must be the concussion, enemy of rational thought. There is no way – *no way* – he can do it. Inch down a long, steep, uneven trail on one leg, with darkness falling. Cross creeks and haul himself over boulders, his broken leg – what? – just bumping along. Sure, no problem. With minimal food and water. In nonstop agony.

He will never, ever make it down. He is going to die here, alone, in a field of stones.

Heart racing, he fights for air. It's all around him, but he can't get enough. Panic grips his throat.

Joe. Joe will come.

Of course!

He sits up, fumbles his cell phone from his backpack, hits Joe's number. Nothing. Checks for new texts. None. Rereads Joe's message from earlier today: *Shook up but ok. Hope ur2.*

Joe's not hurt. He will come. Kyle thumbs a hurried text: *Below Eagle Bluffs. Broken leg. Come help.* Hits send. It may not go through right away, but eventually it will and Joe will come.

Meanwhile he calls 911 again. Then Joe again. Then the clinic. Answer, someone!

Silence.

Tries Joe once more.

He's not hurt.

Prays for Joe's ancient flip phone to ring. Please!

Silence.

Silence.

It comes on him, a vast, yawning emptiness, black as the barren boulder slope, as the shadowy forest below, as the rocky trail that spools down and down into nothingness. Nothingness, and no one. No one is coming. Not Joe, not anyone.

Joe's not hurt. But you hurt him.

Last night. Oh God. The vestiges of hysteria push at Kyle's skull, where nothing is working right.

Last night, it was —

Admit it, you pussy.

No. It's so wrong.

It didn't seem wrong.

Because of the coke.

The coke is new. New*ish.* Kyle has always steered clear of drugs, aware of the stats. No way will he be that doctor, the one who succumbs to pressure and easy access and becomes a full-blown high-functioning junkie before mid-career. Drugs are for the weak. He is not weak.

You are so. Weak-ass faggot. And you're addicted. Just not to drugs.

First it was the legs. That sleepy-eyed American had long, lean legs, clad tight in faded Levi's. Big silver belt buckle, riding low, made you wonder what he was packing down there. Long torso too. Cowboy hat, swagger — God, he had it all, that guy. Made Kyle's saliva run. Doing him was a no-brainer. But doing him like that — it meant turning some kind of corner.

You turned a corner all right. Took a lot of people with you.

The thing is, he didn't give a fuck who saw. All he wanted was that lanky piece of ass, and the wanting filled him and swelled him and made him strong, even stronger than the coke, and so he did it, right there at the table, went over and unzipped himself and hauled down the guy's long-legged jeans and sank his face in, one hand grasping the big American's cock while his head worked, the other holding himself, stroking frantically, the American's friends cheering, a crowd gathering, some of them clapping, all for Kyle Jizz-person, still going strong, still young and desirable, no artificial enhancement necessary, uninhibited and wild and totally crazy and — yes. Free. Free. He needed them to see that, needed them to know.

And Joe?

God, Joe.

Because it wasn't just the American's friends who saw. Joe's friends saw. *Their* friends. Dennis and Sy came off the dance floor. Tyler stood over to one side; you couldn't miss his afro. Shane caught Kyle's eye in the bathroom later when he went in for another line of coke.

What he did last night was say a big *fuck you* to Joe. Without speaking a word, he announced that he was a free man, announced it at the biggest club downtown, through a megaphone the shape of a cock.

The tears come again, and this time they may never end.

Oh, Joe.

He is so ashamed. About everything. Even last night, in the midst of the addictive pull of pleasure, shame burned in his face and in his heart. Afterwards the American buttoned himself up and loped off with his friends, all of them hooting and swaggering, and Kyle stood there, as the crowd thinned and his wet face cooled, his wet hands cooled. Ashamed.

For months he has lied to Joe. So many lies. He has looked straight into his lover's brown eyes, offered a nugget of truth (*I stayed late at the gym*), and withheld key details (*because my trainer gave me a hand job in his car*). Every time, he looks Joe in the eye, and every time, he is blind to the selfishness and lust behind his own gaze —

And the weakness. Weak-ass pussy.

He is blind to the man in front of him, with his good heart and his simple trust.

He loves Joe. He can't get it up for him, and he feels smothered and stuck, and he feels ashamed of his betrayal, but he loves his man.

Liar. Sneaking around, lying to his face. Treating him like a child. That's not love.

Except it is. He loves Joe. It's himself he doesn't love.

Fatigue washes over him, and despair. He will never have the chance to make it right. His body is broken, and his heart, and he is going to die here on the mountain, in the boulders, like a wild animal.

He lets the wave take him, drag him along the ground of consciousness.

Once, after how long he can't say, he is pulled up by the sharp cry of the raven, high in the sky. Then he sinks again. He doesn't fight it, just lets himself go, lets the drawstrings of anguish tighten around him, sealing him off, shutting him down.

∧

The old lady is heavier than you'd think looking at her skinny arms and legs. She must keep a lot of flesh tucked under that polyester blouse, Joe decides, grunting as he manoeuvres Miss Dodie onto her side on the sofa. Between them, he and Anna got the old woman here, and now the nurse is changing her diaper, an intimate operation that's unfolding far closer to him than he would like.

Joe steals a look at Anna. She doesn't seem drunk, though she sure was slugging it back when he found her in the dining room. Sidney, while he changed her bandage in the powder room, had urged him to go help. "She can't move the old lady on her own."

"What about your dad?"

"He's in his *office*. Sitting there at his desk, like he's in some kind of trance."

Great. The big businessman, proving once again that he is completely useless in an emergency.

So Joe went off to help the nurse and ended up scaring the crap out of her. The look she gave him — like a rabbit in a snare.

"Come on, let's get Miss Dodie," he'd said, taking the vodka from her and setting it back in the cabinet. Only a quarter of the bottle was left. Here's hoping it wasn't full when she started.

"But ..." Anna trembled so hard that the loose sleeves of her grey sweatshirt shook.

"What? Let's go."

"No. Please. She cannot know." She hugged herself. "Please do not tell her. She will fire me. I need this job. I need it. I am not allowed to drink."

Joe shrugged. "She's going to smell it."

"No." She fished a piece of gum out of her pocket, then looked straight at him, her eyes wild. "Please, do not tell. I do anything for you." Her gaze slid down his body. "Anything."

He couldn't help it, he laughed. Laughed and slapped his thighs. "No, no, no. For Pete's sake, I won't tell her, okay? I won't tell anyone. But please, no favours."

She flinched.

"No, Anna. You're lovely —"

"*Nyet.*"

"You are, Anna. Lovely. But you're a *woman*." He waited a moment.

Her eyebrows went up. "Oh. *Da.* You are — how you say? — fruit."

"I haven't heard that one in a long time. But yeah, I'm a fruit."

Anna hugged herself tighter. "Joe, I am not good girl. I do bad things. But I am not thief. I do not, I *did* not take money." She holds his gaze. "You must believe."

"I know. Sidney told me."

"The girl? How ...?"

"She says you've been with Miss Dodie the whole time. Since we first came inside the house you've either been with her or near her. You never went upstairs. That's where her dad keeps this money he says is missing."

"Oh. Is true, I do not go upstairs. But then who take his money?"

"Sidney thinks he's confused. He hit his head on the office floor pretty bad, and then he got beaned by something during the aftershock." Joe shakes his head. "So much for the big-brain businessman, eh?"

Anna did an unexpected thing then. She reached for his hand, pressed it between both of hers, and kissed it. "You are good man, Joe. Good and strong and smart. Please, I do need help."

Anna may be a nurse but she's not much of a homecare worker, Joe thinks now as he tries not to watch her clumsy handling of Miss Dodie's diaper. Her technique is nonexistent. Nothing like the stout nurse's aide who helped him that last month with Ma in Newfoundland. Daisy, she was called — laughably, since she was built like a running back, big everywhere, shoulders, hips, smile. Much like Ma, who, never without a cup of sweet tea and a molasses cookie in front of her, had grown so wide in old age that even cancer-ravaged she stayed thick through the middle. Daisy had the build of a heifer but moved like a cat, a graceful, fluid efficiency in every motion. She could flip Ma like a slender fish, sponge her clean all over, adjust her nightgown, and settle her back on the pillows in the time it took Joe to boil the kettle.

Anna is no Daisy, and Miss Dodie is definitely no Ma. Unlike his mother, who didn't waste a word when she was healthy and lost most of her speech at the end, Miss Dodie never stops. He barely knows the old woman, yet he's been treated to a boatload of her rambling stories and confident pronouncements, not to mention her strange outbursts. He's sick of the chatter, unlike Anna, who not only tolerates her employer but seems to get a kick out of her, laughing at Miss Dodie's outrageous comments and shrugging off her criticisms. Maybe it's the language barrier. Maybe Anna doesn't understand half of what the old lady's saying.

Still, as irritating as this strange duo may be, it's good to be needed. Joe has checked the house for aftershock damage, gotten the latest news from Vincent, given the dog a drink, changed Sidney's bandage, and helped to move Miss Dodie. His plan was to pitch in with the firefighting along with Vincent and then walk home, orders to shelter in place be damned, but with Stedman holed up in his office and of no help whatsoever, he's decided to stick around long enough to make sure everyone is settled and safe. Not for much longer, though. He has to get home tonight, to wait for Kiki. Or to open up the door to him if Kiki gets there first.

Kiki. The name is a low wail inside. Joe has heard nothing from his lover and has given up trying to call and text. As long as communications are down, he's better off conserving what's left of his phone battery, now at twenty percent with no hope of recharging until the power's on again. Yet he can't bring himself to turn the phone off. What if one time Kiki gets through? Joe badly needs to hear from him. The uncertainty is unbearable.

At last Anna has balled up the old diaper. The smell is dizzying.

"Don't let him see!" Miss Dodie screeches. "Don't let that man see my bottom!"

Anna grins faintly as she sets the wadded-up diaper on the floor. "Is not necessary to worry. He does not like the ladies' bottoms."

"Baloney. They're all the same. They *live* for ladies' bottoms, sniffing around them like dogs in an alley. Believe me, Annie, I know. I had a lifetime of watching it. My husband—" Miss Dodie stops abruptly and cranes her neck, trying to peer over the sofa whose back she is facing. "This is not my bedroom. You can't fool me. Where are we?" Awkwardly, because she's still on her side, she looks over her shoulder at Joe. "Kelvin? Why ever are you wearing that hair today? You look silly. You look like a white man!"

Joe raises his eyebrows at Anna.

"Saint Kelvin, from the Vietnam," she says quietly. "He took care of my lady before." She runs a washcloth over Miss Dodie's puckered privates. "He did all things right." She raises her voice so Miss Dodie can hear. "Not like Anna. Anna does no things right. She works her toes to the bone but she cannot get nothing right." She drops the washcloth to the floor, on top of the soiled diaper, and pulls a fresh one from the large shoulder bag Joe saw her carrying earlier, on the seawalk.

"It is true, you make terrible coffee, and you never feed me. You make me take the pills. I hate them. But you are a sweet girl, Annie. You are good to me." Miss Dodie reaches up and pats the nurse's face, which reddens.

Was it only this morning he first saw these two and lifted a hand to Anna to say hello? Such an ordinary moment it was, the sky painted with high cloud, the air mild, his work at the Stedmans' nearly done, his mind on the next job, a short drive away in Caulfeild, a stunning rock garden that cascades down a bluff from the spare post-and-beam on top. Is that house even there now, just hours later? Has it collapsed and slid down the cliff? Does an earthquake split rock the way Stedman's driveway split, the way highways and bridges, according to Vincent, have cracked and pulled apart?

Kiki was up high when it happened – did the mountain protect him, keep the trees rooted strong, insulate his body from the shaking? Joe knows so little about earthquakes, but common sense says Kiki should be okay up there. It also says that even the strongest mass, if there's enough stress, is going to give.

Joe shuts his eyes. Kiki will be fine. He always knows what to do. He'll be on his way home and soon, hopefully tonight, they'll be side by side on the sofa, feet up on the big ottoman, swapping stories.

Only he's tired of you. He doesn't even pay attention to you anymore.

The truth hits like an uppercut and pushes out a soft grunt. "You okay?" Anna asks. "Need to rest?"

Joe shakes his head. He's still supporting Miss Dodie's shoulder to keep her on her side, buttocks out, face turned into the sofa back.

"Sniff, sniff, sniff, sniff." Miss Dodie addresses the sofa in a quiet sing-song. "Always sniffing at them. He wasn't even interested at first. I had to throw myself at him. I had to practically open my legs and shove it in!" She looks up at Joe and waggles her left hand back and forth. "He gave me this ring, you know." She holds her hand up for him to admire, but the ring finger is bare. He says nothing. They were searching for a ring this morning when they came onto Stedman's property.

"He was like an old grannie at first, so prim and proper. But once we did it, he couldn't get enough. Morning, noon, and night. He came home for lunch some days, can you imagine that? Lunch!" She cackles. "He wanted to eat all right, but not lunch. He wore me out. I couldn't keep up. Then, just like that, he was done with me and he started in on the rest of them. Sniffing their bottoms and their you-know-whats. Like a dog, always going at the other dogs. Sniff, sniff, sniff."

Joe is surprised to see her eyes glisten. "He said he loved me, but I knew what was happening. I was never enough. He needed all those other dogs." She gazes at Joe. "*You* know, don't you?"

He holds his breath.

"Sniff, sniff," she says. "As if I didn't know."

He knows. Of course he knows.

His stomach falls.

Kiki is young, fit, energetic. Still got the juice flowing through him. It's only Joe who's old, and it's only Joe he's tired of. Not all the other dogs.

Anna must sense something, because she speaks over Miss Dodie's head. "Do not listen to her. All the time she talks this way."

Her gaze lingers. The old woman has just torpedoed him. Can Anna see the hole?

Oh, he is a fool. He's pictured himself going home, trudging up the steep streets to the townhouse where Kiki may be waiting, has imagined the tearful reunion, the flood of relief and gratitude. Kiki is the only man he's ever loved, their home is the only proper home he's known as an adult, but suddenly it's glaringly obvious.

He's got it all wrong. The truth has been leering at him and he's chosen not to see. How long has it been since Kiki looked at him with anything but annoyance? How long since Kiki truly wanted him? He works backward, trying to find the last time it wasn't him, Joe, who did the wanting, who reached out for closeness.

I'm working late tonight, Kiki always says. *I'll be at the gym until late.* The lamest of excuses. How could Joe fall for them? All those times he's phoned the clinic at twilight, the loneliest part of the evening, and told himself Kiki wasn't picking up because he was immersed in paperwork. All his calls to Kiki's cell that have gone to voicemail. Again and again, Joe has chosen belief over suspicion. It's Kiki, after all. Who loves him.

Love you.

Kiki who is also spending more time away from home, more time at the gym, buying new tee-shirts that cling to his biceps, new pants that hug his thighs. Not for Joe, who sees him naked almost never, who sees him in clothes for maybe ten minutes in the morning if he's lucky, since he's always asleep when Kiki comes home.

Miss Dodie has quieted down, her head motionless against the sofa.

Sniff, sniff, sniff. All those other dogs.

The little blue pills. Not for you, you lunk-headed fool.

In his throat rises a dry, awful lump.

He is stupid, just like the old woman said. A stupid boy, slow to learn, afraid to ask questions. A stupid adult, bumbling through life, forgetful, gullible, getting everything a little wrong. He's spent five years with Kiki, five years living so far outside his league that he actually started to think he belonged there. As if. Kyle Jespersen, *Doctor* Jespersen, intelligent and refined and desirable, is done with him, and Joe is an idiot because he swallowed it all, the entire lie. He let himself feel loved and appreciated, imagined himself worthwhile and helpful, when all along he's been what he has always been, a pitiful dunce.

At Anna's signal he releases Miss Dodie's shoulder. The old woman shifts creakily, settles onto her back, and pulls up the woven throw Anna places gently over her.

This untethered old woman, senile, demanding, nuts — all along Joe thought *she* was the fool. It just goes to show. Like with song lyrics, or trying to remember history dates or French verbs or chemical compounds, he got it all wrong.

∿

The snow-cloaked mountains that guard the mighty Fraser River provide the only beauty in this nowhere place, and at ten p.m. they're obliterated by dark. Charlotte's bleak view is of hotel lights and parking lot, the latter stuffed full of vehicles, most of them ugly American models, all of them presumably stranded.

She wraps her linen-cotton blazer tight against the dewy cold. The jacket, which she shrugged on first thing today, is perfect for a morning in the car and an afternoon at the office but will barely register once they're at altitude in the Rockies. If she is going to do this mad thing, exchange her Stedman self, her SUV, and her long list of duties for a few days as carefree, wanton Lottie, she will need clothes.

Not, Lord knows, from here. The sooner she gets out of Hope, with its sparse amenities, fast food, and downmarket accommodations, the better.

Hope. How did such a ruthlessly optimistic name settle on a place like this? The cheery moniker is a false front slapped over a dingy hole.

Tomorrow they can stop in Kamloops and she'll find a Gap or a Zara, maybe a Victoria's Secret if that's not too metropolitan for the BC Interior. Chain stores that are easy on the wallet. Charlotte hates cheap clothes, hates their dangling threads and their factory smell. She has Mother to thank for that, her blue-blood hippie mother who ate wheat berries and yogurt with a century-old Dominick & Haff spoon and donned handmade kidskin boots for the latest protest. She had standards, Mother did, and they did not include garments from a mall. Even though Charlotte concurs, she can endure bargain clothes for a few days, especially when she'll mostly be out of them.

Thank God for that nice bundle of cash in the zipped compartment of her Birkin bag. She'll have to ration it. No credit cards from here on. Whatever story she eventually concocts to explain her whereabouts after the earthquake, there can't be any records to arouse Tayne's suspicion. A few sexy push-up bras and thongs? Well, yes, I needed those while I was waiting for the all-clear. Lucky thing her phone broke at the cheese shop, the last place she was officially supposed to be. From there on, she'll be untraceable.

In spite of the cold night, the thought of lingerie sends summer lightning down her belly and between her legs. Unbelievable, the desire this Australian stranger has unleashed in her. They've had sex three times: once before their afternoon breakfast and twice after. Full-on, multi-position penetration the first two times, then a marathon session in which Bryan proved that, talented as the rest of his body may be, his tongue is the star. Charlotte lost count, knows only that she rose and fell, rose and fell, until there was nothing left to rise. Overused and overheated, she left Bryan curled like a prawn at the bottom of the bed, asleep, and came outside for air.

Sex. She thought she had rediscovered it with Marcus. What a joke.

Now she sees the dull charade she was acting out with him. The real thing has come back to her, the astonishing power of lust, not only its physical sensations but the utter heedlessness of it — plunging in, letting go, taking what she wants, as much as she wants, for the sake of nothing but sheer heady pleasure. She used to be this way all the time, in her old life. Free, adventurous. Unshackled.

Servants shackled to the home — Mother's tossed-off line for women unable to choose when, or whether, to have a child. Charlotte was not one of those. She chose to have Sidney. She chose and got the shackles anyway.

Mother was right to beg her; that was the bitter irony. She barely knew Charlotte, yet somehow she understood that her daughter was no more equipped to nurture a child than she was. Mother was right and Charlotte, in her rash scheme to prove her wrong, made the worst mistake of her life. At least it was a mistake she would never repeat. Following Sidney's second birthday and the two most miserable years of Charlotte's life, Charlotte returned from the procedure — her week at the spa, she told Tayne — determined to buckle down and manage the child she had, and relieved beyond words that, despite her husband's best efforts, there would never be another.

Mother stuck to her convictions. You had to admire that. Her beliefs meant more to her than any sentiment or convention. Despite the obstacles in her path — wealth and entitlement, a husband and a child — Mother clung to her convictions with a steadfastness that ruled out tender moments but also set a formidable example, one Charlotte might have learned from had she been less intent on defying the woman at every turn.

Convictions. Charlotte has a career and a family, and the obligations that go with both. Social status, schedules, and properties. A massive investment in one man and his empire. But convictions? She has done what's expected of her, and what she expects of herself, but none of that, it occurs to her, is the same as what you're compelled to do.

"Penny for your thoughts."

She smiles but doesn't turn. "The moon. Just look at it." Overhead, above the mountain peaks, the clouds have parted to show off a sharp crescent.

Bryan wraps his arms around her from behind and rests his chin on her head. She is enveloped by warmth and the tomcat smell of marijuana. "I don't care about the sky," he murmurs. "I've only got eyes for you."

"God, that's cheesy. Don't try it on your gorgeous young ladies. It only works on the mature ones. The ones starved for compliments."

"Come on, Lottie. You don't need to fish." He tugs a lock of her hair. "You're gorgeous. You know that, right?" He bends close to her ear. "Didn't he tell you that?"

"Who?"

"Your husband. Before you got divorced."

Damn, she keeps forgetting. If she's going to try on another life for a while, like that character who dodged the falling beam, she needs to master the details. She is Lottie the lawyer, an ex-husband, no daughter, no ties.

And convictions? Does she have any of those? Is there anything Lottie believes in?

"You're right, no fishing." She turns around and touches the corner of his mouth. "But maybe fish. I'm starved. Think the restaurant's still open?"

"One way to find out." He keeps one arm around her shoulders as they start back to the hotel. "You've got an appetite, don't you?" He grins.

For a moment, out of habit, she berates herself. She is weak; she has to do better. Then she switches off that soundtrack.

"I do." There's a sharp honesty in admitting to the hunger that gnaws at her — for food, for sex, for adventure. For freedom. And there's something familiar in it. This is the authentic Charlotte, the Charlotte she used to be.

As they near the hotel entrance, she fills her lungs with cool night air. In the morning they will hit the road, first up to Kamloops to shop, then east to Alberta. For a day or two, in this gap left by the earthquake, she will be carefree Lottie, up for a dare, greedy for experience and sensation. The woman she might have been had she not met Tayne.

Bryan's hand slips off her shoulder and brushes one nipple, stiff in the cold air. Sets off more lightning.

"Listen, you. You keep doing that and there won't be any dinner." With one hand she cups his hipbone, the most man part of a man besides the obvious. Feels the joint and sinew shift with each stride.

"And? Would that be so bad? We're free spirits, Lottie. No schedule." Somehow he knows exactly what she needs to hear, this tousled man-boy who appeared out of nowhere. She kisses his nose.

They enter the lobby, which is quiet now that night has come, and pass the so-called business centre, a tiny alcove filled with two ancient computers and a printer. In spite of the laughable equipment, the area has been mobbed with guests looking for news and trying to trace loved ones. Now one of the computers is free.

"Want to try the internet first?" Bryan asks.

For a nanosecond she considers it. Tayne and Sidney? No. She's still pissed at them. Let them wonder. The promotion? She's curious, but in an abstract way.

The warm lobby and the scent of grilled meat wafting from the restaurant draw her in. So she shakes her head. "I checked earlier. My webmail's still down."

"How about Facebook?"

"I saw a few posts from friends back east, but nothing from Vancouver. It's like everything's on pause there."

How effortlessly the words come. This, too, is familiar. The authentic Charlotte was always a great pretender.

∿

Thank God Sidney's out of earshot. At first Stedman was miffed at how fast she left, just delivered the gardener to him in his office as he'd asked, then jogged off without so much as a *Hi, Daddy*. Now, as Joe recounts the gruesome details gathered from the Chinese neighbour, who is apparently alone next door, his wife and daughter back in Hong Kong, Stedman is grateful that his little girl can be spared the updates, however embellished they might be by their unreliable narrator.

The hired man stinks of soil and sweat and, faintly, of shit. Not only is he dirty, and an exaggerator if not out-and-out liar, he is a thief. By the time this encounter is over, Stedman will have his twenty thousand dollars back, every penny of it. He knows this as surely as he knows his own name. But first, because the gardener is the only one who has left the house and knows what's unfolding in the wider world, Stedman will extract all the intel he can, loosening the man's tongue and only afterwards making him empty his pockets.

It's hard to know how much of the outlandish report to believe, but there must be nuggets of truth amid the fairy tales. The city's completely shut down, Joe says. SkyTrain, buses, taxis, ferries, the airport – nothing's running. The train tracks that parallel the Sea to Sky Highway are buried by landslides, the worst of them at Lions Bay, where half the village has slid down the mountain and engulfed the highway and the tracks below. Stedman's eyebrows shoot up at that unlikely image. In Richmond, Joe says, many buildings are off their foundations and the water level's rising. Liquefaction has kicked in – a term Stedman has heard before but doesn't entirely understand – and some of the dikes are breached. Every major highway is closed. Whole sections of road have buckled. All bridges are off-limits, either damaged or closed to traffic until they can be assessed for safety. Local streets are open to emergency vehicles only. No one's allowed to drive. Stedman snorts at this.

"Hey, look. I don't care if you believe me," Joe says. "Those are the orders. The streets have to stay clear. It's the only way crews can get to the fires and start looking through the rubble." He pauses.

"Only there's not a lot of crews. A bunch of firefighters and paramedics can't get to their stations. Too many routes blocked."

Stedman pins Joe with his steely stare, the one that says he means business. "How are you all getting home, then?"

"We're not. At least the women aren't. Like I said, it's official orders. Anyone who's in a safe place has to stay there. But don't worry, I'm leaving. I'm walking home to North Van. It's not that far, a couple of hours."

I bet you're leaving, Stedman thinks. With my money — mine! — in those grubby pockets. But he can't pounce yet. He needs to know more. "What about the North Shore?" Apart from that single early text, Stedman has heard nothing from Marcus or anyone at North Vancouver headquarters. Are his people trapped there? Or have they walked home?

Joe shakes his head. "I don't know. On the CB channels they're mainly talking about downtown. It's total chaos there, glass everywhere, power lines down, gas lines busted. Bodies in the street, people just lying there injured, nowhere to put them. St. Paul's Hospital is gone, it's just a pile of bricks. The brick buildings got it worst. The community centres and churches — they're full and turning everyone away. There's a bunch of people wandering around homeless."

Homeless. Stedman feels a jab of irritation. Just what we need. More deadbeats living on the margins, shooting up and demonstrating, playing bongos in the park instead of earning a proper living.

But what was that about brick buildings? GlobalTech's headquarters, in the east end of North Van, over by the movie studios, occupy a four-storey brick rectangle slapped up in the fifties. Could it be damaged? What about the innovation lab in Burnaby, filled with precision equipment, what's going on there? And the distribution facility out near Deltaport, did it take a hit? And their networks. What if the backup systems failed and they lost work?

He must talk to his people. Only now is it sinking in, the enormity of what may lie ahead. GlobalTech's manufacturing facilities are all overseas, they'll plug along fine for now, but damage to headquarters, and especially the innovation lab, could set the company back big time. They can't afford that, not now.

Merck lost this morning, now their home city rocked — what will the Chinese buyers think? The idea of them backing out and carrying their pots of cash to another tech company, a competitor, sets his bandaged face afire.

Headquarters. He took so much flak over that decision. *Time to move*, Marcus urged him a decade ago, well before the company went public. *We're in the big leagues now and we need an office to match*. But Stedman, ordinarily so fixated on image, felt strangely loyal to the old place. He'd built the business there and had no intention of leaving, so he stood firm. The building's gone through two renos since he bought it, beautified and updated so he can receive visitors in style, but it was never retrofitted to seismic standards. His facilities manager prodded him to get the job done, agreeing it would cost the earth (the guy had laughed at his own pun) but stressing that it was insurance against loss. That argument was doomed to fail, for Stedman does not believe in insurance. Why hand over a bunch of money for nothing when you can invest it in something? This conviction has built him an empire.

But now... Acid reflux from the bitsu-bitsu burns his throat again, and he wills himself not to throw up. If what the gardener says is even partly true, his facilities could need extensive repairs, could maybe be *beyond* repair. And if that is true, he's in deep trouble.

There is no earthquake insurance on any of it. There is none on the house.

He swallows against the oily acid. Focus, he tells himself.

"Here is how it's going to go," he says. "I need to know what's happening at my office. I'm going to turn the power back on. I'm going to recharge my phones and wire up my laptop, see if the ethernet's working."

He will do these things and he will track down Charlotte, and she will know what to do next. Her advice will steady him. He just needs to get online, or to access a working phone. Which services come back first after a disaster, anyhow? He has tried to remember details from earthquakes in other places, like Japan, but he can't. Damn it all, Vancouver is one of those places now, plastered all over the national news — maybe even international, especially if the States got hit. How is he going to sell a huge share of a Vancouver-based company now, to anyone, without taking a gigantic loss?

Joe's hands are on his hips. "You can't turn on the power."

Who is this self-righteous labourer to keep telling him the state of things, what they're going to do and how they're going to do it? In *his* house. "Of course I can," Stedman barks. "You said the lines to the house are still live. They're underground. They're fine." He starts toward the office door, but in two steps feels the gardener's grip on his elbow.

"Hey, did you not hear a word I said? There's broken gas lines everywhere. You've got downed power lines just up the street, which you could see for yourself if you actually bothered to go outside. There's fires, big ones, not under control. Can't you smell the smoke? You switch the power on and this house is like a matchbox. The whole friggin place goes up in a second." Joe steps closer, chin forward like a bulldog. "Come on. You got a fancy education, a big company, you're such a smart guy. Do you need me to explain it all again?"

Arrogant asshole! They're so full of themselves, these guys, with their shop-class wisdom about how to fix leaks and build retaining walls, when to replace a motor and when to repair it, what size screws you need and are they imperial or metric. They scratch their heads and look perplexed. They whip out measuring tapes and pencils like sidearms. They baffle you with jargon: mitres and biscuit joiners, compressors and lathes, Loctite and Tyvek, PVC and MEK. They own that language and they dole it out like misers — not, Stedman knows, out of inarticulateness but out of fear. They are afraid. Afraid that men like him, men of the mind, successful, intelligent men who occupy the penthouses of this world, not the worksheds and the basements, will parse their special language and discover it's based not on complex concepts or intricate procedures but on primitive items like duct tape and pencils and glue, on brainless tasks like twisting and hammering, on techniques that the clean-fingernailed, degree-holding, office-going men of this world could grasp in seconds, and could wield skilfully, if they so chose.

"You stole my money." It comes out a low growl.

Joe smirks. "I didn't steal anything. And neither did Anna, so you leave her alone, okay? No one took your danged money. You hit your head this morning. You're confused."

"Confused? That's a good one, you smug little shit. You know exactly what I'm talking about. I caught you red-handed in my bedroom. Pretending you were there to fill the bathroom sinks. I know exactly what you were up to. Walking around to see what's worth taking. There would've been cash all over the floor."

"There was no cash —"

"Liar! Give it to me!" Stedman lunges.

"Hey!" Joe steps aside just enough to avoid contact. "Listen to me, b'y."

Great, Stedman thinks. *B'y*. A Newfie. He should've known.

"I don't have your money. I don't need your money. I don't even want to get paid for today, okay?" He pokes Stedman in the chest. "You're in your own little world here, with your waterfront house and your *hired men*. You don't see your neighbours, you don't see your daughter, you don't see any of the people around you. I'm a businessman too, get it? Just like you. I own my own company. I own my own house. My partner's a surgeon. We've got loads of money. I don't have to work, I *choose* to work, and I don't want your ... your phoney cyber cash."

"What the hell is that supposed to mean?"

"Lotta good it does you now, eh, b'y? All your big technology, it's totally useless now. *You're* totally useless. You don't know where the shut-offs are in your own house, for Pete's sake. You can't even *understand* the danger we're in."

Stedman casts his bald eagle stare, as Marcus calls it. He will not be ordered around, especially not by a banty little Newfie. "This is my house and I'm turning on the power. And you are getting the fuck out of here."

Again Stedman goes to leave, and again Joe grabs his arm. The gardener is small but surprisingly strong.

"Hey. I can't *wait* to get out of here. You're all a bunch of friggin loony-tunes. But you are not turning the power on. It's not just about you, okay? You've got two women stuck here for the night at least, maybe longer. Even if you don't give a shit about them, what about your daughter? Don't tell me you'd put her life in danger just so's you can stay *connected*." He breathes the word in Stedman's face.

"You fucking asshole." Stedman's chest fills. "You are a liar and a thief, and my daughter is no concern of yours."

"Well, it seems she is. Who took care of her this morning, eh? Cleaned up her cut and wrapped up her hand?" Joe smiles at him, an awful smile. "It wasn't you, the big tycoon, was it? It was me. You may's well not have been here for all the good you did her. Your own daughter and you didn't even show up."

"You prick!" Stedman cannot hold it in. "You arrogant little prick! Don't you dare tell me anything about my daughter! This is *my* house and she is *my* daughter. You don't know the first thing about her. She's a girl, a child." Suddenly he draws back. "Oh, Jesus. No. You sick pervert. You stay away from her, you hear me? I don't want you even looking at her!"

The gardener chuckles — laughs! His eyes are twinkling. "You really got no idea. None at all."

The sick fuck! Rage explodes in Stedman, an aftershock as staggering as any other.

"Maybe if you weren't so busy trying to *connect* with people out there" — Joe waves at the window — "you'd see what's going on right here, in front of your nose."

Not since his Hamilton boyhood has Stedman struck another person. He swore, as an adult, that he would never be like his father, would never let the anger loose. But he is a man of action, and it feels right to be here, it feels good to be on the brink, the last number clicking smartly into place before the lock springs open. He balls his fingers and raises his arm and before he knows it his fist lands, sharp knuckles against soft cheek. Joe's head snaps back.

Then knuckles against spongy nose. Knuckles against hard chin. Joe is down.

Stedman kneels on the cherry floor, his hard, beautiful floor, the one Charlotte laughed at, Charlotte so beautiful and so hard, and his chest is molten hot, a blast furnace — *His own daughter! Under his own roof!* — and it is knuckles against solid gut and knuckles against softer side and his hand is screaming so he switches to the other fist and all he can do is hit and hit and hit.

"Daddy!"

Sidney pulls at his shoulders, then claws at him.

"Daddy, stop it! You're hurting him!"

"He" — punch — "hurt" — punch — "you!"

"Daddy!" She is sobbing. "He never hurt me, he helped me. Joe!" She throws herself on the floor, tries with her body to intercept Stedman's punches, which land weak now, and weaker.

Stedman falls back, panting. Dammit he's tired, but it feels good. He has done the right thing. He has protected his daughter. "He was going to hurt you, Sidney. He wanted to. He's a pervert!"

"What are you talking about?"

"Oh, God. Never mind. It's okay, Sweetpea. You're okay now."

Joe is curled up on the floor, knees to chin, not moving. Stedman is exhausted.

What would Charlotte make of this?

Sidney, still crouched beside Joe, looks over at him. She is so young. So fragile. He did the right thing. He did what a man has to.

He is so tired. He's got to get a hold of himself, has to search the gardener while he's still out cold, has to get his money back.

Sidney's cheeks are stained with Joe's blood; snot shines under her nose. "Daddy, how could you hurt him? Joe looked after me. He's the only one who did." She bends over the gardener and strokes his curly hair. "He looked after us all."

Stedman reaches over to pull her arm away. "Don't touch him, honey. He's a dirty old man, he's disgusting. But he won't hurt you now." Thank God nothing happened. How could he have left Sidney alone with this criminal?

What will Charlotte think? Where is she?

"Daddy!" Sidney looks beseechingly at her father. "How can you say that? Joe would never hurt me. He doesn't even like girls."

Sidney is safe. Charlotte is safe too. Somewhere out there. Why hasn't she been in touch with them? There's something wrong about that, something —

"Daddy, are you even listening to me?"

She doesn't want to be in touch. Like that, he knows. It's irrational, but true.

"Daddy, do you hear what I'm saying? He's gay! For God's sake, he's gay."

She's not coming back. Never. He has lost her.

⌒

NPR MORNING EDITION: That was performance artist Summer Rain, whose new show *Metanoia* has its American debut tomorrow before a sold-out crowd here in Chicago, at the Center for Performing Arts.

Next up, we'll hear from Johns Hopkins researcher Dr. Joanne Mayvin, whose task force on universal health care has stirred up fresh debate in Congress.

[*Extro music*]

NPR MORNING EDITION: And — we're off the air. Summer, thanks for coming in to the studio. It was a pleasure to finally meet you.

SUMMER: Uh-huh. Whatever.

NPR MORNING EDITION: Don't worry, it'll be fine. Those parts that trailed off, we'll cut them for the podcast. It'll sound great.

SUMMER: Trailed off? [*Laughs*] Yeah, right —

JESSE STERNE: Listen, thank you so much. You and all your staff.

SUMMER: Jesus Christ, Jesse. [*Inaudible*] ... kissing ass. It's not like we had a choice.

JESSE STERNE: Truly, it was a pleasure. We really admire what you do here at NPR.

SUMMER: Like anyone gives a shit. [*Loud rustling*] Let me go! Quit, like, *handling* me! Let me just do the stupid show tonight and then I want out of this fucking city. It's just — I can't stand it anymore, you know? Lying, pretending. It's all bullshit. It's America, for fuck's sake! A bunch of greedy capitalists who don't give a shit about anyone else, going around with their guns and their money when kids are starving and ordinary people are dying of, like, infections because they can't afford a doctor. It's obscene. How can anyone live here? How could she ever want to live here?

JESSE STERNE: Summer! Please, stop. I'm so sorry —

SUMMER: And this coffee. What the fuck? It's like they never heard of organic or fair trade or —

[*Smash*]

JESSE STERNE: I'm so sorry. Look, we'll replace the mug, send me an email, we'll take care of everything. I have no idea — She's just, she hasn't slept, the time change and all. And on the way over, she thought she saw someone she knew. It upset her. Let me ... [*Inaudible*]

PART FOUR

Deformation

YOU CARRY THE BOWL EVERYWHERE, ready to helmet your head, because just when it seems the earth has settled and you can trust it again, the shaking starts. The aftershocks are mostly weak now, and over fast. But two are big. Not like the main quake, or the first massive echo an hour and a half later, but scary.

For the first big one you're awake. An hour earlier you'd brought out food, fancy stuff from the kitchen meant for another boring dinner party. You tried to eat with the others but you couldn't, because you're afraid — because God, you came close, so close you could taste it, so close the burn spread through your stomach and your brain — and now you're afraid to put anything in your mouth. You need a meeting. You need to sit in some cool church basement with watery hot chocolate and people who know.

When will life go back to normal?

You're afraid, too, of him. Your father has turned into a stranger, like some kind of psycho. He beat up Joe. He hurt him bad. You can't bear to think what might have happened if you hadn't come along. Your father was an animal, his eyes barely saw you. How could he do that? Since then he has shut himself up in his bedroom. He won't come out, and when you talk to him through the door it's like he doesn't hear you. He says it'll be okay, he just needs some time, his head's fuzzy. You don't believe him. He runs a huge company, he tells people what to do all day. Now it's like he's checked out.

The finger food you set out reminded you of May. Where was she while you were putting the food she had bought onto plates? She took the cats to the vet. Was she still there when the earthquake came, or was she running errands, or on her way home? What about the cats? Do they have food? Are they all together in the Smart car, May and Jasper and Mittens, waiting to be rescued? You worry about them. You worry about Uncle Tim, who'll have heard the news and will be upset because you haven't called. You worry about Anna, the sad nurse, who doesn't see that drinking will only make her sadder. And you worry about Joe, gentle Joe, who's still groggy and has blood on him even though Anna cleaned him up the best she could. How bad is he hurt? You don't really know. Bad enough that he couldn't walk home and had to spend the night. Anna helped you blow up the air mattress, the one your parents used for guests in the old house, and Joe slept on it, in the ocean-facing great room, with the women. You didn't want him sleeping upstairs. You didn't want him anywhere near your savage father.

The one person you don't worry about is her, out there in the Valley somewhere. May's phone, which fell off the kitchen counter but didn't smash, still has some battery left, so you try now and again to call, but nothing gets through. It doesn't matter. You know she's fine. She's always fine. Nothing touches her. It's like she has a built-in metal bowl.

For the second big aftershock you're asleep. You went to bed so jittery you thought you'd never drift off, but as soon as you crawled under the duvet and hugged the velvet whale, you went under. Next thing you know it's the middle of the night and the bed is shaking and all around you stuff is rattling.

You put the bowl on your head even though you probably don't need to. Everything that can smash has smashed. What could be left to hurt you now?

FOURTEEN

∿

People thirsted to understand this act of nature, which struck them, in its manifestation, as unnatural. How was it possible? How could a creeping accumulation of tiny, undetectable forces result in such cataclysmic change?

Art could have explained it, or psychology. Instead, many turned to the hard sciences.

"Stress is a force that affects an object, and strain is how the object responds to it," was one geologist's description online. "Strain is not a force, but a deformation. Everything in the world – everything in the universe – deforms when subjected to stress, from the vaguest cloud of gas to the most rigid diamond."

∿

IN HER THIRTY-TWO YEARS on earth, Anna has slumbered through many an unquiet night. With churning, belching factories for neighbours, she learned early to tune out noise. She could drop off during almost any ruckus, in the middle of a crowd or with the TV blaring. Until she was thirteen and Bohdan moved to Odessa – supposedly to find a job but really, given her brother's lack of skills in all areas, to escape the grimy box they called home – she slept in the cramped, poorly insulated sunporch that tilted perilously over the street below. She was a stork, she told herself, her country's national bird, nesting high and free above the noisy city, and then went to sleep.

On buses and trains she has slept. Under forest canopies. In the back stairwell of a shiny, many-domed church in Kharkiv. In the undergrowth of a Kiev park, once she could no longer show her face. Back home, in Ukraine, she always slept. Every night but one. *Soldaty.* The night of the soldier.

Here in Canada, where nights are comfortable, safe, and noiseless, she cannot sleep. Here the inner din keeps her awake. She lies in her narrow bed, thoughts assaulting her. The evening flask used to help, but even it lets her down now. On nights like last night, an interminable stretch of hours made worse by the aftershocks, strange surroundings, and smoky, chemical air, drinking barely slows the mental onslaught let alone stops it.

That night, the night of the soldier, her mind didn't race. It stopped. She crossed the park. Found a clump of bushes. Cleared a hollow inside and crouched there, knees to her chest, thoughts switched off. Silent, staring, numb, cold, she waited for dawn light to filter through the late-season leaves that hid her.

This morning similar rays push through the glass of her new prison, the waterfront mansion in West Vancouver, and a familiar wretchedness spreads from the pit of her stomach to her heavy, grainy eyelids. On her tongue the sour taste of wine, too much wine.

She glances at her Timex. Only three hours since she finally drifted off, after twice that long spent turning and twisting on the sofa. Throughout the night Miss Dodie's snores from the other sofa alternated between soft and rasping. Joe, on a mattress by the fireplace, scarcely moved thanks to the prescription painkillers Sidney found yesterday — *I busted the lock*, she said with a trace of pride when handing over the pill container. Outside, the whop-whop of helicopter blades broke the still night, along with occasional raised voices from supply ships in the inlet. Otherwise the house was quiet, everyone sleeping off the day of fear.

The girl was the first to retire last night. She went upstairs soon after laying out food she had salvaged from the kitchen: olives, crackers, deli meats, dips, a plastic tray of raw vegetables jumbled but still dewy from the tipped-over fridge. *Dinner party tonight* was all she said when Anna raised an eyebrow at the fiesta of shapes and colours — bright yellow peppers, deep green snap peas, rosy grape tomatoes, orange carrots, slender asparagus, a container of curried mayonnaise in the centre. Imagine such an array of food in your house.

Sidney stayed long enough to nibble a carrot stick and watch while Joe sipped from a straw the Mountain Dew the girl had pressed on him. They were gathered in the great room, seated around the coffee table as if it were a campfire and they a band of ragged pioneers – all but the girl's father, who did not appear for the makeshift meal, who has been unaccounted for ever since he beat Joe. Joe slurped slowly, his lips around the straw purple and puffy, but did not eat. When Sidney handed him a plate of cold cuts, artfully arranged, he shook his head. He has said almost nothing since the attack. Anna fears he is injured inside; he is favouring his torso, which looks swollen, but he will not let her examine him. Really, what would be the point? She is no nurse and she is fairly sure Joe knows it. He is the smartest one here. He is the reason they are all alive.

As soon as Joe finished the Mountain Dew, Sidney disappeared. To her bedroom, no doubt. It is where Anna would go if she could, to the snug room at Miss Dodie's that holds her every earthly belonging. She would clutch the smooth flask and wrap herself in Baba's quilt, tight.

Only Miss Dodie chattered during their solemn meal. Propped up on a leather sofa, from where she could just reach the coffee table, her battered knee elevated on a throw pillow, she praised the offerings of the restaurant, which she continues to call this house, and the restaurateur, who she continues to think is Joe.

"I fell," he said when Miss Dodie asked about his battered face.

"You have to keep the floors clean." She shook her finger at him. "Your kitchen is a disgrace, sir. Too many ponds – puddles ... There is too much ... things on the floor. Where is the woman of this establishment? She is a lazy thing, leaving all these messes. Why isn't she here cleaning up? No one does their job anymore. Except you, Annie."

Miss Dodie ate red meat and more high-fat dip than she should have, but Anna allowed it. It is the least she can do. Her lady has suffered so many shocks in so little time, and her schedule has been overturned. No nap, no afternoon tea, no evening blood thinner pill. Little wonder the woman's brain is badly tangled. Eventually, after attempting a cauliflower floret and pronouncing the golf balls inedible unless you were a llama (where does she get these ideas? and what is a llama?), Miss Dodie slipped into the dreamscape where she sometimes goes, eyes glassy, face slack. Fortunately Anna had talked her into a bottle of apple juice before then. Dehydration, not hunger, is the enemy in times of crisis.

Crisis. Always there is crisis.

Head hammering, Anna turns away from the morning light and tries to get comfortable on her leather sofa, the twin of Miss Dodie's. Anna, too, needs hydration. Not apple juice.

She pushes the thought away.

Crisis. Why must it follow her, even here, to the far coast of Canada? It greeted her when she entered the world, in 1986, the year Chernobyl rained poison over the northern part of her country. It ruptured her family life: her father's lost hand, his drunken rages, her mother's suffering, her brother's escape to Odessa. Then came death, both her parents gone. Then the Russians invaded. *Not an invasion,* people said, including the soldiers who entered and menaced and bombed and installed themselves in a territory where they claimed they were welcome. It was true: they were welcomed by some. Anna's co-workers and neighbours, even Oksana, her family's most steadfast friend, shrugged matter-of-factly, resigned to being once again gathered to the bosom of Mother Russia.

Not Anna. She was five when the USSR collapsed and Ukraine proclaimed independence, just starting school when her city rose up to celebrate the future of the Ukrainian people. Only five, but all her life she remembered it, the quiet jubilation, the flare of possibility. When the Russians invaded, those memories only intensified. Her ears rang with the old songs; she saw the hugs and hopeful smiles; she relived the relief and the passion of a people finally free. She still believed in the future, *her* future, with all her heart. She could not bear to see her country trampled once more, its autonomy squashed like a beetle beneath the oppressor's boot. So she fled. She chose freedom, or whatever meagre form of it she could find while hiding in a foreign land and surrounded by an impenetrable language. Freedom and the faint prospect of, if not happiness, then contentment. Acceptance. Whatever it was she felt that rainy afternoon, a couple of weeks after moving into Miss Dodie's old rancher, when her employer surprised her in the kitchen. Anna was chopping onions for stew, her eyes weeping. "Annie," Miss Dodie said, placing a shaky bejewelled hand over the hand that held the knife. "You don't have to cry anymore. This is a good house. This is a good knife."

Now, halfway around the globe, in one of the richest neighbourhoods of one of the world's steadiest countries, Anna is nose to nose with it again. Crisis, her old friend, has found her.

Unable to settle, she slides off the sofa, pulls on her grey sweatshirt, and pads past the air mattress where Joe is quietly breathing, *slava bogu*. Miss Dodie will need breakfast, and Anna's first order of business, after coaxing the woman into another humiliating diaper change, will be to prepare it.

Prepare is hardly the word, she thinks as she scans the wrecked kitchen. She cannot cook with the electricity off, and at any rate the stove is unusable, covered with slick spills. She peers into the tall pot on the back burner and wrinkles her nose. Old cooking oil. Perhaps money does not always purchase tidiness. She would never leave an unemptied pot in Miss Dodie's kitchen.

As she hunts in the cupboards, Anna tries to ignore the dried splashes of red wine that birthmark the floor. She drank too much wine yesterday. It never sits well with her, but last night, when she carried the dinner remnants back to the kitchen, it was all she had access to. What she wanted then, what she longs for now, is not wine but the real stuff in the dining room.

Across the kitchen, the door of a small beverage fridge hangs ajar. Rummaging in the back, she finds a small orange juice box, pokes in the sharp straw that comes with it, and slurps, not stopping until she has sucked every sweet drop from the corners.

Better.

She steps over glass shards, dented cans, and flower stems on her way to the tall pantry. What could it contain that might qualify as breakfast for a woman who begins each day with a soft-boiled egg, a dry slice of toast, two cups of coffee, and a good sulk about the absence of butter, bacon, or sausage? Anna picks up a box labelled "breakfast bars," lumpy cereal pressed into ingots by the look of it. On another shelf is a bag of dried apricots, which she collects along with a single banana stranded on the oily ceramic stovetop.

No electricity means no coffee, so she pulls two more juice cartons from the small refrigerator, one for Miss Dodie and one that she downs herself. Her head pounds a little less.

Perhaps her lady will accept this dry picnic fare if it is presented on a silver tray, with proper silverware, a plate, and a napkin, laid out the way Miss Dodie is accustomed to.

If there is silver, it will be in the dining room.

She has no choice, then, but to go there. The decision is out of her hands.

The dining room is dim. The narrow windows face west, away from the morning sun. A hush lies over the fallen chandelier, the long table, and the sideboard opposite. Anna sets her supplies on the table and eyes the glass-fronted doors of the sideboard's upper cabinet.

She will go there, find a placemat and silverware, a plate and a napkin. She will not open the glass door of the liquor cupboard. She will not drink.

One step, another, and she is there. She tries a drawer, finds neatly folded napkins inside. From another drawer takes a placemat of quilted cloth, cream with yellow flowers, well suited to breakfast.

The bottles and decanters squat at eye level, hypnotic creatures leering at her through the glass. It is morning, and she is hung over. She must not.

She opens a lower cupboard. A tray — there has to be a tray. She locates a wooden one leaning on its side, but it will not do. It will set Miss Dodie to wailing.

She straightens up. So many bottles, all the way to the back of the cabinet. This rich family can drink whatever they want, whenever they want.

She bends down again. Spies, toward the back of the cupboard, a slim silver tray. It is small, and tarnished she sees as she pulls it out by its curlicued edge, but recognizably silver.

Back at the table, Anna sets the tray down and congratulates herself for her willpower. She pushes the fruit bowl back to the centre of the table, out of reach. To think an innocent bowl, spilling grapes and kiwis and a single green apple, is the reason Miss Dodie is laid up now.

You are the reason, says a sharp voice. *Not the fruit. You. She is a helpless old woman and you left her alone so that you could drink.*

Zatknis! Anna tosses her head as if shaking off a mosquito. Shut up! The movement sets off a cranial helicopter with thwopping blades, as deafening as the aircraft that filled yesterday's sky. She grabs Miss Dodie's juice container, pierces it with the tiny straw, sucks greedily.

It is not enough.

You did it. You left her alone. You are a bad person and everyone around you dies.

But it is morning. Never in the morning.

Just one sip to quiet her head, to help her focus. There are so many problems to solve, so many decisions to make. Somehow, she must get Miss Dodie home. The woman needs her familiar surroundings and her routine, not to mention the blood thinners she takes to prevent clots. Anna must organize the logistics. She owes it to her lady to approach the day with concentration. It is her job.

Her job that she does alone. Always, she is alone, lonely.

In an instant she is back at the cabinet. Reaches for the vodka, uncaps it, and before she can think takes a deep drink. Her blood cells plump, her nerves tingle, her body reawakens.

Two more gulps and it will be gone. There is no point leaving so little. She will finish the bottle and then it will be enough and she will return to Miss Dodie.

By the time she rolls the empty bottle underneath the sideboard, out of sight, her head is clear and her life has purpose. She knows what to do. If by afternoon Miss Dodie has not recovered enough to walk, Anna will ask Sidney to help. The girl is prickly and she nearly exposed

Anna yesterday after smelling wine on her breath, but she is quick to assist. Anna will fetch Miss Dodie's Volvo from the seawalk parking lot, drive it back here, and between them she and the girl may be just strong enough to get Miss Dodie off the sofa and install her in the passenger seat. Joe is too sore to lift the woman, but perhaps he can direct them. In no time they will be home.

And you can drink again.

The cool flask. Will it be where she left it, unharmed?

Suddenly Anna realizes how little she knows about the state of the world outside. Who is to say Miss Dodie's neglected old rancher will even be habitable? The roof could be flattened by the ailing hemlocks that loom overhead, unpruned in the decades since Mr. Dodie's death. In what condition will she find her room, her bureau, and her scant possessions? The quilt her Baba made? Her envelope of money and Bohdan's knife?

If Miss Dodie's house is ruined, where will they go? A church or a school gym, an overfull community centre where people wander under fluorescent lights, clutching blankets, shivering and quivering like abandoned pets? She imagines Miss Dodie in their midst, picking up strangers' belongings, stage-whispering insults about this woman's hairdo and that man's penis, reminiscing about her glorious breasts, coughing up random and frequently pornographic comments because she thinks no one can hear. Anna will have to endure the questions that people like her are always asked. *Where are you from? No, where are you* really *from? What brought you to Canada?*

The idea is unbearable.

They could come back here if the rancher is ruined, but there is no guarantee that Stedman will take them in again. Why should he? He is famous. Until Joe told her, Anna did not realize who he was, but now she remembers seeing him in the Canadian magazines at the hair salon. He is a celebrity. Also an animal. He beat Joe in an attempt to recover his money—that was the only thing Joe would tell her as she cleaned his battered face—which means she could be Stedman's next victim. All for money that none of them, including Sidney, believes is truly missing. Stedman has behaved oddly ever since Anna bandaged his face yesterday. Is it a head injury? Whatever the case, it is unlikely that once he closes the door on a demented, occasionally vulgar old woman and her ragged Ukrainian serf, he will ever welcome them back.

The rows of bottles gleam in the low light. Now that she has broken her rule and drunk in the morning, would it be so terrible to take more?

Miss Dodie had friends once, or so say the silver-framed photos of young and middle-aged women that adorn her lady's living room, prettily made up and dressed in patterned silk scarves, standing before rhododendrons or seated at tea tables. But either the friends have died or Miss Dodie's condition has turned them away, for during Anna's time there have been no callers and no social events. Not a soul has telephoned or come to the house who isn't a delivery person, a repairman, or paid help of some kind.

If the house is ruined, they have nowhere to go. Nowhere.

As the realization dawns, Anna is twisting the cap off the gin. Pleasure flames core deep as she swallows, no longer rationing, no longer caring. With the flame comes elation, pure and electrifying. She can do anything, *anything*, her imagination the only limit.

The bottle is in place and Anna's hand is back at her side when a sound makes her whirl around.

Chort! The daughter.

"Figures I'd find you in here. With the booze."

A night's sleep has not altered the girl's attitude. She assesses Anna from the dining room doorway, hip cocked defiantly, still holding the stainless steel mixing bowl. She has likely not seen the bottle in Anna's hand, but she may as well have.

Anna slams the glass door shut and her heart thuds crazily. She is caught. Just like yesterday, except Sidney is no Joe. She will not keep Anna's secret. She will tell her father or Miss Dodie as she was about to do yesterday, and that will be the end for Anna. The biggest aftershock of all.

"You're busted."

Anna is not sure what that means but it cannot be good. As the girl approaches, Anna flails for useful words. "I — I am getting dishes. Miss Dodie must have breakfast on the silver — on a tray of silver."

Sidney sets the metal bowl on the floor beside the cabinet and smirks. "I bet." This morning the girl is dressed in black tights and an oversized tunic. Heavy kohl pencil around her eyes gives her an elfin look. In contrast, Anna's face in the mirror over the sideboard is drawn and ashen, and her grey cotton pants are wrinkled and, she notices, speckled with red wine.

"You're drinking. Again."

The vibrations are there, far off. The distant train. Anna shakes her head. The girl did not see her drink. She is only guessing. Unless — ? Anna glances at the floor. No. The empty bottle is still hidden beneath the cabinet.

"Come on, just admit it. I won't say anything."

But she will. The girl was on the verge of saying something yesterday. She is lying.

"I know you were drinking. I can smell it."

The train is on its way now, gathering speed. In Anna's ears, the dreadful approaching hum. And between her legs, a sudden sticky wetness. *Nyet.* Not now. She has been expecting it, the days crossed off on her calendar, but amid the confusion she forgot.

The girl tilts her head. "Was it vodka? That's what you drink over there, right? In Russia?"

"*Not* Russian. Ukrainian."

"Whatever. I like vodka. I like it all. Not wine or beer so much. I'm a liquor pig."

The kind sow used to smile, almost. The same pig later hung upside down, slit open, bleeding out, her whole body a ghastly smile.

Blood pounds in Anna's ears, and her crotch dampens.

"You know, just the hard stuff."

How can he be hard?

Sidney must know that Anna is not keeping up. "Vodka, gin, rum, scotch. All of this." She nods at the cabinet.

How can he be hard? Even now, years later, when the train hurtles toward her, Anna pauses on this detail. How could he be aroused? How could he go from whatever he was doing – finishing a cigarette, urinating in the bushes, missing his parents, planning the next airport attack – to being instantly aroused, with no invitation, no encouragement? How could he get hard? How could he stay hard? How was it physically possible?

Anna swallows. She needs to leave, fast. When the train comes, it flattens her. "Your hand, it is okay? Maybe you lie down and rest?" Perhaps sympathy will win Sidney over and keep her quiet.

The girl smirks. "Don't change the subject."

She is dogged, not distractible, this girl. She would make an excellent soldier.

He was completely focused. Methodical, as if executing the steps of a memorized drill. Certain he would hurt her, terrified that his comrades might be waiting nearby to join in, Anna went mute the minute he pushed her down. He ripped the neck of her much-washed tee-shirt, shoved a hand inside, and twisted her nipple. With the other paw he yanked down her jeans. Before she could register what was happening, he was inside her.

How can he be hard? It was her last thought before she took herself away.

"You don't have to drink, you know," Sidney says. "It's a choice. We all have a choice."

Anna is shaking. Who is this rich girl to tell her anything? What does she know of life? Anna cannot, must not, fall apart in front of her.

"We had a huge earthquake. Like, one of the worst things ever. People are dead, the whole city's in pieces. The house where you live could be gone for all you know. And the woman you're supposed to be taking care of, she's hurt because you weren't with her. Just like you're not there with her now. You're here." Sidney opens the cabinet, grabs a bottle, shakes it in Anna's face. The amber liquid sloshes, tantalizes. "This is the only thing that matters to you. You want this more than anything."

Anna shuts her eyes and her ears. She cannot listen.

She envisions Baba's quilt. This is how she readies herself when the train barrels in. It was how she got through that unspeakable fall afternoon. Baba's quilt lay at the bottom of Anna's bed her entire life, except for the weeks when it blanketed her dying mother. Before abandoning the apartment for good, Anna stuffed the quilt into her knapsack, a last-minute decision that meant leaving her warmest pullover behind. She would need the reminder of home wherever she landed. It was the quilt, she told herself, its orange-and-red snowflakes as familiar as her own skin. It was the quilt covering her, its soft backing that had touched her mother's bare arms. It was not the soldier in his scratchy camouflage, some nylon strap from his outfit scrubbing at her breasts as he flattened her, jackhammering with a penis that kept at it and at it and at it. It was cool on the ground and she lay there, limp and silent, doing as she was told, praying that he would finish, just finish, each thrust a file scraping her torn-up insides.

"You're an alcoholic," Sidney says. The girl is tiny and at the same time formidable, a slim rod of unbendable steel.

The train bears down on Anna like the filthy soldier, bringing with it that word — a word she knows but cannot say, not in any language. A word she forces herself to unhear so that she can go on as she does, without judgement. Without fear.

She hugs herself tight, her breathing shallow. A strangled sob escapes her.

"Hey." Sidney reaches over. Her hand singes Anna's arm.

"*Nyet!*" Anna twists away. "Do not touch me! Go away."

"Fine." Sidney shrugs, like nothing in life can surprise her. "It's just, I get it, okay? I understand."

"You do not!" Panic ignites fury inside Anna and she explodes. "You understand nothing!" Where are the words? She needs more of them, so many more, to even begin to say what is inside her. "You are rich girl. You live here, like the king." She waves at the dining room and all its debris. "You have everything. *Everything.* Never hungry. Never work. Never, mm — never hide. You don't have idea, you don't even have the clue."

Her fury is huge, as huge as her need. She is this close to snatching the bottle from Sidney's hand and tipping it to her mouth, to hell with what anyone thinks, then grabbing another from the cabinet and draining it too. Her job, over. Her safe life, finished. In an hour, even less, Miss Dodie will send her away, and she hardly cares. All she wants, the only thing she wants, is a drink.

Sidney sloshes the bottle again. "I'm telling you, I know. I'm the same as you. An alcoholic. Drugs too. Pot, cocaine, oxy, E, prescription stuff. Basically anything with decent chemicals in it."

Anna hugs herself tight. The girl is cruel to mock her this way.

"I was in rehab. You know what that means? Like a hospital but for addicts. Three months I was there. Only it's more of a jail than a hospital, because you can't leave. They force you to stay and they watch you all the time. I haven't had anything since. Not once." This last comes louder, bolder.

Anna does not believe her. This girl lives in a palace and has everything she wants. She is not like Anna. She may choose to drink, but drink does not rule her.

Sidney holds out the bottle. "Here, do what you want. It won't help. It won't make anything go away." She surveys the littered room. "Not any of it."

Anna does not take the bottle. She cannot drink in front of anyone. She is plain and lonely, and she is bad, everything about her is bad, and what she does is private, shameful. It is not for this girl to see. Anna will not be the slaughtered sow, her innards exposed to the world.

Again Sidney reaches out.

Leave me, please leave me, Anna thinks but cannot say. She is too far inside herself now, her heart hammering, her breath hitched.

Sidney reaches out, only it is not the bottle in her hand. It is the bowl. The metal bowl from the kitchen. The girl sets it on Anna's head, so gently that Anna barely feels a thing.

◇

Kyle saw Cirque du Soleil for the first time last summer. Spring had stretched out forever last year, the way it can on the west coast, primulas, daffodils, and tulips nodding for weeks in the cool, moist air. Only in mid-July, when the circus came to town, did the clouds finally lift and the hot weather descend, dropping a perfect blue-sky canvas behind the trailers and white tents and fantastical arenas that mushroomed on the former Expo 86 land near False Creek.

Joe begged him to go. All their friends had seen the Cirque at some point, either in Vancouver or back east or at one of the troupe's permanent venues in Vegas, and everyone swooned over the athleticism, the costumes, the pulsing lights and music, the magic. Even the valet parking attendant from the pharma lunch-and-learn, the one Kyle fucked later with some Hispanic guy near Lee's Trail, was going — his fourth Cirque show, he told Kyle, resuming casual conversation in the time it took to buckle his Diesel belt. So Kyle bought two tickets, made early reservations at Wild, the ethical seafood place his clients raved about, and took Joe on a date.

Entering the tent from the lush Vancouver evening was like stepping off the planet. While Joe scanned for their seats Kyle froze, transfixed by the sprawling main stage, the lights that cast multicoloured pinpricks overhead, the thump-thump-thump from a cluster of hand-drummers offstage, the pockets of shadow that promised surprise — whether pleasant or ominous he didn't know. The big dome swallowed him, so other-worldly and all-encompassing that it seemed nothing else existed outside the closed universe of light, shadow, and rhythm. It was exciting and threatening all at once.

Now he is under the big top again, inside another realm of dark and light and thudding beats. Except this dome brings only pain.

As a doctor he is trained in pain: how to measure it, manage it, medicate it, counsel people to deal with it. All the papers he has read, presentations he has attended, and drug reps he has listened to have taught him, it turns out, zero. What he's experienced since yesterday afternoon, since trimming a second branch and binding it to the first half of his splint, since crawling down the trail until he found another stick straight and sturdy enough to serve as a cane, since adopting the agonizing hop-and-slump gait that gains him inches and costs him torrents of sweat and exhaustion, since learning how searing are the contortions involved in bending to a fill a water bottle when your leg is shattered and splinted – is that what is meant by pain? Is that what drives his patients to plead for drugs, more drugs, new drugs, stronger drugs? He's had little sympathy for these whiners, thinking though never saying that they should just suck it up. He wishes now he could take back every judgement.

Last night he stopped around eleven, after seven hours of what he told himself were sets, like in the gym. One hop after another, until he got to four. Pause to recover, leaning over the branch-cane, shaking and sweating. Then another set. He did it as long as he could: hop-four, slump, often tripping, sometimes holding the slump far longer than he ought to, once thrown agonizingly to the ground, during the big aftershock a couple of hours after he set out, switching on the head-lamp as little as possible after dark so as to conserve the batteries, until his hand where it gripped the rough walking stick rubbed raw and his supposedly functioning leg buckled. Then he lowered himself to the ground, splinted leg straight out in front, the pain mercifully muted. He lay on his thin pack, poor insulation from the night ground, drank half a bottle of water, chewed a gluey power bar, and after another failed attempt to call Joe, entered a wretched state between sleep and consciousness.

As the night wore on and the earth rumbled intermittently beneath him, the pain was joined by regret and guilt. His mind, flitting above slumber, always circled back to Joe. Was he with strangers or alone? Was he – God – was he still okay?

What do you care? Liar. You treat him like shit.

Now, at eight a.m., a beautiful post-quake morning, the sky a blue parody of calm, it's back to the hop-four, slump. The pain has become a steady state in which every moment is unendurable yet somehow is endured. Kyle inhabits his own universe, which must be why he can't quit thinking about Cirque du Soleil. The strobe lights, the thudding drums, the performers jumping and twirling, piling into human pyramids, circling hoops and ribbons. The nervous heat of Joe's thigh that grazed Kyle's as the Chinese boy placed one more chair on the teetering tower of chairs, then elegantly climbed atop it in what must surely be his last moment alive before he stumbled and crashed to the floor below and yet miraculously he did not. The hot grip of Joe's hand when it became clear, as the boy nimbly descended, tossing chair after chair as he went, that the heart-stopping feat had succeeded. It was over. The boy's last moment would come another day.

Which one will be Kyle's last moment? As the morning grinds on and the suffering beats him down, he begins to understand that he will not make it. The drums beat and this hop will be the last. He will sit down and never get up. No? Then this will be the last hop. Then *this*.

One by one, though he cannot take a step, the performers twirl and the steps happen. So much energy from nowhere. Hours of it. Agony.

He is not even halfway down.

Where is Joe? At home waiting? Worrying?

Kyle tries to leave the circus world and instead be in their kitchen, with Joe at the counter making a milkshake. Joe has always been the domestic one. During Kyle's first year of solo practice, Joe would pack him roast beef sandwiches or turkey bagels for the gruelling twelve- and fourteen-hour days; would wait up for Kyle to straggle home, bone weary, brain overloaded by the dozens of details he had to manage now that he was not just a doctor but a business owner; would massage Kyle's neck and shoulders for the three minutes it took him to pitch into sleep. Joe looked after their place, the tiny West End apartment in those days, not just cleaning it but doing the laundry and the shopping, buying Kyle's toiletries, paying the bills. Joe dutifully donned the monkey suit, as he called it, a sport coat and a proper shirt – *with buttons!* Joe always exclaimed, feigning incredulity at a shirt that couldn't be pulled over his head – and allowed Kyle to tame his curly mop with gels and pastes – *product!* Joe snorted derisively – whenever Kyle dragged him to dinner or drinks with the high-rolling gay men who were the clinic's main investors. Two years ago, when Joe's mother was dying in Newfoundland, Joe was the one who moved in and looked after her. Not his aunts or uncles or cousins, who actually lived in the province, but Joe, from the opposite side of the continent.

Five years Joe has given him. Five long years of waiting out Kyle's black moods, cajoling him when the return to equanimity takes too long, whispering *loverpot* and *Kiki*, the pet names that never fail to soften then dissolve the shell that calcifies around Kyle after the longest clinic days. Joe has given him everything, all the love, time, and space he could ask for. Joe gives and gives, and what does he get?

Lies.

It's unforgivable, what Kyle has done. He has wronged Joe. Old-fashioned as it sounds, it is true. Joe has been faithful to him, has made a home with him, has loved Kyle steadily for who he is, faults and all, and Kyle has shoved the love aside like it's a sink full of dishes or a pile of unpaid bills, some irritating duty he'd rather be clear of.

Lies.

The word thumps like a drumbeat, and the Cirque takes over again. Lights and percussion, tumbling and twirling.

Kyle's right hand is chewed up, like pâté. The branch cane that created the wound is of little help. Should he just toss it?

The main problem is one of geometry: with the splint attached, his shattered right leg stays fully extended so that his foot bangs into every protruding rock, every tiny rise. Thank God he's going downhill. Up would be impossible; he'd have to drag himself on his belly. But even a descent involves intervals of up, during which he tries to keep the broken leg slightly lifted from the hip, as if preparing to kick a soccer ball. Between the unbalanced stance and the uneven terrain, he is barely in control minute to minute. So many pain bullets have shot his leg that the agony is constant now. He is a prisoner of his own private big top, his pulsing dome of sensation, with Joe, overheated and vital, by his side.

Joe gives and gives. And what do you give him?

He actually welcomes the obsessive circus thought pattern. There's something soothing about it — it forms a mantra that he grabs onto and rides down and down the viewless treed tunnel of trail that will, he prays, spit him out at the bottom. He is reminded of a movie he and Joe once saw about an injured climber who pulled himself out of a crevasse and dragged his broken body, inch by inch, back to camp. Kyle didn't want to go to the movies, he had mountains of paperwork and it was bucketing rain, but something made him cave. Joe was so excited, the way he was later at Cirque du Soleil. Near the end of the film, as the climber barely clung to life, a pop song began to haunt him — "Brown Girl in the Ring" — and it was the song that prodded him along. The incessant Cirque tableau is Kyle's prod. He hates it, the repetitiveness and tedium and fear, but as long as he stays under the dome, he will stay alive. He cannot endure the next moment, let alone all the next moments it will take to get off this mountain, but somehow the Cirque allows him to endure the present one.

What do you give Joe? Not just lies.

Overhead the raven swoops, the beat of great wings stirring the sky like the helicopters overhead. Fewer than yesterday? Kyle can't be sure. Nor is he sure it's the same raven, though there is comfort in imagining it is.

He wipes his eyes with his free hand, retreats further into the circus tent.

What do you give Joe? Really?

Lies, month after month of lies. And the distance that comes with lying. Criticism and correction. A cold bare back, a dead limp cock, a cock that's been in someone else's mouth, ass, hand, that's been webcammed into someone else's room. Deceit and betrayal. That's what he gives Joe.

And fear. Fear of commitment.

Yes.

Because yes. He is afraid.

It has been with him forever, fear. It's his oldest companion. He cowered before his father, who saw and loathed the softness inside him. He rode the school bus petrified, nose against window while the same kids jeered at him, day after day. He spent recess in the bathroom, lunch hour with his comic books. He didn't touch a man until he was twenty — twenty! — afraid of what might happen if he gave in to his blinding lust. It is fear that makes him airbrush the vain rather than tend to the damaged, their harelips and burns, facial cancers and sarcomas. It is fear that makes him compulsive about the gym, resolved to gird his body against all that is weak within. As for love, real love, forever love — it is the most terrifying abyss he can imagine. To give himself over to it would expose every frailty, and jab every bruise. Real love scares the living shit out of him.

The drum beats and he feels Joe in the seat beside him, gripping his hand, hot and anxious but also exhilarated. The gravity-defying circus act, each step impossible, each step surely fatal, but — look! They did it. Joe squeezes his hand.

It is Joe's hand. No one else's. None of the others, the many, many others.

Kyle takes another step. His last?

Then another, in the only direction that matters. Down.

$\sim$

A man's home is supposed to be his castle. But since the earthquake yesterday, the three major aftershocks since, and the smaller tremors that caught him unawares, Stedman has watched his palace deteriorate into a rude medieval court, a chilly dwelling with no running water, no electricity, and no light apart from the squat candle he swiped from Charlotte's night table; and within its walls, a ragtag entourage of strangers and fools.

He let them stay the night. What choice did he have? The old woman, not exactly spry to begin with, can hardly walk since her fall in the dining room. She spent the night on the sofa, Stedman concludes as he regards her sleeping form now. The same morning sun that sparkles diamonds over the ocean, today glinting and playful beyond the sliding glass doors, falls harsh on the furrowed old woman, whose fish mouth emits a series of light, moist snores.

He is stuck with this woman. Likewise her caregiver, who slept on the leather sofa opposite by the looks of the untidy nest there: coats, sweaters, scarves, even the striped Hudson's Bay blanket, a patriotic adornment that to his knowledge has not covered a human body until now. The early sun catches an object underneath the leather couch — a wine bottle, he sees as he pulls it out. Empty. He kneels, reaches in farther, finds a second, then a third, each drained dry. Damn it all! The third is the 2002 Château Lafite Rothschild he's been saving for an occasion that matches the vintage. An occasion like getting bought out of his company, should that liberation day ever arrive.

Wonderful. The nurse, who may have also pocketed his twenty thousand dollars — he's still not sure which of the hired people took his stash — has gotten drunk on *his* most expensive wine and is wandering around *his* house, her nutso patient forgotten and left to drool on *his* furniture. God, what if the old woman, immobile all night with no one to help her, did worse than drool? He ventures near and sniffs, but detects nothing save a stale smell of soda crackers. There's one thing to be grateful for.

The gardener spent the night too, judging by the air mattress near the fireplace, where sits the telltale ball cap that every handyman wears. Why? To signal to each other that they're of the same tribe? Where the hell is the gardener so early in the morning? Off checking *his* property? Making friends with *his* neighbours? Tending to *his* daughter?

Yesterday's anger flares, then sputters. These are all things Stedman should be doing. He knows it, yet the most he's been able to do so far is get out of bed. This morning, besides an aching face and a mind gone to soup, he woke with bashed-up hands and a deadweight of guilt.

Gay? Could things be any more screwed up? Bad enough that some blue-collar stranger takes over his house and maybe steals his money. Then Stedman has to go and hit the guy, and it turns out he's gay. Now, to the list of head injuries, lost Merck account, untold corporate damage, and general uselessness in his own home, Stedman can add the humiliation of being a gay basher.

Standing over the air mattress, he scuffs at his unbandaged jaw. He hates having a day's growth, but he can't bring himself to shave.

Part of it is the pain – the right side of his head feels like it's in a vice. Mainly he doesn't want to look in a mirror.

He hit a gay man.

How was he supposed to know the gardener is gay? He doesn't look gay; he doesn't sound it. He drives a truck and wears frayed work clothes. He's got a bad haircut and a ball cap, for God's sake. But he is gay, and Stedman hit him. Stedman, who back in Hamilton beat up every snot-nosed kid who dared make fun of Tim. He only had to do it a few times before the word spread: *Leave the little faggot alone or his big brother's gonna whale on ya.*

He scared himself yesterday, he will admit it. The paralysis, the self-pity, the loss of control. Then the shame. He's an achiever, a winner, yet what little he has accomplished since the earthquake he has done badly. Disaster has not brought out the best in Tayne Stedman.

To top it all off, Sidney despises him. Yesterday, before the incident with the gardener, she made several attempts to coax her father out of his office. "What about Mom?" she asked plaintively. "We've got to find her. We've got to talk to her. And May. We need to find them both so we'll know if –" Her voice broke at that point. He didn't reply. "Dad, why are you *here*?" she asked the next time. "How come you won't leave your office? You're acting so weird. Like you're hiding." Then, after he hit Joe, the way she gaped at him – God, he never wants to see that again – like he's a monster.

Since then he's hardly seen Sidney. She appeared at his bedroom door once in the evening, hands on hips, looking pointedly off to the side. "They need food," she said. "We have to feed them. And it looks like they're staying the night. You have to come down and help." Wearily he shook his head, said he needed to think. Still she refused to look at him, and her disdain sapped his last ounce of strength. "You're my big girl," he told her. "You know what to do."

She does know. Sidney is smart and willful, her mother's daughter, and it's apparent that she got everyone settled last night. But every girl needs her daddy. Sidney has to know how much he loves her. He's got to make her see that.

It's true, what Charlotte says — he's been neglecting the home front. *Workaholic*, she spits at him when he begs off some anniversary or school meeting. She's probably right. Years ago, he figured that once GlobalTech went from big to enormous he could ease up, take the odd weekend off, go for drives with the family, which would have expanded by then — he and Charlotte were trying for a baby. Wrong on all counts. Eventually they gave up on more kids, and soon thereafter sex, and as the company grew so did people's expectations, including his wife's. *You can control the market in eastern Europe*, she told him, and she was right. *Ease out of the US*, she warned right before the 2008 collapse. *India and China: follow the growth* is her admonition now. Every year he works more and more, later and later, resigned to the fact that bigger is never big enough. Only lately has he grasped that the only way to unburden himself from the golem he has created is to pass it to someone else.

Damn it all, how did yesterday affect stock prices? Checking the market is one more thing he needs to do, besides getting hold of Marcus and May and Charlotte —

She's not coming back.

— and reassuring his little girl that they will be fine. Sidney may not want to look at him let alone listen to him, but she needs to know that she is safe and that he'll do anything to keep her that way, even slugging that asshole of a gardener.

The morning sun that slants through the glass doors brings him purpose. He will surmount this catastrophe the same way he conquers his business challenges, day after day, year after year. He will devise a strategy; he will retake his castle. *Be a man*, Charlotte hisses whenever he needs whipping into action, whenever he slips a toe into the deep, feathered comfort of passivity. It is her voice he hears now, rousing him.

She's not coming back.

It doesn't matter. He is his own man, beholden to no one. He does his best when he goes it alone.

As if to challenge his solo status, there comes a sound so out of place in this upside-down world that for a moment he fails to recognize it: the doorbell, followed soon by a barrage of pounding.

He arrives in the foyer right behind Sidney, who narrows her eyes at him before standing aside. He swings open the heavy fir door, perfectly intact after all that has happened, to find two helmeted men on his porch. Soldiers – or rather reservists, he deduces from their unlined faces and tidy camouflage.

"Everyone all right in there, sir?" The speaker, the shorter and stockier of the two, can't be more than sixteen. His voice quavers as if still seeking its adult pitch.

"Thank you, yes. All fine." Stedman starts to close the door.

"Wait! Dad!"

"Sir?" The stocky youth wedges a boot in the door, then a leg. He peers around the doorframe at Sidney. "Ma'am? Is there a problem?"

Ma'am. Stedman guffaws. Who do these clowns think they are?

The silent soldier, the tall one, folds his arms and eyes Stedman up and down. Sidney pushes into the doorway. "We don't know where my mom is. Or May, she's our maid. Can you, like, make a call?"

The soldier touches a rectangle holstered at his hip. "All we've got are sat phones. Emergency use only."

Stedman rests a hand on Sidney's head. For once she's not wearing the metal bowl. "Honey, run upstairs. I'll look after this."

The second soldier, the tall one, clears his throat. "Sir, we have several injured parties from an evacuated highrise down the way. We need to keep them somewhere safe until we can ship them to a treatment centre. Their building is not stable. Requesting permission to billet them here, sir."

"Dammit, man, you can't be serious. I've got a house full of strangers already, one of them injured."

"*Two* injured," says Sidney.

Does she mean the gardener? He's got, what, a couple of bruises? Or does she mean him, her father? He touches his bandaged jaw, then shakes his head emphatically even though it hurts his skull. "There's no room here, no room at all."

"Dad!" Sidney looks horrified. "We've got tons of room."

"Absolutely not," he tells the soldiers. "We've got more here than we can handle. Now I ask you respectfully to leave my property before—"

"Daddy, come on." Sidney tugs at his arm.

"You can take them next door."

The soldiers turn to the voice behind them, unmistakeably smug. Half hidden behind the soldiers, standing a step below them, the gay gardener shoots Stedman a laser-like glare. "Vincent has plenty of room and wants to help."

What the hell? The hired man is everywhere.

Joe steps onto the porch and the stocky soldier gasps. "Sir! Are you all right?"

Stedman freezes. Joe's face is like something from a horror film, makeup and prosthetics courtesy of the special effects studios over by GlobalTech headquarters. His bottom lip is split open, a reddish-black gash, his cheeks are purpled, one eye is swollen shut. What the hell happened? Did the guy fall? There's no way Stedman did all that. No way.

"Sir?" The stocky soldier awaits Joe's answer.

"Looks worse than it is," Joe says. "Here, I'll take you next door, introduce you to Vincent. He can help you with whoever's injured."

The soldiers glance again at Stedman and Sidney.

"Ma'am?" The tall soldier steps toward them and raises his voice. "Ma'am, do you need help? Are you going to faint?" He shoulders past Sidney and crosses into the house. Stedman turns in time to glimpse the nurse's back as she disappears from the foyer, running.

Everyone here is crazy, Stedman thinks as the soldiers turn back down the steps, led by Joe, who limps slightly.

"Excellent," Stedman mutters. "Faking a limp. Not enough to take my money, he's going to come back and sue me." He drops his hand onto Sidney's shoulder. At least he took charge this time. It feels good. "Come on, Sweetpea. Let's go inside."

She looks at him, his daughter. Her hair hangs in sheets of gold, her eyes are big and dusky, and her expression is one he has only ever seen on the face of his wife: contempt, pure and withering.

They're in Shuswap country, approaching Salmon Arm. Endless lake, rolling farmland, forested hills, towering mountains. "Bloody beautiful," Bryan keeps saying. "A guy could stay awhile in a place like this."

Charlotte sees none of it. She is on the floor in front of the passenger seat, which she has slid back to create more space, the adjustment mechanism unoiled and resistant. She's not doing what a red-blooded woman riding with an unattached Aussie hunk should be doing on her knees in a moving vehicle. That happened earlier, before they checked out of the motel in Hope. They'd gathered their few belongings and were about to shut the door on the dismal beige room when Bryan grabbed her hand and rubbed it against his denimed bulge. "Gonna be a long drive, Lottie," he said. "Not sure I can make it unless you help me out." They neglected to close the curtains of their ground-level unit, whether out of haste or inclination she wasn't sure. Anyone walking by could have seen Bryan open-legged on the bed, his shaggy blond head thrown back, her brunette one bobbing up and down. The risk of it was electrifying.

"Damn." One arm shoved under the seat, Charlotte brushes against dirt, crumbs, wrappers, and God! something moist. "What the fuck?" She withdraws her hand and sniffs, unable to resist. Fermented apple juice—less revolting than she expected. Bryan smiles and the dent appears in his right cheek, a rugged divot she has traced with her finger and licked clean of sweat.

"It's like a compost heap down here," she says.

"Yeah, I'm hoping for mushrooms eventually. Living off the land, you know." He glances at her again as she shakes dry her apple-sticky fingers. "Make that living off the *hand*."

It's a lame remark, one of many he's come up with. Her Australian's face is chiselled and his pants are full of life, but his attempts at humour fall flat every time. However. She's not with him for his sparkling repartee.

"Any luck?"

"No. I can't find it anywhere." She sits back in the seat and goes through the Birkin bag again, this time removing every object and making a pile on her lap. She put it in her purse yesterday, she knows she did, and she never took it out again. It's got to be here.

"Come on, Lottie, who cares? It's over, right? You're rid of the guy."

She stares at the tube of lipstick in her hand. Rid of the guy. Bryan is right: Lottie wouldn't care. She is divorced and on her own. Why fret about a wedding ring that has lost all meaning?

She quits rummaging and gazes out the truck's pitted windshield. They've arrived in Salmon Arm, which despite the quaint name looks like a generic highway town: gas stations, fast food chains, strip malls, mattress shops. There's supposed to be beauty in small towns, but all she ever sees is this part, the grimy commercial spine.

No husband, what would that be like? Charlotte has contemplated it after a bad fight or when Tayne goes ghost and hardly comes home, but her thoughts always run toward separation or divorce. Being rid of him — somehow that's different. It's like erasing him and all evidence of him, an entire folder deleted from her system.

"I give up." She starts to refill her handbag. "I can't find it."

"Want me to help? You know, fresh eyes. Someone else looks, sometimes they see things you can't. Want me to pull over?"

Fucking hell — the money.

"A lady never lets a man look in her purse." Charlotte believes no such thing, but she has neither the time nor the desire to concoct a plausible explanation for why the zippered compartment of her bag holds twenty thousand dollars in cash, actually a little less after her purchases in Kamloops. The truth will sound ridiculous: *I took it from my husband to buy an orange Birkin bag. Because the money's mine in the first place.* No, the truth will sound like a lie. She's not supposed to have a husband.

She reaches over and gives Bryan's thigh a squeeze. "Sweet of you to offer."

Being rid of Tayne. She could go anywhere. She could start over, like the man she read about in the Chicago airport. Say adios to BC, where she lives only because of Tayne, and head for a proper city like Montreal, a grande dame that throws shade on the pimply adolescent that is Vancouver. She could have her own schedule, her own choices. Maybe — her own convictions. No household to run, no office either, no parties to organize, no scavenger hunts for cheese, which she and Bryan have been nibbling but can't seem to make a dent in. No need to supervise May — no need for May at all. No booking painters and window cleaners and moss removers and gardeners, people to put up the Christmas lights and people to take them down again. No making doctor's and dentist's and eye and hair appointments for her husband and her daughter, no twisting her days to get them there on the right date at the right time. No monitoring Sidney's state and mood and smell: Is she sober or high? Truthful or lying? Sullen or ready to detonate? No having to manage the girl, set expectations, and enforce consequences, because — and here the penny drops — there is no girl.

That, of course, is the distinction. That's why being rid of Tayne is so different from leaving him. Leave him and he's still there, and so is Sidney. Charlotte is still a wife, just a divorced wife. She is still a mother, because you can never divorce your child. But erase Tayne and he never existed. And neither did Sidney.

Bryan's window is down a few inches. The breeze stirs her hair and takes the edge off the funky smell emanating from the bag on the floor. The goddamn cheese — will she never be free of it? Irritation at all things goat, and all that the cheese stands for, makes her squirm.

"How about some music?" Bryan fiddles with the scratched-up console and the CD kicks in, simple plodding drumbeat, twangy guitar. The Black Keys, a band Charlotte recognizes from Sidney's playlists.

She balls up her hands, nails biting into her palms.

Sidney is her flesh and blood, and Charlotte is a monster. That's the only word for a mother who wants to erase her own child. It's one thing to crave a break now and again. What parent doesn't? It's another entirely to wish away your only offspring. Mothers abandon their kids every day, but they are drug-addled mothers, abusive mothers, crazy, suicidal, schizo mothers. Charlotte is none of those. She is healthy, successful, organized. She excels at every challenge, whether she enjoys it or not. There's no question Sidney tries her patience, mocks her, hurts her — even, a few times, physically — and now humiliates her on social media. But for Charlotte to actually desert her daughter means entertaining a ghastly admission — that she is the worst, most unnatural kind of woman: a mother who doesn't want to be one. It means accepting that she has turned into her own mother, who once told her, *It was never my job to love you, only to make you independent.*

A different song begins, mellow and moody, a Coldplay tune from ages ago. Salmon Arm is behind them now, and the Trans-Canada unrolls, smooth, wide, and slow. Cars, motorbikes, even transport trucks whiz by in the passing lane. Bryan's battered Dodge Ram putters along. *She's an old gal,* he said when they hopped into it this morning; *she doesn't like to be pushed.*

I'm not even old yet, Charlotte thinks, and I'm tired of being pushed. So tired.

She shivers.

"You okay, Lottie?" Bryan palms the back of her neck. "Your ring — want to head back to Hope, see if you left it at the hotel? We're not in any rush. I'll turn around right now if you want to."

She shakes her head. "No, you're right. It doesn't matter. That part of my life is over."

The low hills of the Shuswap slip by, green and eternal, unlike the dramatic Coast Mountains that rise above West Vancouver. What does that horizon look like now that the city has been held by the neck and shaken?

You think certain things are immutable — mountains, marriage, motherhood — that they are what they are and nothing can sway them. Then something does, and you're left blinking, gasping, in a void that feels more real and true than any solid thing that was there before.

〰

LISA JACOBS: Welcome back to *Toronto Art Beat*. We're in conversation with renowned performance artist Summer Rain. A survivor of the Great Vancouver Earthquake, she has transformed her personal experience into an explosive body of work that has the international art world buzzing.

Summer, your new creation, *Metanoia*, which we saw a clip of before the break, marks the tenth anniversary of the earthquake. The show debuted two months ago in Victoria and opened here in Toronto last Friday. In between Canadian dates you crossed the US, and after your next show, in Montreal, you'll finish in Vancouver on the anniversary day. That's quite a run.

SUMMER: Thank you. It is.

LISA JACOBS: You must be delighted with your reception here in Toronto. But there's some curiosity about your American tour. Why the cancellation in Chicago?

SUMMER: You're right, Lisa, the show has been so well received here. It's great when you have loyal fans who've been following you since the beginning. I'm grateful to every single one of them.

LISA JACOBS: Unlike the critics? A few in the States have been lukewarm about your new piece, saying it goes too far. Did the mixed reviews have anything to do with you pulling out of Chicago? We also heard rumours that something upset you, that you saw someone ...?

SUMMER: I try to ignore the critics, Lisa. You know, I'm really looking forward to Europe this summer. We kick off the tour in Barcelona. That city is jumping, the whole street-art scene, the Twitter art, the guerilla tags. It's what you might call the people's art. It's alive and well in Barcelona.

LISA JACOBS: Let's talk more about *Metanoia*. It unfolds much more calmly than your previous shows, but the ending! No spoilers here, folks. Let's just say that when you emerge from the forest, with the flames, the actual *fire* onstage, it's truly shocking. Partly because it happens so fast, and partly because of how you – well, who you are. It is without question your most daring act on stage. You told the *New York Times* that the final image was inspired by someone from that time, someone who meant a great deal to you. But you've never spoken about that person publicly. Who is it? Or who *was* it?

SUMMER: I can't ... It's nobody. No one.

FIFTEEN

‸

Vancouver was not the only spectacle on the world's screens. Across the water, the east coast of Vancouver Island was rocked just as hard. Nanaimo, population 91,000, equally close to the quake's mid-strait epicentre, folded in on itself. Waterfront and downtown cordoned off; university closed, campus evacuated; high-tech and construction firms shuttered, also the malls, the big-box strips along the Island Highway, the fish cannery, the Costco, the gas stations. Up the coast, Parksville and Qualicum Beach, retirement havens for seaside golfers, were raked through, adult-only condos slammed, modular homes slanted off their foundations, roads and driveways jagged with crevasses. Great swaths of the nearly three-hundred-mile-long island went dark, the aging submarine cables that carry electricity from the mainland wrecked by the rupture.

Most afflicted yet least publicized were the northern Gulf Islands, oddball settlements too tiny and self-contained to grace the global stage. Victoria, too, escaped the spotlight: tucked into the southern tip of Vancouver Island, the provincial capital was wounded, but less deeply than the metropolis on the mainland.

No earthquake respects a border. Northern Washington and the San Juans took a hit: buildings canted over, electricity knocked out, secondary bridges collapsed, death toll surprising. Sections of the I-5 shut down, stranding motorists and cutting off towns. Highway 11, the coastal route, was littered with trees and debris and abandoned vehicles that no tow truck could reach.

Farther down the Pacific Northwest, relief swept the coastline like a video gone viral. Big all-American cities filled with big all-American citizens, living in glorious wealth and abject poverty, at the back of their minds knowing, yet at the same time not, that the Big One will come one day. But not this day. All of them – like all of the spared – off the hook, breathing, righteous.

‸

IT IS RIDICULOUS TO FEAR a teenager, especially one who has not grown into her age. Look at the bed, piled high with stuffed animals. A blue velvet whale, a tan monkey gone bald where the plush has worn away. Look above the scalloped wooden desk at the bulletin board, pinned with faces of joyous girls, long straight hair and polar-white teeth, each photo affixed to the cork with a pink heart-shaped tack. Look at the butterflies in the photos and drawings that fill the spaces between gleaming-haired girls. Look at the walls, postered with boy bands, animals, and a curvaceous, big-haired woman holding a microphone. *Beyoncé* say the letters along the bottom.

How can Anna be afraid in this room overscented with spiced vanilla, no doubt spilled by the shaking? It is the refuge of a girl — not even a true teenager let alone an adult. Anna knows. She once owned stuffed animals: a giraffe strangely more legs than neck, and a pink pig that reminded her, not altogether comfortably, of her uncle's sow. She taped up magazine covers of Green Grey and the Nu Virgos and a school photo of Irina, her closest friend. She did what she could to personalize the sunporch where she slept until her brother left for Odessa and she inherited a real bedroom, with a door. Then began a new era, purged of childhood. Instead of celebrity faces, up went Impressionist paintings she clipped from magazines discarded by the library. A shoot from her mother's spider plant softened one corner of the bureau. The stuffed animals went to a young cousin, who rode the giraffe around his apartment, giddyupping with glee. She kept only the photo of Irina, which stayed on the wall for a year until her friend moved to Kiev. When the new decor was done, Anna stood back and took stock. She saw the shift for what it was: a rite of passage, her first foray into adulthood. A sparse room, uncluttered, mature — the room of a young woman. She was thirteen.

Forget the fear and look all around. So many *things*. Jars and tubes and spray bottles line the top of the bureau — the girl has tidied up since the last aftershock. A striped loveseat covered with clothes and purses. Sliding doors to a closet that spans an entire wall. A flat-screen TV bolted to the opposite wall. Piles of cast-off clothing on the floor, also hair clips, brushes, sandals, loose-leaf notebooks, pencils, the snaking white wires of earbuds. The room is filled with all a girl could want, plus items Anna would never think of—a horseshoe-shaped pillow in one corner, a sequined backpack, a squat black apparatus with a screen and microphone that Anna cannot identify.

"Karaoke machine," Sidney says as she emerges from the ensuite bathroom, tampon box in hand. "Don't they have those where you come from?"

The term means nothing to Anna, so she does what she always does when tumbled by the surf of English: waggles her head, a mixture of no and yes, and changes the subject. "Is bathroom out there?" She points to the hallway and sees, on the floor near the doorway, a lace bra, lipstick red, stiff cups defying gravity. Maybe there is some young woman in this girl after all. Does she ... Is there sex in her life? The racy undergarment, against the backdrop of plush toys and juvenile furniture, turns Anna's stomach.

"You can use mine. I don't mind."

With a tiny nod, Anna takes the tampons into the ensuite, locks the door, and shuts her eyes.

It is ridiculous to be afraid of a child, even when the child knows your secret.

Nyet. Not every secret.

Anna is afraid. Sidney has told no one about the drinking—yet. The girl has been unexpectedly kind, giving Anna her metal bowl, which Anna thanked her for and gave back; offering a tampon when Anna asked for pads. But kindness is fleeting; Anna knows better than to rely on it.

She is afraid, too, of the soldiers. Will they come back? One of them, the tall one with piercing eyes, lunged toward her at the front entrance. She thought she would vomit. Instead, she ran.

Besides the fear, she feels *it*. It is there, beneath the embarrassment of being caught drinking and the anxiety over losing her job. It is there, faint but growing. Whether her blood-soaked panties have summoned it, or the girl's scarlet bra, the low, awful thrum has started again. Anna feels it vibrate throughout her body. She hugs herself, digging her fingers into her upper arms, hard enough to leave bruises. Like the soldier did.

Look at the girl's bathroom, bigger than any in Miss Dodie's house, which has three full baths plus a two-piece off the back door. Look at the long wooden cabinet that lines one wall in lieu of a counter, two ceramic sinks set on top, both of them filled with water. Arching like a swan's neck over each sink is a silver spigot.

Two sinks for one girl.

Look above the cabinet at the wide rectangular mirror that spans the wall. Look into the mirror. Who – ?

She draws back, disoriented. The last clear hit of alcohol has diffused, and once more she does not recognize herself. The new pixie cut has surprised her, its feathering remarkably undisturbed by all that has happened.

She fashions a smile. The stiff expression thins her lips and pinches lines into her cheeks. Hers is the face of a hand-carved puppet, whose mouth trembles.

Durnukha, the soldier said, her chin in his calloused hand. Plain-faced, ugly woman.

You are beautiful, Miss Dodie said yesterday. Only yesterday.

The distant thrum gathers steam. Go away, Anna tells it. Not now.

She sets the box of tampons beside one of the sinks. To take her mind away she opens a lower cabinet, revealing a bank of built-in drawers. *Vot eto da!* Unbelievable what is in this bathroom. She opens a drawer filled with hair elastics, headbands, clips, ties. Another drawer holds a dozen cream-coloured washcloths, folded in neat squares. She fingers the top one, soft, like velour.

"Everything okay in there?"

She bangs the drawer shut. "Yes, please. I will finish soon."

Her underwear, when she pulls down her pants, is soaked with watery red that has leaked onto the grey cotton crotch of her trousers. In a few hours the blood will run thick, black, and clotted.

Blood. So much blood.

The train picks up speed. Please, no. It must not hit her now.

Blood. The word pulses in her head, its own insistent heartbeat. It was not her first time, the time in the park, yet she bled as if it were. Blood trickled down the inside of one thigh. The smell of it now, like coppery earth, carries her back against her will.

The sharp knock makes her jump.

"You coming out? You better not leave her alone too long."

Miss Dodie. She must get back to her lady, help her recover so that they can go home, clean up, and start again.

There is no saving the bloody panties, which Anna wraps in toilet paper and tosses into the wastebasket. Afraid to ruin the off-white washcloths, she unrolls more tissue and mops herself clean. She removes a tampon from the box.

"Pads?" Sidney had said when Anna requested some for the blood down below. "Um, who uses pads? I've got tampons."

Anna sits on the toilet, legs spread, staring at the cellophane-wrapped plug. It is small and bullet-shaped, not the long tampon inside a cardboard tube that Anna used in Ukraine. She cannot imagine inserting it.

Hard. How could he be hard?

She has let nothing inside her since the soldier.

Durnukha, he called her. She hated him for that. She hated him for everything he did to her and everything he stood for, but she especially hated him for saying that. He had already ruined her. He did not have to insult her too.

You are beautiful, Annie, Miss Dodie said yesterday at the hair salon. Anna's life has emptied itself of people, one by one, until now there is only Miss Dodie, who scolds her but also laughs with her, who says things like *you are beautiful.* Miss Dodie's life, too, has contracted. She depends on Anna, and Anna can never leave her.

The tampon is all there is. She has to.

She holds her breath, closes her eyes, and shoves her finger and the tampon inside. Bites back a sob. The girl must not hear. She knows too much already. She cannot know this too.

At the sink, as she scrubs and scrubs her bloody hands in the saved water, Anna looks squarely in the mirror. It is not true, what Miss Dodie said. She is not beautiful. But neither is she ugly. Here, today, she is merely different.

You are not strong, she tells her reflection. But maybe all you need is to be strong enough. She empties the sink, watches the pink water swirl down the drain.

When Anna emerges, the girl is standing by the bed, picking at her bandage. "Where is your mother?" Anna asks. "She is coming home soon?"

Sidney shrugs and continues to dig at the gauze. "I don't know. My dad and I couldn't get through to her yesterday. Now our phones are dead."

Anna places one hand over Sidney's. "No, it will ruin. You must keep it covered."

"I don't care." But the girl allows her hand to be stilled.

"You will find your mother. Or she will find you."

"You don't know that."

The girl is right, but if Anna has learned anything in thirty-two years, it is that the truth offers all the comfort of a pincushion. "I do know." She makes it sound definite. "You will find her."

"That's what Joe says too. He gave me this." From inside the neck of her tunic, Sidney withdraws a metal disc on a chain. "Some saint. It's supposed to help you find stuff that's lost."

Somehow, in the bathroom, Anna's fear of the girl went away. She knows Sidney will not tell anyone about the drinking. She touches the medallion, warm from Sidney's skin. "When you smell the alcohol, do you ... do you want to drink it?"

"I've been sober nearly five months."

"Is not long time."

Sidney shrugs, her shoulders under the long-sleeved tunic like the wings of a delicate bird. "Long enough. But I came close yesterday. Way too close. I had my hand on the door of the liquor cabinet, standing right where you were. I was going to break the lock and drink everything in there. Everything! Only we had the big aftershock and

Miss Dodie got hurt and I was okay for a while. Then I went to my mom's office to get the painkillers for Joe." She closes her long-lashed eyes. "I had to break the lock there too. She keeps them locked in a drawer, she thinks I don't know. I stared at that pill bottle for like five minutes before I brought it to you."

As she leans toward Anna, the scent of vanilla intensifies. She must have dabbed on some perfume. Something about that, the girl comforting herself in such an ordinary way at such an extraordinary time, makes Anna want to weep.

"I need a meeting," Sidney says quietly. "I really need a meeting."

"She must love you very much. Your mother."

Sidney shakes her head. "She just wants to fix me. She wants me cured so I'll stop embarrassing her. Then she can work all the time and have dinner parties and go running and belong to her committees and not have to ... you know, think about me."

"No. You do not believe that."

"It's true." The girl twirls a lock of hair around her blue-nailed forefinger. "My grandma, my mom's mom who's dead now, she came from Montreal to visit years ago, and they were sitting out on the patio. They must've thought no one was around. She told my mom that the women in their family weren't cut out to be mothers and that my mom should've never had me. She said my mom should've listened to her and had the ... you know. Abortion." She brushes the ends of her hair against her lips. "I'm never having kids."

Anna feels a deep pang. "You do not know. You are too young. So much will happen to you."

Sidney lets go of her hair. "I do know. I'm going to be an artist. I'm going to live downtown and spend all day doing my art. No hiding it or, like, keeping the door closed because I don't want anyone to bug me about it. No husband, no kids, nothing. Well, maybe a dog, if they're allowed in the building. A small dog. But I'm not getting married or having kids just because you're supposed to. People are scared all the time, they're scared to do stuff a different way. Their own way. That's why none of my so-called friends will talk to me anymore. They think

I'm different and that it's contagious or whatever. I'm not going to be like that."

This is the most the girl has said to her, the most she has said to anyone within Anna's earshot. But Anna must go back downstairs. Miss Dodie is waiting.

"Are you scared?" Sidney's question comes out soft, like her stuffed animals.

Anna swallows, remembers the pointlessness of truth. "No."

"Never?"

Blood. The burning eyes, the rough hands. The distant train, thrumming, thrumming. The loneliness of being one and being invisible. It all rushes through her mind. She stares at the wall over Sidney's head. "Do you know anything that happens in my country?"

The girl is silent. Anna is not surprised. For people here, when the Ukrainian crisis left the headlines, the conflict disappeared also.

"Always there is fighting. When you are from my country, you are scared and so you stay, or you are not scared and so you leave. For me, I left." She recounts this, the edited version, with a bravado she does not feel.

"If you're not scared, then why do you drink?"

This is the problem with lying. Too easily caught.

Anna thinks a minute. "I come to Canada for new life. Because it is hard in my country, too much poor people, too much bad. Here, everything is good." She pauses. "Until now. But soon it will go good again. All this will fix, as good like new. For me, everything here is new. I am in your country, like … how you say? The worm that will be the butterfly. But I must go down now. My lady —"

"Wait." Sidney crosses to her desk and returns with a notebook, its shiny cover marbled with green and black. She holds it carefully, as if it might come apart in her hands. When she opens it something moves. It is a drawing, a remarkably detailed coloured-pencil sketch.

"Metamorphosis," Sidney says.

The drawing is of a butterfly nearly out of its cocoon. In the background, in lighter pencil strokes, the corner of a garden, the branch of a tree whose trunk is not on the page, fern fronds and tall flowers bending in a breeze Anna can almost feel. The perspective is off, the butterfly too large against the background, but this makes the fragile creature look stronger. Sidney flips through page after page of butterflies, all in various stages of emerging.

"Meta …" Anna tries but cannot remember the rest.

"Metamorphosis. *Meta* means a change. This one," Sidney stops at a page that blooms with colour, "this came out close to how I wanted it."

The outlines of the drawing are filled in with vibrant colour, deep and almost wet, made with markers maybe. A shape, roughly oval, occupies the bottom third of the page; streaming from it, rays of colour that trail off the page. Along the bottom, a word in block letters. Anna tries to pronounce it. "Meta-no —"

"Metanoia." Sidney angles the notebook toward Anna. "Metamorphosis, that's when the shape of something changes, like the body. Metanoia is a change of heart. Or, like, your mind."

Anna touches the oval, in which she now sees a face, its features indistinct. "The body." Her fingers brush the exuberant streams of pink, orange, fuchsia, green, lavender. "The mind?"

"Exactly!" Sidney pages through more drawings that dance with colour. "I did these at the end of rehab. I kept thinking about it, *metanoia*, and there was this moment when I realized that sure, I was supposed to fix my body, all the drinking and drugs and the physical addiction, and that was important, but if I was ever going to be more than a tragic little rich girl who" — she draws quotation marks in the air — "struggles with substance abuse, it was my spirit that had to change. The drawing, well, it helps."

Anna knows better than to believe in any gods. But if she did, she would ask that just once in her life she might look the way Sidney looks now, eyes and skin and hair alive, belief radiating off the girl as surely as electricity must spark from the downed lines outside. Anna is filled suddenly, inexplicably, with a sensation she barely recognizes. It is hope. If energy and passion can thrive here, now, in the room of this troubled girl, in the middle of a smashed-up world, then surely anything is possible.

Joe crosses the west side of the Stedman property, returning from another check-in with Vincent next door. The white terrier, calmer than yesterday, trots obediently at his side. It's straggly, this part of the yard, the part he didn't get to yesterday. He mowed and fertilized the lawn, but the boxwoods need a good trimming. He rubs the end of a slender branch, one of the many tails and antennae that spring from the hedge. He hates to leave a job undone.

Dang it all, get a grip. He shakes his head. It's not like he's ever coming back here again.

He glances back at Vincent's house, an ornate two-storey mansion, built recently and built strong by the look of it, largely spared by the earthquake. Not so the seven injured people from the highrise down the shore, who are waiting inside for an ambulance or a van or even a visiting medic. A couple of them are in dire shape, resting on the queen-sized bed in the main-floor guest room, in and out of consciousness. Internal injuries, the soldiers guessed.

Joe considers heading back and asking Vincent if he can stay there instead of returning to the Stedmans'. He felt less conspicuous in the midst of so many wounded, just another limping, bashed-up casualty of the quake. But Vincent's got his hands full, and Joe can't bear any more inquisitive looks. Though Vincent's eyebrows shot up to his scalp when he saw Joe's hamburger face, he never asked what happened. Good thing, because Joe doesn't want to discuss it.

It's not that he's embarrassed. Stedman may be tall but he's soft, a mediocre fighter compared to some of the bison-built straight guys who've clocked him in the past. Joe could've fought back, and judging by how his body feels today he should have, but the spirit had gone out of him. One minute he was furious at Stedman, ready to lay him low in no time; the next he gave up. It's like he wanted the pain, wanted his body bruised up to match the soreness inside. It's not something he feels like explaining to anyone.

He needs to leave. He can't keep skulking around here, trying to hide from the man who beat him to a pulp. Only where's he supposed to go? He can't help the firefighters anymore, not in this condition. His left side hurts the worst. It's like an industrial stapler shoots him every time he breathes. Cracked ribs, probably. Who knows how long they take to mend? There's no way he can walk home until he's healed up some.

Home. The idea, which lifted his heart high just yesterday, slams it to the earth today. What the townhouse will look like he can't imagine. He's tried to prepare for the worst: their unit flattened or tilted, one of the tall cottonwoods out back slammed through the roof, each room a trash-heap of belongings. But his mind won't hold the images, any more than it will let him contemplate the ringing emptiness of the place — emptiness when he gets there if Kyle hasn't made it back yet, and emptiness forever when Kyle leaves for good. He can't think about it. That part of his mind and heart and future needs to stay shut against the loss to come.

The white dog has collapsed in a heap at Joe's feet, as if tired of waiting for him. The poor thing must be exhausted, racing around in circles since yesterday, plus a day or two before that by Sidney's reckoning. Too sore to crouch, Joe tries bending from the waist to stroke the sweet spot between the terrier's ears. The stapler goes off inside and he catches himself.

What if they'd gotten a puppy, like they talked about years ago? Another body beyond themselves to care for, to glue their lives together. Would Kyle have thought twice about leaving Joe alone at home? Would it have been harder for him to stay away all those evenings and weekends, pretending to do paperwork at the office, pretending to be at the gym, when he was really — just say it — *screwing around*, if there was a sweet little dog like this one wagging its tail at home, ecstatic to see him at the end of the day?

"You knew it was coming, didn't you, boy? You felt it." The terrier shudders slightly, on the verge of sleep. "That'd be a good thing to be able to do."

Would it, though? Would Joe be better off if he'd known before now, if he had sensed the end was near? Can you ever prepare yourself for the end of love? What would you do, exactly? Harden your heart bit by bit, the way you callous up your hands when you're new to gardening? Try to love a little less every day, draw away a little more every night?

The dog twitches, now fast asleep. Look what this poor guy got for his premonition: a bunch of pointless frenzy followed by total collapse. Joe figures he's in for a stretch like that whenever it sinks in that Kiki is gone. It wouldn't be any easier if he'd seen the future long ago.

He stretches, massages his back, watches a throaty Beaver dip toward the harbour, yet another floatplane loaded with emergency personnel and equipment instead of commuters. Every seaplane operator in the region has been pressed into service, what with Vancouver International officially shut, its control tower in ruins and its runways either submerged or buckled. Even the small local airports, like Pitt Meadows and Langley, have been declared unusable. The reports are worse all the time, says Vincent: thousands dead, road and rail access blocked, potable water scarce, supplies and troops arriving slowly and mostly by sea. It's starting to sink in all that lies ahead, how thousands will be homeless for the foreseeable future, how they're not counting the days but the years it will take the city to recover.

Wherever Joe goes, at least he can leave this strange, sad place with a clear conscience. The basics are taken care of — utilities off, water stockpiled, hazardous objects stowed, exits cleared. The house and its occupants are as safe as they can be under the circumstances. He's concerned about Sidney, what with her father not thinking straight. The nurse too. What if Stedman goes back to suspecting Anna of stealing his make-believe money? Is he unhinged enough to attack a woman?

The thoughts skate across Joe's mind, but none of them stick. Nothing, it seems, can touch the great frozen pond of his sorrow. It was there when he briefed Stedman yesterday. It was there when he sat in the great room last night, unable to talk or eat, barely capable of swallowing the soda that Sidney pressed on him. It accompanied him to Vincent's, sat by him as he absorbed the worst of the news.

The sorrow mingles with the smell of smoke, stronger than ever now, intensifying his guilt at not joining the crews that are battling the fires. The sorrow is everything; it is everywhere. Kiki, sweet centre of his life, is gone. Now there is only Kyle — stone-faced liar, doctor to the rich, hundred percent fag and deeply ashamed, philanderer, betrayer.

It's the betrayal that claws at Joe, the betrayal that makes him feel like a patsy. Like a one-winged dove. A stupid lunkhead who deserves to get hit.

I can't do this, Kiki said yesterday. *I feel like I'm living a lie.*

He said it and he meant it. He said it but Joe didn't hear.

A low, terrible rumble, faint at first, then louder and louder until Joe's ears fill with thunder. This time the earth stays still. No buildings fall, no people scream, no streetlights hit the pavement. It is a silent devastation. Beneath Joe's feet the grass he has lovingly tended gives way, his solid footing falters, and the earth cracks open, and with it, his heart.

〜

The air hangs thick with suspended particles; whether from the seventies chenille spread, the soot from the cast-iron woodstove, or the patina of age on the tongue-and-groove ceiling, it's hard to tell. A breeze stirs the cheap horizontal blinds but does nothing to ease Charlotte's swollen lips, her rigid nipples, her slick and shaky runner's thighs.

Two hours ago they'd set Lake Louise as their destination for the night. They never made it. As the kilometres sped by, they went from flirting to trying to top one another's description of what they'd do later in their hotel room. Talk led to Bryan's right hand down the vee of her new Banana Republic blouse, his fingers caressing her through her bra until in desperation she pushed her breasts up and out of their cups. Soon she unzipped Bryan's straining jeans. Careful not to go too far — she didn't want him to come now in the truck instead of later inside her — she circled and stroked languidly, stilling her hand when his breathing sped up. The few semis that passed them honked enthusiastically, the high-seated big-riggers saluting the x-rated view. At the first blast, embarrassment stained Charlotte's cheeks and she covered her breasts. Then the old recklessness took hold. Fuck it, she thought. Let them look. They don't know who I am and they'll never see me again. She felt as strong and boundless as the upthrusting mountains.

They were nearly through the Monashees, the town of Revelstoke ahead, when they decided a motel was needed, urgently. Lake Louise would have to wait. They checked in at the first place with a vacancy sign, a three-storey Swiss-style chalet, hearts carved out of the wooden overhang, window boxes of fake geraniums on the balconies. "Pure kitsch," Charlotte whispered as they humped their luggage – Bryan's backpack, her shopping bags from Kamloops, the inescapable sack of cheese – up two flights of stairs, past warped prints of alpine creeks and narrow-gauge railways, to the sloped-ceiling top floor. "I dunno," Bryan said, running a hand along the cheap wood panel. "It's got its own sort of charm, doesn't it?" At the end of the threadbare corridor he put the key in the lock – "An actual key, with the room number on it!" Charlotte exclaimed – and they fell onto the bed, the chenille spread grooving her soon-bared skin, mapping networks of corduroy road onto her body. As he pulled off her panties, Bryan flashed the dent in his cheek. "You're an open book, Lottie. A good rooting's all you need. A hard fuck, then a big meal."

Now, crusted with salt, so hot that she's flung the covers to the floor, Charlotte listens to Bryan snore lightly beside her. Irresistible, even with mouth breathing and spittle. Also dead wrong. She is no open book. More like a padlocked diary. She feels a stir of unease at how easily fooled is this sweet traveller, how readily he accepts any version of herself she cares to offer.

There is one book she'd like to open: the novel she read that night in the business lounge at O'Hare Airport, sluggish from free wine and hours of delay. The title torments her from the far edge of her memory. She'd paged through the paperback quickly, but when she hit the story about the man who dodged death and fled his stale life, it was like a wave breaking over her, cold and bracing. Do people really do that? she wondered back then. Go about their business until a single dislocation, a piece that flies sideways, prompts them to run?

People disappear all the time. She's heard the news stories, read the details online, collected tales of the friend of a friend who went to a bar or a neighbour's house or drove around the corner to buy juice, did something ordinary and unremarkable like going off to buy cheese, and they're never heard from again. The young man last seen at a Yaletown party on Halloween – did he stumble off a pier in a drunken stupor? Or was he beaten to death, his body dumped in another town? The new mother who vanished in Stanley Park, the only trace a woven bracelet that her sister had given her placed neatly – deliberately? – atop a weathered stump. Was she driven to suicide by postpartum depression? Or imprisoned as a sex slave? The municipal politician with ties to the gang world who flew to a Victoria meeting but never showed up. Was he murdered and his body dissolved by acid as legend has it? Disappearances result from crime or drunkenness, despair or pure accident, she always assumed. What if, she wonders now, the so-called victims actually escaped? Turned their back on the life they knew and decamped to some remote outpost where a new, secret life awaited?

There must be real-life people like the man in the story, fed-up people who flee burdens they can no longer carry, messes they don't want to tidy. They must start over, these people, with a new name, a fresh identity, a different job, accumulating friends and colleagues and lovers who know nothing of their past. It would be easier to do it that way, to disappear rather than leave. Easier and somehow purer. A clean break, no leash jerking you back to your former life. Saying no to slow death, saying yes to new life.

She gazes at Bryan's tousled hair. I escaped, she thinks. I could be trapped in Vancouver right now, cowering in my office, worried about blown deadlines and clients and broken computers. I could be at home, ignored by everyone except May, who will be freaking out. I could be adding up the months and dollars it'll take to restore the house and agonizing over what can never be fixed, like Grandmama's antique Spode. I could be dead. Instead I'm here, unscathed, alive.

Life. Charlotte flips her pillow, hoping for a cool underside. Every successful life is a front — she read that in a magazine and it incensed her, stayed with her like a buried coal she could breathe into anger in a flash. Typical, she thought then. Like the world needs another apology for mediocrity. The only people who tear down success are the ones too lazy to work for it.

Now she understands. Her successful life? It's a forgery of beauty and balance, each detail painstakingly brushed in, each colour deliberately chosen, each flaw, like Tayne's neglect and Sidney's addiction, painted over. Real life is not like that. It's not a beautiful canvas. It unfolds in a dusty room with hideous furniture and an ancient chenille bedspread. Life smells, and not of perfume; it's salty and tangy, a little gamey, like the blond tangle of Bryan's armpit. Life tastes of butter and bacon and Boston cream, not lettuce and sparkling water. It thunders past with the honking semis, booms like the loudmouths in the hallway who are shouting about the earthquake, drunk in the afternoon. Life is the lazy, elongated vowels of Aussie English; the sharp, goaty smell of cheese; the mouldy flavour of a joint smoked in bed.

She's been wrong about so much. She was convinced that Tayne and Sidney were the liars, hiding behind their excuses of career and drugs, and that she was the honourable one, making a home, managing the details, excelling, being her best self. Yet after all this time what she's built is not a monument to truth or beauty or conviction, but a front, as fake and gaudy as an old-time movie set.

My mother the liar, Sidney wrote on Facebook.

Charlotte's anger is gone. Her daughter may be a sullen, ungrateful screw-up, but she is also right. Charlotte is a liar. She has been one all along.

~

Come on, Kyle thinks. Come *on!*

Since their one successful call yesterday, every time he has tried to phone Joe he's gotten dead air. How many attempts? He lost count ages ago.

This time it's ringing. Is it for real? Or is his concussed brain playing tricks on him?

Leaning against a tree trunk to rest his hands, raw and blistered from the walking stick, Kyle actually hears the rings. He imagines Joe's hip pocket singing "Benny and the Jets." His heart races. With hope or fear?

"Kiki?" Joe's voice is muffled but real.

"Joe! Oh God, I've been trying and trying to get through."

"Me too. How – ?" Joe sounds far away. "I'm on the west lawn of the house. Maybe there's reception here. Or maybe they finally got some of the cell towers –"

"Joe, this has to be fast. The connection could go anytime."

"I know. Where are you?"

Joe sounds strange. Like he's been to the dentist and his mouth is still frozen.

"I'm on the mountain. I don't know, two-thirds down? Three-quarters? I'm all right. I'm – Well, one leg's smashed up. It's not great but I can make it. What about you?"

Nothing but the sound of breathing.

"Joe? You there? I've been so worried about you."

"Uh-huh. I'm fine. Just fine."

"Still at the waterfront place?"

"Yeah. Could be here awhile. If you're safe, you're supposed to stay where you are. That's what they're telling people."

"Oh, God, I saw yesterday, from Eagle Bluffs. I saw the whole city. It's – Jesus, it's bad."

"Tell me about it. I'm in the middle of it, right?"

Joe sounds so strange. Like his mouth isn't moving right and … frankly, like he's pissed off.

And? Wouldn't you be?

The last day comes back into focus: the fight yesterday morning, the things he said to Joe. *Love you.*

"Joe, at home yesterday, it was awful. I need to explain."

"No. Not now."

"Yes now."

"No! I don't want — Wait, I can't hear you, Kiki. You're cutting out." Kyle's reception is crystal clear. "Long as you're okay, that's great," Joe says quickly. "Let's just —"

"Joe, I haven't been honest with you. Not for a long time."

"Shut up, okay? Just shut up. This is not the time."

"It *is* the time. It's got to be now. Who knows what's going to happen?"

"No! Don't say it!"

"Joe, I am so sorry. For everything. We'll get home, both of us, and I'll tell you everything —"

Joe inhales sharply. "Look, you're breaking up. I can hardly hear you. I'm going to hang up."

"No, don't! Joe, listen to me. I am going to get off this mountain and I am going to make it home and I am going to tell you —"

Joe is shouting now. "Shut up, shut up, just shut up!"

"No, you have to —"

"I won't! I love you! Don't you get it? You're everything to me, you're my whole life." Joe is crying, sobbing. He has never heard Joe cry. "You can't break up with me now, you can't —"

"Oh, Joe." How can he get it so wrong? "Come on. I'm not breaking up with you. I love you. Please, please forgive me. I've been such an asshole. You're the only thing that matters to me, the only thing —"

The line goes dead.

Kyle stares at the device he has willed for over a day to connect him with his lover. He is shaking. What just happened?

Will Joe call back? He sounded so upset, so ... hurt. Wasn't he glad they were talking? Wasn't he relieved?

He knows.

Kyle hits redial. Nothing. A squirrel hops from branch to branch overhead, the scratching an eerie echo off the trees.

He knows. You're a weak-ass liar, and he knows it all.

Tries again. Nothing. Stares at his phone, waiting.

At least Joe is okay. At least he's not injured.

Now that the squirrel has gone, the forest is silent. Not a rustle in the trees, no rush of distant water. It's been hours since he crossed the last creek and dragged his water bottle through the spouting wet.

The phone sits in his sweaty palm. Did he really just talk to Joe or was it some elaborate hallucination? The injured climber in that movie they went to, while he was hauling himself toward camp, saw and heard things that weren't there. Has the pain quit nibbling the edges of Kyle's sanity and taken a chomp from its core?

The phone battery. It's gone down, only thirty percent left now, proof that the call was real. It *was* Joe. It was Joe's voice and he is okay.

And Joe loves him. Joe loves him and that's all Kyle needs to know. He's been a fuck-up, a selfish, horrible person, and yet he is everything to Joe, he is Joe's life. Joe said so. It means Joe will forgive him.

It starts, familiar as his own heartbeat: the circus drumline that has accompanied him for hours.

He stows the phone in his pack, fumbling, his motor coordination worse than ever. He returns all his weight to the walking stick. Pain snaps its jaws at him — the raw meat scrape of his palm, the rub of his blistered feet, the gargantuan agony of his leg. But with the pain comes a flare of elation.

Joe.

Bring on the pain. He deserves every second of it and he will take it. And if it eases, he will ask for more. Because Kyle knows that if he can power through the pain and get himself off this mountain, Joe will forgive him. The tattoo of pain, the rhythm of the drum, and now Joe's name echoing every beat, the strong syllable — *Joe* — they are the thrust he needs to keep moving.

He hops once, twice, three times, then slumps. The old hop-four, slump is gone; he can't go more than three without a rest. It doesn't matter. It may take many more hours, it may take days, but he is going home.

A raven lifts off from a Douglas fir, its caw filling the sky as it wheels and turns down the mountain, toward the city, toward Joe. The raven's sky is Kyle's sky, and it is Joe's sky too. They are only a bird flight apart.

He takes another hop. Grimaces, smiles. The two expressions feel the same.

Home.

∿

In the great room earlier, bathed in morning sun and taking stock of his situation, Stedman had resolved to get it together: to shake off his paralysis, rein in his wandering mind, and take charge. Since then, other than dismissing the soldiers, he has spent the better part of four hours – as best he can determine, his watch having stopped yesterday and the ormolu masterpiece lying in shards – shut away in his office.

It is not a retreat or a withdrawal, he reminds himself; it is a strategy session. He is not a hundred percent, his edges are blurry, but he has identified his priorities. Now he must rank them, formulate a plan, break it into steps, and do what it takes to execute those steps going forward.

God, planning takes time. So much time. He's never been good at the details. Anything micro level – that's Charlotte's domain.

Whenever he thinks of her now, his thoughts float like whispers. *She's not coming back.*

Why does that idea keep niggling him? Of course she's coming back. He needs her. Sidney needs her. And Charlotte needs them. Surely.

She's never happy anymore.

Yesterday in the kitchen she was so stressed, the hurricane on the verge of blowing. You could almost imagine her walking out.

And never coming back.

It crawls further over him, the sensation that's been visiting since yesterday, more frequently now that he turned the soldiers away and saw the contempt on Sidney's face. It's not a feeling so much as a vision. A premonition.

It's here this minute, right beside him. Now on top of him. God, it's bleak. A celestial palm holding him down. The press, the weight, of all he has lost: his wife, his daughter's respect, Merck, the sale of his shares, the freedom that crooked its finger only yesterday, the drive up the highway in his sweet MGB. His old life, before it got huge. A simpler happiness. Another child. A kinder love.

He closes his eyes, runs a hand over his face, finds the place on his jaw where it hurts most. Presses it, hard.

Focus, he tells himself. Take charge, for yourself and for Sidney. No more orders from the hired man. He may be gay but he's an asshole. He stole your money, your decisions, your little girl.

No more. Whatever needs doing, Stedman will do it himself. Starting with the electricity.

He leans back in his chair and takes in the harbour view, so different from Montreal, where there was so much to hate: the sign wars, the bone-cold winters, the supercilious francophones who detested anglos like him. He was in the city for one reason: the MBA tuition was the lowest in the country, so between his savings from part-time jobs and the sums his mother put aside, he could scrape by. What he hated most about Montreal, even after he met Charlotte and his future turned gold, were the random power outages. He never told Charlotte, who even then mocked all weaknesses, how their shadowy apartment unnerved him, its refrigerator mute, its radiators cold. Telling her would mean dredging up memories better buried. How his mother, partway through frying sausages or boiling potatoes when the stove shut off, would pause, then say they'd be having a picnic again for dinner, crackers and peanut butter and jam, and wouldn't that be fun? In summer it *was* fun, but in winter, when the thermometer plunged low, there was no adventure to be had. He and Tim huddled close on those nights, the two of them in thick flannel pyjamas, their twin beds pushed together and topped with every blanket in the house, Stedman's father nowhere to be found, the reason the bills had not been paid.

Stedman's father. Sober, he was the hardest worker you'd ever meet. On a tear he was another creature entirely: unreliable, short-tempered, forgetful, absent. *Waste of skin* is how Stedman sums up the old man, though it's a private assessment. To Charlotte and her mother, and to the media during his meteoric rise, he has recounted the same well-composed story of a working-class upbringing (he never says *poor*) and an unpredictable father (he never says *drunk*). To do otherwise would be to court pity, which is the last thing he wants. Tayne Stedman, CEO and Chief Innovator of GlobalTech Communications, is a self-made man. He has dined with two prime ministers and one US president. He has headed up boards and national councils, founded a global think-tank on cross-cultural pollination. Bill Gates's direct number is in his phone. He has built a glittering life, one he will not tarnish with spots of bygone woe.

You done good, he tells himself each day. He is nothing like the old man. He loves his little girl and he will make sure she knows it.

Focus, he instructs himself. The plan. Go online, connect with his people, find Charlotte.

She's long gone.

No. He will find her. He is a man of action, and he will reclaim what is his. He will show them – his daughter, his wife, himself – that no matter what has happened out there, their world has not shattered.

SIXTEEN

∿

The world watched Vancouver, eyes glued then averted then drawn back to the giddying horror: the precisely calibrated city, glass highrise centre ringed by ocean and mountains, tolerant blending of cultures and colours, perfect mix of society and solitude, of American-style capitalism and European-style socialism, a model metropolis ranked among the world's cleanest, safest, greenest, wealthiest, healthiest — unseated by the fierce swat of nature's hand.

Once the earth stilled, the looting began. First on the Downtown Eastside where the rougher element, the indigent and the addled and the addicted, shouldered their way into unstaffed corner stores to load up on cigarettes and Pepsi, chocolate and mouthwash. Then the lawlessness spread. What produce remained in the markets' sidewalk displays disappeared, a few oranges here, a cabbage there. Soon liquor stores in Surrey and Burnaby were raided; drugstores too. Hooting, cheering teens snatched running shoes and tablets, set fire to trash bins. On Robson, plate-glass windows shattered and burly men scooped out Coach bags and Jimmy Choo shoes. Across the Lower Mainland a homeopathic recklessness set in, as if the only response to destruction was to counter with more of the same.

∿

THE WORLD IS WATCHING THEM, says Joe, relaying the news from the neighbour's radio and the injured highrise residents now staying next door. Twenty-four hours after the forty-five seconds that upended the region, global media are consumed with the Vancouver tragedy. Rescue efforts are unfolding. Canadian troops have been joined by US militia, and more are on standby. The numbers of dead and injured are climbing, yet there is no room for them in the hospitals left undamaged. Community centres, arenas, school gyms, and churches have turned into treatment centres and morgues, but are filling faster than they can be set up. Fires rage, fuelled by ruptured gas lines. The sulphur piles in Port Moody are blazing, spewing out an unbreathable chemical fog. The looting continues. Even the tony Whole Foods market on Marine Drive, scant blocks from this house, has been broken into. People — *what people?* asks Miss Dodie, but Joe can only shrug — are running off with goji berries and tamari almonds, organic arugula and floral wreaths.

The news is appalling, yet in the minds of the castaways gathered in Stedman's sun-bathed great room — except for Miss Dodie, whose thoughts run an unusual course — it is also inevitable. Each one of them, even Sidney, who has been forced by the school system to read literature, recognizes the stuff of tragedy: the mighty have fallen, society is crumbling, order has given way to chaos. Of course the world is watching. The world is riveted.

They, in turn, watch each other, these shaken, sequestered souls, fearful of what might come, barely comprehending what has passed.

Anna watches Miss Dodie, out of duty and also concern. The old woman cannot get up to much trouble, confined as she is to the sofa, though earlier she tottered to the bathroom surprisingly quickly, with Anna's help. Extreme vigilance may be unwarranted, but Anna is nonetheless worried about her lady. Miss Dodie misses home, and these unfamiliar surroundings and people are straining her few mental resources. The woman's wistful expression stirs Anna's heart.

Because attentiveness is her habit, Anna also watches Joe. His swollen mouth tells the news, but his mind is elsewhere. From the beginning he has taken charge and watched over them, calm and helpful and practical. He has made the decisions and done most of the work. He is the only sensible adult here besides herself. But now, back from the neighbour's, he seems preoccupied. Whether he is worried or in pain from his beating or simply distracted, she cannot tell. Do not despair, Anna wants to whisper to him. The worst has happened. It will only get better.

Sidney would watch her father, hoping for a sign that he is on top of things, getting a handle on this disaster, acting like a caring human being instead of a cold-hearted tyrant, except that Stedman is still barricaded in his office. In the room he calls his own, its Brazilian cherry floor mercifully steady and perfectly aligned, surrounded by furniture that he selected, not Charlotte, he surveys the totems on his magnificent desk — photos of himself with world leaders, the Governor General's Innovation Award, books on chaos theory and disruptive innovation — and reviews the steps that will restore his power.

Because she cannot watch her father, Sidney watches Anna, in the slant-eyed, undetectable way she mastered in middle school when she first understood that survival depends on observing without being observed. Fingering the medallion Joe gave her, on a cheap chain around her neck, she tries to read the nurse's rigid, anxious face. Something is bobbing near the surface there, something that troubled Anna earlier, in Sidney's bedroom. She has a secret, this quiet alcoholic with the accent, a secret besides her drinking. Sidney — out of curiosity? sympathy? kinship? — wishes she knew what it was.

Miss Dodie, awkwardly installed on the strange leather sofa, a cushion supporting her lower back, knee throbbing like a heroine's heart, runs through all the unimaginable things that have happened — an earthquake! like in Japan and other parts of the world that she cannot name but where the people are small and brown; and a sleepover! in a stranger's restaurant, but my, it's dirty, all the smashed objects and spilled wine and no woman here to keep it clean, yet it's on the ocean and there is fruit, though nothing actually delicious, like bacon — and she is watching a creature (a Steller's jay, but she does not recall the name) that preens and poses outside, just beyond the glass doors that open onto the patio and the sea-facing lawn. The bird looks cheerful. It may be the uptuft on its head, a feathered paintbrush that flicks a short, quick stroke on the sky each time the jay twitches. The sight pulls Miss Dodie's thoughts away from the restaurateur's lengthy account of the news to her late husband's penis, which kinked up like that thing's plumage, full of life and perky. She misses him, her Marty, despite the lies and infidelities, the drinking and the roaming, the foreign orifices he felt compelled to enter with that upturned penis. She rubs the wrinkled finger where her love should be. Whose skin is that, so loose and papery? But she knows. It is her skin, her finger, and the ring is lost. That much of yesterday she remembers. They walked by the sea and saw that thing ... that insect, like the one outside now — a bird! With its neck grotesquely wide. Then the swell-necked thing stole her ring and ate it up. She glares at the Steller's jay, which appears to her no longer jaunty but malevolent. Sooner or later, whether husband or bird, one's true nature surfaces. Everyone is a fuckster in the end.

The jay intently watches the glass, but sees nothing beyond its own reflection. The sight is admirable, for the jay is healthy and in the prime of life, but of fleeting interest. The bird hop-hops farther onto the lawn, drawing closer to the sea, which is ruled by other birds. Cocks its head, assesses. The world is still full of strange noises. The insects remain plentiful, as if shaken to the earth's surface. The air is worse. Thick and particle-laden. Waiting.

Joe watches the women, three generations of them in the great room, and sees that they depend on him. The old bag will never get off the sofa without his help, injured as he may be. Anna needs the news he brings. When will it be safe to drive, she wants to know. And she needs his silence to keep her addiction safe. Sidney needs his reassurance. What do we do next, the girl keeps asking him. Her father is still missing in action — just as well, because her celebrity dad is a clueless good-for-nothing hothead. Stedman, whose house is now safeguarded and whose daughter is cared for, has relied on Joe the most, and will be the last to admit it.

As Joe watches the women, the yoke of responsibility at last settles on his shoulders. He is not accustomed to being in charge, yet here he is, the leader of this oddball band. He is not smart, yet in the worst disaster imaginable he has done everything right. *Almost* everything, his ribs remind him as he shifts on his chair. He will be fifty soon. Maybe that is not so bad. Maybe it will be an age of more confidence, more certainty. Of greater love. For Kiki spoke of love, and Joe must hold on to that. Kiki spoke of forgiveness. That much Joe heard before he ended the call, afraid to hear the awful truth. *Sniff, sniff, sniff.* Whatever Kiki has been doing, Joe does not want to know. He only wants his lover back.

Less than twenty kilometres away, Kyle watches the stony trail ahead, blocking out all sights on the periphery. The circus drums mark the beat: hop-three, slump; hop-three, slump. He has sidelined the pain, whether through discipline or exhaustion. It is still there, and it skewers him each time his broken leg fails to clear a rock or a rise, but by and large he has entered a trance. He ate the last bite of power bar hours ago but is no longer hungry. He got water at the last creek but feels no urge to drink. His searing moments, the ones he is sure he cannot bear, no longer bring pain; they burn with remorse and also with hope. *Joe. Home.* Each hop with his good left foot releases his lover's name into the air; each swing of the shattered right leg says where he's headed. The forest on either side of the interminable mountain trail rings with the rhythm.

More than five hundred kilometres away, Charlotte watches Bryan, naked, beside her in the bed. How can he still be asleep? Is it the sex? The dope? Or does he really, really like to sleep? She considers waking him to remind him that in a day or two she'll be off, that their time together is limited so they should make hay and so forth. But he is a big boy. He knows all that. How many more times will they lie together like this or (because why limit yourself) stand or sit or kneel? Three? Five? She tries to memorize her Australian's beautiful profile. She will miss him when she goes. The world shook this virile, vital man into her lap, and she will never forget him.

SEVENTEEN

∿

Some of the city stood strong. Buildings, some new, some old, whether through engineering or good luck, escaped the buffeting, toppling, and pancaking. For every resident clipped by a wall unit or trapped beneath a caved-in roof or entombed by a landslide, dozens more remained unscathed.

The world, however, was gripped only by reports of loss, not by who and what survived. It was an earthquake: destruction was the theme.

Thousands died. Tens of thousands were injured. An untold number could not get home, or no longer had a home, and waited out the hours, clutching blankets, clutching plastic water bottles, in gymnasiums and community centres, in churches and arenas. A few of the unseen did the unexpected: they turned their backs on the wreckage and fled, leaving history behind.

All of them — the injured, the stranded, the separated, the disappeared — wanted to know, will we ever be the same after this? The answer was: never. Also: always.

∿

HER LADY HAS AT LAST ACCEPTED a glass of tonic water and after a few sips has quieted down, much to Anna's relief. Whether it is the unaccustomed surroundings or her injuries from the chandelier, Miss Dodie's off-colour tales have grown louder and more lurid. It is more than a little unsettling to hear an eighty-six-year-old matron go on about how her husband's penis sprang up at the slightest touch, how passionately he kissed her, how some nights he begged her to remove her blouse at the dinner table so he could gaze on her glorious breasts and watch the nipples stiffen. Anna may not follow every word, but she knows *glorious breasts*, the term Miss Dodie always uses when telling this story. Based on the drooping, crepey mounds that Anna harnesses into one stiff bra or another every morning, she questions how faithful her lady's memory is in this regard. Did Saint Kelvin have to hear such sordid details when he was in charge? Not likely.

Anna's understanding of Miss Dodie's mental state is limited to the few facts she has gathered from the woman's family physician. Dr. Mason, a white-haired gent only a few years her employer's junior, has pressed pamphlets on Anna, but she cannot understand the stilted English. She has studied the pictures, photos of doughy seniors who appear vacant and cheerful at once, and drawings of brains and arteries, but they tell her little. Most of what she has learned about Miss Dodie she has gleaned through trial and error, plus her short experience nursing her mother, whose brain tumour mimicked dementia in the beginning.

Anna can therefore not explain why Miss Dodie's mental acuity fluctuates so drastically. There are times the woman forgets her own address or what to call the thing Anna runs through her hair. There are others when she peers into the very heart of matters. She pretends, for example, to have seen proof of Anna's credentials, when there is no proof because there are no credentials. Should anyone question Anna's background — which, given her blatant lack of skill, happens all too often — Miss Dodie insists that Annie's papers are around somewhere. Then she winks at Anna as if to say *I know you are a fraud but let's pretend I don't*. Miss Dodie's complicity is worth as much to Anna as her pay, and Anna will endure no end of pornographic stories in exchange.

The endurance of others, however, is limited. Nose wrinkled, Sidney drifted out of the room some time ago. The gardener limped out soon after, a dreamy look on his face, whether amused by the old lady's indiscretions or caught in his own thoughts, it was hard to tell.

"They're all gone, Annie," Miss Dodie says now. "All the waiters and waitresses. Only you and me left."

It is unusual for Miss Dodie to accept tonic water. The only thing Mr. Dodie fancied more than the glorious breasts of his wife (and, apparently, the breasts of many others' wives) was a stiff gin and tonic. To this day Miss Dodie reviles not only alcohol but the various mixes associated with it. Anna has nonetheless convinced the woman that the tonic will repair her injuries, a fabrication concocted purely to support a visit to the liquor cabinet. As she filled Miss Dodie's glass,

Anna drank as much as she dared of the gin she had sampled earlier. Each swig, though essential as water, brought her less enjoyment. The drinking has now crossed over to the medicinal stage, no more pleasurable than Miss Dodie's pills, which the woman has been without for over a day now. A day without blood thinners will not harm her, but what if the interruption stretches another two, three, even four days? Anna imagines her employer's heart firing a clot of blood into her brain, as fatal a shot as any execution.

Miss Dodie's head tips back and she stares at the ceiling, mouth open, eyes too. She has shifted to a seated position so that she can set the mostly full tumbler on the coffee table, a sign that her mobility is improving, but at the same time she has slipped into her dream world. Dreaming of what? At least she is doing it quietly – for now. A restlessness is building inside the woman, Anna can sense it behind the acting out. Miss Dodie needs to go home. Anna does too.

Please let the house be livable, she thinks. As long as it is, Miss Dodie will continue to need her. If their home is destroyed, Miss Dodie will be off to a care facility and Anna will be out on her bum. Nowhere to go, needed by no one. Completely alone.

She sits forward on the sofa, arms on her knees, and examines her rough, red hands. She is a blank sheet on which life marks its lines. She pictures Sidney's art book and all it contains, from simple drawings to whole worlds of colour, every one created from nothing. Will a day come when she, Anna, holds the pencil? When the lines of her life are of her own making?

$$\wedge$$

What is the name of that book? Like her itchy foot yesterday, the title worries at Charlotte, tickling her memory. The name of the author too, one of those hard-boiled writers from the thirties or forties. Mallory? Malcolm?

She draws the bedsheet over her cooled-off body, careful not to disturb Bryan. The phone, she thinks for the hundredth time. Why the fuck did I throw my phone?

The lament is more rote than anything. She could have bought a new cell phone in Kamloops this morning. She considered it briefly before deciding that if she went off with Bryan for a few days, it was better to leave no trail. Now she is relieved she held off. If she's going to disappear for good, she needs to do it right.

The how — that's the easy part. Her busted phone will tell no tales; the GPS died with the rest of the device in Agassiz. The SUV in the long-term lot back in Hope will be as far as anyone can trace her. Bryan, with his Australian notions of masculinity, has insisted on paying for their hotel rooms and food. In Kamloops she shopped with cash from the twenty thousand she lifted from home. What's left, which is most of it, will last her awhile, certainly long enough to contact the Montreal lawyer who oversees her private trust fund, the slice of Pettigrew fortune that she alone has access to. Once he signs an oath of secrecy, he can do the rest: move her money to the Cayman Islands or Switzerland, put it in numbered accounts, whatever it is that lawyers do to hide their clients' names and fortunes. There's not much in the fund, just a few million, but she won't need a lot. A small, chic condo where every room is hers and hers alone. A basic wardrobe, a few decent pieces she can mix and match. New passport and ID, of course, but that can't cost much. People buy identities all the time.

Doing this right means leaving no trace. Tayne, Sidney, their friends, her colleagues at Diamond & Day — everyone must assume she was killed. They'll wonder how, since her car is outside the damage zone, and they'll look for answers, but they will never find them. There's no record of her staying in Hope, and given the crowds that swarmed the motel there, it's unlikely anyone will remember her face. If someone does, so what? It won't change the conclusion they reach. It was a major earthquake, people died and will never be found, and she will be one of them. Just like the man in the book, she will step unseen from an old life into a new one. The earthquake is her falling beam.

Enough. She has to know the title. Even an ersatz mountain lodge will have a computer. She eases out of bed, pulls on her wrinkled clothes, grabs the kitschy room key, and slips out.

It took a long time to work out, what with his mind tending to wander —
he is more and more convinced that his head sustained some serious
damage yesterday — but at last Stedman has written down the steps,
rearranged them, rearranged them again. Locate Charlotte and make
a plan to get her home. Tell Sidney what he's done and restore her faith
in him. Contact the office to see how his staff have fared, what shape
the facilities are in, how and when they can get back on their feet. Do
a quick check of the markets. Send his unexpected house guests home.

Step one: turn on the electricity. Not for good — much as he hates
to concede anything to the smart-ass hired man, he knows there could
be a fire risk. Just long enough to connect: to recharge his phones and
laptop, get the home internet going, and scan email, texts, Twitter, and
newsfeeds. He will move swiftly. He will retrieve and send messages.
He will unearth clues as to the fate of his people. Given the scale of the
devastation, if the gardener's accounts are to be believed, there will be no
news reports on the wife of Tayne Stedman, no photos of a maid in a flattened Smart car. But there should be messages from both women by now.

She's not coming back.

The idea continues to haunt him, but he swats it away. He has no
evidence that Charlotte has left him, other than a nagging feeling that
it is so. The idea is ludicrous when he considers it rationally. Her whole
life is here: family, home, career, money.

As for work, even if the local staff have gone to ground, the company
reps outside Vancouver will be posting to social media. Communication
is everything: it's a message he's drummed into them. They know the
value of a swift announcement that all is well, that GlobalTech has been
impacted by a tragic event, as have the citizens of this city we're proud
to call home, but together we will rise above the ashes — no, make that
rubble — pivot in the face of adversity, redouble our efforts, yada yada
yada. His people will think of the right words, put them in a stirring
arrangement, and issue the statement in four languages.

"We like to go home now."

The words, strongly accented, startle him. Ah, the nurse.

He swivels his chair and takes in her bedraggled appearance: the shapeless cotton clothing, the sturdy peasant build, the drab skin. Worn out as an old slipper. Is she the one who stole his money?

"Sure, go home." He stands up and arches his back. Time for everyone to move along, time for Stedman to forge ahead. "I don't think we need you here. I'm feeling much better." He touches his bandaged cheek.

"I can drive there?"

Stedman is puzzled. "Do you have a car?"

"Yes, but is in parking lot at Ambleside Beach. Is too far for my lady to walk, now she hurts her knee. I can bring it here, then drive home?"

Irritation needles him. He has more important things to do than play guessing games with kooks. "Go ahead. Be my guest."

Anna nods. "Yes, I am your guest. Thank you, and from Miss Dodie also. But I must know, is possible to drive in the road now? You hear on the news?"

"Oh." How the hell is he supposed to know? The nurse's face remains flat and expressionless. She'd make a damned fine poker player. Maybe she does have his money.

"Go ask the gardener. He's keeping up with the news. Though I guess I'll find out too, once I turn the power back on. I can go online then and see what's happening." The nurse continues to stare at him. "He's still around, isn't he? The gardener?"

"I do not know. Fifteen minutes ago or twenty, yes."

"Well, go find him. He probably knows about the roads." He peers at her broad, impassive face. How good is her English anyway? "Do you understand?"

"Fine." She looks straight at him. "You look at me. I do many things bad, but I do not have your money." She turns and heads off down the corridor.

A woman of few words. What would it be like to live with someone like that? A marriage of quiet instead of badgering, where exchanges are to the point rather than loaded with subtext. The nurse is homely, though. Could he sacrifice attractiveness for peace? It's an intriguing question, but one that will have to wait. He has things to do.

The sun has traced its way across the sky, and Joe has crossed to the east lawn where the grass is cool. Classic Kentucky bluegrass, not the most practical variety, needing even on the west coast loads of water, not to mention fertilizer, aeration, and top dressing. But he understands its appeal, especially for people like Stedman who can pay others to do the tending. The dense dark-green blades give off a fresh-cut scent — unbelievable that it was only yesterday he ran the mower — and form a thick, glossy carpet underneath him. Now that he has made himself sit down, testing the limits of his injuries, he can't imagine getting back up again. He rests his hand on the head of the terrier, fast asleep at his feet. Ever since Joe came outside again after briefing the women, the dog has been by his side.

"Hey, boy," he whispers. "Who's a good boy?"

There's still so much effort ahead, and he's trying to convince himself that he can handle it. More aftershocks could bring more injuries. Miss Dodie is getting agitated. Who knows what will fly out of her mouth next. The nurse is keeping an eye on her, but she's also drinking on the sly and could end up too tanked to be helpful. Sidney has gone further inside herself, probably because her father, the big-shot businessman, is still ignoring her. What is he doing holed up in his office all this time? Sulking? Obsessing over his precious money?

Joe can wait for the roads to open and drive home or wait for his body to heal and attempt the long walk, but either way he's not going anywhere soon, which means Kiki may get home first. One leg is smashed, Kiki said, but if he's on his way down, it can't be that bad.

Joe didn't have it in him to tell Kiki about his own injuries. The bruises on his body were nothing, then, beside the pain in his heart. But now, after what Kiki said, the pain is less. Joe strokes the terrier's head. Joe wants to believe that Kiki loves him. Wants it desperately.

Anna is nearly on top of him by the time he notices. That's Kentucky blue for you, thick and silencing. She crouches beside the sleeping terrier.

"Have a seat. Relax." He waves expansively.

"No. Is time to go home. Miss Dodie and me."

"Okay, but you can't drive there. No traffic allowed on the roads, remember?"

"*Da.* I remember. But is changed now, maybe?"

"No, it's going to be a day at least, probably more. Can she even make it out of the house, your ... Miss Dodie?" The name still feels foolish on his lips. What self-respecting woman would call herself that, as if she were a southern belle from the Civil War?

"I think yes. She moves more now, she even walks a little. She is getting better. Her knee is blue and black all over but is not so big."

Joe doesn't correct her. King of the bungled song lyrics, he's the last person to nitpick. "We'll all get home soon enough. Got to face it eventually, see what sort of mess is waiting there." He scratches the sleeping dog's head. Its ears flick as if twitching off an insect. "See if we've still *got* a home."

Anna watches him gravely. "Something is different. You are ... you are thinking much since you are back from over there." She nods toward Vincent's. "There is something you know?"

"Nope." He lifts his head. "I don't know anything. I'm always the last to know."

She holds his gaze, her grey eyes washed out but steady. He thinks of his mother. "Is not true," she says. "You know the most of everybody. So smart, so ... so kind." She reaches toward the dog's head and places her rough hand on top of his, gives it a gentle squeeze. "You are strong, Joe. I feel this from you. Whatever will happen, is not important. You always are strong."

Maybe I am, thinks Joe. I made it this far. Ma would be proud of me, at least.

"Your man, he is lucky."

Joe shakes his head. "How do you know I have a man?"

"I know." Anna smiles. "You love him, is plain as the day. And he loves you."

I love you was what Kiki said. *I love you with all my heart.* "Maybe."

"Not maybe. He does. You are good man. Any person would love you."

Please forgive me.

The breeze runs fingers over Joe's reddened face. Brings the briny scent of low tide, an unremarkable, everyday smell. A smell from yesterday, from the pre-earthquake world. The smell of life as it was, and as it could still be.

"Oh, the man, Mister Steed-man."

"Yeah. The big-time businessman." Joe snorts.

"He is not right in his head. He has, how you say? The percussion."

"Concussion?" Joe has never considered that. It would explain a lot.

"He is turning on electricity."

What?

Joe's mind wrenches back to the moment. Jesus! Is he crazy – ?

He barely has time to form the thought before the first sounds come. The initial cry is so muffled he's not even sure he hears it. The second is unmistakable. A wail of pure fear.

Anna is on her feet.

"Miss Dodie!" she cries. "Come!"

∧

CBC RADIO ONE: Summer, we're delighted to have you back on *Imagine Nation*. You have legions of fans here in Montreal. You of course moved here after the earthquake and you made your artistic debut here. We're always excited when you bring a new performance to town.

SUMMER: I'm thrilled to be back. *Bonjour, tout le monde.*

CBC RADIO ONE: I don't want to give away too much about your new piece, *Metanoia*, but I would like to ask how it relates to the last show, *Idols*. The performances are very different. *Idols* comes across as so ... angry. Am I off base?

SUMMER: *Idols* is definitely angry. From the first glimmer of an idea, I kept picturing these huge pieces of wood, all rough and weather-beaten. The texture of the wood, and the sound, like a deep bass drum, wouldn't leave me alone. Then the whole series of carvings emerged, and the soundscape too, just like that. There was a frightening force bound up in it. It was anger, you're right. Tremendous anger. Even rage.

CBC RADIO ONE: Did that come from the earthquake and what it did to you and your family?

SUMMER: Does it matter where emotion comes from? Anger is anger. The trick is to recognize it for what it is and not disguise it as something else. I mean, look at me. [Laughs] When you look like this, you're going to understand anger. And disguises.

CBC RADIO ONE: Have you worked through your anger, then? Metanoia is a more tranquil piece, at least until the end, when you emerge from the Fire Grove. Then – well, it's staggering. The flames all around you, and of course your, your –

SUMMER: It's fine. You can say it.

CBC RADIO ONE: I just mean – Well, the sheer rawness of the image completely undoes the calm that's been building. Up to then we sense that something has been resolved, or at least accepted. Like a bitterness that has been diluted. Then the ending throws it all open again. The darkness, the anger – all the feelings from your previous installation, they come rushing back.

EIGHTEEN

⌃⌄

There is no way to predict an aftershock, no way to prepare.

Just when you think it's over and you have borne the final blow, once more it hits: the tremors, the instability, the fear. Once more you are thrown.

Later, when it's over, you think again: surely. Surely this is the last time. And once more it is not. And there you stand, taking it.

⌃⌄

IT'S A STRETCH TO CALL a circa 2001 beige tower and CRT monitor a business centre, but at least the internet works. The browser homepage, a promo for Revelstoke tourism, is topped by a banner about the earthquake. *Our hearts are with our neighbours in Vancouver ...*

Charlotte types in all the search terms she can think of. Combinations of *hard-boiled, mystery, story within story* yield nothing, until she includes *1930s* and gets Dashiell Hammett. That's the writer, she's sure of it. When she adds the falling beam that nearly killed the character, she gets the hit: *The Maltese Falcon.* That's why she kept thinking of *M* names! How could she have forgotten? The movie's supposed to be a classic.

More hunting and she discovers that the story within the story, the part she remembers so well, is so famous it has its own title: the Flitcraft Parable, Flitcraft being the name of the man who disappeared. Briefly she feels let down. She'd imagined the tale was obscure, that she was one of the sensitive few to dwell on it, yet here it is, widely discussed by readers, critics, and scholars.

She scans the long description of the parable on one site. It's just as she remembers. The man walking, the beam falling. Partway down she stops dead. Backtracks a line or two, rereads.

No. That can't be right.

Returns to her list of hits and selects another. Reads.

What the fuck?

A father is supposed to set an example. Of all people, Stedman should know that. Yet he's been nothing but weak and indecisive. Hiding in his own home. Ignoring the injured neighbours. Letting a know-it-all take over his house and his daughter. Letting someone — who? — get away with stealing his money.

He will make it up to Sidney. He owes her that much after she's worked so hard to get her life back. It's been tough for his little girl. Staying sober. Giving up her gang of friends so she doesn't get sucked back into the partying. Everyone aware she was in rehab, casting her that pitying look. Not to mention dealing with her mother. It's hard to live with someone who confuses love with quality control, who measures and assesses and expects, and always, always finds you wanting. Charlotte's constant picking would erode the sturdiest individual. When Sidney began acting out, he urged Charlotte to ease up and give the girl some space, but she wouldn't. Look what followed: addiction, truancy, promiscuity, theft. He's managed people his whole career and he knows it's inevitable: feed anyone a diet of denial, and they will rebel.

Well, Charlotte's not here, so it's up to him. He will make it better. And Sidney will see: he will be himself again.

〵〴

It takes a moment for Anna to realize that the scream, lower-pitched than Miss Dodie's but just as urgent, is coming from her own lips.

She is only thirty-two, still young by North American standards, yet she has seen a lifetime of alarming sights. Her father passed out on the kitchen floor, his naked body atop a reeking pool of urine and liquid shit. The skeletal man who entered their Donetsk apartment and clawed at her mother, pleading for food, until Bohdan rocketed out of nowhere, a ferocious nine-year-old ball that knocked the intruder out the door. The sheet-wrapped infant amid the peelings and vodka bottles in the bin behind their apartment, its tiny cheek and nose the only clue that the cold, rigid bundle was human and not a wad of rags.

The neat bearded man in her neighbourhood park three weeks before she fled, jabbing the air with his hand-lettered anti-Russia sign, shot point blank by an assassin in a police officer's suit.

So many sights for a woman of thirty-two. Not one of them as horrific as this.

The tall pot at the back of the stove, the one filled with cooking oil: on fire. The burner beneath it, glowing: also on fire. A frypan of food on a red-hot circle in front of the pot: on fire. Flames creep up the backsplash behind the stove, eating the accumulated grease spots. Only the counter beside the stove does not burn. The items on it — a few broken dishes, an open packet of bacon — are less digestible as fuel.

The ceramic stovetop: on fire. Flames dance a trail down the appliance and onto the floor. The floor itself: on fire. How? A spill — cooking oil? — all over the stove and floor.

Fire licks at, then eats, the fanned-open cookbooks, the clipped recipes, the bills and papers and magazines the earthquake has thrown onto the terracotta.

But what calls forth Anna's scream is Miss Dodie: on fire. Polyester-clad Miss Dodie, in front of the stove, spatula in one hand — she is cooking bacon? — twirling like a Sufi, flames ribboning off her blouse in all directions.

"Joe! Come fast!" Anna scans the room and sees not a tablecloth, not a curtain, in this sleek industrial kitchen. Pulls off her grey cotton sweatshirt. Runs.

∿

The stiffening breeze is unkind to Kyle. Already chilled from shock, inadequate clothing, and the slow creep down the mountain, he curses every gust. Curses the rocky ground and the oppressive forest, the trail that will never end.

He is weaker all the time. More often than he can count he's had to stop and tighten the straps around the tree-branch splint. His fingers, long ago numbed, will not obey. The foot of his broken leg has swollen so huge that it threatens to burst the suede skin of his hikers. The other foot is blistered and bruised from hundreds – thousands? – of lurched steps that have stubbed rocks and roots. His back, which ached and throbbed yesterday after the aftershock draped him over the rock, shrieks each time he bends to adjust the splint. His tongue is a sticky cotton ball, and he has no water. He crossed a creek a ways back – a kilometre? half that? – but was too exhausted to lower his body to fill the bottle.

Joe.

His eyes itch with fatigue and his head weighs heavy, an overblown peony bent toward ground. But the drumbeat continues, and he takes one more step.

Home.

Selfish! He's been so selfish he could puke. Once he's off this mountain he will make it up to Joe. From now on it will be about the two of them. It has to be. He will learn how to give: his time, his attention, his innermost thoughts. He'll even give Joe a dog if that's what it takes. He'll let go of his fear, his crippling, ruinous fear, and he will be brave, or at least try to be.

∧

Where is it? There's got to be one in the garage, but where?

The flames are spreading fast, and the old woman –

No time! Joe has no choice but to leave the woman to Anna. He's got to get the fire under control before it spreads beyond the kitchen.

There has to be a fire extinguisher in here! He rushes from one side of the garage to another, scanning, scanning. The stapler in his ribcage fires with every step, but he barely feels a thing.

Stupid, stupid, stupid! He saw the pot of oil yesterday, but as long as the power was off and the stove stayed cold, he figured it was fine. He should have emptied it. He should have emptied it.

It has to be in here. He kicks aside a spill of cardboard.

What was Stedman thinking? He warned Mister Big Shot about the risk of fire. He's sure he did. Yet the big tycoon flipped the breaker anyway.

Unless Joe forgot. What if – ?

God, he forgets so much, not just song lyrics. Could he be remembering wrong? What if he didn't tell Stedman, only thought about telling him but didn't actually do it? What if he screwed that up too, like everything else? Then he would be the reason the kitchen is raging. He would be the one —

No. He can't bear the thought.

Kiki would have done the right thing. He'd have emptied the pot of oil right away, Joe would bet on it. Kiki always knows what to do.

Please forgive me, he said. Oh, Kiki, Joe thinks wildly. My Kiki. I forgive you. I do.

"'He went like that,' Spade said, 'like a fist when you open your hand.'"

This description of the character Flitcraft disappearing is the most-quoted line in all the articles and blogs on the story. Charlotte remembered that part right — the man escapes death, experiences a moment of clarity, and vanishes.

But the ending.

She leans as far back as the rigid wooden chair will allow, eyes closed, trying to process.

It's not the way she remembered.

How could she have gotten it so wrong? The man was supposed to make a different life for himself. That's what she thought. A split-second choice and he chose. Left behind his family and his house and his job. Chose a better, more authentic life. Exactly what she is poised to do.

Yet that is not what Hammett wrote. The man makes a *new* life in the story, but not a *different* one. By the time he surfaces years later, he has married another woman, had another child, taken a good job, bought a house. His new life in a new town is an exact replica of the life he fled.

This is the story that transfixed her in Chicago? Guy survives random accident, glimpses truth, then escapes — only to end up in the same prison as before? This is the story that's guiding her pilgrimage east?

The old woman's thin hair: on fire. Her mouth a frozen O as she continues to gyrate.

Oh, my lady!

Anna lunges at Miss Dodie and knocks her into the stove. Wraps the sweatshirt, impossibly small, around as much of the woman's burning blouse as possible.

The heat of the fire is freezing. *How can this be?*

Flames on Anna's face, eyebrows sizzling, the ends of her hair, her newly shaped hair. Every molecule in her screaming *run!* Something deep inside her, an anchor, making her stay.

She moves the sweatshirt to Miss Dodie's head, blindly patting her lady everywhere she can, eyes shut tight against the heat and smoke. Hands white-hot, knife blades searing through her palms. *So this is how it feels to be stabbed.*

Joe, come! The words echo.

She knows the term *fire extinguisher*. Knows the location of every one in Miss Dodie's house. There will be one in the rich people's house because they have everything —

Easy times.

— everything. Joe will find it.

Joe! Come! Her lips are burning. Did she speak the words out loud? *Easy times.*

She has seen it all. A drawer of her own, cherry pie that costs the earth, two sinks for one girl. An old woman who touched her cheek.

Her sweatshirt burns. *Miss Dodie! No!*

So much she has seen. Outstretched palms that no one fills, mouths twisted with hate, nostrils flared in terror. A life of longing, a life alone.

Pain, like stabbing.

Please, Joe! Please!

And the soldier.

〜

The hop-three, slump has slowed to hop-two. Impossibly slow. Impossible. At least the trail is levelling off. Soon it will break out of the dense screen of cedar, fir, and hemlock and deposit Kyle at the highway, which the path then parallels for the last kilometre back to the Gleneagles Community Centre.

The highway is right there. The other side of those trees. He should by now hear the rumble of a tour bus or semi, the gunning of a motorcycle, some old beater without a muffler. But there is nothing. Only the far-off whine of aircraft.

Panic grips him. He stops, braces himself against a tree, breathes deep to steady his pulse. What's waiting down there, in the open air? What will he see when he clears the trees? How much horror, how much death?

Joe?

But he is okay, he said so. Joe is safe and waiting and he loves Kyle. Still, Kyle's heart thuds, his mind races.

Chickenshit. You're scared to leave. All this work and you want to stay where you are.

For a moment that is exactly what he wants to do. The thick forest is his prison but also his shelter, and the idea of emerging from it into – God knows what – shakes him to his core.

Such old friends, fear and he. He is afraid of getting old (*Kyle Jizz-person*). Afraid of weakness (*Flubber, Princess*). Afraid – *Joe, I'm sorry, I'm so sorry* – of love.

The voice is right. He is a weak-ass chickenshit.

He is tired of that voice. So tired of it. Look at all he has achieved in his life. He can find it in him to do this one thing. Can't he?

It remains eerily quiet. Where are all the cars?

〰

Joe is frantic, rushing around like the addled white terrier. The garage is as much of a mess as the house. Tools everywhere. Containers, jars, and cans spilled. Storage boxes upended. A moped lying on its side.

For God's sake, where is it?

Everything wrecked. Just like their townhouse will be. The Fiesta-ware smashed, the antique highboy ruined. Everything that belonged to them, that they chose together and cherished, gone.

But not Kiki. Doctor Kyle Jespersen will be there, waiting for him. Waiting for forgiveness, waiting for love. And as long as Kiki is there, Joe will have it all. The whole wide glorious world.

It has to be here. No man has a garage full of flammables and doesn't have a friggin fire extinguisher. Come on! Find it.

A smashed cardboard box full of plastic oil containers. A blue recycling bin knocked over, clamshells, cans, bottles everywhere. Wild colours on the floor where a carton of paint cans spilled. Brushes and tins of acetone and a shop vac in a jumble on the floor. The air heavy with fumes.

From the kitchen, a scream that rips him through.

She has spent her whole life running. She ran from her mother, ran to Tayne, ran headlong into motherhood. She runs an office, runs a household, runs to stay fit, runs errands, *runs*. So much running only to stay in one spot. Now, at last, she is running to a real destination, a new future, a new self—

The man in the story ran to something, only he ended up right back where he started. Like a boomerang. Something else Australian.

A chill crawls up her spine.

"There you are." From behind, Bryan lifts up her hair and kisses her neck. "I thought I lost you."

Tayne wanted her in the beginning. He made her feel strong, desired, a concentrated version of herself. Now he barely tolerates her. Marcus made her feel the same, for a week, maybe two.

The man went back.

Her mother never wanted her.

Bryan pulls over the other chair and straddles it backward. "Checking the latest?"

"Yeah." She quickly closes the search window. "More of the same. Damage everywhere. No messages for me."

Bryan squeezes her arm. "There are people missing you, Lottie. Just you wait till everything's up and running. You'll have loads of messages."

She is fully chilled now. The lodge's air conditioning breathes down her neck, assaults her with the reek of mildew.

"This place is a dump." She stands up. "Let's go to Banff."

He mustn't lay it all on Charlotte. She wasn't sold on marriage, wasn't even sold on kids when they met. Shell-shocked, no doubt, from her mother, who preached that every child should be wanted but never applied the sermon to her own.

It was only when Charlotte got pregnant that her maternal instinct kicked in. He knew it would. He'd done his research. It's all about hormones with women; Charlotte's just needed a kickstart. It was no big deal, just a pinprick in her diaphragm to see what would happen. He was confident. And he was right. Once she was carrying Sidney, that was it: she was going to keep that baby and no one, not even her mother, who flew all the way to Vancouver to talk her out of it, could tell her otherwise. He knew his wife and her stubbornness. Once there was a baby, Charlotte Pettigrew was his for good.

No, it's not all on Charlotte. He has to shoulder some of the blame for Sidney's problems. What gives him hope – and now, when he needs it, strength – is that never during her troubles did his Sweetpea lash out at him. She stayed loyal and civil, even defended him at rehab, the two of them against the force that is Hurricane Charlotte. For his daughter's personal demons, Stedman feels sorrow; but for this, her abiding love in the face of his many mistakes, he feels shame. Because now he has let her down.

Which is why he owes her. It is time to act.

~

Wildly, Joe scans the overturned garage for a flash of telltale red.

Yes!

No. It's a jerrycan on its side, trickle of gas from its mouth. Bad, very bad, with flames so close. No time to do anything about it.

Another scream.

Forget the garage. There'll be an extinguisher by the fireplace in the great room. For Pete's sake, he knows there is! In a flash, it comes to him. He saw it last night from his air mattress near the hearth. Last night, when he thought he'd lost everything. Now he knows better.

I love you with all my heart.

Nostrils burning from the fumes, but euphoric that he remembered, he heads for the door into the mudroom. Breathes deep, gets a lungful of bitter air, coughs.

He will handle this, like he's handled everything since he set foot on this property. He will handle it and it will be over. And soon he will leave, once and for all. Take himself home to Kiki.

His heart soars. Home, and Kiki.

~

The soldier. Always and everywhere, she sees the soldier.

How his head went high and his mouth turned down at the sight of her tee-shirt, the logo that branded her an artist and a traitor. How he bore down on her, one hand shoved down her shirt, the other foraging in her pants. His grunts like those of her uncle's sow, for a time her only friend. His hips as he ground her deep into the duff. The wide pores that pocked his cheeks, the dirty blackheads that speckled his nose. The heavy eyelids that flew open at the sudden, explosive surge, then closed as the fluid flowed, the final, peaceful climax.

Help me, Joe! Please!

The blood black on her silver blade. The flower of soldier's blood on her tee-shirt as she wiped herself. Wiped the wet knife, Bohdan's, hidden in the bureau drawer with the money and the flask, all the things that matter, all in one place. The leaves that clung to the September shrubs, which would hide the body for a time. The coarse flesh which she prayed (though there are no gods) the crows would gore and strip. The bloody tee-shirt she left behind – the error that changed her life.

Please Joe! Come!

All she could do was hide. In Kharkiv until she saw the police posters, in Kiev until she heard the news bulletins, in the vast Polissya wetlands as she made her way, on foot, to Poland.

Now she does her hiding in Canada.

Miss Dodie has gone silent. Her body still thrashes, but weakly. *Nyet! My lady!* There is only fire.

Count to ten: *raz, dva, tri*. Hold on …

She makes it to six, her flesh excruciating. The sow hanging upside down, split open.

I can't do it, Mama. Her mother's face seamed with exhaustion, her body frail, *Annie, oh Annie*, the delicious pie, the glorious breasts.

Donetsk, the park – *nyet, nyet!*

The factory, the apartment. Home.

Her arms around her lady to the end. Not alone.

Pebble by pebble, a slow tide raking a gravel beach, it slips away – so much that was hard, so little that was good. No beauty, no easy times. Only life.

∿

All quiet, save for the raven, which calls from somewhere out of sight. No highway sounds. No human sounds at all.

Hop-two, slump. So quiet.

With the next hop Kyle's concussed brain sloshes and he remembers what he saw. The collapsed cliffs below Eagle Bluffs, the highway buried in earth, cars with – God! – people screaming mired in the landslide.

The highway is impassible. There are no vehicles on the highway. That's why it's so quiet. No one to flag down, no one to stop for him.

How could he have forgotten? For hours he's thought only about leaving the forest, getting off this eternal trail, as if that will end his ordeal. How could he have forgotten that the highway will be deserted?

He could cry.

Joe. Home.

He has to try.

He cannot. His head spins, his body shakes. He cannot imagine covering the final kilometre that winds along and under the highway, to Gleneagles and people and help.

He can't imagine it, but he has to. He will not let Joe down again.

〰

The weight pulls at Stedman's arm; the handle bites into his hand. Dammit, he got lucky. The five-gallon bucket was just sitting there on the side patio, filled to the brim with water. Probably the gardener left it there yesterday, the careless bastard.

"It's okay!" he yells in the direction of the kitchen. "I got you covered!"

Water beads the sides of the bucket.

"Dad! What's happening?"

"Sidney!" She's behind him, pulling at his arm. He shakes her off. "Get back, Sweetpea. Now!"

"No, Dad —" Her fingers claw at his arm. The pail jerks, water sloshes over the top.

"Sidney, listen to me! There's no time. Get back!" With his free hand he shoves her. She bangs into the deacon's bench and, knocked off balance, slides to the floor.

No! He hurt her! But he had no choice. It's the only way he can save her. The only way he can show her that for all his flaws, absences, preoccupations, he is a good man, a good father, not like the old man, not like Charlotte. He is a father who adores his little girl.

Hefting the pail, he steps into the kitchen, where the stove and counter and debris-covered tiles blaze hot. On the floor the two women are rolled in a tight embrace, the nurse's body wrapped around the old woman's. Shielding her, like he will shield Sidney.

They are out of the flames, but — oh God, their bodies are so black, so still. The smell of it hits him. The sickening char.

Stop, focus, stick to the plan.

The moment he traced the screams to the kitchen and saw what was happening, he knew the priorities. First get the blaze under control, then worry about the women.

He concentrates on the stove, clearly the source of the fire. Smoke spills from a frypan on the glowing front burner, from carbon strips of whatever was frying in it. The tall pot at the back shoots flames, towering orange licks. He swallows, steps closer. Ready.

∧∨

Joe braces himself for pain and shoulders open the door from the garage into the house. Sees, in his path, Sidney on the mudroom floor, hunched over, crying, stainless steel bowl on her head. In the doorway to the kitchen, Stedman. With a bucket of —

No, no, no!

"Get outside, now!" he yells at Sidney. Hauls her up, shoves her to the side door, prays she will leave, prays to Saint Anthony to look after her.

He doesn't hesitate. Doesn't think of his injuries. He runs.

∧∨

Stedman holds the bucket in both hands. Takes aim.

"Get outside, now!" It's the gardener's voice behind him. What the hell is he doing here?

"Stop!"

Stupid Newfie, always underfoot.

"You can't throw water —"

Oh, yes, I can. Stedman clenches his jaw and the pain that shoots up his face hones his concentration. Smart-ass know-it-all. This is my house, I'm in charge, Sidney is my daughter, my little girl.

He eyes his target: the burning pot, the towering flames.

Takes aim.

The gardener comes at him in a blur. "Stop!"

Throws.

High above, mid-turn, the raven cries. He has been with Kyle for so long now. Hours? Maybe. Or it could be minutes, or days. For a time the sky goes silent and Kyle is sure the raven has left. The abandonment is overwhelming.

I'm weak, Joe. I'm afraid. But I love you.

Hop-two, slump.

Another cry pierces the sky, fills him with hope.

The splinted leg catches another rise in the ground and he feels the sickening thud, feels the rub of bone on bone, far away, all so far away. The raven, the circus drumbeat, Joe — they circle in his mind, a lazy incomprehensible eddy.

I'm the weak one, Joe. You're the rock that never shifts.

He pictures Joe up ahead on the trail, small and powerful from years of labour, slightly bow-legged in his favourite Levi's, turning around to tease Kyle, to urge him on. Don't be a pussy, he'd say, echoing Kyle's inner voice, which he knows nothing about. You hate pussies.

Kyle smiles. He *does* hate pussies, none more than the one inside himself.

Up ahead the image of Joe advances toward him. Except there are two Joes. Wearing camouflage.

A throaty chuckle from a bough somewhere high above. The raven is with him.

Hop-two, slump, as the men run toward him.

"Stop!" they yell. "We're coming."

He can't stop now. One more agonizing hop, one more ragged breath.

Joe.

∿

The sun sets late in May in the Rockies. Nine o'clock and there's still plenty of light outside the truck window. The mountains flaunt their majestic beauty. Relentless beauty. Too much beauty.

The feeling that clamped onto Charlotte in the run-down chalet in Revelstoke will not let up, and no amount of deep breathing will help. She feels sick. The reckless energy that filled her since Hope has been replaced by a euphoria hangover: dry mouth, low-grade headache, scoured-out insides. The smell of goat cheese, putrid enough on its own, is overtaken by the old coffee stink from the van's cupholder. Fuck! She loathes used coffee cups and their disgusting dregs, so dark and hot and delicious to begin with, a disappointing oily puddle at the end.

Bryan sees her discomfort and misunderstands. "We'll be there soon, babe. You hungry again?"

She shakes her head.

"I don't mean for food." He reaches over and squeezes her knee. His hand feels heavy and dead on her leg. She wants to fling it away.

Miserable fucking story. She should have never looked it up. The ending she remembered was so much better than the real one. Who would write that ridiculous boomerang ending? Who would open up a fresh future for a character and not let him follow it all the way? It's tragic, and it's wrong.

Road signs whizz by. So do other vehicles. Everywhere she looks, motion. Life.

Fuck it all, and fuck everyone. Tragic outcomes are for other people. Charlotte knows what to do and she will do it. And do it right. She is stronger than some stupid fictional character, she has discipline in her DNA. Her world exploded and gave her back herself, and it's a gift she will protect at all costs. She is only going forward, never back.

My mother, the liar.

Charlotte is done with lies. No more script, no more front. Only truth from now on—truth, and road. More and more road, crossing mountains and prairies, bridges and borders. All directions are there for her. The only question is: which one.

Bryan fiddles with the radio controls, dials in a news station. Even here, in Alberta, the earthquake is the only story, though it's a story made of many narratives. How Vancouver will be shut down for weeks to come. How potable water is running dangerously short. How the Vancouver Aquarium is working frantically to keep its marine life from dying. How a high school in Prince George has closed for the week so students and teachers can raise money for the disaster. How an explosion claimed the waterfront home of entrepreneur Tayne Stedman, leaving no survivors.

PART FIVE

Reformation

VANCITY BUZZ: Summer, I know you never dedicate your performances. But seeing as this is the tenth anniversary, is there anyone special you'll be remembering tonight?

SUMMER: So many people have helped me in my life and my career. That's why I don't like to single anyone out. Tonight – today – naturally I'm thinking about the people from that time. My parents, peace be with them, the others in the house, the emergency workers. Later on, my doctors. I'm especially grateful to two people I've never talked about before, not publicly.

VANCITY BUZZ: Oh, intriguing!

SUMMER: One is my neighbour from back then, Vincent Leung. We didn't know him, my family. We never took the time to meet him. He found me on the ground after the explosion and took me to a treatment centre. There was a lot of confusion. I had no ID and no one believed who I was because the news said everyone in the house had died, but he sorted it out. I owe Vincent a huge debt of gratitude for his quick action. I tell him that whenever I'm in Hong Kong.

VANCITY BUZZ: And the other?

SUMMER: Well – He ... [*Pause*]

VANCITY BUZZ: You know, it's okay. You don't have to.

SUMMER: As you can see, I have trouble talking about him. It's just ... it's weird, but I can't actually say his name. It makes me too sad. He's the one who, you know. Saved my life. He –

VANCITY BUZZ: No, really. It's okay. We can –

SUMMER: No, I – [*Pause*] Seriously, you'd think after ten years I could talk about it without crying, right?

VANCITY BUZZ: Why don't we –

SUMMER: No, I want to say it. I need to. See, he tried to stop it. He didn't know any of us, he never laid eyes on us before the earthquake, but he tried to stop it, and he … he died. But not before he pushed me out. He's the reason I'm here today. If I could have one wish, it would be to thank him.

VANCITY BUZZ: This is obviously hard for you, Summer. Thank you for sharing. You know, I'll share something too. I'm such an admirer of yours. You and I were the exact same age, seventeen, when the earthquake happened. Did it change you completely?

SUMMER: Well, yes and no.

VANCITY BUZZ: [*Laughs*] Is this the part of the podcast where you become difficult? Because word is, you've got a reputation to uphold.

SUMMER: No, no. I mean it. Obviously the earthquake changed me. It altered my appearance, it turned me into what I am –

VANCITY BUZZ: Which is gorgeous, if I may say.

SUMMER: You may say, Jordan, you may say. On the surface, everything changed. My family was gone, my home. God, you know how it was. So many families, so many homes. There was nothing special about my situation, not at all. I changed my name too, of course. I wanted to be known as myself, not the Stedman heiress. But I – you know, the real me – didn't change in any fundamental way.

VANCITY BUZZ: Really? Your life took such a turn. Becoming a gifted artist, a celebrity, a model for the alternative appearance movement.

SUMMER: But that's all external stuff. On the inside I'm still me. I'm that seventeen-year-old who lived through the earthquake and then the explosion. All the things and all the people I am today were inside me then. Every one of them.

VANCITY BUZZ: Forgive me if I'm pushing buttons here, but your new piece is called *Metanoia*. Doesn't that mean a fundamental change, like on the inside?

SUMMER: You got me! [*Laughs*] I know it seems contradictory. In psychology, metanoia means healing yourself after you've had a meltdown or breakdown. The parallels to my situation are obvious, right? But the healing you go through, sure, it changes your behaviour and your attitude, at least you hope it does, but it doesn't change *you*. That part, the *you* part of you, is always going to be the same. That's why I keep coming back to butterflies. You look at one and think, how could that have ever been a hairy caterpillar? Well, it was. Everything that's in that gorgeous butterfly was in the makeup of the ugly worm. Their appearance is totally different, their behaviour too. I mean, God, one of them flies. But they are the same being.

VANCITY BUZZ: What can we take away from that?

SUMMER: I guess that you can change a lot about your situation, but there's no getting away from who you are. You can't run from yourself. That's what I'd say to anyone listening to this who might think they can escape themselves, anyone who might have tried. And it's why in this performance I show myself fully, the way I really am.

NINETEEN

〰

Only mid-May yet the dawn sky, heavy and haze-brushed, foretells another scorcher. The sea lies calm and motionless, no sigh of breeze to stir the heat. The earth, too, is calm, has not tremored beneath the city these past ten years. It is not the stillness of before, as certain and unremarkable as skin over bones. Within it now, at its core, are rustlings of breakage, whispers of instability.

Along Burrard Inlet, and out to the smoke-blurred horizon of Vancouver Island, cruise ships ply the waters, their international cargos waving from the decks. Among them tankers, fewer now and smaller with oil and gas in retreat, but enough to placate the industry's proponents and incite its protesters in equal measure. Dwarfing them all, the new supercontainer ships that feed the swelling population's hunger for wardrobes and home renos, electric vehicles and 3D printers, lighting and e-bikes and padlets and robotics. Shaken first by the earthquake, then by the time of sickness, Vancouver is rising again, and it is starved for consumer goods.

The decade of exodus is over, the years when traumatized citizens fled, foreign investors pulled out, businesses shuttered, trade and tourism dwindled. Following the earthquake, cordoned-off buildings and unsafe zones pockmarked the city's once vibrant sectors. Commercial real estate staggered. The glut of residential listings, one in three damaged from the quake, emptied the retirement nests of homeowners who had till then thrown every dollar at the mortgage. Values tumbled, communities shrank, the tax base withered.

Then, like a long-delayed aftershock, came the time of sickness. People perished, more than should have in this era of science. Wild bee species dwindled, touching off panic about food crops. An unknown fungus afflicted the cedars; more whales died. In Vancouver, morale plummeted. The city withdrew deeper into itself.

Many in those years feared that all was lost, that the jewel of the west coast was gone. But those who stayed, the resilient ones, nursed hope. They looked after one another. They courted innovation. They welcomed immigrants and ideas, brilliant outcasts and wealthy eco-tourists. They fought back the sicknesses and began to rebuild.

Vancouver ten years after still bears scars, but it is coming up healthier, greener, and kinder than the ruins beneath. Despite the wildfires of hotter, drier summers, and an ocean still finding its balance, the region has for now held back the worst of climate change. Nature in this decade has hit other places harder, places with less rainfall and more sun, with barrier islands and glaciers, prone to floods and blizzards and category-defying hurricanes. As the globe's habitable regions shrink and its populations seek stability and tolerance, hope is slowly building in Vancouver. The city has begun to glitter again. Diamonds need heat and pressure to form; also, time.

$\wedge$

THE SUN IS BARELY UP and already the West Van seawalk teems with runners, far more than in the days when he used to paddle past on the flat early sea. Back then people waited until seven or eight a.m. to run, or else squeezed in a route over the noon hour or after work. Now, with each year hotter than the one before, the only reasonable time to exercise outside between May and September, assuming no air quality advisories due to wildfire smoke, is early morning or night.

That leaves him little choice about when to hit the pavement. Even though his client roster is once more full to bursting, the clinic doors shut faithfully at five. Evening is home time, together time. No working late, no going to the gym, no walking alone on the trails to check out who might saunter by. Some nights they go to dinner with friends; once in a while, if there's anything decent playing, they take in a movie. Every Friday through spring and summer they barbecue chicken and ribs, make pitchers of margaritas, and entertain two or three other couples on the big covered deck of their house in Lynn Valley. They got lucky with the 1970s split-level. It sits on a generous corner lot on a quiet, treed street below the North Shore mountains. The neighbours are great: a few families, two retired couples, a middle-aged welder who's off hiking every weekend, the deaf old preacher across the street who insists on calling them *roommates*. They bought the place three years ago, just before prices ticked up.

Housing was bleak for a while there. God, everything was bleak.

West Vancouver, where the wealthy could afford to simply leave, cleared out in months, and his practice nearly folded. Often in those early years he considered packing it in himself: the townhouse, which he hung onto for a while and rented out, the west coast, career, relationships. In the time of sickness, he came close. He would go to ground, he decided, hide out in some small, isolated town up north, live off his savings. But then the sun would come up and the skyline would glow and he'd tell himself to just keep going — take one more step, then another.

The air across his face is thick with the sultry day to come. He adjusts his stride slightly. As always, ten or fifteen minutes into the run his IT band tightens and tugs at his knee. The leg never fully realigned despite an intensive physio and stretching regime that he's followed for a decade. He thumbs the outside of his right thigh, massaging the tendon, inviting the blood.

The split-level in Lynn Valley is solid, the only earthquake damage a tilted deck, which the previous owners fixed. But it's dated. They've replaced the decades-old cabinetry, much of it veneer, and ripped out the shag carpeting and vinyl flooring. Still, there's a green-and-brown bathroom to deal with, straight from the disco era, and a panelled rec room that no amount of white paint can fix.

Most of their spare cash goes to renovations. Most of *his* spare cash, though he's never bitter about that. He knew when he married Robert that he was signing on as breadwinner. An artist's income is tenuous at the best of times, and it adds up to little more than pocket change in the depressed Vancouver art market. Things are improving — people are spending again and luxury items have rebounded — but that's not important. What he cares about is supporting Robert's passion. He works full days and covers the necessities so that Robert can paint, network with galleries, and teach the occasional workshop to keep his name out there.

Hard work is something Kyle Jespersen has never shied away from, and in the last ten years he's learned that when the work enriches people beyond himself, it brings its own rewards. His volunteer time after the earthquake, a year-long rotation of heartbreaking skin grafts and facial reconstruction, shuffled his priorities, made him value service more and reputation less. Once a month he still pulls a Saturday shift at the Metro Area Burn Unit, treating those who can't produce a health-care card. It's good work even if it's depressing; the homeless population, they say, may never fall back to pre-quake levels. When someone whose ravaged face he has smoothed or whose nose he has rebuilt tears up while thanking him, or emails him months later to say they've finally gone clean or landed a job, he's convinced that what he accomplishes in a single downtown Saturday matters more than all the injecting and sculpting, the trimming of jowls and lifting of eyelids, that he performs the rest of the month.

As he rounds the point and passes the latest luxury highrise, a year from completion but already fully sold, Lighthouse Park comes into view. The tall beacon that once graced the rocky point was demolished in year one, to the chagrin of West Van old-timers. Even with the flood of international aid, budgets were tight, and the municipality couldn't justify repairing a structure that time and technology had rendered more of a historical attraction than a true navigational aid. Yet the park's name is unchanged and the lighthouse footings remain, ghostly reminders of that other time. He picnicked beside the crumbling concrete with Keith, his lover at the time, on the third anniversary of the quake, along with others who remained healthy that first spring of the sickness. As they toasted Vancouver's rebirth, sipped Prosecco, and ate ham and Brie gone runny in the sun, Kyle's mind was full of that morning three years earlier: skimming past the point, kayak slicing the water, his nervous energy and passions, his confusion and betrayal, and his fear – underneath it all, fear – pressing him onward. He was inexpressibly sad on that clear anniversary day, and none of Keith's banter could cheer him. Soon after, they broke up. He wasn't ready, he told Keith, it was too soon. He'd known that from the outset, knew it with every man he picked up in those years of trying to stifle the memories and dial down the pain.

Like the lighthouse footings, there are still traces of the earthquake on his body and in his life. This twang that kicks in whenever he runs, his aching back on low-pressure days. The mountain he refuses to set foot on, the old phone that stores the text message he can't delete. The school gym turned hospital, not six blocks from his clinic, that after three days of bone-setting, rehydration, and drug-induced rest he insisted on leaving. Their townhouse, filled with breakage but more or less intact, the air dusty and stale when he unlocked the front door that long-ago morning. No sign that anyone had been there. No sign of Joe.

Ten years gone and the emptiness on the other side of that door still plants a fist in his gut. He knew Joe wouldn't be there, but knowing never stopped him from hoping. They'd misreported the girl's death at first; they could have done the same with Joe. In the three weeks it took to pull dental records, Kyle quizzed everyone he could think of, all their friends and family, but no one had heard from Joe or knew for sure whether he'd been in the house at the end. Pressing the coroners was futile too. Like everyone else who waited, he learned that a city rocked by disaster is slow to release its stories.

In the meantime he texted his lover every day, sending all the words he needed to say: *You are my life, Joe. Please forgive me. I need you. I'm sorry.* Each time he hit send, he reread the single message he'd received from Joe that day: *Shook up but ok. Hope ur2.* He gave up only when the coroner service confirmed what everyone else had accepted. They delivered the news in person — they'd recruited volunteers for the task, like in wartime, to make the notifications more humane. As if death could ever be kind. The smooth-faced young man was calm and matter-of-fact, already experienced in the script of death; Kyle, in the doorway of the echoing townhouse, crutches biting into his armpits, trembled with rage. It's the closest he's ever come to striking a person. *Don't you talk about him like that*, he screamed inside. *Dead? Like you know anything about him. You know nothing.*

A day later, still shaky and deep inside unconvinced, he took a cab to the West Van waterfront.

"You sure this is it?"

"Oh, yes." The driver's orange turban bobbed. "Yes, yes. This is where the Stedmans lived. Very famous here in West Vancouver. Very terrible what happened. This part of the house, here by the driveway, it blew up like a bomb – whoosh." He threw both hands in the air. "The rest burned to the ground. The fire trucks could not come in time. Oh, yes. Very many houses gone that way."

Awkwardly, Kyle manoeuvred himself and his crutches out of the backseat and up the driveway. He stared at the deep pit, the blasted ground, the blackened remnants of framing at the opposite end of the house, where an immense riverstone fireplace and chimney still stood. Even after a month the smell of charred wood and melted plastic lingered over the hole, the pungent stench of loss. He stayed there twenty minutes, bent over his crutches. The cab driver, professional through and through, switched on the radio to cover the sounds.

Joe. He says the name silently every time he runs the seawalk and passes, as he's doing now, the fifteen-storey condo building that sits on the old Stedman property. Every time he wonders: what did they find when they excavated the site? There must be particles of Joe – a few curly hairs, a scrap of Levi's, some molecules of heart – mixed into the earth, maybe right over there, near the woman wrapped in scarves. The clean-up crew collected pieces of the old Toyota pickup, but apart from the licence plates, which were returned to Kyle, there were no mementos of his man.

The police reported that besides the bodies of Joe and Stedman, the remains of two females were removed from the premises. One was Mrs. Dorothy Lydell, eighty-six-year-old resident of the British Properties, not related to the Stedmans, not a friend, not connected to the family in any determinable way. Her presence in the Stedman home could not be accounted for. The other female was never identified. Younger than Stedman's wife, somewhere between thirty and forty, and bearing no resemblance to the lady of the house, the woman remained a cipher. Smirks were exchanged between the two officers who briefed Kyle. Clearly they had their suspicions.

As for the so-called lady of the house, Stedman's wife was never found. Kyle kept abreast of the search, a pointless yet necessary thread that tied him to Joe's last days. The police did their best given stretched resources. With help from Stedman's brother, who pitched in from Toronto, and the GlobalTech executive who'd been Stedman's right-hand man, they contacted relatives, friends, and colleagues. They blitzed social media, put Charlotte Stedman on all the missing-person sites, checked credit card and cell phone records. The daughter's Facebook post immediately following the quake had suggested the mother was in the Fraser Valley that morning, a supposition confirmed when Stedman's Porsche Cayenne turned up in a motel parking lot in Hope. Beyond that, no trace of the woman could be found: no witness accounts, no bank records, no body. After multiple dead ends, the search was called off and she was presumed dead. She had slipped through the cracks, the way so many did in that confused time.

I let you slip, Joe. But I will never let you go.

Far off, a sound echoing from the mountains: a raven, crying out to the sky.

Joe.

He thinks of him for so many reasons. Another earthquake anniversary looms. The Upper Lonsdale street where they lived comes into view. A landscaping truck lumbers by, loaded with mower and spades and branches. That Stevie Nicks song plays and he thinks of the version Joe invented on purpose, to crack him up: *Just like the one-winged dove.* Some shirtless specimen, like the one running toward him, touches the spark of lust to the tissue paper of guilt, and the flare-up sears him in a way no physical injury ever will.

He thinks of Joe, too, though it may be deeply wrong, when he looks at Robert, in their queen-size bed, over salmon burgers on the barbecue, or as they lay hardwood in the rec room, and thinks, we are part of each other, and I'm not afraid. When Robert looks back, knowing it all — Kyle's lies, his betrayals, his fears and devastation — and loves him anyway, Joe is there in that wide-open gaze.

Sometimes he takes the Saint Anthony medallion from his office drawer. For years it has lain there, next to a stapler, gathering tarnish but retaining a glow just the same. Today he will take it out for the last time. Shirin — still his office manager; she stuck with him through the worst — will step out and buy silver polish, no questions asked. By this evening it will look good as new.

Overhead the gulls float and glide, scanning the sea for their unsuspecting breakfasts. As always when the past entwines him, Kyle tells himself to release it, just let it go. Today his thoughts become seagulls, free, with only the vast sky to contain them. Think of what's to come, he tells himself, not what has been.

Tonight they're going out: an early dinner at the Korean place, then over town to the new show by Summer Rain. Critics say it's her best yet, reported Robert, a shocking yet elegiac masterpiece suffused with strength and heroism. Kyle asked him not to say more. He would rather be surprised.

He's had the tickets for months. Summer sends him a pair whenever she comes to town, an ongoing thank-you that he insists he doesn't need. She refuses to listen.

Hers was a heartbreaking case: seventeen; burns all over her body, some third degree; the left side of her face barely touched — she'd lain with that side to the ground — the right beyond repair, or so thought the surgeon he took over from two months after the quake. The doctor was only too happy to refer the girl to Kyle, who was gaining a reputation for taking the hardest cases, the most severely disfigured, the ones deemed hopeless. Kyle always had hope and he worked tirelessly, methodically, graft after graft, operation after operation. It was so different from his private practice. No one emerged beautiful. That wasn't the goal. The goal was to be unremarkable, to walk among others without provoking ridicule or revulsion.

The Stedman girl, as she was known back then, tugged everyone's heartstrings in the burn unit. Her famous father was dead, her mother was missing, and the only other relative, an uncle from Toronto, came to her bedside once, then turned away, visibly shaken, and sent cards thereafter.

Kyle knew when he requested her case that he'd extract from the girl only an outline, not a full account. She could barely speak because of the pain. The right half of her mouth had burned away, along with her right cheek, jaw, nose, and ear. The right side of her neck was a mass of crimson. The top of her head, from her crown to her eyes, had been spared; she'd been wearing some kind of helmet or other head covering. Robert still mentions this and shudders: thank God; imagine an artist of Summer Rain's calibre blinded before she found her calling. Her hands, like most of her lower body, were badly damaged. She lost the fine motor coordination needed to paint or draw, which led her, in the end, to performance art.

Kyle only had so much time with her — the casualty list was long — so he concentrated on her face. Clothing could hide her other scars and ridges, but she had to look the world in the eye. He gave her his fullest concentration and his most excellent work, and she repaid him twice. First, in a word here, a phrase there, with the story of Joe and his final, heroic act. And second, though she never knew it, with the medallion he palmed from her bedside table as she lay sleeping on her last night in hospital. It wasn't theft, he told himself. He needed it more than she ever would.

It's a cardinal rule of medicine that you don't treat patients you have an emotional attachment to. Working on Sidney, Kyle understood why. Every surgery, every refinement, was an atonement. Every time he laid hands on Sidney it was to honour Joe, to love and repair what little he could reach through surrogate means. Every time it tore him apart, and after each session it took days to recover. No one knew the agony it cost him, because no one knew of their connection. Especially not her. He would never tell her. Any pity she might feel for him, any stirring of her heart, was a balm he had not earned and could not accept. The mere idea of it turned his stomach.

They never talk, now that she is Summer Rain, or correspond. The tickets — a third and unexpected repayment — arrive at his clinic every couple of years with no card or message. He likes it that way. He understands as well as anyone the fear of reanimating unbearable loss. He has never tried to see Summer or meet her backstage. He has been content simply to watch her.

And what a thrill it is to watch her. Excitement and affection and something more intimate, like pride, fill him each time she appears in her tableaux, powerful and mythical — and alone. In every show she is solo. Though of average height, she somehow towers before her audience, her body in its draperies slender yet strong, willowy yet buxom; her long hair a sweep of honey; her neck made sinuous by the scars that contour it; her eyes huge and kohl-rimmed. The rest of her face would stop your heart — half as nature made it, half a canvas of her own design. When he saw the publicity photo she enclosed with his first tickets, for her debut piece, *Ghosts*, he laughed aloud in shock and delight at the swirling, full-colour flames — or are they wings? — that climbed the right side of her face. In that moment, arrested by the resplendent tattoos, he understood that she had accomplished through her art what he had never managed in a career of surgery: she had created beauty. Not salvaged it, restored it, or improved upon it, but *made* it, and from raw material that even his considerable talents had left unusable.

Whatever role she plays in her art, whatever position she strikes, she never disguises her face. It is always there, a symbol of all that is ruined and remade, a testament to the harrowing beauty destruction can produce; and her disfigurement, unsettling and powerful, only entrances audiences, never alienates them. He can't wait to see what she has created this time.

This time, for the first time, he has something for her. Ten years — an eyeblink and also an eternity. He has hung on to Saint Anthony long enough. Has hung on to it all: his ringing grief, Joe's act of grace, all they had, and all they lost. It's time that she knows. It's taken him a decade to be ready for her. A decade to fully understand that no matter what he keeps or gives away, Joe will always be with him.

Here, at last, comes the Dundarave Pier, the turning point in Kyle's route. Gulls wheel over the pier, where two men stand with cast lines. His right leg has stopped speaking to him, his breathing has gone deep and regular, as if the air, as he pushes through the warmth, contains more oxygen. It's always this way. It takes the first half of a run to truly warm up, to test your heart and find your pace. It's only in the second half that you hit your stride.

TWENTY

∧

For years to come, for decades, the forensic work occupied seismologists and geologists, city planners and emergency workers. What forces gathered, at which points, and why? Were there early signs that next time could be read? Why did this structure stand while that one, outwardly solid, crumbled?

Artists, too, plumbed the wreckage. What traces does such ruin leave behind? What marks does it etch upon you? Does your vision change? Does your skin smell different? Are you diminished, or could you in some way expand? Some messy, supercharged part of you that's been locked in place for years — could it stir? Could it wake and grow and, in one astonishing moment, blaze forth?

∧

TEN YEARS. Nearly a third of your life. Yet you remember so much.

Sitting at the kitchen island looking at Rebecca Lee's Instagram, listening to that old Taylor Swift song you were tired of, the memory of May's bitsu-bitsu sweet and fatty on your tongue.

In a heartbeat, the shaking, the hurling of the world. Barstools flying, dishes crashing. The terracotta floor where you curled up, holding for dear life to the cupboard frame. The pain of your bandaged hand, the wail of the house alarm. You remember every thudding appliance, every broken plate, every shattered wine bottle. The butcher knife stabbed into the cabinetry inches from your head. Charlotte's smashed MacBook, the final shutdown of a mind never open to you.

You remember it all as if it were now. How it's just another day until suddenly it's not. How you're someone with many possessions who actually has nothing. How you're part of a family yet the loneliest person you know. How you're certain that one day, maybe not this day, but soon, you will fly, you'll ride the highest draft of the best buzz until you're soaring, when in reality you are pinned to the earth.

Ten years have passed, yet every day you remember them. You say a prayer, or what passes for one in your vague spiritual life. You pray for Anna, the inscrutable nurse who in exposing her need taught you more about your own. You pray for Miss Dodie, because the human pageant needs its odd souls. You pray for Joe, the gentle gardener, who saw into your frightened self, who watched over you, and who saved you. It was an act you try to honour in your art, except that you can only come at it sideways; it still hurts too much to remember.

Standing here, in the shadow of fifteen storeys, you remember the house, one of the last single homes to line the seawalk. They're all gone now. The Stedman house, Vincent's too, the other half dozen down the way, bulldozed one after the other to make room for luxury condos, their buyers foolishly gambling that because no tsunami materialized a decade ago, one never will.

In the warm morning air, fourteen hours from revealing to your home city, for the first time, your bare ruined body, crisscrossed neck to feet with hard, angry runnels of scar, you take in the view that was once all yours, the inlet, the seawalk, the early-morning runners lost in thought, and you remember the family that lived here. You'd forget them if you could, the way you left behind their name, but it's like trying to forget that you have fingernails, or lungs.

Your dad, who did the best he could — you know that now — but who shut himself away, lured by growth and wealth and fame. You marvel at the irony, which you've explored in your work: a communications leader with no clue how to communicate. And Charlotte, as you call her now. The soft name cuts your tongue yet the sting is bracing, and from it you extract energy as you do from every laceration that has shaped your life.

That first year after you checked out of the burn unit, outwardly improved but readdicted to painkillers, you fell into a void of alcohol and drugs — just one more broken soul on Vancouver's broken streets, a disfigured castoff who never gave her name, who avoided mirrors and other reflective surfaces, who talked to no one.

You thought then that she would come for you. During that lost year, you misplaced many cell phones and lacked the organizational skills to keep your plans paid, but your Facebook page stayed up. You never updated it but you checked it now and then, knowing that if she was out there, it was the easiest way to contact you.

Uncle Tim never heard from her. Not the day of the earthquake or any of the days that followed. After he hauled you off the street, took you to Toronto, and got you on your feet again, berating himself for not having taken you on in the first place, he made you talk about her sometimes. It was part of your recovery, he reminded you, to make amends. You talked about her when asked. You made no amends.

He took your money, Uncle Tim, lots of it, in exchange for housing you that year. You invested in his tech start-up, and all the business ventures after that. You don't care about the money. You never have. Once the lawyers sold your dad's assets, even devalued as they were after the earthquake, there was always more than you needed. Now money matters even less. Now you make your own.

From Toronto you went to Montreal, in theory to learn more about your late grandmother, still revered in feminist circles, but in reality, if you are honest with yourself, because you thought Charlotte might be there. You fell in with a couple of your grandmother's acolytes, a pair of sun-wrinkled motorcycle dykes, tough and unsentimental. They surprised you: gave you a home for a time, helped you stabilize, signed you up for art classes – as long as you made no emotional demands on them. It was a fair arrangement, and it was honest. If only Charlotte could have spoken that plainly.

As months went by, then years, and you created Summer Rain the artist, you told yourself that everyone was right: Charlotte must have died. She'd been on a bridge that collapsed and her body washed down the Fraser. Or she'd been crushed in a rock slide and was never dug out. None of the scenarios you dreamed up, however, fit with the SUV being left in Hope. Sometimes, in your weakest moments, you imagined that she had abandoned the vehicle and was taking another route home when she met her fate. That she was walking or hitchhiking, heading back to you.

The ridiculousness of your imaginings now astonishes you.

What you know for certain is this: the great earthquake swallowed countless people, leaving no sign or proof that they were gone, but not all of the swallowed are dead. Some merely shifted with the ground. It happens with every disaster — hurricane, tsunami, terrorist attack. You've looked it up; you can google with the best of them. For the countless numbers who die, a few slip away. They see a channel open and they sail through it to another sea. It would be easy: a new name, a new identity, a new appearance even. Easier still with money. As long as you kept your past to yourself, no one would know who you were or where you came from.

You also know this: everyone says she died because the alternative is too disturbing. What mother, especially in a time of crisis, walks away from a family that needs her? What mother erases her only child?

Charlotte was not a monster. She never hit you, starved you, put out cigarettes on your arm, or bombarded you with hateful names. Her lack of attention was sewn into her nature; her matter-of-factness and overwhelming schedule didn't allow for the hugs, endearments, or general attention your friends got from their mothers. She was not a monster, and yet part of you — on certain days an overwhelming part — believes she did a monstrous thing. You believe — and on certain days you *know* — that she is alive, out there somewhere, occupying another life.

Why are you so sure? Is it because you sense her presence through your body, through some innate genetic signal? Or because you crave the pain that comes from believing, the way a person bites down on an infected tooth?

Once or twice a year, as you walk the streets of New York, Edinburgh, Rio, Hong Kong, swathed in the scarves and sunglasses that keep people from recognizing you, or as you enter a busy square or bustling restaurant, or wait for a delayed flight at an airport, you see a flash of upright carriage, hair swept into a controlled knot, impeccable business attire, head held high in certainty or superiority, and you know it's her. It happened only weeks ago, in Chicago, on your way to the NPR studio. You were so positive that you followed her for two blocks, Jesse clamouring at your heels, before you lost her in the early-morning rush.

Each time it happens you are rattled to the core. Your self-creation collapses. The years fall away and you are once again that lonely, hollow girl, adrift in a too-large world, starved in the midst of abundance. You crash, you flame out, sometimes for hours and sometimes weeks.

Until a day comes. It's like any other day, except it isn't. You wake up and wait for the despair to hit. When it doesn't, you get up, you make coffee. You give thanks for your independence, rejoice in your solitude. Feel the strength in your bones, draw power from your scars. Plant your feet on the ground, firm and steady. For now.

Careful readers will notice that I've altered the details of certain real-life locations and events that appear in this book. Of particular note, the stretch of West Vancouver shoreline where the Stedman property is located is a creation of my imagination. I have played with the sight line from Eagle Bluffs. And I have changed the sequence of some events in the Ukrainian crisis. These and other liberties I've taken, as novelists will do, for the sake of the story.

Characters and events in this book are fictitious or are used fictitiously. Any similarity to real people, living or dead, is coincidental and not intended.

ACKNOWLEDGEMENTS

When I began this book, I knew nothing about earthquakes except they're scary and I don't want to be in one. For patiently answering my random, often ignorant questions (while keeping a straight face) and generously reviewing parts of the manuscript, I cannot adequately thank John Clague, PhD FRSC OC, Professor Emeritus with the Department of Earth Sciences, Simon Fraser University. All seismic errors and distortions are mine.

For their priceless road maps through the twisty, turny world of publishing, my deep appreciation to Caroline Adderson, Jesse Finkelstein, Nancy Flight, Sally Harding, Eve Lazarus, Amanda Lewis, Barbara Pulling, Susan Safyan, Kelly S. Thompson, John Vigna, and agent extraordinaire Stephanie Sinclair. For believing in this novel and launching it into the world, I am forever indebted to the team at NeWest Press: Matt Bowes, Claire Kelly, Christine Kohler, Carolina Ortiz, and the insightful and intelligent Leslie Vermeer — perceptive reader, tireless advocate, in all ways an editor's editor.

For other technical help and content reviews, heartfelt thanks to Rob Bittner, Iryna Iudina, Eve Lazarus (again), Elena Ouliankina, Dr. Jonathan Peck, and Delaney Steel.

Thank you to my early readers and editors for your feedback and support, especially Richard Babin, Jennifer Glossop, Ron Richardson, Shaun Shelongosky, and Janice Zawerbny, who at a critical juncture stopped my heart by saying she loved this novel.

Who knew that after three decades of confidently writing and ghostwriting for clients, I would turn into a pool of quivering gunk when it comes to my own material? For their unstinting encouragement, I thank my family, friends, colleagues, and students. A special shout-out to the partners, present and past, of West Coast Editorial Associates, for abiding friendship and a work environment in which dreams matter as much as the bottom line; to Flo and Harold Gienger, for offering a quiet place to revise and (thank you, Flo) endless soup; and to Jim Peck, for always listening.

To Lois Richardson and Barbara Tomlin, cherished friends, astute readers, and indefatigable cheerleaders, without your regular injections of confidence, I would be snivelling in a corner clutching an unpublished manuscript.

Finally, and forever, to Travis Shelongosky: no thank-yous (as requested), only loves.

FRANCES PECK wrote fiction and poetry until her early twenties, when the realities of adulthood and rent steered her toward a career as a freelance writer, ghostwriter, editor, and instructor. Known for her writing and workshops on the finer points of language, she's the author of Peck's English Pointers (an online writing tool), a co-author of the HyperGrammar website, and an occasional essayist and blogger. Frances returns to her first love, fiction, with *The Broken Places*, part of the Nunatak First Fiction Series.